GIRL IN THE RED HOOD: A RETELLING OF LITTLE RED RIDING HOOD

THE CLASSICAL KINGDOMS COLLECTION, BOOK #4

BRITTANY FICHTER

WANT FREE STORIES?

Sign up for a free no-spam newsletter for short stories, exclusive secret chapters, discounts, and sneak peeks at books before they're published.

Details at the end of this book.

To my mommy, for all the hours you let me hide in my room and write. You encouraged me to explore. You taught me to love the library and to hoard new notebooks and pens. And most of all, you believed in me.

Thank you.

CHAPTER 1
GRANDMOTHER'S WARNING

"You don't understand!"

Liesel watched in alarm as her grandmother ran after her father and grasped his arm. She'd never seen her grandmother so upset.

"People that go to that town . . ." her grandmother pleaded, "they never leave! You can't take Liesel and Amala there!"

"And why not, old woman?" Warin yanked his arm out of her hands. He tossed another sack into the wooden cart before turning to face his wife's mother, crossing his arms across his chest defiantly. "Once and for all, if it's so dangerous, surely you're willin' to share those secrets you guard so closely, if only to keep your daughter and granddaughter near."

Liesel didn't know what secrets her father spoke of, but she wished her grandmother would tell him. The thought of moving to a village her grandmother hated terrified her.

Despite Liesel's wishes, however, her grandmother just stared up at him, her mouth open and her jaw trembling. No words fell from her lips, just a silent fear that Liesel could feel from where she stood. A strange pain that the girl had never seen before filled her grandmother's hazel eyes.

Warin watched Amala as well, nodding when she failed to answer. "That's what I thought. Liesel, make sure your mother's comfortable. We're goin'!"

Liesel hurried to the back of the cart to make sure Amala was snugly tucked beneath the blankets she and her father had piled upon her. As she did, Liesel could hear her father muttering about superstitious foolishness under his breath as he stalked back inside for another bag.

"Just an old woman making up stories to keep her children near." He threw another disgusted look at his mother-in-law as she paced back and forth in the darkness of the early morning.

Liesel wished it wasn't so early. She would have liked to see the large cabin once more in the glow of the morning sun rather than just the flicker of torchlight. This darkness felt foreign.

"I know why you're leaving so soon!" Ilsa suddenly stopped pacing and yelled, her voice shaking. "My husband is gone hunting, so you think you can sneak away like a thief in the night!"

"A thief?" Liesel's father stormed over to where Ilsa stood and glowered down at her. "We finally hear of a healer that might be able to cure your daughter, and when I take her there, you call me a thief?" His face was red, even in the light of the flame, and each angry word cut Liesel's heart like a knife.

She wanted so much to plead for him to stop, to wait until her grandfather came home. He knew much more about the forest than her father did. Shouldn't they ask him if he knew about this village in the great forest before they set out for it? But she knew from experience that her pleas would only make her father even more determined to go.

"Liesel!" Warin barked, still holding Ilsa's glare. "We're leavin'!" With that, he threw the last bundle into their rickety cart, jumped in, and clicked at the horse. Liesel stood, frozen in her place as it began to roll away.

Without a word, Ilsa turned and ran inside the house.

"Grandmother!" Liesel shrieked, still unable to move her feet. She could hear the cart stop behind her. Her father would be angry that she wasn't obeying, but she didn't care. She couldn't leave her grandmother. Not like this.

As the shriek left Liesel's lips, Ilsa sprinted back out of the house clutching a large, colorful, leather-bound book to her chest. She shoved it into Liesel's arms.

"Whatever you do," she sobbed fiercely, "you *must* escape those woods!" Warin's large arms closed around Liesel's waist before lifting her and roughly dropping her into the back of the cart. Ilsa still cried out, "Come back to me, no matter what!"

Tears streamed down Liesel's face as she watched her grandmother fall to her knees, wailing as she grew smaller and smaller in the distance.

CHAPTER 2
MARK OF THE WOLF

By the time the sun rose, Liesel knew the fields they passed were not her grandfather's. They were flat, unlike the rolling hills of her grandparents' land that lay at the foot of the mountain. Her mountain.

She watched sadly as its sharp crags softened into blurs, and her eyes strained to see them as their cart rolled steadily along. The dark blue shadows became less pronounced, and the green tree line turned gray. Green rows of vineyards gave way to golden wheat and barley as the land slowly dipped down. Eventually, the trees came into view.

The trees were nothing like Liesel had ever seen. Her grandparents' vineyard had small clusters of wooded land here and there on their property, large enough for her grandfather to find some game in, but they were mere brush compared to these.

These woods towered so high they looked even from a distance like a great, dark cloud hovering over the ground. Their depths seemed measureless, and they stood blacker than anything she'd ever seen before. And unlike her forests closer to home, no smaller trees led up to the giant trunks. The grass simply ended at the bases of the ancient sentinels that guarded the entrance to their wood.

A chill moved down Liesel's back as they turned right, off the main road onto a smaller one that led into the dark domain. As soon as they were inside, the sun disappeared. As they moved deeper in, Liesel noticed that there were few flowers growing beneath the trees. She could only imagine that the lack of light choked the life out of anything that might begin to sprout here beneath the twisted canopy.

By the time they had been in the forest for an hour, no sunlight reached the forest floor at all, just the shadows of branches, which intertwined themselves with a surprising thickness.

As her courage thinned, Liesel tried to focus on her mother to remind herself just why they were venturing into such a strange place. Amala didn't stir as her daughter tucked a stray piece of hair behind her pale ear. But then, Amala hadn't stirred in a long time. After watching her for a moment more, Liesel sighed and pulled out her grandmother's book.

It had shocked Liesel when her grandmother had pressed it into her arms. The book was Ilsa's most guarded possession.

"Reading is a privilege, Liesel," her grandmother had sternly told her when she was a young child, protesting the reading lessons Ilsa insisted on giving her. "Most people do not have such a privilege. But believe me, in all the places I've been, in all the disasters and miracles I have seen, reading has been the key to unlocking the most wonderful of secrets."

Opening the book to a random page, Liesel began reading to distract herself from the increasing darkness they continued to ride into. The words were hard to make out in the deepening gray, but Liesel knew them well enough not to need the tiny script. Written in her grandmother's own hand, with pictures drawn by her grandfather, the book brought Liesel again to marvel at all the places they had journeyed to where they could record such wonderful adventures. If she tried very hard, it was possible sometimes to pretend the path her family traveled on now was a story in her book. But then some strange sound from the trees would startle Liesel, and she would have to start trying to pretend all over again.

When night fell, or Liesel guessed it had fallen as it was darker than she had ever known possible, Liesel's father stopped the carthorse and started a fire, cursing quietly into the night as he fumbled with the tinder. When the flames were finally of a decent size, he began to roast some salted fish they had packed, and Liesel once again checked on her mother.

What had become a year of endless sleep for her mother had begun more abruptly than Liesel could have imagined possible. They had been working in their herb garden together, a task that both Liesel and Amala enjoyed. The garden had been small and neat, nothing compared to the size of her grandmother's garden out on the vineyard, but generously sized for a garden in the city.

"Keep working that mugwort, will you?" Amala had slowly risen and begun to walk back to the house. "I'm feeling a bit overheated. I think I will lie down for a few moments."

"Are you sure, Mother?" Liesel stood to follow her mother inside, but Amala had waved her back down, her brown eyes smiling.

"Thank you, no. I'll be fine. I just need a bit of rest, that's all." That was the last smile her mother had given her. A moment later, Liesel had heard a thump and the sound of pottery breaking. Running in, she'd found Amala on the floor. She feared the worst at first, thinking her mother dead. But then she saw the shaky, shallow breaths Amala still forced in and out.

Sprinting into the street, Liesel had screamed for someone to get the town healer. Women had gathered to do what they could, but upon the healer's arrival, nearly all hope was lost. A *slumber malady*, the healer had called it, a sickness without a cure.

"These things happen from time to time," he'd said as he wiped his hands. "Little bits of dark power seep into our world from the places we least expect them sometimes. Best you can do is make her comfortable." Liesel had felt as though she might pass out as she stared down at her mother on the bed, white as the holy man's robes and as still as glass.

Upon their friends' urging, Warin and Liesel had moved out of their city cottage and into Amala's parents' home on their vineyard at the foot of Liesel's beloved mountain. From there, Liesel's father and grandparents had sent word to towns near and far, begging the healers to come up and examine her mother. And many had come, although Liesel sensed it was generally in hope of the reward promised by her grandparents to the one that could cure Amala, rather than a common sense of integrity. Despite the generous reward, however, soon there were no more healers, just a woman clinging to life with little more than the ability to swallow and breathe. There had been little hope.

"We have seen this before, Warin," Liesel had once heard her grandmother whisper softly to her father.

"Yes, yes," her father had said. From the corner that she'd hidden in to eavesdrop, Liesel could imagine him rolling his eyes. "And the fairy of the land healed the fair maiden and they lived happily ever after." His voice was thick with mockery, but Liesel knew too well that it was how he hid the pain.

"But it's true!" her grandfather had insisted. "If you would only be willing to go to them and ask for the fairy—"

"I'll not be runnin' about the land chasin' after a daydream while my wife draws her last breaths!" Warin had bellowed. "We have been through this before! There is no magic!"

The stubborn outburst had been no shock to Liesel, who had heard Warin's countless rants before. That was why it had surprised her so much then when her father had listened to the stranger instead.

The day before their secret escape, Liesel had been chasing a runaway chicken in front of her grandparents' house. Out of the corner of her eye, she'd been watching a man walk up the long road from town. Considering the vineyard was the last piece of land before reaching the mountain, she knew he could only have been heading for them.

He'd stopped for a moment before starting up the path to their door, studying her for an unusual length of time. Hesitantly, Liesel had waved, which seemed to give him the courage, or audacity, as Warin had put it later, to come up to the house and talk to her as if she was of age. Liesel had found it quite enjoyable, despite her father's later grumbling. Thirteen was a strange age to be. She was expected to do the work of a woman but was ordered around as the babies were. And this man had seemed to read her mind.

"You're a little old to be chasing chickens, aren't you?" He smiled easily as he walked up the dirt path to the house.

Liesel felt herself blushing as she returned the smile. "Yes, but if I do not, no one will."

"Well, that is a good way to think of it, if nothing else." He'd laughed. His clothes were simple but clean. In fact, their detail suggested a bit of authority, someone with more influence than a simple tradesman. He spoke clearly and smiled pleasantly, but Liesel hadn't missed how his eyes traveled up and down her person the way her grandfather examined his grapes.

"Is your father nearby, perhaps?" he'd finally asked.

Liesel had fetched her father from the field, wondering the whole time what the stranger could want. He answered her question when he introduced himself to Warin.

"Good morning, sir! My name is Izaak," he had greeted her father enthusiastically. "What a lovely vineyard! And your name is?"

Liesel nearly let out a giggle. Whatever he wanted, this man was not off to a good start.

"Warin," her father grunted. "What do you want?"

Izaak looked slightly taken aback by Warin's brusqueness, but recovered his smile quickly. "I'm not familiar with this countryside, I must admit. I've never seen anything quite like your land—"

"It's not mine." Liesel's father had turned and started walking back to the fields. The thin stranger followed.

"So, you aren't a farmer?"

"Blacksmith."

"And you're out here because...?"

Warin turned sharply to face the man. "Look, I'm busy. Are you going to stand there babbling, or tell me what it is that you want?"

"I must confess," Izaak finally lost his smile and sighed, "my village suffered a great sickness last winter. Many died, and there are few to take their places. I am looking for strong men who could move out to work in our village."

Liesel felt the first ripple of unease when she saw her father's eyes light up at the mention of moving. While Warin had agreed to live at the vineyard, everyone knew he hated living with his wife's parents. Then disappointment settled into his face.

"Interestin' as that sounds, my wife is ill. We've had healers from all over to see her, but none could help."

The man's eyes brightened again. "Ah, but since the sickness, we have a new healer! She came to us from the Far East with herbs and salves that few around here have seen! And I know she hasn't been to see your wife yet, as she refuses to leave our village."

The moment he mentioned the new healer, Liesel knew they were going. And it wasn't long before all of the details of the move were settled between the two men.

"Liesel," her father had called to her as the thin stranger left, "don't tell your grandparents quite yet. I'll tell 'em when it's the right time."

The right time had been that night, apparently, when her grandfather was gone hunting, and her grandmother had been powerless to stop Warin. And now, they were in the middle of a forest without light.

"We're almost there," Liesel whispered to her mother before laying a goodnight kiss on her cold cheek. Leaving the vineyard was the last thing Liesel had wanted to do. As she stared into the fire her father had built, however, Liesel decided that maybe it was worth a try. She would do anything to have Amala back.

They rose early again the next morning and continued along the road. The further they traveled, however, the more uncomfortable Liesel felt. These woods seemed sick. Though no direct sunshine had penetrated the trees the first day they'd entered the great forest, it had still been light enough. But on the second day, even the brightest spots made the forest appear the way the sky had during the darkest storms back on the vineyard. Liesel looked down at her bright red cloak, suddenly glad for the vivid color in such a dull place.

They arrived at the town late that afternoon, or what Liesel guessed to be afternoon, at least. Glad to see signs of life after their strange, solitary ride, Liesel smiled at the first passersby that she saw. Men, women, and children came out of their thatched roof cottages to stare at the newcomers, but oddly enough, no one returned her smile. Farther into town, a small child raised her hand to wave, but her mother pushed it down and hurried her out of the street. Soon the houses grew closer, and shops, stalls, and larger buildings all blended together until they could see what looked like a town square up ahead.

"Father," Liesel called in a low voice, "it doesn't look like there was an illness here recently."

"What do you mean?"

"All of these people... the shops are full, and the people are everywhere."

"Bets are, they're like us," Warin said with a shrug. His nonchalant attitude didn't fool Liesel, though. She could see him looking at the people after that, as well, a small crease furrowing his brow.

When they reached the well in the center of the main town square, Warin pulled the horse to a halt and instructed Liesel to stay with her mother. He was on his way to the steps of the largest building Liesel had yet seen, when a rather rotund man walked purposefully toward them, Izaak trailing nervously after him.

"You must be our new blacksmith!"

"Which is odd, considerin' I just passed one up back there." Warin frowned at Izaak, his lilting accent making his displeasure even more obvious. "You said there had been an illness that wiped out the village."

Izaak paled a bit, but the other man, unfazed, stepped forward with an overly friendly smile. "We can always use another blacksmith, especially as ours is getting along in years."

"And you are?"

"Odo, town mayor."

"Well, Odo, we're here to see your healer."

The mayor's sweaty smile faltered for a moment before reappearing on his face. "Surely you would like to see your new home first—"

"The healer. Or we're leavin'."

Liesel felt a small flicker of hope in her heart. Perhaps this healer might know something the others didn't. And when Amala awoke, she could convince Warin to leave the forest and take the family home.

The mayor looked a bit unnerved, and paused before answering. Finally, though, he glumly nodded and turned, motioning for the family to follow. Warin hopped back up into the cart and clucked at the horse. And just two streets over, they stopped before a small cottage.

It looked no different than the other cottages, with the exception of a herb garden that lined the path to the door. Liesel felt another stab of unease, though, as she glanced at its contents. The garden itself was barely larger than her mother's had been, and she recognized every plant in it. Most of the plants looked sick, though, which Liesel guessed was from the lack of direct sunlight.

The weedy plot hardly looked like it belonged to a herbalist from another land, just as the woman walking out of the house to greet them hardly looked like she was from the Far East. She had pale skin, as did everyone else in the forest village, mousey brown hair pinned back carelessly beneath a dirty blue cap, and a thin face with dull eyes.

As Warin gently lifted his wife from the back of the cart, the mayor fairly sprinted over to whisper in the woman's ear. Her eyes widened a bit, and she looked over the mayor's shoulder to glare at Izaak. By then, Warin was heading up the path, and Liesel didn't miss the look of panic that flitted across the woman's face as she opened the door for them to walk inside.

The cottage room was dark with just one candle to see by, but there really wasn't that much to see. Liesel had been inside the healer's house back in her old city, a building that was full to the brim with dried plant pieces in jars, other plants hanging upside down to dry, a large variety of mixing bowls, mortar and pestle, and a large pot to boil mixtures in. This house had only one shelf of jars, and most of them were covered with dust.

The mayor cleared the table so Warin could lay Liesel's mother on top of it.

"What–" the healer began to ask, but Izaak interrupted her.

"Duffy, remember the sleeping sickness I told you about?"

The woman stared at him blankly until a look of nervous recognition came to her face.

"Oh... oh, yes." She walked over to her shelf of jars and stared up at them for a moment before pulling four down. Grabbing the dirty mortar and pestle from another dusty table, she went to work grinding and mixing the herbs.

Liesel watched intently as she worked, running through the plants and their uses in her head. Her mother had been an expert with herbs. Although this mixture of herbs that the woman had concocted seemed a bit simple for the kind of illness her mother was suffering, nothing was too alarming until she pulled out a dried clipping of a dark green branch with spiky leaves and fluffy orange buds.

"No!"

Everyone jumped at the sound of her voice.

"That's fox heel!" Liesel cried. Even the healer stared at her as if she'd spoken another language. Only then did Liesel realize how rude it must seem for a girl to correct a grown healer. But Liesel knew all about *that* plant.

She'd nearly eaten it when she was two. Her mother had looked over just as Liesel had raised it to her mouth. They kept it in the garden because it could heal skin wounds, her mother said, but it was absolutely never to be eaten. Amala had run so fast she had dropped and broken a bowl to keep Liesel from touching the plant to her tongue. When Liesel had gotten older, Amala had shown her how to safely apply it to a bruise, but never was it to be eaten or drunk.

"Crushing the flowers into the herb makes it poisonous," Liesel explained softly as her father's look of shock turned into a glare.

"Liesel, outside. Now." Liesel felt her face redden with embarrassment as she followed her father out the front door like a small child. When they were safely out on the walk, Warin bent down to look her in the eye. "Just what do you think you're doin'?"

"I told you," Liesel whispered, "Fox heel is dangerous."

"You think their healer doesn't know her own trade? That a girl of thirteen knows better than she does?"

Liesel felt resentment rise in her throat. Glaring back at her father, she huffed. "They lied about the sickness. There has obviously been no blight here. They lied about their healer being from the Far East! Doesn't it seem that they might lie about this, too?"

"One more word out of you, girl, and you will regret it!" Warin gave his daughter a withering look.

"I don't care!" Liesel shouted, tired of watching such foolishness play out. "If you let them give that rubbish to Mother, she will die!" She could be just as stubborn as her father when she wanted to be.

Warin stared at her in awe for a moment before giving her a sneer and stalking back inside. Liesel took off after him, darting around his large frame, just in time to see Doffy prepare the mixture for a tea. Liesel knocked the spoon out of the woman's hands.

"I don't know what you think you're doing, but I'll not let you poison her!" Liesel yelled.

Two strong hands grabbed her from behind, however, and Warin said, "I apologize for my daughter's behavior. She's just upset about her mum being sick. Please, do what you need to do. She'll see eventually that she needs to trust those who know better than her."

After giving the mayor a nervous glance, the healer lifted another spoonful of the mixture to prepare the tea again. Liesel felt like her heart had stopped beating and dropped into her stomach as she watched the woman mix the poisonous orange-tinted tea. Tears began to slide down her face as she realized she was going to watch her mother die. She shrieked for her father to stop them, pleading with him to save Amala's life. Warin put his hand gently but firmly over his daughter's mouth as he continued to restrain her.

"It'll be all right, Leese," he whispered kindly into her ear through her weeping. "I know you're frightened, but this woman will save her. She'll be better. I feel it in my gut."

All too soon, the deed was done. Amala had swallowed the tea, and the family was taken to their new cottage.

"The old tailor lived here," the mayor explained. "He passed on three years ago. It's yours now. Let Izaak help you carry your wife in so she can rest."

Liesel watched it all with dead eyes. The mayor and Izaak soon left, and then it was just their family. Liesel sat with her mother, holding Amala's hand as Warin emptied the cart.

"Is she showing any signs?" he asked hopefully. It was all Liesel could do to stay silent in response, when all she wanted was to scream. She glared instead and shook her head. "Well, then," he said, "I'm off to the butcher's. Take care of your mother. I'll be back."

Liesel silently loathed his chipper tone, ignoring his wave as he left. It wasn't long after that Amala's breathing slowed and her hands grew cool. Through the blur of her tears, Liesel finally saw her mother's gray-blue eyes flutter open for the first time in a year.

"My Leese." Amala's hand shook as she lifted it to touch Liesel's face. Her voice was rough, but it was sweeter than Liesel remembered. Liesel grabbed her mother's hand and held it to her cheek.

"I tried to stop them," she sobbed, "but they wouldn't listen! Father wouldn't listen!" As she spoke, Liesel wondered why she was blubbering on about the tea when her mother's eyes were finally open. Didn't that mean she was better? Besides, there were so many other things she wanted to tell her mother about that had happened in the last year, but all Liesel could do was cry.

"I know, sweet girl." Amala's voice was faint. "I couldn't see you, but I could hear."

"You could hear?" Liesel frowned in confusion. Coughing, Amala nodded.

"I could hear everything."

"Since the day you fell sick?"

Amala nodded, wincing as though in pain.

"But are you well again?" Liesel held her breath. Amala coughed deeply again in response, as if to answer her question.

"No, love. I will be gone soon." She drew a shaky breath. "But it seems the Maker has given me a few moments with you before I go." Liesel felt a new flood of tears wash down her face.

"Now, there's no time for that," Amala gently scolded her daughter, a tear sliding down her own face. "Your father will need you. He won't take care of himself without your help. And you," she gently tapped Liesel's nose, "be careful. You're so beautiful...

and men will notice. Men aren't always what they seem." She drew in another rattling breath and caressed her daughter's face once more. "I love you, my sweet girl."

And with that, Liesel's mother was gone.

LIESEL SAT PERFECTLY STILL for an immeasurable time, staring into her mother's ashen face. But deep inside, the part of her that dreamed couldn't be still. It couldn't accept that this was how it ended. Words began to echo in her head, some from her mother. There were other voices, too, however, and eventually there was one command that drowned out all of the rest.

Whatever you do, you must escape those woods! Her grandmother's voice commanded desperately. *Come back to me, no matter what!*

Grandmother had been right. They had come to this wicked village, and the healer was either completely incompetent, or she had just poisoned Amala purposefully. With all of the lies that had been told, all of the desperate looks the townspeople had been giving one another after seeing her, something in the town of Ward was very wrong.

Without knowing what she was doing, Liesel found herself out of her chair and running. Night darkness was beginning to cover everything, but it didn't matter. Liesel knew which direction the vineyard was in, and she wasn't stopping until she got there. It didn't matter that she could no longer see more than five feet in front of her, nor did she care that she had no supplies. All Liesel could think about was going home, running into her grandmother's arms, and leaving this wretched forest behind forever.

But soon it grew too dark, and Liesel's skirt caught on a low branch, causing her to trip. Her hands stung as they scraped against unseen sticks and dry pine needles, and she stubbed her toe on a rock. Wet earth stuck to her as she began to rise, but something made her freeze halfway up. Her breaths were ragged and heavy from her run, but she tried to quiet them as she strained to listen. She was almost sure she'd heard breathing that was not her own.

Turning slowly, still on her hands and knees, she nearly fainted.

The silhouette of a creature stood out against the shadows. A growl slipped out, so slight she wasn't even sure she'd heard it. Fear made her blood turn cold, and with all thoughts of the damp ground and her scratched palms forgotten, Liesel took off again, even faster this time. A tiny voice in her head wondered what she was doing, why she was even in the forest, and screamed at her that no sane girl of thirteen years would be where she was, but she ignored it completely.

She'd gone only a little ways, however, before she was flat on her stomach, the creature crouching on her back. For the first time, Liesel found her voice, screaming as loudly as she could for help.

A heavy paw was shoved expertly onto the back of her neck, shoving her face into the ground, cutting off her cry as a snout with gleaming white teeth lowered itself down beside her face to growl. It occurred to Liesel that she was going to die.

A part of her wondered if this was the Maker's way of secret mercy, saving her from a long, miserable life in that horrid village without her mother. The rest of her, however, was terrified. What kind of pain could a creature like this inflict upon a human, particularly one that wasn't yet fully grown? What kind of gruesome things could those teeth do?

In the brief second before the bite, Liesel wondered which side he would attack her from. The neck? Or perhaps a leg?

A warm pang from her right hand surprised her, however. She turned her head as best she could to look through the darkness at her hand as the warm blood trickled down it. It hurt, but it wasn't the killing lunge she had been expecting. And even stranger was that the animal wasn't continuing the attack. As soon as he had bitten her, he had moved a few feet away, a low growling still in his throat.

Despite the blackness of night, she could make out the contour of a wolf, the biggest she'd ever seen. His coat was silver, and it almost gleamed in the gray haze that filled the dark woods. Liesel had seen wolves before, but only from a distance, and with the comfort of her grandfather's expert crossbow nearby to protect her. This beast's claws were difficult to see, but they looked longer than anything Liesel could have imagined.

At that moment, she locked eyes with the beast, and as soon as she did, she began to shake. The eyes into which she gazed were unmistakably human.

She didn't have time to linger and ponder his unusual eyes, however. In one second, the wolf was watching her intently, as if surveying its strange work, and in the next moment, it was lying lifelessly on the ground, an arrow in its heart. Liesel watched in horror as the human eyes closed.

"Are you all right?" a man's voice called from a distance.

As heavy footsteps approached, Liesel found herself incapable of answering him. She couldn't even lift herself up off the ground. She could only lie there trembling uncontrollably, scrunching her eyes shut as though that would make the horror disappear.

"That's a nasty cut there," the deep voice said. Gently, Liesel felt herself lifted by strong arms and cradled like a child. "Do you live in Ward?" he asked.

Liesel racked her memory, trying to remember the village's name. Ward sounded right. Even if it wasn't, she didn't really care. She just did her best to nod.

"What are you doing out here all alone?" She could hear the frown in his voice.

Liesel finally opened her eyes and looked at him, but her chattering teeth made it impossible to answer.

His expression softened. "Well, no matter. We'd best get you home. I'm sure your mum's worried something awful. I know my wife would be." He didn't see, but Liesel felt a tear roll down her cheek. Yes, Mother would have worried.

As he carried her, he talked, and Liesel found his voice to be soothing. He was a hunter, he said, and his name was Paul. He didn't usually come this far east, but the buck he'd been chasing had led him outside of his normal grounds. He had a family back in higher country, including a daughter about her age, and he didn't like to leave them for long.

Liesel began to drift in and out of slumber as he carried her back and chatted away. It wasn't until they were at the edge of the village that she realized she'd fallen asleep.

"You, sir!" The hunter called out. "I have a girl here, and she's not well! Do you know where I might find her family?"

"I'm new here. I wouldn't know." Liesel's eyes were closed again, but she recognized the worn, rough tone of her father's voice. Instead of its usual arrogance, however, it was hoarse and broken. A small piece of Liesel's senses returned, enough to feel pity for the man. But with the pity came rage as well. It was he who had dragged them to this place of death, and he had been the one to hold her back when Amala still could have been saved. And he knew it, from the sound of his voice.

"If you please," the hunter said, shifting her weight in his arms, "I found this girl in the forest. She was being attacked by a wolf–"

"Girl?" Warin's voice lifted slightly. "I've been missin' mine since I came home and found her mother dead."

"I... I'm sorry," the hunter said softly. "I found this child in the woods, like I said, bitten by a wolf. Perhaps the pain of losing her mother was just too much..." He stepped forward again. "If you would just look and see if she's yours." Liesel heard her father rouse himself from the stoop slowly and walk toward them.

"Aye, she's mine. Don't know what the fool girl was thinkin', runnin' into the woods alone at night." Despite his harsh words, his voice was soft and gentle. Familiar arms lifted her from the hunter's. Liesel wished she could find her voice to thank the stranger for his kindness.

Her father didn't put her into the bed, and Liesel couldn't look to see if it was because her mother's body was still there. Instead, he simply carried her to a chair in the corner of the room and cradled her as he had done when she was young. The last sound Liesel heard that night was Warin's quiet sobbing as he held her close. Her last thought was a desperate one.

She still hadn't escaped the woods.

CHAPTER 3
FINDING THE SUN

"You're not readin' that book again, are you?" Warin called through the doorway.

Liesel paused, trying to come up with something to say. She had nothing, however, by the time her father walked inside.

"You've read that blasted book every day for the past month." He shook his head at her. "You're goin' to bring both of us to madness if you don't leave this house sometime."

Despite Warin's rare show of paternal love the night her mother died, he and Liesel had spoken less than ever in the month that followed. He'd never even asked about the wolf, just accepted what the hunter had told him. Then he had gone on as if nothing had happened. The wolf attack, her mother's death, even his new job at the blacksmith's stall merited only a few words.

And Liesel was fine with that. In fact, she was more than fine. She knew he missed Amala, and she knew he was grieving, but it did little to lessen his accidental participation in her mother's death. Warin had never even apologized. He had simply carried on as if the whole thing had been just an accident.

The funeral had been small, just a grieving husband and daughter, the holy man, and the aloof mayor, although Liesel wasn't sure exactly why he was there. Perhaps Odo felt some guilt for playing a part in Amala's death, she thought at first, although one wouldn't know it from the number of times he yawned while her mother was buried. It was about all Liesel could take to have him present, and it helped her realize even more how much she needed to escape Ward.

The night after the funeral, Liesel was desperate enough to leave that she broke the silence she'd kept toward her father since Amala had died, and she begged him to take them back to the vineyard.

"You could even move back to the city." Liesel had followed him around as he mucked the tiny horse stall that stood behind the cottage. "You would never have to worry about me. I could live with Grandmother and Grandfather! We—"

"No." Warin had been sudden and fierce in his refusal. "We are not goin' back." When he turned to see the glare she gave him, he leaned down to look her in the eye. "And don't you even think of naggin' me about it, 'cause my mind is made up. We're stayin' here. Best for you not to question the wisdom of my decision."

"Mother would have hated this," Liesel had hissed at him, trying desperately to keep her tears at bay. Immediately, she regretted her words. He turned away silently, but not before she saw the raw pain in his expression. Still too angry to apologize, however, Liesel had stomped away and had gone for a walk instead.

Ward was not a large village, but there were enough people milling about to call it bustling. The mayor had mentioned that while they couldn't farm for the lack of sunlight, the townspeople made their living by hosting travelers who were taking the shortcut through the forest to the capital city. Instead of growing their food, the people had their supplies brought in by wagon from the sunnier places outside of the forest. This struck Liesel as quite expensive, but she quickly realized that they could afford it, due to their many inns, as well as animal stalls, taverns, and wells.

Liesel passed by the tailor's shop, the swordsmith's, the butcher's, two bakeries, and the church as she'd walked. It should have been a pleasant outing. The market was full, and neighbors chatted happily as their children scampered through the streets. The longer she walked, however, the more Liesel realized she was not the only one looking. The villagers were looking right back at her as well. The adults didn't even attempt to hide their stares, and some of the children pointed.

Liesel felt herself blush, probably red enough to be visible even in the gray of the forest evening. Had word gotten out about her fit at the healer's? Or was this how they treated all new arrivals?

It wasn't long before she had decided to return to the cottage as quickly as possible, and since that outing, she hadn't left the cottage except to get water from the well, gather kindling for the fireplace, or attend Holy Day worship. In her time at home, her grandmother's book had been Liesel's sole comfort and companion. Warin didn't allow reading in the evenings, as he said it wasted precious candles, but during the day, the book was her only friend. And now her father wanted to take even that.

"Why don't you go outside?" Warin frowned at her beneath his dark, bushy eyebrows.

Liesel raised her own eyebrows in response and looked pointedly at her hand.

Her father snorted. "Won't do you any good hidin' inside when the entire village is in the forest, girl. Wolves mostly stay to themselves. You probably just surprised the one that got you, that's all. Now I want you out of this house for the time bein'. Go."

It wasn't without irritation or the temptation to say something sharp that Liesel left her beloved book in the cabin. But arguing with her father would be pointless while he was in such a mood. Slowly, she made her way down the narrow dirt path to the main road. She was not going back to the town by herself, that was for sure. The open stares she was sure to encounter made her feel as if she had the plague. So she began down the road in the other direction, the one that would eventually lead her toward the sun. She might not be able to escape the town for now, but she could pretend, even if just for a while.

After about twenty minutes of walking, a change brought her to a halt. It took her a moment to recognize it for what it was, though. On the other side of the road, deep in the foliage, almost too deep to see, one thin beam of sunlight shined down through the otherwise canopied ceiling. Liesel felt her breath catch in her throat. After a month in the depths of an eternally gray forest, she was starved for something bright.

After pausing for a moment, Liesel set her jaw and lifted her skirts delicately to begin chasing the bit of sun before it disappeared completely. The forest floor was littered with dead branches and dry pine needles. As she slowly hiked over pile after pile of dead brush, Liesel started to wonder at the wisdom of her decision to make the journey in a dress, but when she finally reached the spot, it was worth it.

The sun was weak by the time it stretched through the treetops, all the way to the ground, but its warmth was delightful. Liesel stood where it trickled down onto her face, imagining she was back on the vineyard, when a rustle in the bushes behind her made her heart stop.

Nearly frozen with fear, she turned slowly toward the sound. The forest was eerily silent as Liesel held her breath and waited. Was it a snake? Or perhaps a wolverine? There was a story of one of those vicious little creatures in her grandmother's book, one that had attacked a man and taken his arm. Or could it be another wolf? Unable to wait any longer, Liesel tried to gather her wits, and lifted a large stick. She tried to sound fierce, but her voice came out dry and hoarse.

"Who is it? I know you're there." She immediately felt rather foolish, considering the noise might be an animal, waiting to pounce. It was no animal sound, however, that came from the brush in response.

"Only if you put down the stick."

Before she could put the stick down, Liesel nearly dropped it in shock. It was a boy's voice.

The boy stepped forward slowly, his eyes wary. His dark brown hair was messy, roughly chopped off as if cut with a dull blade, or perhaps just cut very carelessly. The clothes he wore had holes in several places, and looked just a little too short, although that wasn't unusual for boys about Liesel's age, which was what she guessed him to be. The way he moved, however, was the most unusual thing about him. The grace with which he placed his feet as he cautiously stepped toward her was almost feral.

Neither of them spoke for a long time. After her legs began to hurt from standing so still, Liesel finally gathered the courage to speak again.

"Why were you watching me?"

"I was wondering why you were in the forest alone. Women don't walk these woods alone." His voice wasn't deep, but it wasn't a young boy's tenor either.

Liesel raised her chin a bit defensively. "And what if I like to walk in the woods?" It was a strange thing to say, as Liesel did not actually like to walk in the woods, these or any others. But it annoyed her that this boy would tell her what she could and couldn't do.

He just made a face and shook his head. "It doesn't matter. Women don't walk these woods alone. Actually, they don't walk in them at all. It's not safe." The way his brow furrowed made Liesel feel somewhat foolish. Of course she knew it wasn't safe. Her first night there had proven that.

She sighed in resignation. "We just moved here, and my mother died." Her voice cracked a bit. "No one will talk to me, and I don't know why. Then I saw this patch of sunlight, and I just... I needed something familiar. I needed to escape, even for a little while."

Suddenly unable to stand, Liesel fell, crying, onto a low boulder nearby. The boy watched with wide eyes as Liesel shed the first tears since the night her mother died. Along with her sorrow, she also felt anger for herself, for she had sworn not to break, not to give her father another reason to reprimand her, and now she was doing just that in front of a complete stranger. Sniffling, Liesel wiped the traitorous tears from her face and tried to give the boy a confident smile.

"I'm sorry." This time, his voice was less suspicious and his expression was softer.

"Thank you, but it is I who should be sorry. I'll be fine. And my name is Liesel." Liesel struggled to make her voice less tremulous as she looked back up at the small patch of sunlight filtering through the distant treetops. "I just wish there was more sun. It would be a little more like home."

"You lived somewhere with lots of light?" The boy still sounded cautious, but Liesel could tell his curiosity was getting the better of him.

As she nodded, a sudden longing took hold of her. She desperately wanted him to stay, where just a few minutes before, she had hoped he would just let her run back to her cottage. Though he still looked tentative, his eyes were kind, and he was giving her more attention than anyone else had since she had arrived the month before.

"I lived on a vineyard with my grandparents."

Unconsciously, it seemed, the boy stepped closer. "What did it look like?"

"Their vineyard is at the foot of a mountain, so you can see for miles from their front door." She smiled a little at the memory. "The sky is endless. Below it, you can see the city, as well as other towns that lie down the road beyond. The vineyard is green, and laid out in rows, and the air is warm and dry."

"You miss it," the boy stated matter-of-factly.

Liesel nodded again. "I never knew I could miss someplace so much."

"You don't like it here?" This time it was a question, as if the thought had never occurred to him that someone might not want to live in the woods.

"No." Liesel shook her head so emphatically that a tendril of yellow hair fell out of her hood. "Not even flowers grow here. I miss the sun and the colors. I miss my grandparents." The boy frowned thoughtfully at this. "Besides," Liesel said, giving one final sniffle and standing to dust off her dress, "as I said, no one in town will talk to me."

The boy dropped his eyes immediately, and looked away. Liesel almost asked what was wrong, but stopped herself. She wanted at least one person to talk to, even if he was an odd boy from the forest. So instead she asked, "Do you live in town?"

"I live in the woods with my family," he said uneasily.

It took everything in Liesel not to ask all of the questions building up inside of her, but she decided against it, fearing she might frighten the shy boy away.

Why *was* he so nervous? She wasn't threatening in manner, at least, in a way that she knew of. She had picked up that stick, of course, but really had not the slightest idea of how she would have used it had he been an animal. He must simply be shy.

Unsure of what else to say without overwhelming him further, Liesel finally said, "I suppose I should go home soon. It's getting dark, and my father will be expecting supper."

"Wait," he half-turned toward her as if waking from a stupor, "will you be coming back tomorrow?"

Liesel weighed his expression before answering. Was she trying to avoid her, or did he really want to see her again? She sighed. "Truthfully? Not if I can help it."

"Why?"

"I..." She paused. "I'm afraid of the wolves." It felt foolish to talk about the beasts in the middle of the day as they stood there together, especially as he lived in the woods. But she needed to. She'd tried to tell her father, of course, tried to describe the fear that had filled her as she'd stared into those human eyes. No matter how hard she worked, however, the moment she tried to talk about the actual wolf, aside from what the hunter had said, her voice caught in her throat, and she could not get the words out.

To her surprise, the boy snorted and shook his head. "I'm here. They won't attack."

Liesel thought that this was one of the strangest things she had ever heard anyone say. She looked dubiously at the boy again. His voice was beginning to change, but he certainly didn't have the body of a man yet. What did he expect to do if one of those giant beasts found them? He looked so confident, however, that she decided not to challenge him.

"Well," Liesel bit her lip hesitantly, "do you want me to?" Her heart beat unevenly as the question rolled off her tongue. If he said no, she would be spared the dangers of the forest that might come with a companion who thought himself impervious to wolf attacks. And yet, there was something about him that drew her nearer, made her want to look more deeply into those kind eyes and draw out their secrets.

"I suppose it would be all right." He shrugged carelessly, but

Liesel didn't miss the nervous glance he threw up at her while staring at the ground. She couldn't hide her smile.

"Then I suppose I will be back." Liesel turned to head toward the road.

"One more thing."

She turned to see him staring after her with a quizzical look.

"Why is your cloak red?"

"My mother liked red. Why?"

He shook his head. "It's just an odd color to wear in the forest, unless you want everyone and everything to see you."

Liesel touched the cloak gently. He was right of course. And yet... "It was my mother's when she was a girl."

"Huh. I still think it's strange." And without another word, he was gone.

For the first time since she'd arrived in Ward, Liesel felt warm, and it wasn't from the rays of the sun she had basked in, either. Having someone to talk to, and better yet, someone who wanted to see her again, made her feel just a little more at home in a way she hadn't felt since her mother's last touch.

By the time she got home, Warin had returned from the blacksmith's stall. He was already pulling his boots back on, however.

"I forgot the cornmeal today while I was out. Come with me. You can tell me what else we need." Then he muttered, "Your mother always did these things."

As angry as Liesel still was with her father, she felt another stab of pity for him. He had depended on Amala in so many ways. Nodding, she smiled, and for once, it wasn't forced. As they left the cottage, though, she decided not to tell him about the boy just yet.

Their walk was quiet, which suited Liesel, until an unwelcome voice startled her.

"So, lass, have you made any friends?" Mayor Odo was suddenly at her elbow, and his proximity made Liesel jump and then cringe. How had he found them so quickly? His house was on the other side of Ward.

"Ah," he laughed, "I can tell you have by that expression. Who did you meet?" His smile was friendly enough, but there was something in his eyes that made Liesel think otherwise. Unfortunately, her father chose that moment to suddenly be as interested in her welfare as the prying mayor. She could see him giving her a long, sideways look as they walked.

She sighed. "I don't know his name, actually." It was only as she spoke, however, that she realized it was true. She had given the boy her name, but he had never shared his. An idea quickly formed in her head, though, so she continued to talk. "He's about my age, and he has hair the color of bark, and brown eyes. He is probably a handspan shorter than my father. Do you know him?" Perhaps the nosy mayor might be helpful after all. She was dying to know the boy's name. "Oh," she added, "and he says his family lives in the forest."

At this last comment, the mayor's face suddenly paled. Even Warin noticed.

"Is there something wrong with his family, Odo?" He scowled at the short man. But the mayor shook his head vehemently.

"Oh, no! Kurt's family is very nice."

Liesel allowed herself a small smile. So his name was Kurt. It fit him, she decided.

"What do they do out there?" Warin asked.

"They're hunters." Odo took a sudden interest in a passing cart of potatoes while he answered.

"I thought you said huntin' in this area is forbidden!"

"It is, but... Kurt's family is very old. In fact, they own much of the land around the town. It is best just to leave them be."

Her father was already shaking his head. "Liesel, I don't want you—"

"No, no, no!" Odo interrupted him. "She will be perfectly safe. The family just tends to keep to themselves, that's all. The boy needs a friend, though. He's a good boy. Liesel will be the perfect companion, with you living at the edge of town and all."

Liesel held her breath as she looked at her father. While she had never been one for disobeying direct orders, she didn't know if she could keep her sanity and live much longer without some conversation. To her relief, however, Liesel's father finally nodded his head in assent.

"I suppose that will work then, if it gets you out of the house sometimes."

Liesel grinned in spite of herself. Her father had succeeded in separating her from her beloved book, but Liesel was suddenly very glad to have a reason to leave the cottage. Besides, she thought, she might not have to give up her book after all. She had an idea.

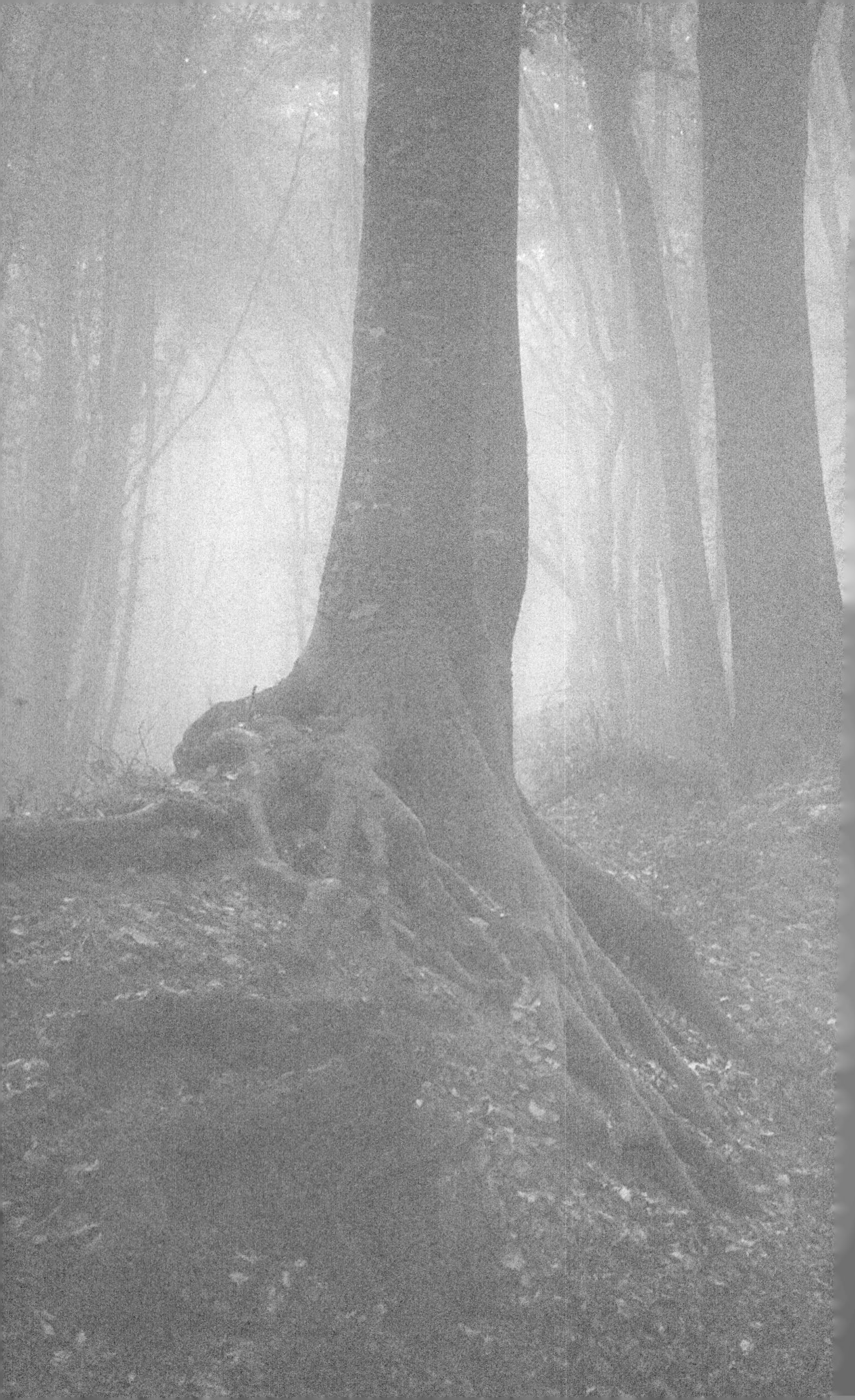

CHAPTER 4
NO GOOD MAGIC

Liesel seemed to drop everything she touched the next day as she finished her chores. Her mind just wasn't on the work. What if he didn't come? The boy was certainly unusual, but there was a warmth about him that Liesel found herself craving as she finally set off into the woods. She really didn't see how she could survive much longer without a friend.

Loneliness had held little meaning for Liesel before her mother died. She had grown up with friends all over Weit. Even after Amala had fallen ill, Liesel had always been able to find one of her grandparents to tag along with around the house or follow through the fields. And while Liesel wasn't prone to idle chatter, she liked hearing other people speak. Living with the silent Warin was beginning to take its toll on her. She walked even faster through the brush as she sent up a prayer to the Maker that Kurt would indeed return.

When she got to the clearing, she nearly passed out from relief, for he was already standing exactly where she had left him the day before, staring up at the small patch of sunlight and wearing a thoughtful look.

"You said yesterday that your grandparents' home has much sunlight. There are other places around the world like that as well, are there not?" He continued to stare up at the canopy as he spoke.

"Yes." She came as close to him as she dared and looked up at the beam, too.

Without turning, he simply nodded. "I knew it. Father was wrong. You know how I knew?" He finally turned his serious golden-brown eyes upon her, and without waiting for a response, grabbed her wrist and took off running, dragging her deeper into the forest behind him.

Liesel allowed him to lead her, although a wiser voice in her mind that sounded much like her mother's wondered how far she should let this strange boy lead her into woods she barely knew. And yet, the heat of his hand was comforting in a way Liesel had never felt before. Besides, she reasoned as she bumped along, she didn't want to hurt his feelings, so she allowed herself to be yanked along until she heard water.

They burst out of the trees and into a clearing. In the center of the clearing was the largest waterfall Liesel had ever seen. She gaped up at the waterfall's short cliffs to find a large patch of blue sky above them. Unfiltered, blinding sun spilled down into the water that lapped the sand not far from their feet. The roaring of the water was a shock, compared with the near silence of the forest, as it crashed down into a sparkling blue pond three times wider than Liesel's cottage. The waterfall itself was about as tall as the church steeple back in her old city, and it was nearly as majestic in its bearing.

But the sky... Liesel found herself grinning ridiculously as she looked up in awe at the clear blue sky.

"What is this place?" She had to nearly yell over the crashing water. He waved her over to a log on the other side of the clearing a bit further from the noise.

"I found it when I was small. My mother told me stories of places with lots of open sky, and I wanted to see for myself. My father says this is as big as it gets, but I never believed him." He looked at her, his eyes suddenly burning with curiosity. "Tell me," his voice was reverent, almost too quiet to hear over the water's roar. "Tell me about all of those other places!"

"Well," Liesel thought for a moment, "I haven't been to many of them myself, as I've only lived by the mountain, but I've read stories of the places my grandparents visited..." He nodded eagerly, so she continued. "In one kingdom, the rulers have greater powers than our king, or any other king, possesses. They can make blue fire with their hands and use it to heal as well as fight! Then there–"

"Wait, they have good magic?"

"Of course it's good magic. Then next place they went–"

"But there is no good magic!"

Liesel huffed, finally tired of his interruptions.

"Are you a magician?"

"No." He made a face.

"Well then, how do you know that good magic doesn't exist? Now, do you want to hear the stories or not?"

Nodding, he got up from the log and flung himself down on the sand at her feet, closing his eyes and putting his hands behind his head.

Mollified, Liesel continued. "One of my favorites is of the kingdom where the ocean meets the land, and the ocean folk are half-human and half-fish."

Kurt sat straight up, sand spilling out of his wild hair and down the back of his shirt. He didn't seem to notice, though. "Tell me about that one!"

"I could tell you better if I had the book my grandmother gave me. It's filled with drawings and stories from when she and my grandfather traveled the world. I could bring it tomorrow, and you could see for yourself. If you can't read it, I can–"

"I can read," he scoffed as he stood up and skipped a rock across the water. Liesel felt a bit guilty. She knew the story by heart, as she did every story in the book, but she hadn't been sure he would want to see her again after this. By promising to bring the book, she knew she could buy herself at least one more day with him.

With the promise of another meeting, she leaned back on the log and lifted her chin toward the sky, allowing the heat of the sun's rays to wash over her whole body. She couldn't remember the last time she had been this gloriously content. Time quietly passed as they sat in silence.

Still, the longer they sat, the more Liesel fought to quell the questions that were raging inside of her, and finally she gave up. "If your father is so sure there aren't places with open sky, why doesn't he leave the forest to see for himself? It's only a day and a half's ride to the edge of the trees." To freedom.

"My father doesn't ever leave the forest. He is too busy taking care of the family."

"Oh. Do you have a large family?"

"You could say that." He stared out at the waterfall, but Liesel shook her head to herself in confusion. Never had she met anyone so determined to remain mysterious.

Not long after, it was time for her to leave. As they stood to go, Liesel hated saying goodbye to the waning sun that was now beginning to sink. More slowly than the first time, they made their way back to edge of the clearing, and Liesel realized as she lifted her skirts that their run had put more tears in her dress than she would be able to mend in one night. It had been worth it, though, she smiled to herself.

When they were near the path, Kurt stopped. "Don't forget to bring your book tomorrow," he said before turning to go.

"Wait!" Liesel had an idea, and spoke before she had time to lose her nerve. He turned and looked at her with an open expression. "Would you like to come back with me... just for a few minutes? You could meet my father, and I could show you the book there." But he was already shaking his head.

"My father wants me to stay out of the town." The disappointment must have been evident in her face, however, because he added more gently, "But I will be back tomorrow." And with that, he was gone.

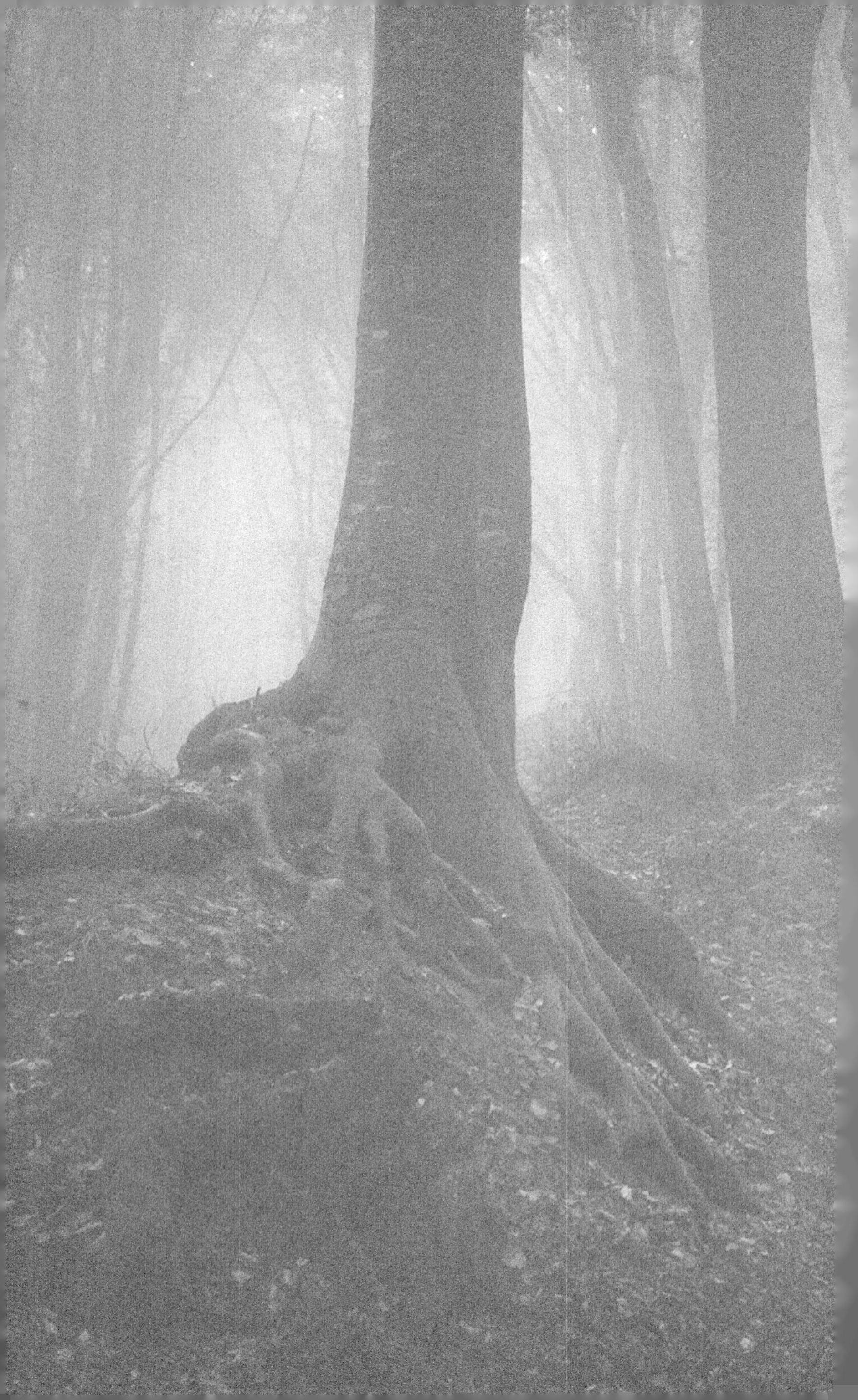

CHAPTER 5
FORGOTTEN DAUGHTER

"I don't think you could stand out anymore if you tried." Kurt shook his head as he handed the book back to Liesel. It had nearly met disaster the first time she had tried to carry it to the waterfall. She had caught her dress on a bush and nearly dropped the book in a puddle. From then on, Kurt had taken to carrying it for her.

Every day, they read another story, and every evening, he asked her if she was coming back the next day. Liesel enjoyed it immensely, having someone else as interested in her beloved book as she was, but she was somewhat concerned about what she would do when they ran out of stories. It had been a week already, and there were only a few dozen left. The more she got to know the boy, however, the more she dared to hope that he would want to visit even after all the stories were gone.

"A girl walking alone through the forest, wearing a red cloak and carrying a book nearly as heavy as she is just begs for trouble," he continued with a frown.

Liesel smiled and stood up straighter. "Not so much a girl. I am fourteen today!"

At this, Kurt held his hands up and gave a mock bow. "My apologies, my lady. Happy birthday. Now, may I have your permission to return to my home?"

Laughing, Liesel curtsied and turned back toward her own

home. It had been the best week she had lived since her mother had been well.

Kurt had proven to be different from any boy she'd known back in the city. He had an untamed look in his eyes, and his walk could only be compared to the great mountain cats Liesel had seen from afar when her grandfather had taken her hunting several times. He also had an uncanny ability to navigate the forest. The paths Kurt led her down were imperceptible to her eyes, and he would often stop and listen for sounds she never heard. But for an inexplicable reason, she felt safe whenever she was with him, something her grandmother might not have approved of.

Even Liesel's mother had warned her about boys when she'd turned twelve. "They're like wolves, Leese. They have little on their minds aside from eating and chasing girls. You're turning into quite the pretty young woman. Don't be giving them reasons to think you want them to chase after you. When you are old enough to marry, your father and I will find you a good one, but don't be paying these hooligans any heed now while you're young." Amala had nodded at some of the boys Liesel had once played with as she continued to hang up laundry on the line in their yard.

"What about Father?" Liesel had asked. "Wasn't he a hooligan once?"

Amala laughed loudly. "Now where did you hear that?"

"Grandfather."

Amala had rolled her eyes. "Fathers always think young men are hooligans... all of them. That's why the Maker gave girls mothers, to help them find the true men among the boys."

Liesel sighed. How she wished Amala could meet Kurt. She was sure her mother would have liked him. He was different from the boys she had grown up around. His wild ways were a bit alarming at first, but he was gentle. And he was careful with his words. Liesel could see him weigh each of his thoughts before speaking. How she just wished she could hear more of what he really thought instead of having to guess at his silence so often.

As Liesel neared the cottage this evening, though, her thoughts of Kurt disappeared. The door was ajar, and she could hear a strange wailing from the inside. Sucking in her breath, she steadied herself for what she was sure to find. It was the fifth time that week that her father had come home in such a state.

Sure enough, as soon as she pushed the door open, he let out another wail. She set the book in a cupboard where it would be safe, before turning to face the mess behind her. Warin lay stretched out on the floor, flailing his arms about as he groaned. Liesel could smell him from where she stood.

"Where ha' you been?" he moaned when he finally realized she was walking toward him. "I been callin' you all day to make it stop!"

Liesel's cheeks flushed at the loathsome way he slurred his words. "I wouldn't have to make it stop if you didn't spend so much time at the tavern," she muttered as she grabbed him behind the arms and started dragging him toward his bed. His hair was covered in dirt, and one eye was black. Liesel could only guess he had said something foolish to one of the burly travelers who often frequented his favorite tavern.

"Don't you sass me, Daughter!" he yelled and tried to point at her.

Choking back a gag from his stench, she managed to haul him up onto his straw mattress before removing his boots and shoving his feet onto the bed with him. Without his boots on, he smelled even worse.

"There are some people in this world who can handle a drink now and then," Amala had told her once, shaking her head after Warin had spent too much time at a tavern back in the city. "And your father is not one of them."

Liesel had always thought her mother to be wise in every way, but she was tempted to wonder sometimes where that wisdom had gone when Amala had accepted Warin's marriage proposal at the tender age of seventeen. Her grandparents certainly hadn't approved of the match, not even her grandmother.

For all Amala's talk of listening to a mother's sense in choosing a good man, it seemed she hadn't followed that sound advice herself. To be fair, Warin wasn't a bad man. Even in his drunken stupor, he'd never once tried to hit his wife or daughter the way some of Liesel's friends said their fathers did. He had always seen to it that they were well provided for, even if that meant spending hours nearly freezing in the woods in the dead of winter just to bring meat home for supper. When she was little, he would even lift her up onto his shoulders as they walked through town so she could see everything from above.

Far behind were the days, however, that Liesel and Warin had shared any kind of special bond. Amala had been the love that tied them together. And now Amala was gone.

When Warin was finally quiet, passed out on his bed as if death had taken him, Liesel cut a few slices of bread and cheese and went to sit on her own mattress, tucking her knees beneath her chin. Her chest tightened, and the food suddenly felt dry in her mouth.

No. Liesel tightened her jaw and then began chewing again. She wouldn't let the sadness take her. She would not let the tears have their way, because if she gave them permission to come now, they would never stop. So she tried to think about home.

If she had been at home and her mother had stayed well, Amala would have served Liesel a blueberry tart for breakfast in bed. The day would have been spent looking at cloth in the tailor's shop, and Liesel and Amala would have chosen a color for Liesel's new dress. They would have gone out to her grandparents' home for supper then, and her grandmother would have made her favorite sweet bread with honey and milk. Then her grandfather would have told her tales of when he was a young man traveling the world, and her parents would have presented her with a new pair of shoes and some little bauble they'd picked up from one of the traveling merchants who came to town from distant lands.

Instead of making her feel better, however, the memories only made Liesel feel worse. Tearless sobs shook her body as she lay on her mattress in the dark. There was no blueberry tart or sweet bread this year, no new dress or new shoes. Her mother was never going to push the hair back from her face and greet her in the morning with a smile. She would never see Amala's face again. Instead, she was stuck in a forest without light. The people ostracized her, and her father seemed to need the drink more than he needed her. Her grandparents were miles away, and she hardly knew her only friend. Maybe fourteen wasn't so special after all.

THE NEXT MORNING didn't start out any better.

"No need to be tellin' folks about what happened here last night," Warin said as he rubbed his head. "A man's entitled to a drink every now and then. Best we forget about it and begin anew." With that, he'd pulled on his coat and left for work, not looking at his daughter to see the glare she'd been aiming at him all morning.

She didn't know why she'd hoped he would remember her birthday this morning. It wasn't as if he was ever likely to remember something so trivial on his own. And yet, she'd foolishly hoped.

Liesel spent the rest of the morning cleaning the cottage and tending to the horse. She slammed the cupboards and cottage door as much as possible, and their loud protests made her feel just slightly better. Not enough, though, to remove from her the same sour mood as she set out for the woods to meet Kurt, and only when she'd nearly reached their meeting spot did she remember that she'd forgotten the book.

Sure that Kurt would want nothing to do with her without the book, she decided to dawdle as she went, not paying attention to where she was really going.

"There you are." Kurt's voice broke the silence as she kicked a pebble. "Why are you all the way over here?"

"I forgot the book."

"So you're getting yourself lost instead?"

Liesel sent him a scathing look before turning back to find the pebble. Kurt reached out finally and took her by the elbow, forcing her to look at him. His voice was quiet this time. "What's wrong?"

Liesel felt her chin tremble as she weighed up whether or not to tell him. "I hate this place!" she finally spat out. "It's dark and ugly here! Not even the flowers grow, and everything dies!" She wanted so badly to tell him about her father, but the shame was just too great. Anger directed elsewhere was much easier.

"Well, at least you're in a bright red cloak." Kurt's voice was teasing. "I still think it's strange, but at least I'll be able to find you if you make a habit of getting lost like this."

She just glared at him.

"I'm sorry," he said, all jest gone from his tone now. "It was a stupid tease." He paused for a moment before taking her by the wrist. "Come with me. I want to show you something."

She said nothing, but allowed him to lead her.

The invisible path he took seemed to have no markings or reason to its twists and turns, but she was used to his odd methods of getting around the forest by now. After what seemed like an endless walk, he let go of her wrist and bent down next to an old hollow log.

"What do you think this is?" he asked softly.

Liesel stared at the log with contempt. She could feel a lesson coming on, but she really couldn't have cared less. "Something dead."

Kurt gave her a faint smile. Silently, he lifted the log enough for her to spot something furry beneath. In spite of herself, Liesel leaned in to get a better look. Then she gasped in delight. A fawn was curled up in a small hollow below, hidden by the aging wood's shadow. It looked soft and sweet as it stared up at them with trusting eyes. Carefully, Kurt lowered the log again.

"Her mother will be back soon," he whispered. "It would be best for us not to distress her." For the first time that day, Liesel allowed herself a small smile. The fawn stayed nestled in its bed as they left. The little animal was the very picture of serenity, something Liesel had enjoyed little of since her mother had fallen ill.

But even more comforting than the baby deer, however, was Kurt's affection toward it, the care he took to keep the creature comfortable and the desire to spare the mother anxiety.

"Thank you," she mumbled as they walked, suddenly embarrassed of her petulance. It wasn't Kurt's fault her father was a drunk, and although she truly did hate the forest, there was no reason to insult his home to his face.

To her relief, he gave her a broad smile, the biggest he'd worn since they'd met. "I'm not done yet."

They continued exploring for the rest of the day. Liesel was in awe at the amount of life the shadowy woods sheltered. A nest of baby birds hidden in the shelf of a crooked tree, and flowers that bloomed without sun were all placed near her normal path, but without help, she never would have seen them. He showed her how to find berries that were safe to eat, and a poisonous plant with healing milk.

"It looks lifeless at first," Kurt conceded as he held his hand out to help her climb the cliff face beside the waterfall. "But these woods harbor more life than one could ever know."

"I believe you," Liesel puffed as she struggled up the steep incline behind him. "What exactly are we doing up here again?" The sun that covered the ground near the base of the waterfall was warm and unadulterated. There were enough trees surrounding it, however, that most of the forest floor was shaded.

Still, Kurt pushed them higher. "Just think of it as your birthday gift."

By the time they reached the top, Liesel could tell the cliff was much higher than she had originally guessed. Her dress was stuck to her body with sweat, and she was breathing so hard she could barely speak.

"What," she huffed, "are we looking at now?" As she straightened herself, she had to work to keep her face from showing her disappointment. All she could see was more forest on both sides of the thin river that fed the waterfall. Kurt just smiled, though, took her by the shoulders, and turned her around.

Liesel shrieked. From the top of the waterfall, she could see that they were surrounded by miles and miles of green treetops. But to her left, to the west, she could see the outline of a mountain.

"My mountain," she whispered as she fell to her knees. "You gave me my mountain." Tears coursed down her cheeks, but she let them fall. The contours of the four peaks were mostly hidden behind thick gray clouds, but she could see just enough to recognize it as hers.

"Why?" She turned and looked up at him. "Why are you being so kind to me?"

He didn't answer immediately, just returned her gaze as a troubled shadow came over his eyes. His young face suddenly looked old.

"It's the most I could do," he finally mumbled. "The life you were chosen for is hardly the one you deserve."

Liesel had no words with which to reply. Instead, she frowned as she looked back over the many treetops that separated her from the road home. Her first reaction was to attribute his cryptic response to her mother's untimely death and unattached father, but something more, an undertone in his voice, sent a shiver down her spine. An instinct somewhere deep in her stomach warned her that something was very, very wrong. But what could she do? She had already tried to escape once.

She looked back at Kurt one more time. He was staring out over the treetops again, however, and didn't see her gaze. His set jaw looked as if it had turned to stone, and he had his lanky arms crossed defensively across his chest. If nothing else, she decided, she could take comfort in knowing that he cared. They might be powerless to stop the lonely end that seemed determined to take her, but through it, at least she would have a friend. And for that she would be grateful.

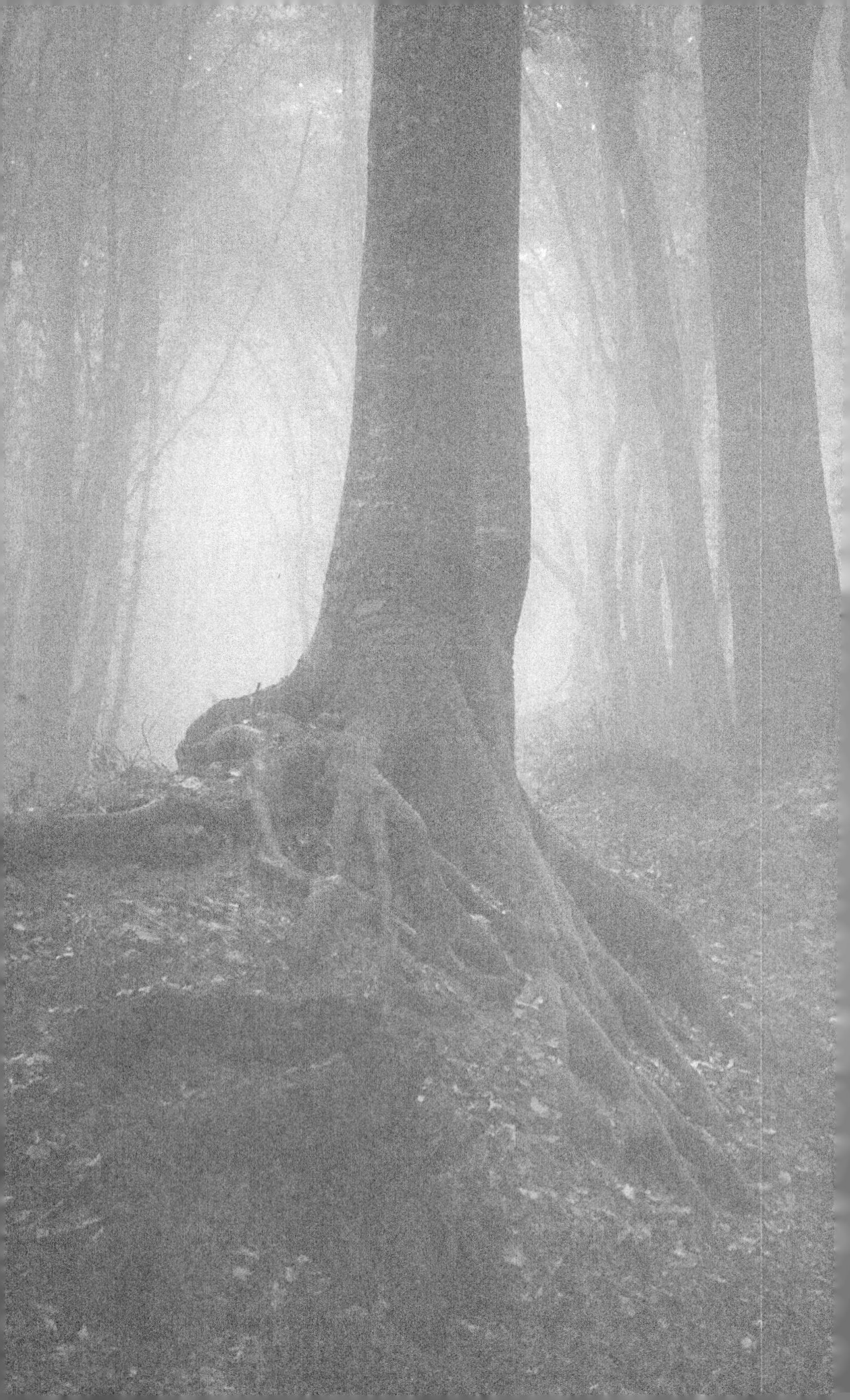

CHAPTER 6
RUMORS

"I don't care how evil the rulers of Tumen are." Liesel shook her head and pointed again at the map. "Being a prisoner of the Wasp Dunes would be much worse." Kurt grabbed her hand and moved it to another section of the page.

"Apparently, you've completely forgotten everything your grandmother wrote about how the Tumenians treat their slaves."

Liesel pretended to be annoyed, but secretly relished the way his hand felt on hers. Of course, she couldn't let him know that. Slapping his hand away, she made a grab for the book, but Kurt was too quick and had it high above her head before she could blink.

"You could be wrong!" She made a grab for her book. An unsuccessful one. "My grandparents haven't been to Tumen since they were young. Tumen might have changed since they wrote the book, but the dunes will never change!"

"What are you doing?" A young voice called.

Liesel froze, her arm still outstretched, and she could feel the tension rolling off Kurt as he momentarily froze, too. Then, without warning, he slammed the book shut and held it tightly to his side. Liesel peeked back over her shoulder to see a boy a few years younger than Kurt.

"Is this her?" The boy looked at Kurt.

"Who else would it be?" Kurt's reply was harsher than she had ever heard it.

The boy turned and studied Liesel unabashed, seemingly unaffected by Kurt's dangerous tone. And Liesel couldn't help but stare back.

The boy's hair was cut roughly, as Kurt's always was, and his face was angular, too. His appearance was a bit softer, though, and his voice was still young and unchanged.

"Liesel, this is Keegan, my brother. Kee, Liesel," Kurt said with a dramatic wave of his arm.

"Hello." Liesel found herself strangely shy.

The boy didn't respond at first, just continued to study her. Finally, when he spoke, he nodded at the book. "Why are you looking at maps?"

Liesel opened her mouth to respond, but Kurt cut her off. "Liesel's not from around here. She likes to see where she came from."

This was true, as they'd looked at maps of the mountain earlier that morning, but Liesel wondered why Kurt was being so careful with his words.

After a brief silence, Keegan added, "Father doesn't like it when you're up here."

"Well, who is going to tell him?"

They stood for another moment, eyes locked, until Keegan turned his gaze to the ground.

"Father says we need to be home early tonight," he mumbled.

"I haven't forgotten. I'll be there."

Keegan looked past Kurt at Liesel once again. "Can I stay with you?" he whined, and this time, she sensed he was trying to persuade her. "Uncle Lothur wants me to help him when I get back."

This time Kurt's answer was gentler. "We've talked about this, Kee." They shared another long look in which much was said, but Liesel understood none of it. Finally, the younger boy nodded sullenly at the ground and began to shuffle away.

"Actually, I need to go soon." Liesel took her book from Kurt. She laughed at his confused look. "My father realized this morning that he had missed my birthday, so he's sending me into Ward to order some new dresses and a new cloak. Mine are getting too small."

Kurt snorted. "Three months after is a bit late, isn't it?"

"Yes, but it is preferable to him not remembering at all." She gave a small sigh. "My mother was always the one who remembered those things."

They began climbing down the cliff beside the waterfall. The climb no longer taxed Liesel the way it had the first time she'd made the trip up, but she wasn't tall enough yet to use the footholds Kurt used, so she still needed his help. As they made the descent, she thought about the evening before, when Warin had finally realized his mistake.

"Liesel!" He had barged in the door, so excited he'd nearly run into the table she'd just placed supper on. "I have somethin' special!" He had then proceeded to tell her all about the annual Autumn Festival that was approaching, something she'd known about for weeks after overhearing some neighbors' conversation on Holy Day. "Now you're not old enough for the jigs," he had mused. "You have to be fifteen for those. But you can still dress up like your mama used to. Your birthday is comin' soon, isn't it? You will be what, fourteen?"

"I am already fourteen." Liesel couldn't bring herself to look up as she'd sliced the bread, the old anger returning.

"Already? When did that happen?"

"Three months ago."

"What was I doin' then?"

"Drinking," Liesel had responded icily, finally putting the knife down to glare at her father. "You were drinking, Father! Now sit down. The fish is growing cold."

Warin had obeyed, but he kept sending confused, wounded looks in her direction as he ate. Neither of them had said anything else the rest of the evening, and Liesel had thought he'd forgotten the exchange again the next morning until he dropped a small bag of coins next to her porridge.

"Go to the tailor," he'd said quietly. "Have 'im make you some dresses that your mum would be proud of. Get whatever you think she would like."

Liesel had gaped at the amount of money when she'd opened the pouch. "Father, I can't—"

"Yes, you can." He turned away as he stuffed his trousers into his boots. "I can do without a drink for a while." And without another word, he had stalked out of the house.

"What color will your new cloak be?" Kurt's question drew Liesel from her musings as they reached the bottom of the cliff. "Red again?"

"I don't know. Red was my mother's favorite color, but perhaps it's time I choose something different." And yet, moving on in even such a small way was still painful to consider.

"But if you get a different color," Kurt's eyes twinkled, "I won't be able to find my strange little friend the next time she gets lost."

Liesel felt herself blush pleasantly. "Will you be at the Autumn Festival this year?" In her heart, she begged him to say yes. The idea of being around all of those villagers who stared at her made her uncomfortable. It was bad enough to muster the courage to attend worship on Holy Day every week, but at least she and her father had a purpose when they went into town then. Going to a giant celebration to do nothing but watch others dance and be watched herself sounded like torture.

Her father would be there of course, but he seemed oblivious to much of what made her uncomfortable. He still thought she was imagining that the townspeople stared at her. Besides, she allowed herself to admit, she wanted Kurt to see the fancy new dress she was going to have made. She would never be able to wear it out in the woods without tearing it to pieces on the bushes and briers. When she looked at Kurt, however, she realized he looked discomfited.

"I don't think so."

"But you are fifteen, aren't you? Father says when you're fifteen you can dance at the festivals."

"Almost." He looked even more uncomfortable, staring down at the ground and shifting his weight from one foot to the other.

Liesel tried to swallow the disappointment that burned in her throat before it could show on her face. She wasn't sure why she was so disappointed, but the feeling of rejection was there.

Kurt must have sensed something, however, because when he looked up, his eyes widened just a hair. "It's my father," he said. "He says that it will one day be my duty to take care of the family, and he thinks it is a waste of time to go to Ward."

"Oh." She thought about that for a moment. "Is that why he doesn't like for you to go to the waterfall either?"

"Yes." Kurt sounded bitter. "He says there is no use dreaming about impossibilities. I'm needed at home."

Liesel had the sudden urge to reach out and comfort him. It made her angry that someone could care so little about Kurt's dreams. Again, the sudden swell of emotion took her by surprise. What was wrong with her? Liesel fought the urge to shake her head and clear it as they stood there awkwardly.

"Well," Kurt finally took a deep breath and put on a smile, although Liesel didn't think it seemed real, "you go get your new clothes. I need to find my little brother."

"He seems nice enough."

"He's not too bad. Spends too much time trying to be older than he is, but I keep him in line." Kurt's smile was more genuine now. "See you later, Liesel."

Liesel was always sad to leave Kurt, but today she couldn't help the extra bounce in her step as she hurried to order her new clothes. It was a good thing her father had given her so much money. She wasn't tall by any means, but she had managed to grow out of all the outfits her grandmother had taken her to get fitted for the year before, and her shoes were so small they hurt her feet. And without shoes, she would never be able to follow Kurt around the forest.

As she walked, Liesel wondered at what had possessed her to ask Kurt if he would be attending. She hadn't planned on asking him. The question had just popped up without her permission. But once she had even considered seeing Kurt at the festival, the desire had all but overwhelmed her.

It wasn't as if she even knew what she would do with him if they somehow met at the dance. They were both too young to participate in the jigs, as Warin had reminded her. It would simply be, she reasoned with herself, nice to have a friend there to talk to. Even when they weren't talking, Liesel found Kurt's presence calming. Still, a little voice nagged, there was something beyond having a friend present that she desired. Her hand reminded her of that, still tingling delightfully where he had touched it when he'd helped her down the cliff.

It took entering town for Liesel to shake off such confusing thoughts. As she walked through Ward alone for the first time since the disastrous first encounter, she tried not to look anyone in the eye until she had reached the tailor's shop.

It was a small building with a thatched roof, just like her own cottage, but its interior had real wooden floors, rather than stone or dirt floors like most of the other buildings in town. The wooden floors were also meticulously clean. Bolts of fabrics sat on shelves. The choices weren't as varied as the cloth in Weit had been, but they would serve the purposes she needed.

"Hello?" she called out.

The tailor appeared from the back, wearing a welcoming smile until he saw Liesel. "Oh," he fumbled with his spectacles, "what can I do for you?" His words were polite, but strained. Liesel took a breath to steady herself.

"I need two new dresses... and a cloak." Her father had given her enough money for three or four dresses, but Liesel was already uncomfortable. It would be more agreeable for both Liesel and the tailor if they spent as little time together as possible.

"I see. Let me... let me fetch my wife. Just a moment. Millie!"

The woman who responded to the call looked just as shocked as her husband had when she walked in a moment later. She recovered from her shock more gracefully, however, and immediately began asking Liesel a number of questions about the styles of dress that she wanted. Despite her politeness, however, it seemed that she also took care to say as little as possible.

By the time Liesel was being measured, she was wishing for the hundredth time that her mother was there with her. She would have known how to put these people at ease. Liesel chose her fabrics as quickly as possible before darting out of the shop at the first chance she got.

Her visit to the cobbler's shop went no better. By the time she was done being measured for new shoes, she was ready to scream in frustration. What could she have done to make these people fear her so? It wasn't until she was out looking at ribbons in the square that she found a smiling face.

"What are you searching for, lass?"

Liesel looked up from the booth she was inspecting to see a stocky man in a green suit. His weathered face made him look as if he spent much of his time in the sun, something no resident of Ward ever did. What also was odd, Liesel thought, was that he was grinning at her. Liesel was so surprised she nearly forgot to smile back.

"I... I am looking for a ribbon."

"Ah, for the ribbon dance, eh? You'll win that one for sure, my dear. You are pretty enough by far!"

"No, but thank you." Liesel blushed at the compliment. "I am only fourteen. Next year, I will be old enough."

"My cart is next over." He gestured to the cart filled with trinkets just a few feet away. "You might see if there is something to your liking."

Liesel felt a rush of joy. Perhaps this town wasn't hopeless yet. Beaming at him, she followed. As she brushed through the odds and ends that were laid out on the back of the cart, however, she was startled by the sudden sharpness of his voice.

"Lass, where did you get that?" He was staring down at her hand. In her haste to leave the tailor's shop, Liesel had forgotten to replace the gloves she usually wore in public. He was looking right at the scar on the back of her hand.

"I..." she stuttered. But she couldn't bring herself to utter the words. The dread in his face told her that he already knew it all, though. Fear moved through her as it always did when she remembered that night, and suddenly, finding a ribbon didn't seem very important. All she wanted to do was get back to the cottage. "I think I need to go," she whispered faintly as she began to walk away. He grabbed her by the elbow, though, and drew her near enough for her to smell his rancid breath.

"You must leave this place!" he whispered urgently. "And not just this town. You need to escape the woods!" He gripped her arms so tightly it hurt. "You don't know the danger you're in!" Liesel glanced around her and saw people staring at them. No one moved to free her, though. "They can't help you!" he whispered, giving her a small shake. "They can't even talk about it!"

"Why?" She knew she should shake the man off and run as fast as she could, but the urgency with which he spoke, the fact that he was speaking to her at all, compelled her to listen. This was the answer she had been waiting for.

"I don't know." He shook his balding head vigorously. "It is as if they become mutes the moment the secret is breathed about!"

"Then you tell me! Why am I in danger?" Liesel was becoming quite frustrated by the man's cryptic hints. And her arms hurt where he still gripped her.

"I can't!"

"Then why would you tell me—"

"I don't know what happens when girls here get that mark." His gray eyes bulged as he leaned even closer. "All I know is that they all disappear. Every single one."

"Mr. Gaspar." Mayor Odo was suddenly beside them. He promptly pried the merchant's hands off Liesel, for which she was quite grateful. "Just what do you think you're doing?" His words were loud and decently friendly, but there was a dangerous undertone to them. And while Liesel was thankful to be free of the peddler's grasp, she realized with dismay, however, that the mayor's involvement also meant she wasn't going to hear what the peddler had to say about the wolf bite.

"When I'm done walking this young lady home," the mayor said, "I will be having a word with you!" Odo's face was even redder than usual as he glared at the peddler, and despite the cool air that hinted at an early autumn, sweat dripped down the side of his face as he nearly shook with anger.

"Please," Liesel tried to get his attention, "I am well, truly. And

I have not yet finished making my purchases. You need not trouble yourself."

"Are you certain?"

Liesel nodded enthusiastically, and to her relief, the mayor let her go. As soon as she was on the other side of the cart, she ducked down behind one of its giant wooden wheels to hear the mayor as he confronted the peddler.

"I don't know how you found out about the wolf, but I am warning you now to let it go. I do not want to hear that you've breathed one more word of this to Liesel or her father or any other living creature!"

"It's not as secret as you think it is," the peddler said, his voice resentful. "All the other woodland villages have their own version of the story. They know something evil lives in your part of the woods, and that you assist it! Girls go missing from your town. They have been doing so for generations! I don't know which story is closest to being true, but they're all nasty in my own opinion. If you ever left your beloved hole in the forest here, you might have learned that a long time ago."

"You think you are something special, don't you?" The mayor's voice was mocking. "Heroic, even! But know this. If you tell Liesel's father, and they run, it will not end there."

"But she is his daughter!"

"They're all someone's daughter, someone's sister, someone's betrothed. If you save her, you'll only be dooming another." They were quiet for a moment before the mayor sighed. When he spoke again, his voice was quieter, weary, but also more menacing.

"If I find out that you've talked, I will make sure you never trade in this town ever again. And I mean that, Gil. I don't care how many generations of your fathers have passed through here, but it will never happen again if you don't pay heed. You'll be denied access to the road as well as the town and its troughs."

With that, Liesel could hear Odo's heavy, uneven footsteps approaching her, and she had to leap behind a group of women to keep him from seeing her as he passed by. She tried to calm herself as he walked away. She needed to go home. There was no reason to draw even more attention to herself by running back like a terrified lunatic.

But it was hard to breathe, let alone stop the shaking of her hands. It took all of her focus to put one foot in front of the other enough times to get back to the cottage. As she neared the house, however, she spotted a familiar green suit. She must have been even more distracted than she thought for him to have passed her without her notice. Throwing herself against the nearest tree, she peered out to see the man in the green suit deep in conversation with her father.

"You are not understanding me! Your daughter will be lost to you if you don't leave! She was bit by a wolf. Women bitten by wolves in these woods have been disappearing for generations! Do you not care?"

"I do care about my daughter!" Warin's voice thundered across the way, loud even where Liesel was standing. "I care that she's had enough hurts for three girls her age, and she doesn't need you scarin' the life out of her with your tales!"

"But if you would just—"

"You're an old fool with superstitions. Now, I'm goin' to call the bailiff if you don't leave my home!"

The peddler slapped his cap back on his head and stalked back to his horse, nearly stumbling upon Liesel's hiding place as he did. He was so absorbed in muttering to himself, however, that much to her great relief, he seemed to miss her completely.

She was shaking all over by the time he was gone. There were too many thoughts racing around in her head to even begin sifting through them. Her grandmother's words, however, were louder even than before in her mind.

People that go to that town... they never leave!

Liesel looked down at the mark on the back of her hand. It had healed, but the scar would be there to stay, silvery lines against the whiteness of her skin. She stared at it for a long time, wondering if it could have some sort of evil magic that could trap her there in the forest. The scar looked normal enough, at least as far as scars were concerned. Could there be a magic in it truly powerful enough to never let her go? The thought was too frightening to even entertain. She would leave these woods someday. She had to.

She also had to face her father now in the cabin, and the last thing she wanted him to do was think she believed the peddler's warnings. He meant well by trying to protect her, she was sure, but her father was often less than keen in considering the possibility of the unseen.

Kurt. She would ask Kurt the next day. He had lived in the woods all of his life. Surely he would know something, or at least be able to let her know if she was in danger. This thought gave her enough courage to walk through the door and pretend nothing was amiss. When she did, he said nothing about the peddler's visit, and she knew better than to ask. Instead, they made small talk about her new clothes and the upcoming festival.

By the time supper was over, however, the pretending had exhausted Liesel, and she was very ready for bed.

Deep sleep would not come, though. Instead, restless dreams harried her, trapping Liesel between consciousness and true rest. Images of wolves and the sensation of wandering toyed with her mind all night, and when she woke up she felt as if she had never laid down at all. Instead, she felt empty. Her fears had wreaked havoc with her mind for hour upon hour, and she felt as though there was no rational part of her left. All she could think about was finding Kurt.

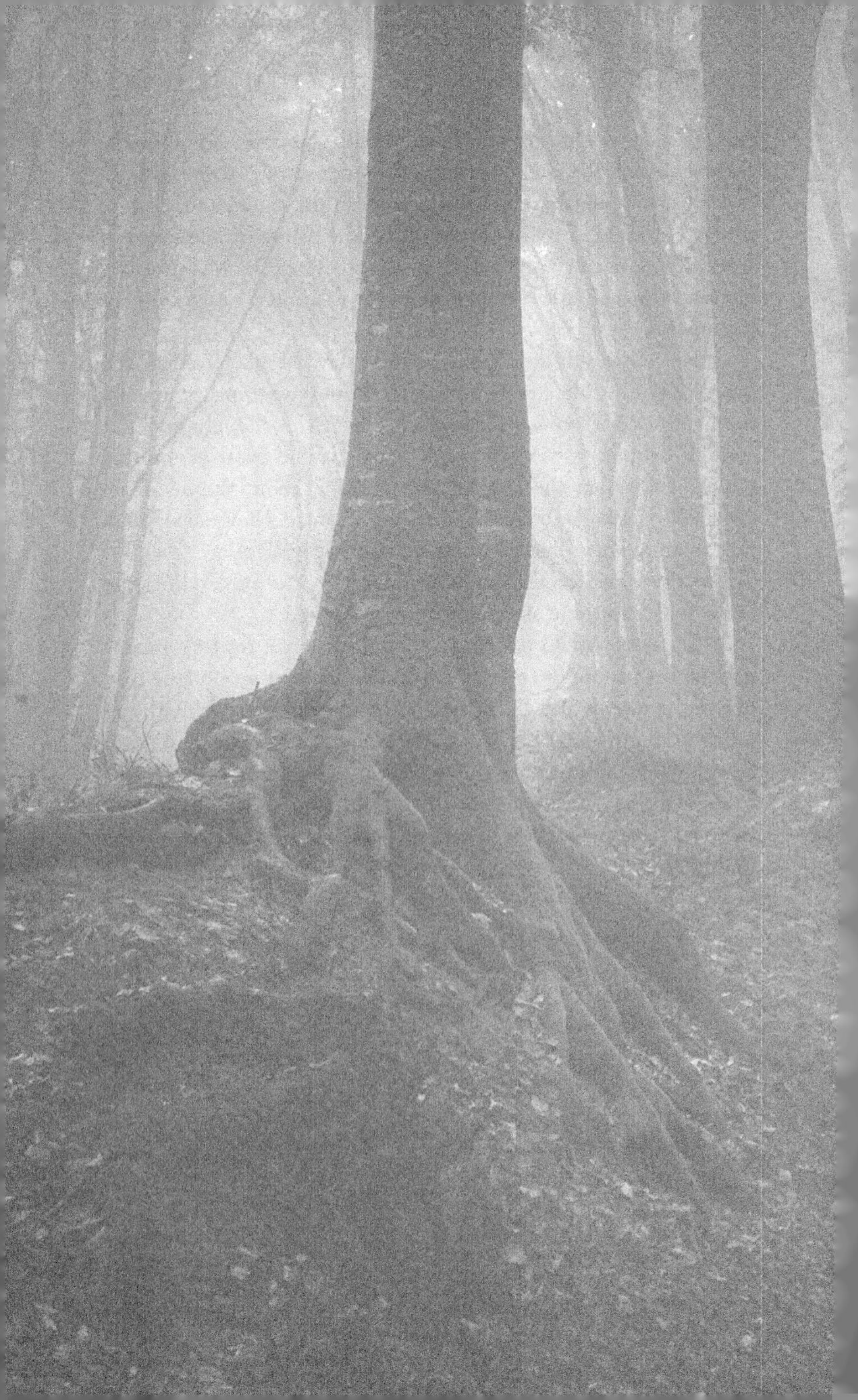

CHAPTER 7
A BOY'S PROMISE

Liesel managed to remain in bed until after her father left. She could hear him pause at the door before he went to work, and she could feel his eyes upon her, but she thanked the Maker when he said nothing and simply left. She didn't think she had the fortitude to smile this morning.

Finally, long after the gray light outside had signaled the rising sun above the forest, Liesel aroused herself and crawled out of her mattress and blankets. Once she had splashed her face with cold water from her mother's old white and blue basin, Liesel left the cottage and headed for the forest.

It did not occur to her until she was near their meeting spot that she was much too early. Usually, she was busy with all the chores she had chosen to ignore that morning, such as drawing water from the nearest well, making bread, and mending torn clothes.

None of that mattered now, though. She had to find Kurt.

When she reached their meeting place, Liesel plopped herself down on a boulder to wait. As she sat, however, all the sounds that were usually indistinguishable grew deafening. Liesel stood back up and without thinking began to walk in the direction that she thought Kurt usually came from.

Somewhere in the back of her mind, Liesel wondered if walking alone through the forest really was advisable, particularly after learning she'd been marked to disappear, but she was too tired to pay much heed to the warning. She was simply going to meet Kurt halfway, she told herself. Or at least, that was the best explanation for her impulsive behavior.

As she walked, the trees began to thicken, adding to the gloom of the ash gray forest. Why would Kurt's family live so deep in the woods? Then she remembered what the mayor had said. Kurt's family was comprised of hunters. Perhaps the big game only lived in the darkest parts. It made sense, as Liesel had never seen any game worth hunting near the village.

She had been walking for what felt like hours before she was finally forced to stop and admit that she was lost. Without the sun, there was no way to tell which direction she was going. She'd heard once that the moss grew on a certain side of the trees, but the moss in this forest covered everything. Tree trunks, stumps, and even the boulders had their lowest parts covered all the way around by the soft, yellow-green skin.

She stopped and stared up at the distant forest canopy in frustration. No matter how hard she tried, though, there was no way to tell the time of day or one direction from another. Liesel considered calling out in the hopes that someone might hear her, but that seemed just as likely to bring harm as help.

Finally, unable to think of anything else to do, Liesel began walking again. Her legs were sore, and her feet ached by the time the forest began to thin again the way it did around Ward. She had begun wondering if she might have wandered around to the other side of the town when she saw the house.

It was rather large compared to most of the other homes she'd seen since moving to the forest, nearly as large as her grandparents' house. Made of stacked timber, it sat at the top of a very gentle slope.

Liesel didn't bother to look beyond the house, however, as she spotted a woman hanging laundry on a line that was strung between a corner of the roof and a tree. She hurried toward the woman, grateful to have found another living person.

"Madam," she called out, hoping she didn't appear too

disheveled from her walk, "I was searching for my friend, and I am afraid I got lost. Would you mind telling me where I am?"

When the woman turned around, however, Liesel was pleasantly surprised. She had the same deep golden-brown eyes and bark-colored hair as Kurt. Instead of greeting her back, however, the woman's eyes went wide, and she dropped the shirt she had been hanging. An odd reaction.

Liesel tried again. "My name is—"

"Heavens, child, I know your name!" The woman darted over to Liesel and, grabbing her by the arm, dragged her back into the trees away from the house.

Liesel opened her mouth to protest, but the woman silenced her with a threatening glare. So Liesel stayed quiet until they came to a stop.

"What are you doing here?" The woman no longer sounded severe, only frightened. "How did you find us?"

"I was looking for my friend, and I got lost..." Liesel let the words die in her throat as she watched the woman's face. She was still holding Liesel's arm, and her grip was tight. Someday, Liesel thought with a bit of irritation, people would stop grabbing her as if she were a small child that might run away.

"You cannot let them see you!" the woman said, glancing over her shoulder. "They already think it's a risk allowing you to live with your father! Seeing you here would only give them the excuse they need to keep you here forever!"

Liesel felt her mouth drop open in horror. "Who are *they*?"

But the woman was already shaking her head. "There is no time! You must leave!" Then she paused for a moment and closed her eyes, tilting her head to the side. Her face fell. "They've heard you," she whispered. "Get out of here! Go home as fast as you can!"

Liesel didn't need to be told twice. Gathering up her skirts, she began to run in the opposite direction, but then she stopped and looked back. "Which way?"

Before the woman could answer, two gigantic wolves bounded up and began to circle Liesel. They were followed by a very tall, lean man. Something about him reminded Liesel of Kurt, but in her fear, she couldn't say what.

"Lothur, no! She is too young!" the woman called out, her hands balled at her sides. "Garrit said so, and you know it!"

The tall man said nothing at first, simply walked toward Liesel with a strange, smooth stride. It was then that Liesel realized that he had Kurt's gait, animal-like and silent. Finally, he stopped and spoke, his voice quiet and composed.

"But she's already here."

"P–" Liesel's voice was hardly more than a breath. She swallowed with some difficulty and tried again. "Please, just let me go home! I promise not to make any trouble. I just got lost, and–"

"No." The man shook his head, a few strands of silver in his otherwise dark hair glinting in the low light. "It is too risky. Surely Garrit will agree with that." Seeming to speak more to himself than anyone else, he began to walk again, circling Liesel the way the two wolves were. They took turns growling at her. One even snapped at her heel when she stumbled backwards.

"Liesel!"

Liesel nearly began to cry with relief when she heard Kurt's voice from the top of the ridge that separated them from the house. To her amazement, he ran right between the wolves without hesitating and drew her behind him, glaring at the man.

The man frowned slightly. "This is the one that believes in magic, is she not?"

"It doesn't matter," Kurt said through clenched jaws. As he did, Liesel realized his voice was really beginning to get deeper. If she hadn't been so frightened, she would have found it quite impressive. "I will take her safely home. You may leave us now." The man looked as if he was about to argue, but Kurt cut him off. "I will tell him that you disobeyed his orders. Is that really what you want?"

"You're rather cocky for a boy," the man said in a flat voice.

Kurt didn't blink as he continued to glare. "And *you* are disobeying orders."

After the man and the boy had scowled at one another for what seemed like an eternity, the man inclined his head just slightly and let out a short whistle. The wolves immediately turned and followed him over the ridge and back toward the house. Only when they were gone did Kurt look at the woman.

They shared a sad smile before she climbed back over the ridge as well.

Liesel felt her knees buckle. Kurt caught her awkwardly just before she collapsed on the ground. As he held her upright, Liesel realized she felt oddly even dizzier than before.

"We need to get away from here," he muttered tersely. "Can you walk?"

But Liesel was trembling so hard and felt so dizzy that she could barely answer. "I don't know."

When he started to pick her up, however, her embarrassment was greater than her fear and disorientation. If Kurt hadn't thought her addled before, he certainly must now.

"Let... let me see." She tried to stand again. This time, her legs wobbled, but she was able to hold herself upright. He kept a hand on her elbow, though, as he led her away from the ridge, and she saw him sneaking worried glances at her often as they went.

It was only half an hour later that they made it back up to the waterfall. Liesel realized with dismay that she must have walked in circles for hours before finding the house.

Kurt said nothing as she sat down and caught her breath. She tried to read his expression through glances she sneaked when she thought he wasn't looking.

Was he angry with her for venturing into the woods alone, despite his warnings? What was his relation with the man named Lothur?

When she finally looked enough times, however, she was surprised to realize that he only looked... sad. He stared out at her mountain quietly, the look on his face much too old for a boy of almost fifteen years. Before a piece of hair fell over his right eye, Liesel could have sworn there was a tear glistening in its corner.

Guilt burned down the back of her neck, and she could suddenly stand the silence no longer.

"I'm sorry."

He finally turned to look at her, seeming genuinely surprised. "What for?"

"I didn't sleep well last night, and I just needed to see you, so I tried to find where you lived."

Kurt shook his head, stood up, and kicked a rock absentmindedly. "None of that was your fault. My family is... different from most other families. It's why we live so far from Ward."

"You mean with the wolves?"

Kurt raised one eyebrow, so Liesel explained.

"Lothur had wolves that listened to him. You ran right past them, and they didn't even notice. They nipped and growled at me, though." Liesel trembled at the memory. It suddenly made sense. Kurt's family must be able to influence the wolves. It was why he'd scoffed that first day at the thought of wolves attacking him, and it must have been why he could run past the wolves without blinking. "But what do they want with me?" she finished with a whisper. Why had *she* been marked?

"Liesel, I told you before. The magic here is not good magic like you have in your stories. It's dark, and it seeks to do evil."

"How do you know there is dark magic here?"

"You keep forgetting. This is my home."

"But why did the wolf bite me? And why won't anyone talk about it?" Liesel heard her voice rising, but suddenly, she didn't care. None of it made any sense. It was like a confusing dream from which she couldn't awaken. Everyone knew. The peddler, the mayor, and even Kurt's mother knew. Everyone but her. And yet, she had the awful feeling that she was still being hunted, and they were just watching, waiting for her to stumble.

"That's how the magic works. They're not allowed to talk about it. They might want to, but most of them can't. Not to you, at least."

"But the peddler!"

"What peddler?"

Liesel related to him all that had happened the evening before. As she spoke, Kurt's face paled.

"Kurt, what's wrong?"

He grabbed her by the shoulders. "Liesel, you cannot tell anyone about any of this! Do you understand?" When she was too frightened to respond, he gave her a shake and asked again, "Do you?"

Liesel would have been angry with him for the shake if it

hadn't been for the terror in his eyes. She had never seen him frightened. He was often oddly quiet, and he sometimes liked to strut around the way most boys his age did, but now all the playfulness and bravado was gone.

"Liesel," he whispered tightly, "I am trying my best to protect you, but there are powers at work here that you've never imagined, not even with that book."

"Tell me," Liesel whispered. "Tell me why that wolf bit me, and why the peddler said I was in danger."

Kurt shook his head. "I can't."

She glared at him. "You are just as bad as the rest of them!"

The hurt in his eyes was unmistakable, but she was too frustrated to apologize.

Neither of them spoke for a while. She stood next to the roaring waterfall, just at the edge where it plunged over, and she stared at the outline of her mountain. She wanted to look at him, to see if he was still sad, but her pride wouldn't permit it. She remembered some saying her mother used to quote about the danger of pride, but she ignored it. Pride was all that was holding her together. Without the indignant fold of her arms and her raised chin, she would crumble to pieces. The knowledge that Kurt had known and not told her was jarring. He had been her rock.

He finally spoke again, though, his quiet words interrupting her thoughts. "I can't tell you, but I can promise to do my best to keep you safe."

Liesel finally turned and looked for a long, long time into her friend's anxious face. His brown eyes were repentant, and she was reminded that he was not yet a man. He might be rather proud sometimes, and could act as if he owned the forest, but in reality, he seemed no more in control than she was.

She sighed. "How can you promise that? You're just a boy, and I'm just a girl." She didn't miss the flash of annoyance that moved across his face.

"I promise!" He moved closer, his expression suddenly fierce. "I can't make it all stop, but I can keep you safe. Would you just believe me?"

Still feeling a bit resentful and defiant, her first impulse was to say no. But the longer she looked at him, the more she remembered. He was the one who had found her. He had brought her as close to her mountain as she could get. He had found her in the forest and saved her from Lothur and his wolves. Kurt was all she had. And deep down, she somehow knew that that would be enough.

Against her will, a small smile crept to her lips. As she nodded, she felt a foreign sensation wash over her. It took her a moment to realize it was peace.

They stared out at the massive ocean of treetops for a long time before she remembered another question she couldn't shake.

"What did that man mean when he said I was the one who believed in magic?"

Kurt grimaced. "My uncle has always been far too obsessed with magic for his own good, my father says."

"Your uncle?" Liesel shivered. How Kurt could be related to that frightening man was beyond her. But Kurt didn't seem to hear.

"We've had enough of *that* around here, thank you very much!" he muttered underneath his breath. The look on his face was so ominous that Liesel didn't dare ask what he meant.

Instead, an idea formed, and where there had been none before, hope suddenly surged in her heart. Aside from her mother's healing, she knew instantly that she had never wanted anything more in her life.

"Come with me!" She grabbed his hands without thinking.

"Where?"

"Away from here! Anywhere! We can see the mermaids! We can climb the mountain and see what lies beyond it. We can go anywhere we want... together!"

"Now?" He was looking at her as if she had lost her mind.

"No." She shook her head and gripped his hands more tightly. "When we are older. We'll escape this place and never look back! No dark magic, no more secrets. We can see the world!"

"Leave the woods?" He shook his head, his golden-brown eyes sorrowful. "Liesel, I can't. My father will need me to help with the family."

"Your brother can help!" Liesel was desperate. She had seen this imagined future so clearly, as if the faeries themselves had crafted a vision just for her, one of Kurt walking beside her as they left the forest behind, their faces pointed toward the sea. And although it had existed for just a moment, Liesel clung to the scene like the air she needed to breathe. She couldn't bear to live trapped in this existence, forever in this wood haunted by secrets. Liesel needed hope.

And, she realized, she needed Kurt as well. He filled the void she hadn't known was there until that moment.

"You deserve more than this," Liesel whispered up to him, suddenly very aware that his breathing had sped up as well.

After an eternity of staring into her eyes, he finally gave her a small, sad smile.

"Very well," he said softly. "I promise."

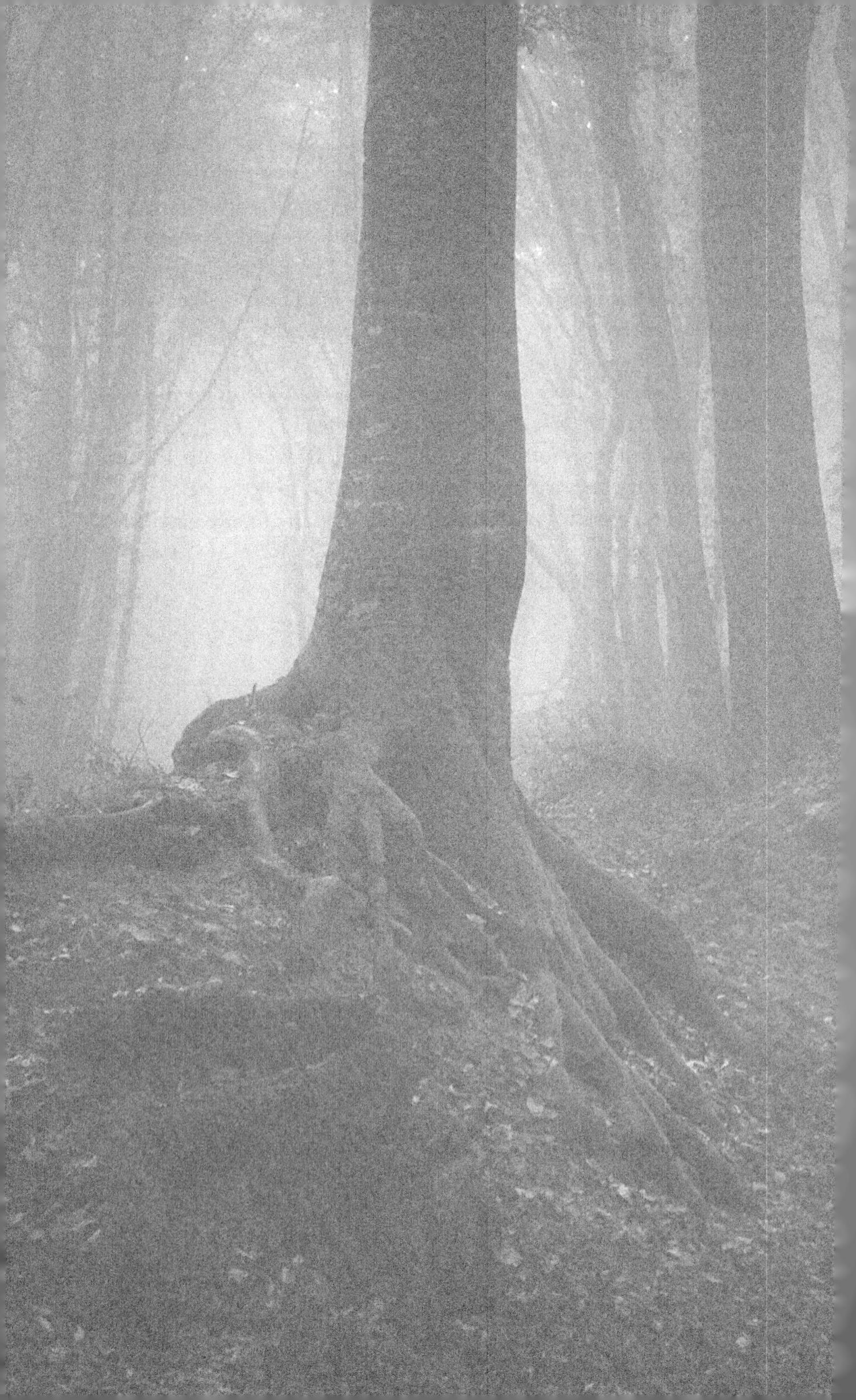

CHAPTER 8
MY FRIEND'S KEEPER

The winter came without warning.
"There's going to be snow tonight," Kurt said, standing up and craning his neck to see around the trees.

Liesel stayed seated as she finished patching the hole in Warin's second pair of trousers. If she had to mend, the cliffs were a most enjoyable place to do so.

"How do you know?" she asked.

"I can feel it." He continued searching the skies.

"The sky looks the bluest to me that it's ever been. And the Autumn Festival isn't even for a few days," Liesel said with an ornery smile.

Kurt glanced down at her, looking slightly annoyed. "I mean it. Bring extra wood in with you tonight. You're going to need it tomorrow."

"All right, then." She threw her arms up in mock defeat. "When my father asks, I'll just tell him that my friend is a seer, but only of weather. That will put his questions to rest." Kurt did not seem to find her joke funny, but Liesel laughed at herself, sure she was quite clever.

If she'd truly doubted his abilities at all, however, the next morning all her doubts were put to rest. Two days, the ice storm lasted. Warin wasn't even able to come home, as he was, Liesel assumed, lingering in the tavern when it hit, but she wasn't worried. In spite of her teasing, she had done as Kurt said, and her pile of firewood was stacked tall and neat as the cutting winds began to howl outside.

If she was honest, the force of the winds frightened her more than once, and keeping the fire lit was sometimes a struggle. Though the forest ceiling was too thick to allow much light through, it certainly let the ice in uncontested, it seemed. But she had a good store of grain and cheese, and gratified herself with reading her grandmother's book by the light of the fire, as Warin wasn't there to tell her otherwise.

When the third morning dawned, and the gray light returned to the forest, she wandered outside, breathless at the woodland beauty. Icicles hung from every branch, roof, and window like ornaments of crystal gleamed white and blue in their glory, even in the dim light.

The silence was eventually shattered, however, when the curses of her father could be heard echoing down the snow-laden road. To Liesel's surprise, they weren't slurred.

"Run out of money?" she asked as he tromped up the road.

"The tavern keep says this winter'll be a bad one," he said, ignoring her question. "Better keep some extra grain in store for nights like the last ones."

"We have enough for a few weeks more," Liesel said, taking his coat and helping him inside. She probably should have been annoyed at his absence, but Warin could be surprisingly pleasant when he wasn't drunk. And though he looked flummoxed, Liesel decided she was enjoying his sobriety greatly. "When will the next grain wagons be in?"

"Just the thing," Warin said, plopping down at the table to wait as Liesel carved him some bread. "Talked to Odo myself. He says the wagons won't be through till this ice thaws and they can brave the mud. Mud like this'll break wheels, y'know."

Liesel frowned a bit. "Surely the roads will be thawed in two weeks!"

"We'll see," Warin said, staring into the depths of his tea as though it held an answer.

Perhaps, Liesel thought, *it wouldn't be so bad to be iced in every now and then.* Warin seemed more concerned about their present state than he had since Amala had died. Perhaps, if he was kept away from the ale enough, he might remember how to care.

But as the ice came again and again, and the food came through less and less, it seemed Warin found the answers to his woes more than ever in the tavern. During one of his rare appearances at home, he told Liesel that everyone in the town was assigned rationed amounts of grain. Unfortunately, Liesel found out, Warin was often *in* the tavern on the days the grain arrived. And by the time he made it to the main square for their share, it was all but gone.

For Warin, it was simply an inconvenience. The tavern keeper had stored much ale in preparation, he said, but that didn't help Liesel any. For the cottage, she'd discovered early on, was riddled with cracks and holes, and though she tried to stuff them with rags and mud, cold air continued to blow all through the house.

Days went by without a sighting of her father, and Liesel found her will to leave the cottage slipping away. The constant ache in her belly and the fatigue of her muscles made her lethargic and unable to walk far from the cottage. She began spending most of her days on her mattress beneath her covers, leaving its mild warmth to do only what she must.

It was on those days that Liesel missed Kurt the most. He wasn't allowed to enter the village, she knew, and she couldn't make it into the woods to meet him. She missed reading her stories with him, and she missed planning their adventures. She wanted so much for him to take her by the wrist and drag her through the trees and brush once more, and she longed to see her mountain. Oh, she missed her mountain.

Two months after the first ice storm, Liesel opened her eyes to find, much to her dismay, that the hearth's fire was nearly dead. Somehow, she had thrown the second to last log on just hours before without realizing it.

It was harder than ever to get out of bed, but Liesel roused herself enough to put on her cloak and venture out to the wood's edge to gather sticks for kindling. Her face was quickly chapped by the wind, and she slipped twice before very nearly uttering a very unladylike word.

"Where have you been?"

Liesel was so startled she very nearly slipped again.

"I've been looking all over for you!" The familiar voice, a little deeper than it had been last time, sounded indignant. When she looked up at him, however, Kurt stopped talking and just stared.

Only then did Liesel realize what he must be seeing.

Her hours in the cottage had made her drawn and pale. And weak. The last time Liesel had dared to look in her mother's mirror, it hadn't been her face that had stared back. It had been a thin, sickly girl with dry, yellow hair that fell limply down her back. Dark hollows beneath her eyes had looked like bruises against her white skin, and her eyes themselves looked dead. She bent back down and began gathering sticks again, her cheeks burning with shame.

To her surprise, however, he grasped her shoulders and stood her back up so he could study her more. His hands were warmer than any fire she'd sat beside in months. She hadn't realized until now how much she missed human touch.

"What happened to you?" His voice was kinder this time, but it didn't lessen Liesel's embarrassment.

"The ice has kept the supply wagons out of the forest." She spoke to the ground, not willing to look him in the eye.

"But your family is supposed to get rations, are you not?"

Liesel shrugged. "I tried. I couldn't carry the grain back to the cabin."

"But your father can get it, can't he?"

Liesel didn't answer.

Kurt's voice hardened a bit. "Liesel, why won't your father get it?"

"He might remember if he wasn't so busy at the tavern!" Her words were sharper than she'd meant them to be, but the bitterness in her heart was too great to hide any longer. How she had wanted to keep her father's habit a secret from her friend. It was one thing to have an absent-minded father, but it was another to have one who forgot all else in his quest for comfort.

"He doesn't hunt either, does he?"

Liesel finally gathered the courage to look her friend in the eyes. His expression was as judgmental as she had expected, but his appearance overall took her a bit by surprise. Despite the uneven stubble on his face, and the fact that his pants were even shorter on him than usual, Kurt looked fine. The constant want that was painted on her face, and on most of the villagers' faces the few times she'd seen them, was nowhere to be seen on him. He was healthier than ever, and had easily grown an inch in the long winter months.

"No," she finally said, "the mayor told him hunting is outlawed in these parts." Except for Kurt's family, of course.

"I forgot about that," he muttered, scratching his head.

"Well," Liesel began to stand, "I hate to go, but–"

Kurt's eyes opened wide as he looked around again. "It's cold out here," he exclaimed, as though he'd somehow forgotten. "You had better go back inside."

Sadly, Liesel had nodded. Leaving Kurt was the last thing she wanted to do, but her toes were beginning to lose their feeling.

"I wish I could..." Kurt frowned in frustration at the road that separated them from her cottage.

"I don't want you to get into trouble with your father," Liesel said. As she turned to go, though, he called her once more, and she looked back.

"I'm glad you kept your cloak red." His eyes were still unhappy, but he wore a lopsided grin. "I'll be able to find you next time you get lost."

Liesel smiled in spite of herself.

She could feel his eyes on her back as she went inside. She set the sticks down by the sputtering fire so they could dry. It would be quite a while before they were ready to burn. She hoped her final log would last until then. Liesel plopped down to wait in the chair that was drawn as close to the hearth as she could get it without setting her legs on fire, and she wrapped herself more tightly in her cloak.

Her father's booming voice awakened her several hours later.

"Liesel, what's this now?"

Liesel tried to blink the sleep from her eyes as she stumbled groggily toward the door. When she opened it, she saw her father holding up a dead rabbit and a bundle of small log bits wrapped in a cloth. "Where did you get these?" he demanded.

"I... don't know," Liesel stuttered, although she had a pretty good idea. "They weren't there when I last went out." The more she thought about it, though, the more she had to fight to keep the smile from her face.

Warin, however, was not amused in the slightest. "You know huntin' is illegal in these woods." He held up the rabbit and shook it at her. "I don't want them to be thinkin' *I'm* breaking the rules now!"

"I think it might be from my friend, Kurt," Liesel hastened to explain, afraid he might throw it away. "His family owns the land, remember?"

Warin gave her a long, hard look. But much to her relief, he finally handed her the rabbit. "Fine, cook it up," he said. "I suppose it won't hurt anythin', as it's dead already. Besides," he followed her inside and began removing his muddy boots, "the dried meat stew they serve in the tavern is gettin' mighty old."

Liesel mashed her lips together so the words on her tongue stayed there. So he had been eating at the tavern, too. What kind of rations had *they* received? Liesel hadn't tasted meat since the winter had begun.

The soup Liesel made that night was the most delicious she could remember ever eating. Liesel tried hard to wait up for Kurt after that, as the meat continued to come every night, along with a small bundle of kindling. But her benefactor was either too stealthy or Liesel was too tired, for she never did catch him.

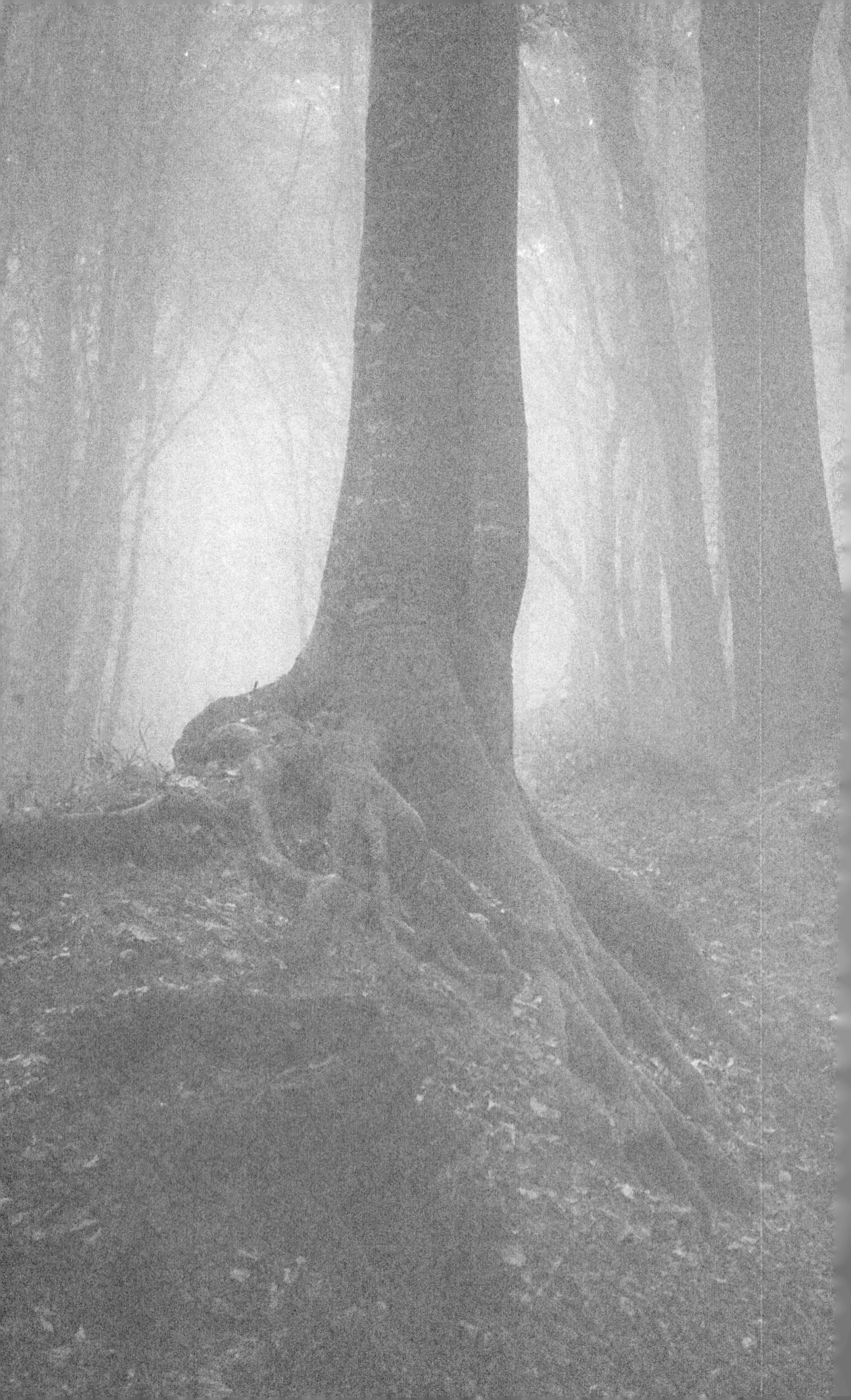

CHAPTER 9
RIBBONS

Liesel sat back and wiped her forehead on her sleeve. For a forest without sun, it could get mysteriously hot. Nevertheless, her garden was full of life, and Liesel was proud of her work. The plot was small compared to the one she'd shared with her mother, but it would keep Liesel and Warin fed through the next winter.

Liesel wished again that Kurt's father would let him visit her garden. She didn't get to see him as much as she had the year before, now that she had her garden to tend, and his father kept him busy with the family. Still, she would have liked for him to see it. The garden would have never come to life if it hadn't been for Kurt. Of course, Liesel and her father wouldn't have survived the winter without Kurt, either.

When they'd met up again after the first spring thaw, nothing was said about the food or wood, but Liesel had seen the satisfaction in Kurt's eyes when he saw her walking steadily toward him.

As soon as the ground had thawed completely, however, Liesel had begged Kurt to teach her how to garden in a place without sun, or at least to take her to someone who could. For though she was grateful for all Kurt had done, she had also determined sometime during those lonely winter months never to be so dependent upon others again.

"Your mother had a lovely garden," Liesel had recalled from her quick glimpse of his house. "Perhaps she could—"

"Absolutely not!" Kurt's voice had been so sharp it startled her. "You are going nowhere near there."

"But how else will I learn?" Liesel had whined. They were sitting up on the waterfall's ledge for the first time since the snow had thawed. Liesel knew he was trying to protect her, but she was desperate. "You don't know what it's like to have nothing in the cupboard to eat."

"Nothing?" Kurt had given her a hard look.

"You know what I mean."

"Look, when I get the chance, I'll bring some seeds and teach you what I know."

"*You* know how to garden?" Liesel had raised her eyebrows. Kurt seemed too wild, too antsy to have ever had the patience to grow much of anything.

He rolled his eyes. "When I disobeyed my parents as a child, my punishment was working with my mother instead of playing."

"Is it still?" Liesel hadn't been able to keep the small smile from her lips. For some reason, the picture of adventurous Kurt being forced to garden was funny.

He wiggled his eyebrows mischievously. "I just make sure not to get caught."

True to his word, Kurt had returned with an assortment of plant bits and seeds the next day. He'd explained how to bury and water them and when they would be ready to harvest.

And true to *her* word, Liesel had worked faithfully all summer, and now that the warm days were growing old, she was proud of all she had done. If only Kurt could see it.

"Liesel!" Her father interrupted her thoughts.

"You're home early," she said as she stood and wiped her hands on her apron. Whatever he wanted must be important for him to skip the tavern for the day.

"I'm here to take you to buy your ribbon!"

"My ribbon?" Liesel stared at him blankly.

"Yes, Girl! For the festival! The one that got snowed out last year. It will be here soon, and you're old enough to dance this time!"

Despite her hesitance to attend the dance, Liesel had to smile. Warin really had felt guilty about missing her birthday the year before. Oddly enough, once summer had arrived, it was as if the winter had never happened, and Warin had happily stepped back into being a father. He'd taken it upon himself to accompany her to town whenever she needed something. Sure that her reluctance to go into Ward stemmed from shyness, he even attempted to get everyone they met on the way to have a conversation with her. Every time they greeted her, upon prompting from him, he was pleased, sure he'd made her a new friend. She didn't have the heart to tell him otherwise.

"That's thoughtful of you," Liesel gathered up her garden tools, "but I doubt that any of the boys will be very keen on dancing with me."

"Nonsense." Warin followed her as she put the tools away. "You're turnin' out just as pretty as your mum."

"Father, they won't even talk to me. I hardly think dancing is something they desire." Especially if they thought she was marked for some sort of evil.

"That's because you haven't given the foolish rascals a chance." Her father continued to follow her around as she went inside and began to slice the bread for supper. "You spend all your time in the woods with that friend of yours. Might do him some good to see he's got some competition."

Liesel felt the blush rise to her cheeks. "Kurt is just a friend." As she said the words, however, she felt their inadequacy. It was hardly mere friendship that moved one person to keep another fed all winter. A friend wasn't really what Liesel would call Kurt.

But if not her friend, what was he?

"Daughter." Her father finally took the knife from her hand and placed his own hands on her shoulders to face him. "Come here."

He went over to the wooden chest in the corner and knelt beside it, taking a small brass key from his pocket. Liesel felt her throat tighten as he did. The chest had once been painted in bright colors, paint from the western shores, her mother had said. Liesel's grandfather had made it himself when Amala was a baby. He'd carved the shapes into the wood, and her grandmother had painted it. Its colors had begun to dull when Isa was still a baby, but Amala had loved that chest. No one had touched it since they'd taken it out of their little cart.

"I was noticin' the other day that your dresses are too short again." Warin reverently pulled something out of the chest and held it lovingly in his lap. He swallowed hard. "I think you're tall enough to wear your mum's dresses now."

Liesel didn't move. After allowing her to nearly starve the winter before as he drank away his pain, her father had somehow managed to notice her height. Anger and pain mixed in her stomach, and she couldn't have uttered a word even if she'd wanted to.

It didn't matter, though. Warin didn't look up, just continued to caress the item in his lap as if it were a pet.

"I know I been drinkin' more than I should. When I saw that your dress is too short the other day, I realized I don't have enough money to buy you new things like I ought, and it made me think—" His voice hitched, and it was a moment before he could speak again. "It made me think of what your mum would say if she could see you now. She would let me have it for not buyin' you new things, and for spendin' so much time away."

He finally looked up at her, his eyes rimmed red. "I haven't been there when you needed me to be. I know... in truth, I've been a lousy father. Your mum, she kept me on the straight and narrow. I just... I don't know how to live well without her. I'm tryin', but that's the best I can do."

Liesel couldn't seem to move her feet or her mouth or her hands.

"The night you ran away..." Warin continued, "the night we lost her... I nearly ended it all then and there. Knowin' I had let her die, even though you tried to warn me, and then knowin' you were out in the woods alone. I was so close to givin' up. Then that hunter brought you back, and I had to go on. But I couldn't, not without help."

Not without the drink, Liesel thought wryly.

"I thought I could bury it all. But then I saw that your dress is too short..." he faltered again, finally holding up the object in his hands.

As it unfolded, Liesel realized it was not just any old dress, but it had been one of her mother's favorites. Tears streamed down her father's face as he looked at her beseechingly.

"I can't imagine all the awful thin's she'd say if she could see all the ways I've hurt her girl."

As if in a daze, Liesel drew just close enough to touch the dress. She had never seen her father cry, other than the night she was rescued from the wolf, and she couldn't be unaffected by his tears. And yet, the vestiges of the last two years were still with her. If she closed her eyes at night, she could still feel the hunger in her belly and the weakness in her legs. She was still haunted by the afternoon in the healer's house, where Warin had held her back as she tried to save her mother's life. She still heard her grandmother's screams as she watched the cabin fade in the distance.

How many times had he hurt her? How many times must she forgive him? Liesel scrunched her eyes tightly to block out the sight of her broken father begging her forgiveness. She didn't want to forgive him. He'd hurt her too many times.

You never know, my Leese. Amala's voice echoed in her mind.

Immediately, Liesel was back in their old kitchen in the city, helping her mother roll out dough. She was young, only five or six, and she had just asked her mother why Amala always told Warin she loved him when he left in the mornings. Her parents had carried on a loud disagreement the night before, although Liesel couldn't recall what it had been about. She just remembered asking her mother why she would tell her father she loved him even when she was mad at him.

Amala just shook her head and gave Liesel a wry smile. "You never know when you'll see someone again. I may be angry, but if the Maker calls him, I don't want to regret my last words."

Liesel opened her eyes again. She was still angry, and she knew she would be for a long time. But deep down, she knew her mother had been right.

"I... I suppose we could get a ribbon," she heard herself saying in a faint voice. "We could get one that's dark blue, to match this."

Taking the dress from her father, Liesel buried her face in it. It smelled a bit dusty, but her mother's scent lingered there as well. As she stood there clutching the dress, she felt Warin wrap his arms around her.

"I'm goin' to do better, Leese!" he whispered fiercely. "I promise."

Amid all the emotions Liesel felt flying around in her heart, in that moment she wanted to believe him. A sad voice inside, however, whispered that it would be a long time before she could.

***

Two weeks later, Liesel had her ribbon. It was the only silk she had ever owned, and deep down, she had decided the moment they'd purchased it that she would have rather kept it for herself and simply wear it than ruin it with embroidery for the dance. But if it would please her father, she was willing to give it a try.

Since the day he'd noticed Liesel's newfound height, Warin truly had been making an effort to spend more time with her. In fact, he was around so often she could hardly leave the house without him trailing after her like a colt. In desperation, she finally sent him to the tavern one day with enough coins for two drinks so she could sneak out to see Kurt without her father following along. Kurt's opinion of her father was one that involved words Liesel couldn't repeat.

While Liesel was grateful that her father was finally taking an interest in her, she had finally begun to harvest her garden, and she desperately needed Kurt to teach her how to preserve the food. At least, that's what she told herself.

He was sitting in their usual spot atop the waterfall's ledge when she arrived. She'd been tall enough to climb the ledge without his help for some time, so the waterfall had become their place of meeting. There were days when she'd climbed up alone, days when his father had kept him home, helping with the family. On those days, she would sit still and think, or sometimes mend a piece of clothing. The water's rushing sound was relaxing, as was being able to see the contour of her mountain in the distance.

From the look on Kurt's face today, however, it seemed he'd spent more afternoons waiting alone for her lately, and they hadn't brought him the same peace they brought her. Suddenly feeling guilty, she went to her usual sitting rock and avoided his gaze. The fire he'd lit and the frying pan he had brought with him piqued her interest, but she didn't ask.

"You've been busy." His voice was resentful, sullen.

"I'm sorry, Kurt." Liesel sighed. "Things have been... different lately."

"Different. I see."

Taken aback by the anger in his voice, Liesel peeked at her friend. He was glaring into the fire. While she did feel bad about being gone so much, Liesel couldn't help but wonder what had brought this storm on. Frowning, she drew out her ribbon and began to embroider her name onto it, a task she had been putting off as long as she could. The dance was the next evening, however, and her father had been asking when her ribbon would be ready to cast.

"So what's his name?" Kurt spit out.

"His name?" Liesel looked at him blankly.

"The one that ribbon is for. The one that's so interesting."

It took Liesel a moment to realize what he was really saying. "You're jealous!" she exclaimed.

He frowned even harder at the flames. "I am not!"

But Liesel couldn't keep the smile from her lips or the blush from her cheeks. While his guess was wildly off, she couldn't help feeling a bit smug. A year ago, she had desperately worried that Kurt would tire of her. She'd never expected him to be the one to fret.

"Kurt, why can't you come to the dance?"

"You know that. My father won't let me."

"And my father is precisely why I am going."

He raised his eyebrows at her, and when he spoke, his voice was sarcastic. "Your father is *making* you go to the dance?" He shook his head and went back to poking the fire. "Now I know you're making things up."

"No, truly." Liesel seated herself beside him and crossed her legs. Her grandmother had always fussed that sitting in such a way was improper, but neither Kurt nor the woodland creatures had ever seemed to mind. "He thinks I am going to have fun at this awful escapade. I am only going because he wants me to."

"So why the sudden interest in whether you live or die?"

"Something reminded him of my mother," Liesel said softly. Kurt didn't respond. "I know he has been awful," she said, "but–"

"He almost let you starve! And he would have if–" Kurt stopped himself before he went on, but Liesel knew what he was going to say.

"I haven't forgotten about that," she said quietly. "I never will. But my mother is dead, Kurt. Isn't it understandable that I might want something with the one parent I have left?" She looked down at the ground. "My father will never be able to love me like my mother. He *wants* to love me, though. Wouldn't you want that from your father?"

"I suppose," he mumbled.

Liesel breathed a sigh of relief. He would come around. He was too good not to.

"But are you sure you are only going to this dance because he wants you to?" He finally looked up at her, no longer scowling, but not yet happy, either.

She gave him the most reassuring smile she could. "I promise, that is exactly why." She gave a dark chuckle. "I told him no one will want to dance with me, though. It's a waste of time."

"Look, are we going to do this or not?" Kurt grumbled.

"Do what?"

"I was *going* to show you how to cook and preserve the vegetables, but if you're too excited about this dance–"

"Kurt!" Liesel finally grabbed her ribbon and tried to smack him on the head with its tail. "I will happily beat you to death with this ribbon if you don't let it be!"

"All right! All right!" He threw a hand up, and laughing, reached down for the large pan at his feet. "I brought some of the early produce from my mother's garden to show you how to cook them, even before I show you how to keep them. You probably didn't have all of these foods in your fancy city kitchens, so you need to know how they taste."

Relieved and happy, Liesel spent the rest of the afternoon and evening watching her friend show off his unusual skills. She'd never heard of a boy that knew how to cook and preserve food. The city boys would have frowned upon that as womanly. But, she considered, Kurt was an unusual boy.

As she was beginning the walk back toward her own home that evening, Liesel turned one more time.

"Just so you know, when we have our adventure one day, we can go anywhere we want. Then we'll only go to dances if you want to!" She meant her words to be reassuring, but Kurt only frowned a little before nodding silently and turning to go.

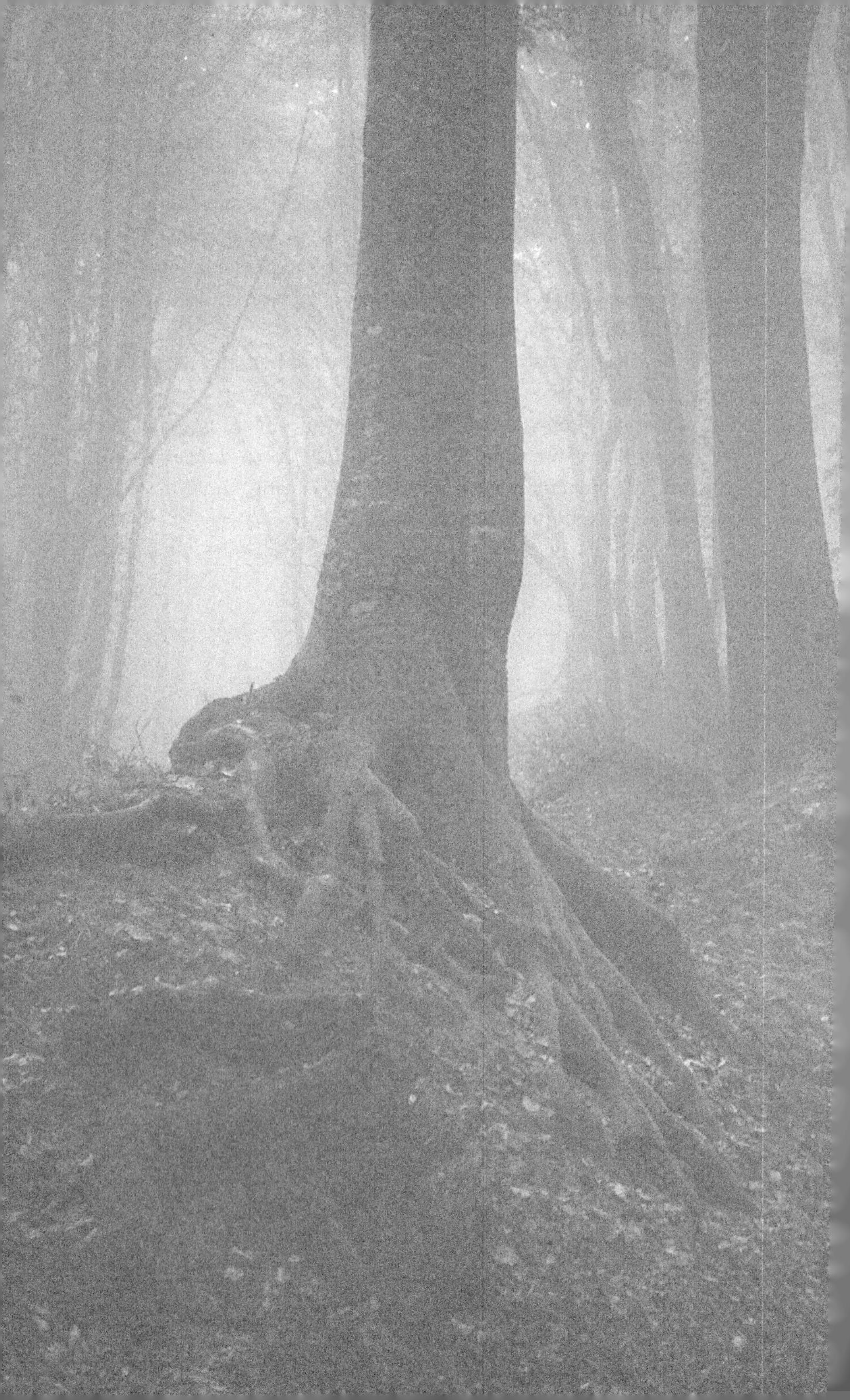

CHAPTER 10
STAY

The next evening, Liesel and her father prepared to leave, with Liesel trying desperately to look more composed than she felt.

Wearing her mother's dress to this festival had been hard enough. It was like discovering all over again that she was dead. As long as the clothes had stayed in the trunk, it had seemed like they were simply waiting for their owner to return. Taking them out, washing them, and even fixing the moth holes hadn't been so bad. They had still smelled of Amala, a scent Liesel had spent hours breathing in before she'd washed them.

Wearing them, however, had been a different story. Her father had been right. She was finally tall enough. But donning her mother's clothes was admitting that Amala was never coming home. And though Liesel had admitted it before, it killed her to do so again.

The idea of trying to catch a dancing partner, too, was nearly too much. She'd almost feigned an illness to stay home, but when she saw the way her father looked at her in her mother's dress, she knew she couldn't. Even now, as they stood at the door, tears gathered at the corners of his eyes, and a genuine, gentle smile lit his face.

"You look just like her, Leese. I always said that hair was a halo of its own." With that, he offered her his arm, and they left for an evening she knew was a huge mistake.

"You know your mum was the best dancer in the city." Warin's eyes were bright with the memory.

Liesel couldn't help but be intrigued.

"That's how we met. Her ribbon was pulled, and I got the first dance."

"She told me you met on Holy Day!"

Warin's grin just grew, and he wriggled his brows mischievously.

"It's true that I first saw her then, comin' out of the church, but we didn't meet. Your grandfather took one look at me and dragged your mum straight home. He couldn't get rid of me that easy, though! From the moment I laid eyes on your mum, I knew I was goin' to marry that girl. You should have seen the look on his face when he saw me pull her ribbon at the dance!" Warin was laughing now, his big voice booming down the quiet road as they walked.

Liesel had to smile along with him. When he found something funny, which was highly unusual outside of the tavern, Warin's laugh was catching.

"How did you manage to pull her ribbon?"

"I bribed the mayor."

"You what?" Liesel gasped. The ribbon dance wasn't by any means sacred to her, but she knew of some couples who had wedded solely because of the ribbon dance. They believed the Maker had coupled them that way, and so it was meant to be. The priest had preached against such superstition, but there were a good many families that still held the dance as much more than a mere festival tradition.

Every town in the region had its own ribbon dance, according to Liesel's grandmother. That her father would interfere with something so important shouldn't have surprised her, but she'd thought even he had limits. Apparently not. Still, from the joy the memory brought to his face, she could see that he believed it had been the right thing to do.

"Your mother was so lovely, Leese. Your grandmother had

insisted on puttin' her hair up in some ridiculous curls before they arrived. Said it was only proper. But as the evenin' went on, and we danced into the night, her hair fell out of place more and more until it floated around her. It was like seein' waves of golden wheat rollin' in the wind. We danced the whole time, and when it was all done, I tried to kiss her. She would have none of that, though! Said I'd have to marry her before she let me steal any such sweetness from her.

"Bein' the young, wild man I was, I had nothin' to my name but the clothes on my back and the few coins I earned doing odd jobs here and there. Your mum changed all that. After that night, I found a blacksmith and hired myself out to him. I'd learned to smith from my own father back in my county, and in a year, I'd married your mum. You came along not long after that."

Liesel listened, spellbound, to the story she'd never heard a word about from her mother. She could only suppose the way Amala and Warin had met was probably a bit embarrassing to her proper mother. Or perhaps, Liesel wondered, Amala had feared it would give Liesel the idea to follow in her footsteps. Whatever the reason had been, it would remain forever hidden now.

Liesel turned to study her father as he walked beside her. His eyes were distant, and the smile he wore now was a sad one.

"Your mum was good to me, Leese. She brought me back when I strayed, and she always forgave me when I stumbled. You're a lot like her. Don't you forget that."

"Thank you, Father." And she meant it. For all his faults, Warin had loved her mother faithfully. A compliment such as this was the greatest he could have given.

The sound of a crowd pulled her from her reverie, and Liesel felt her heart quicken as they entered the town square. A few people had passed by them as they'd headed into town, three or four neighbors who also lived on the outskirts of Ward, but it seemed now that the whole town was gathered around the stage that had been set up in the square. Mayor Odo was standing on it, along with Izaak and a few other dignitaries.

"Don't look so ghostly now." Warin gave her a small shove

from behind. "Drop your ribbon in the bucket before they start to draw!"

Liesel nodded and did as she was told, trying to ignore the terrified stare of the woman holding the ribbon bucket. Only then did it occur to her that she could have embroidered someone else's name on it. Then, even if her ribbon was picked, she would be saved from having to make a fool of herself before the entire village.

But it was too late for that now, and her father was watching her with a delighted grin, so she dropped it in with a sigh. There were lots of other ribbons, she tried to comfort herself. Surely they wouldn't pick hers for Summer Maiden.

"Good evening." The mayor's voice boomed across the square. "Welcome to the Autumn Festival! I'm Mayor Odo, and for those of you visiting our town, I hope you find your stay here pleasant."

Liesel wondered who he was talking to, as she recognized every face in the crowd from their Holy Day visits. That she was aware of, she and her father were still the newest people there. The only less familiar faces she could see were some of the traders and merchants, and she even recognized most of them immediately.

One of them seemed to feel her gaze. When he turned his head to return her stare, she realized it was the peddler who had tried so hard to warn her, Gil. She gave him a hesitant smile, and he nodded. Just then, her father nudged her, moving her attention back to the mayor's speech.

"I know most of you are familiar with our tradition of choosing our Summer Maiden, but I will explain it for our youngsters."

Oh, to be young again, and not to have a care in the world, she thought with a pang of envy.

"Each eligible lass," Odo continued, "has brought her ribbon this evening. Whomever has her ribbon chosen first will be our Summer Maiden, and this year, she shall have the first dance with Landry Stu, winner of last week's archery competition."

The young man named Landry walked up to the top of the stage. His eyes were hidden by the hair that drooped down in front of his face, but his grin was wide and full of pride.

"Are you ready, Landry?" The mayor pointed at the bucket

Liesel had dropped her ribbon in. Reaching in, the boy pulled a ribbon out, though Liesel couldn't see what color his prize was. Landry handed the ribbon up to Odo, and the mayor began to read it out loud.

As soon as he started, though, he stopped immediately, and much to Liesel's surprise, somehow managed to pale in the light of the surrounding torches and the fading gray light of the forest evening. Liesel still couldn't see the ribbon he held, but she did hear him mutter to the young man, "Pick another one."

"Hold on, now!" Warin shouted out, his voice indignant. "He pulled out my daughter's ribbon! Why would you have him pull another?"

"Really, Father, it's—" Liesel tried to stop him, but Warin was already charging up to the stage. Before anyone could react, he'd snatched the blue ribbon from the mayor's hand and was waving it in front of the crowd.

"The rule is that the first ribbon pulled is the name of the first Summer Maiden, and that's my Liesel!" He looked around at the people, expecting their support.

The sinking feeling in Liesel's stomach only intensified when her father realized no one was agreeing with him. Instead, they simply stared. The fear in the air was palpable.

Liesel had expected nothing different, but it was clear that her father had. Long ago had she accepted her place as the town pariah, but Liesel could see the rage growing on Warin's face as he looked for support at all the people he had assumed were his friends. Turning back to the mayor, he held the ribbon up and shook it in Odo's face.

"My daughter was right about you people! You're all addled in the head, thinkin' somethin' like this is acceptable. I thought perhaps my wife's death was an accident, but I can see now that Liesel was right. There is evil in this town, and I won't stand for it! Come, Liesel! We're leavin'!"

Murmurs arose as he stormed off the stage, and Liesel nearly had to run to keep up with him as he stalked back toward the cottage.

She felt nervously giddy as they arrived home, and Warin began throwing everything into piles.

"Where are we going?" Liesel was almost afraid to ask, terrified her father would change his mind.

For a moment, he didn't seem to hear her, so frenzied was his packing. Finally, however, his shoulders slumped, and he came to a stop.

"We're goin' back to Weit. No, rather, we're goin' to your grandparents. I've done a fine job of makin' you miserable here." He turned and looked at her, his eyes repentant.

Unable to hold herself back, Liesel flung herself at her father and wrapped her arms around him. She felt him hug her back, hesitantly at first, but then his grip tightened.

"You're much wiser than your old man, Leese. Your mum would have been proud of you tonight." Liesel felt tears sting her eyes as he pushed her back to look at her face. "And I don't mean just your beauty. You held yourself together with dignity, even when they tried to hurt you. I mean it. Your mum would be so proud."

It took Liesel a moment to recover her voice. "So when are we going?"

"Tonight." As he spoke, however, a wolf's howl sounded in the distance. It made Liesel shiver, and even seemed to chill Warin a bit. "Although, I suppose it wouldn't hurt to wait until the mornin'. We'll get a bit of rest tonight instead."

Liesel nodded emphatically before helping him pack the few dishes they had in the cupboards.

As they worked, though, a strange sensation overtook her, muddying the joy she'd felt so deeply just moments before. She couldn't help but feel torn. It was awful to think that she could be second-guessing their decision to leave, but the memory of Kurt's face began to nag at her mind, distracting her as she worked.

It would be incredibly wrong, she decided, to leave without at least saying goodbye. And reminding him of the promise he'd made. Since they were leaving in the morning, she decided, she could sneak out early and meet him at the waterfall. He usually didn't arrive that early, but if he didn't make it in time, perhaps she could leave him a letter explaining what had happened.

After Warin finally went to bed, Liesel took a quill, ink, and a piece of parchment from her bag. She rarely used the writing materials, as they were nearly impossible to afford, but such an occasion merited a whole book, she decided.

But what could she tell him? How could she truly thank him on paper for saving her life? A few neatly penned lines seemed sinfully inadequate to convey that sort of sentiment, and it made her sick to think she was going to try now.

As best she could, Liesel related to Kurt all that had happened. As she wrote, she thanked the Maker again and again that Kurt could read. In her letter, she promised that she would still keep her side of the bargain. She would meet him when they were older, and they would explore the world together. He'd better not forget, because she was going to hold him to his promise whether he remembered or not.

After she'd finished writing, Liesel sat back with a sigh. Her words were even emptier than she had anticipated. And yet, they would have to do.

It seemed so strange, she mused to herself, that she could feel any sort of sadness about leaving the woods. She'd wanted nothing more than to return to her grandparents since they'd arrived in Ward. In the time that they'd lived in the forest, she had lost her mother, been ostracized, and nearly starved. And yet, a piece of her mourned leaving this boy behind. Through it all, he had been there. Leaving her savior without saying farewell in person seemed so wrong.

And yet, she sighed as she put the quill down, what else could she do? Warin's mind was made up. They were leaving at first light. He was determined to be out of the forest, he'd told her, before the next nightfall, and to do that they would need to ride steadily, stopping only to rest the horse.

Liesel had nearly nodded off with exhaustion by the time she sealed the letter with wax. Getting into her little mattress for the last time, she decided to leave the fire burning. They wouldn't need the fuel tomorrow, she thought to herself as she smiled. And in just two nights' time, she would be lying on her bed at her grandparents' house.

Never would she take the feeling of safety in their home for granted again.

Liesel didn't even realize she'd fallen asleep when the door creaked open. The events of the evening had taxed her more than she'd expected. Rolling over, she decided to let her father start loading the bags into the cart without her. She wasn't strong enough to lift most of them anyway.

She awakened fully, however, when she heard a strange guttural sound from Warin's bed. Then she opened her eyes.

A large wolf was standing over her father's body, blood dripping from its black muzzle. Warin's face was ashen. And he wasn't breathing.

The wolf stared at her for a long moment, and Liesel quickly realized that like the first wolf, its eyes were hauntingly human. Even worse than that, they were familiar, although Liesel had no idea where she had seen them before.

She and the wolf stood like that for a long moment, Liesel silently daring it to come at her. Instead of attacking, however, the wolf finally turned and simply ran back through the door.

In an instant, Liesel was out of the bed, and had her father's arbalest in her hands. Because of the cold, Liesel had taken to sleeping in her shoes, and was morbidly grateful for this tonight as she plunged into the darkness.

The foolishness of trying to hunt a wolf in the night evaded Liesel as she sprinted after the beast. It didn't matter either that she was terrible with the arbalest. Her grandfather had only given her a few lessons with the weapon before Warin's surprise move to Ward.

Still, she tried to load the bolt as she ran. Thanks to her time with Kurt in the forest, Liesel had become better at navigating the brambles and stumps that tended to trip one on the forest floor.

But it wasn't long before Liesel could no longer hear the sound of the wolf as it ran, and she was forced to stop.

"Are you afraid?" she screamed after it into the night. "Are you too cowardly to come and finish the job?" Sobs began to escape her chest in gasps as she tried to shout, the lifeless form of her father filling her mind once more.

Without a plan, she started to run again, but strong hands caught her and held her tightly.

She thrashed. "I have to find it!" she sobbed to whomever held her. "I have to kill the wolf!"

"No, Liesel!" Kurt's voice was cautious, but controlled. "You'll only get yourself hurt."

"But he killed my father!" she cried. She quit fighting him, however, the long run making her suddenly lightheaded.

"I know," he whispered into her hair, his voice strained. "I know."

Liesel no longer had the strength to run or stand or even wonder how Kurt already knew. Instead, she collapsed into the young man's arms.

She felt dead inside. Just when she had dared to hope that her life was turning around, that she was getting her family back once more, those hopes had been dashed to pieces. As terrible a father as Warin had been, she had loved him, and he had loved her. There was no reason that this injustice should have happened. None of it made sense.

Kurt had been right. A dark magic lay over the forest. Nothing but evil had befallen her family since they'd arrived. She clung to Kurt's shirt as he tried to comfort her. She didn't care that she was half-sitting in the dirt, or that she was in the middle of the forest at night. All she knew was that Kurt was holding her together, every little broken, bitter piece that was left of her soul. She could do nothing but hold on tightly and cry.

***

Liesel couldn't recall ever returning to her cottage. All she knew was that somehow, she awoke the next morning in her own bed.

Though her father's blood still stained the floor, his body was gone.

The mayor arrived shortly after to offer his condolences, and Liesel didn't even ask how he already knew or what had been done with the body. All she wanted to do was lie in bed and remember nothing of the world that had been taken from her.

"Did you hear me, Miss Hirsch?"

Liesel slowly turned her head to look at him.

"I asked if you want to move in with someone. We have a number of families that are willing to take you in after such a grave accident. You wouldn't have to live on your own."

So they all knew. Somehow, Liesel wasn't surprised. She stared at the rotund man with contempt. He had so many words when all she wanted was silence.

"No."

"Pardon?"

"I said, no!" Liesel snapped. "I will be fine on my own." It wasn't as if the townspeople had been any help thus far. "I won't be staying here anyways."

The already nervous mayor looked as if this troubled him more deeply than her father's death.

"Where will you go?"

"I am going to board the next grain wagon that comes through town. I'm going back to my grandparents."

"I wouldn't advise that—"

"I do not care what you would or would not advise!" Liesel made sure to enunciate every word. "You and the rest of this wretched town have been nothing but a blight on me and my family! I'm leaving, and there is nothing you can do!"

Eventually, when he must have realized he wasn't convincing anyone, the mayor stood and left, looking much more disconcerted than he had been when he'd arrived.

As soon as he was gone, Liesel began to ransack the cottage, looking high and low for their money. Surely they had to have some coins stashed somewhere. It was only when she reached his blood-stained mattress that Liesel realized Warin must have kept the money on his person when he went to sleep. He always kept the money with him when they traveled. And Liesel had no idea where his body was or who had taken it.

Angry, but undeterred, she slammed the cottage door shut as she marched back into the town. She approached the first grain wagon she saw.

"How much to hitch a ride back to Weit?"

The man loading his wagon looked at her incredulously before shaking his head and chuckling.

"The city by the mountain? That will cost you at least two hundred francs, love."

Liesel nearly lost her composure. Two hundred francs was more than her father made at the blacksmith's in a year. Swallowing hard, she tried again.

"What about just to the edge of the forest?"

"Two hundred francs."

"But that's much closer!" Liesel protested. The trader rolled his eyes and bent down to whisper in her ear.

"Look, it's nothing personal. This morning, before dawn even, your mayor came round to warn all the travelers, such as myself, that an addled girl would be asking for rides out of town. He threatened our allowance out of town if he caught us trying to take her."

"Addled?" Liesel growled.

The man shrugged. "Didn't say I believed him. But to risk my right to trade in this town, I would have to know I was guaranteed something decent for my troubles."

Speechless, Liesel whirled around and stalked over to another trader. And a third, and then a fourth. Somehow, either the mayor or Izaak had managed to speak with every single tradesman in the town. Unless she was able to come up with two hundred francs or more, as some of the others had asked, she was going nowhere.

Without realizing where she was walking, Liesel ended up back at the cottage. Everything was still in disarray, bundles and bags thrown haphazardly about from when Liesel had searched for the coins that morning. She stood in the doorway for a moment, uncertain of what to do.

Part of her wanted to find Kurt. The other part of her wanted to fall into her bed and sleep and never wake up. As she hesitated, however, an ice-cold determination settled in her heart. A plan was already forming in her mind.

Night had fallen by the time Liesel's plan was complete. She would find work in Ward. If they were so determined to keep her, they would have to give her some way to survive. Garden or no garden, she needed a way to buy grain. She wasn't going to live long on turnips, onions, parsnips, and the few potatoes her little plot had produced that summer. She would save and scrimp everything she could, buying only what was necessary. She would get the two hundred francs if it killed her.

A wolf howled in the distance, and Liesel fetched the arbalest once again. Laying it beside her bed, she glared at the door, mentally taunting the animal, daring it to burst through. If she couldn't leave now, it didn't matter. Somehow, she was going to escape.

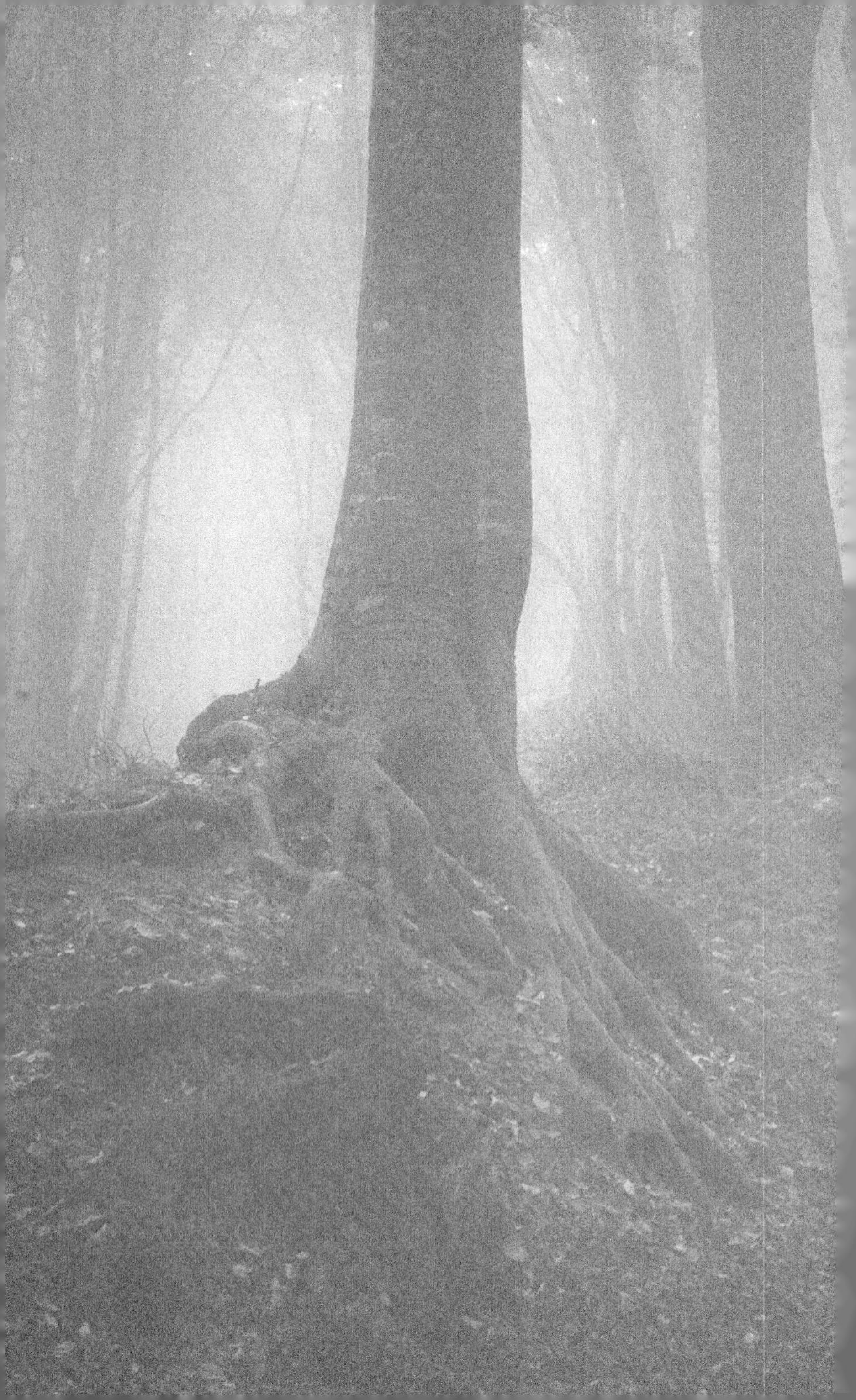

CHAPTER 11
A FORTNIGHT

"I want Armen to win, but I think Bruno will probably pull the ribbon." Mitsi tossed her red curls.

Karla shook her head and scoffed at her sister. "Dirk can beat Bruno any day. Besides, who would want Bruno to win? He is pigheaded enough as it is. No one needs to give him another reason to strut about like a rooster." She looked down the table where all three girls sat as they kneaded dough. "Who do you want to win?"

It was a long moment before Liesel realized the girl was actually speaking to her.

"Oh." Liesel flashed an apologetic smile. "I'm sorry, but I don't really know."

Mitsi went back to the conversation as if Liesel had never spoken, but Karla continued sending curious looks her way every few minutes.

Though she had little to contribute to the conversation, Liesel appreciated the girl's attempt to draw her in. After nearly a year of working in the bakery, it was nice to have someone who didn't treat her as if she had the plague.

"Karla, come here." The baker's voice had an edge to it.

Liesel gave a small sigh, knowing what was about to happen. Karla knew, too, but instead of looking abashed, she lifted her chin a bit and stomped out the back door.

Liesel knew their words weren't for her, but it was impossible not to listen. Usually Mr. Huber wasn't so careless as to rebuke his youngest daughter where Liesel could hear, but all the windows were open due to the warm day.

"Karla, are you trying to get someone killed?"

"I'm just being friendly, Papa." Karla sounded impatient.

"You have a kind heart, Daughter, but if you don't take care, you could be the one they mark if something happens to Liesel! Or it could be your sister! How many times must I tell you about Ilsa? When she ran away, it was her closest friend who was marked instead!"

Liesel nearly risked a glance out the window. How strange that a girl with her grandmother's name should have been marked.

"It's so unfair," Karla whined. "Liesel works hard, never misses a Holy Day, and even stays late to help clean up, and all we do is ignore her. She must be lonely."

"Aye, it is unfair." The baker's voice was sad.

Liesel had to remind herself to keep kneading the bread. She'd never heard anyone from Ward speak about her with such sympathy before. Since she had requested work from the mayor and had been assigned to Huber's shop, the most kindness she'd received was getting to take home dry, unsold pastries sometimes after the shop closed. Not that overhearing this discussion would change anything. Still, it helped a little to know that it was the mark they feared. At least they didn't hate her.

When she'd first met the family, it was strange to learn that the father and youngest daughter were in any way related. Huber was a tall, fat man with an unusually nasally voice, and he was slightly inclined to be dramatic. Karla, on the other hand, was skinny and practical, just two years Liesel's junior. Liesel often felt a twinge of jealousy about the situation, that she should have been great friends with the girl if it hadn't been for the terrifying mark on her hand that everyone in town somehow seemed to know about.

A few moments later, Karla and her father walked back in, and Karla said nothing more to Liesel the rest of that morning or the afternoon. She did, however, sneak her a smile as the sisters left the kitchen at the end of the day.

Liesel procrastinated as much as she could after they left, sweeping the floors and wiping the windows until Huber told her she needed to go home. She stood quietly as he counted out her week's pay, then turned silently to go after she'd pocketed the coins. Huber's conscience must have gotten the better of him, however, because he called out to her once more as she opened the door.

"Liesel?"

She turned back to him, wide-eyed.

He paused nervously for a moment before whispering, "Good work."

Shocked, Liesel could barely get herself to nod as the baker ducked back into his pantry. She wondered again as she left the shop at how peculiar it was that a marked girl from years before should have had her grandmother's name.

What was it that Ilsa had told Warin the night of their departure? *People that go to that town... they never leave!* How had she known that, especially when so many were bound to secrecy by the strange magic?

Liesel huffed. It would have been the perfect question to ask Kurt if she hadn't been trying to avoid him.

Warin's death had changed Liesel. It had made her even more determined to leave Ward. She had asked the mayor the very next day to help her find work. It sickened her to have to ask him for anything, but she knew that without him, no one would even consider giving her a job. Also, it would convince him of her intentions to stay.

She'd hoped that in time, he would relax his reign over the travelers' wagons. Apparently, though, he was still sniffing around, asking which ones Liesel had approached. A full year later, and not even the peddler, Gil, had been willing to speak with her. They wouldn't even carry a letter to her grandparents.

As soon as Liesel had taken the new job, she'd had little time to see Kurt. One day, however, she'd gotten the feeling she was being watched as she walked home. Turning down the bend to her own cottage, she had nearly passed out from fright when she saw someone waiting in the shadow of the trees. When she realized that it was Kurt, however, she had nearly smacked him for scaring her so.

"Why haven't you been coming out?" he'd demanded.

"I got a job," Liesel had said without looking at him. "I'm working most days now. I don't get out until it is nearly dark."

"Why do you need to do that?" He had looked so confused that Liesel had nearly told him of her plan to escape, but an instinct warned her not to. She wasn't sure why, but somehow, she knew he would react badly. It felt wrong to hide something so important from her only friend. But she had to escape. So she used the next best excuse.

"I need to eat," she'd said in a low voice.

Kurt had frowned. "You have your garden. And I can still bring you meat."

"And that is very kind of you... but I would still like to be able to buy grain sometimes. And clothes, shoes, feed for my horse–"

"All right," Kurt had sounded annoyed, but at least stopped arguing the point. "Will I get to see you anymore at all?"

Liesel's heart had sped up, and her cheeks felt warm. For some reason, she'd smiled. "If you wait for me at the edge of the forest like this, you can walk me home. Would your father mind that?"

"It doesn't matter," Kurt had scoffed. "I can walk you home if I want."

And so they'd continued in that manner. Liesel hadn't dreaded going to the bakery so much after that, since she had her time with Kurt to look forward to at the end of every day. She would often save the pastries they gave her to share with him on the way home.

It must have looked odd to any passerby who might have glimpsed them. Actually, the passerby would have only seen her walking on the edge of the road, talking to herself, passing baked goods into the trees. The passerby wouldn't have seen the lanky boy accept the morsels and devour them greedily as young men do. The passerby would have missed the boy looking hard at the girl's face, studying her expressions, hanging on her every word.

But Liesel saw, and that was why it was so hard now to try and avoid the one person in the world she wanted so much to see.

After a year of working, scrimping, and saving, Liesel nearly had the two hundred francs. She needed just one more week's wages before she would have enough. As she walked home on this particular night, however, she realized she felt unhappier than ever.

She should have been rejoicing. After three years in the miserable forest, she was finally close to returning to her grandparents and her beloved mountain. And yet, a part of her mourned. Soon she would have to face Kurt and tell him the truth. And if she was honest with herself, she thought it just might break her heart.

"It's a bit late, don't you think?"

Liesel's heart stopped then started again as she recognized the deepening voice that came from the shadows. He'd caught on to her. Liesel closed her eyes and sent a prayer up to the Maker, asking for words. This was a conversation she wasn't yet ready for.

"Yes," she said slowly, turning toward the voice in the trees. "It is."

A hand reached out and caught her arm, drawing her into the forest. It was a bit unnerving to see only darkness, but Liesel had long ago given up fearing the forest when she was with Kurt. She was discomfited this night, however, by the tone of his voice.

"Liesel, what are you up to?" He sounded impatient and tired. When she didn't answer, he said, "This wouldn't have anything to do with running away, would it?"

"Is it really running away when you're just trying to run home?" Liesel spat out, dangerously close to tears. She heard him let out a gusty breath. "I wanted to tell you, I promise," she hastened to explain. "I just... didn't know how."

"Why?" His voice was barely above a whisper. "Why do you need so badly to go?"

"I need a life, Kurt! I miss my grandparents! I miss the sun! I miss talking to people, and walking by them without them thinking I have some wretched curse!"

"But I've given you the sun... by the waterfall!" His voice was worried now. "I... I can make sure they treat you better!"

Had he lost his mind? How could he make sure that happened? Liesel shook her head, trying to find the right words, when an idea hit her. Reaching out, she found his hands and held them tightly.

"Come with me!" she urged. "My grandparents are kind! They would give you work until we were ready to go on our adventures! We could leave this place behind and never look back! Please, Kurt!" Tears streamed down her face. "I need you, too!"

"And what about my family?" He sounded resentful. "Am I just supposed to leave them behind?"

They were quiet for a moment until Liesel finally whispered, "That's exactly what you're asking of me, isn't it?" Another awkward silence ensued, but Liesel was sure she felt her heart breaking.

Finally, Kurt spoke again, his words slow and agonized. "How long?"

"One week." The coins in Liesel's pocket had never felt quite so heavy.

"Give me two," he pleaded, his voice suddenly passionate. "Give me until the festival!"

"Why? I hate that stupid dance. No one will dance with me." Liesel was beginning to loathe the festival with a passion she'd not known herself capable of. The girls at the bakery had talked of nothing but the Summer Maiden for the past two weeks. But Kurt's hands tightened their grip on hers.

"I would."

"But you're not allowed into the town!"

"Hang the rules." Kurt's voice was husky. "Just... just promise me you'll wait until then. Give me two weeks."

Liesel's breathing hitched with surprise when fingers gently brushed her cheek. It was the most gentle touch she had felt since her mother had died. Her heart raced as she wished there was enough light to see his face by. Faintly, she felt herself nod and whisper, "Very well. I will wait."

To her even greater surprise, he drew her forward. A quick, warm kiss was placed on her cheek before she found herself back out on the road alone. It was so dark by the time she reached her cottage that she tripped twice, but it didn't matter. She was smiling like a fool the whole way. Why Kurt wanted to meet her at the dance, she had no idea. But she was willing to wait and find out.

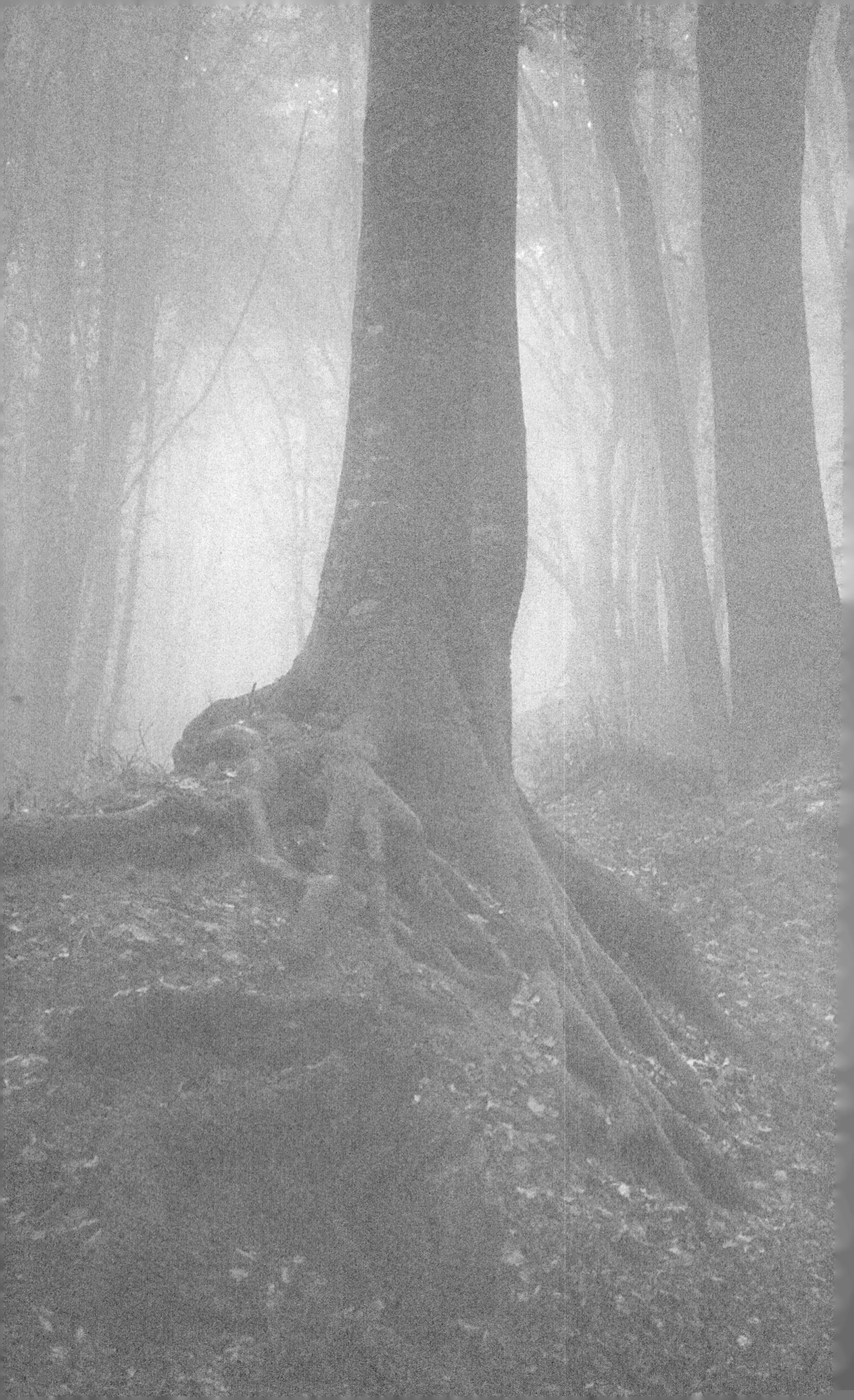

CHAPTER 12
DON'T LOOK BACK

Liesel fastened the red cord beneath her chin. Usually she wouldn't need her cloak this early in autumn, but it had been an exceptionally cool summer. That winter would make short work of the fall was the popular prediction among the people of Ward.

A knock at the door made her jump as she readjusted her gown. She glanced in the mirror once more, still a bit shocked. It had been a while since she had paid any heed to the girl who lived there. In her absence, the girl had gone, and a woman that looked frighteningly like Amala had taken her place. Liesel took another deep breath and turned to answer the door.

If her own reflection had startled her, it was nothing compared to the surprise she felt when she saw Kurt. The stubble that constantly darkened his jawline was gone for once, and the clothes he wore were abnormally clean. His hair even looked as though he might have attempted to brush it. The trousers were brown, and though old, appeared to be without the usual holes. He wore a white shirt tucked in beneath a dark blue coat that reached his knees.

Kurt looked out of place in the clothes, uncomfortable in every way. His obvious discomfort didn't stop him from looking quite manly, though. It took her aback a little. The night in the forest didn't count as a visit, as she'd hardly been able to see a thing, but she had only been avoiding him for a few months. And yet, he seemed to have aged years.

Kurt's own eyes grew large when Liesel opened the door. He cleared his throat twice before speaking. "I, uh... I don't suppose you have a ribbon."

Liesel smiled timidly and pulled one from her hair. A faint grin cracked his anxious face as she handed it to him.

"It was my mother's," Liesel answered the unspoken question softly as she stared at the red silk in his hand. "She wore it the night she met my father."

Liesel had considered using her old blue one, but had quickly decided against it. It held too many memories, and buying a new one just seemed a way to invite disaster. She had nearly told Kurt she wasn't coming until she'd found this one wrapped up in one of her mother's dresses, the scarlet dress she wore now beneath her cloak.

"I like it," Kurt mumbled. After hesitating for a moment, he tied it around his forearm the way tradition insisted before offering her his other arm to hold. Her heart beat fast as she accepted. His arm felt warm and strong.

As they reached the edge of town, they began to pass more people, each person staring more boldly than the last. Kurt looked straight ahead without meeting any eyes, but Liesel couldn't help grinning smugly as her neighbors gaped.

Kurt was unquestionably the most handsome young man she had ever seen. And it was obvious from her neighbors' expressions that they hadn't expected to see her with anyone at all. Suddenly buoyant, Liesel's cheeks burned pleasantly when she thought of the kiss he'd given her two weeks before. And before she caught herself, a wild wish wondered if he would kiss her again tonight.

And what will you do then? the unpleasant voice of reason asked. *Will you still be able to leave? And will you ever forgive yourself if you do?*

Liesel decided to ignore that voice as much as possible. Instead, she focused on the way it felt to hold on to his arm.

As they neared the town square, the crowds gawked even more

than her neighbors had. Liesel felt a shred of uncertainty wind its way around her stomach as she watched the people around her. Something was different, and she was suddenly sure that it wasn't just her presence this time. Something else was wrong.

It only became clear, however, when she saw the mayor up on the stage. He appeared to be preparing for the same kind of speech he'd given the year before when he looked down their way and startled. That was when she understood the change. They weren't looking at her. They were looking at Kurt. And they all looked terrified.

"Kurt," the mayor said after quickly regaining his composure. "What a surprise. It is an honor to have you here with us tonight." Despite his words, the mayor seemed anything but happy to have the young man present.

Glancing around, Liesel noticed families on the outskirts trying to edge away. Regardless of the way they had treated her for the past three years, she felt a sudden pang of sympathy for the townspeople. They were truly afraid. Looking back at Kurt, she tried to understand why.

He was different from them, of course. He moved like one of his beloved animals, and he didn't seem too keen on being in the middle of the crowd himself. But as Kurt's father didn't allow him to come to town it seemed odd that they would all know him enough to fear him. In that moment, Liesel heard her mother's words about men.

Be careful, Leese. Many men are not as they say. If something feels wrong, follow your instinct. The Maker is trying to warn you. And suddenly, every instinct in her was screaming that she should run.

And yet, she balked. This was Kurt. He had befriended her when she was alone and brought her as close to her mountain as she could get. He had kept her alive through an entire winter when everyone else would have let her starve. Kurt had promised to keep her safe, and so far, he had.

He might even love her.

Could this be about his family, rather than just him, she wondered. Kurt had always been mysterious, but his family, even more so. She shivered at the memory of meeting his Uncle Lothur.

The question, she decided, was knowing to which side he truly belonged, to the mystery or to the companion she had come to know and rely on. Drawing in a shaky breath, she glanced up at him again.

Kurt's face gave little away, but his breathing was a bit deeper than usual, and his arm shook slightly. He swallowed hard before answering the mayor.

"Thank you."

It would have been imperceptible to anyone else, but Liesel detected a slight tremble in his voice as he spoke.

"As a treat for us," the mayor gestured to the open space that had been cleared for the festival, "won't you lead us in the first dance?"

Even with all the turmoil of Liesel's thoughts, her heart skipped a beat. That was an honor reserved for the Summer Maiden, the only dance in which all would be watching. Kurt hesitated for a split second before looking down at her. The fear in his eyes was clear, although Liesel couldn't imagine why he might be afraid. This had all been his idea. And yet, taking her by the hand, he slowly led her toward the center of the dance floor.

The people, though tightly packed, gave them a wide berth as they moved forward. Scanning the faces in the crowd, Liesel quickly located Karla and Mitsi with their parents. Karla slipped her a small smile. Farther down the row, Liesel also spotted the peddler in his green suit. Out of the corner of her eye, she saw Kurt give him a slight nod as they passed. To her surprise, the peddler returned it.

How did they know one another? Liesel wanted to puzzle over such a friendship, but she had no time. They were suddenly in the center of the dancing space, and everyone was watching.

Liesel's heart hammered as the musicians began to play. Kurt placed one hand on her waist and took her right hand with the other. Both her terror and her exhilaration soared as he led them through the first steps of the dance. She shivered slightly with delight and nerves as she realized he'd never held her this close to him before, not even when he'd kept her from falling, or had sneaked that kiss. The night her father had died didn't count. She had practically collapsed on top of him.

As they continued to dance, the world began to change. It felt as though the air around them shimmered. Colors wavered, and Liesel's stomach felt as though she might be spinning too fast. The muscles in her arms and legs tingled, and it was as though she could suddenly run forever and never tire. Smells were abruptly stronger. Liesel could tell exactly where the bakery and grain storehouses were, even as they twirled. Curious, and a little troubled, she searched Kurt's face to see if he felt any of the changes, too.

His golden-brown eyes were staring right back at her, but he didn't appear to be confused or disoriented in the way she felt. He wore instead an expression she couldn't quite read, one of sadness, wonder, and determination. The emotion in his face made Liesel's already jittery stomach flop even more. She tried to focus on how it felt as he led her expertly through the dance, but even that grew impossible. Dizziness took hold of her senses, and soon it was all she could do to hang on and follow along.

Eventually, much to her relief, they finished the dance. She knew it was improper, but she had to lean on him as they left the dance floor. Once they were well away from everyone else, he sat her down on a bench, watching her closely as she tried to catch her breath.

"Are you feeling well?"

"What was that?" she gasped.

"What?"

"Colors." Liesel shook her head to clear it. "Sparks, as if the breeze was alive. And why am I so dizzy?"

"You feel that?" He seemed shocked.

"How could I not? But what is it?" She repeated the question. Before Kurt had time to answer, however, the piercing cry of a wolf filled the air. It was distant but unmistakable.

"It's not time yet! What do they think they're doing?" Kurt muttered, all talk of Liesel's strange spell seeming forgotten. Face taut with frustration, he bounded a few paces back toward the crowd and motioned to someone that Liesel couldn't see.

As the howling grew louder and closer, the crowd noticed as

well. Murmurs broke out, and the music stopped. Rather than freezing in fright, as Liesel had done and expected everyone else to do, however, the crowd reacted with expert calm and purpose. Parents grabbed their children, and everyone began to quickly clear the square.

Gil Gaspar's covered cart broke through her thoughts as it came rambling toward them. Kurt had Liesel off the bench in an instant, carrying her in both arms.

The dizziness and disorientation returned.

"Kurt, what's happening?" Despite her strange sickness, terror was rising fast within her.

He didn't answer, though. Instead, he spoke to Gil. "Take her to Tag. Make sure she stays safe."

"This is a dangerous ride," Gil said nervously. "Before we go, I will need the payment we spoke about." With Liesel still in his arms, Kurt managed to pull a bag of what sounded like coins from his boot. After tossing it up to Gil, he ran to the back of the cart and pushed her inside. As he began to cover her with blankets, she grasped his hand to stop him.

"What's going on?" Fear strained her voice and made it sound strangled. Was he truly sending her away? Tag was in the opposite direction of Weit, nearly at the other end of the forest, the woodland town nearest the capital.

"I'm sorry, Liesel." Kurt squeezed her hand with both of his. Pain lined his face as he reached out and hesitantly stroked her cheek. "I promised to keep you safe, and that's what I'm doing. Now get under these blankets and don't let anyone see you until Gil gets you to Tag."

"At least let me get my book!" Liesel sobbed. If he was going to push her even farther from her grandparents, the least he could do was give her the one piece of them that she had left.

But he shook his head. "There isn't time! I'm sorry!" With that, he began to pile the blankets back over her head, pushing her gently, but firmly into the bottom of the peddler's cart. "And Liesel?" He paused. "Don't look back."

"Aren't you ready yet?" Gil sounded nearly frantic, even from

Liesel's spot beneath the thick blankets. The howling was growing much closer.

"This is Johan," she heard him say to Gil. "He will follow you to make sure she gets there safely."

"You're sending *him*?"

"He understands," Kurt said firmly. More quietly, he said, "Only to the border, and no further, all right, Johan? And thank you." With that, the cart jolted forward, bumping Liesel's head in the process.

Liesel was horrified to be going in the wrong direction, especially as she had been just one day from her own journey back to Weit. But the sounds of the wolves and the fear she'd seen in Kurt's eyes scared her too much to protest anymore. What did they want? Another jolt nearly sent her flying out of the cart. When she landed, however, she landed right in front of a knothole in the wood, one that gave her a perfect window to the town that was already shrinking behind them.

To her amazement, a gray wolf ran alongside the cart. Liesel almost cried out to Gil until she realized that he was running with them, not at them. That must have been who Kurt had meant when he'd introduced Johan. But he'd said Johan understood. How could a wolf understand?

Just then, another wolf broke through the brush that bordered the road. He headed straight for Liesel as if she wasn't hidden at all. Sure she would die, Liesel closed her eyes and waited.

But nothing came. Peeking through the knothole again, she gasped. Johan had brought him down to the ground, where they rolled and writhed in a whirl of fur and snapping teeth. She watched in horror as they grew smaller and smaller in the distance. Burying her face in her hands, she sobbed for Johan. No wonder Kurt told her not to look back.

A terrible thought struck her as another howl sounded somewhere to their left, and then their right. If Kurt's family... at least, Liesel guessed it was his family due to the wolves... was willing to send their wolves to attack Johan, one of their own, what would they do to Kurt?

She nearly told Gil to bring the cart to a halt right then and there. But first she asked herself, what then? All of Kurt's planning would be for naught. She obviously had no idea as to what they wanted, or if she could even give it to them. Kurt seemed to think she couldn't, or shouldn't, rather. So she let the cart continue to fly down the road. But a small piece of her that wouldn't be silenced was deeply ashamed. Kurt would surely pay for saving her.

Eventually, Johan caught up to them again. By the time he did, the peddler had slowed the horses, and Liesel was relieved to see that he was still alive. She felt another stab of guilt, though, when she saw splotches of blood matting his silver fur. She prayed it wasn't his.

After an hour more of riding, the wolf cries began again. Johan stopped running and disappeared into the thick brush. He never reappeared.

LIESEL DIDN'T REALIZE she'd fallen asleep until they stopped. As she hadn't left Ward since moving there, she had no way of knowing for certain where they really were. She waited under the blankets until she heard Gil climb out of the driver's seat. Instead of uncovering her, however, she heard him call back to her as he walked away.

"You can let yourself loose now. Best find somewhere warm to sleep. It'll be a cold one tonight."

Pushing the blankets off of her head, Liesel sat up and looked around anxiously. He really wasn't going to abandon her, was he?

"You can't just leave me here!" she called after him, trying not to stumble as she climbed down from the cart, her legs numb from being still for so long. The darkness told her that it was still nighttime, but the sky was strangely light for the late hour it must have been.

It took Liesel a moment to realize that the forest canopy wasn't nearly as thick here as it was in Ward. Moonbeams moved down through the trees and hit her face for the first time in three years. A bit overwhelmed, it took Liesel a second to shake off their hypnotizing beauty and continue after the peddler.

"You're surely not going to leave me all alone!" she cried breathlessly as she followed him. "I've never been here! I haven't any money... I don't even know where the church is!" She was already regretting her failure to hide a few coins in her skirts before leaving the cottage.

Gil paused at the door of a place that from the outside sounded and smelled like Warin did after his nights at the tavern, raucous and sour. "Here." He took a coin from his pocket and flipped it at her before going inside.

Liesel hesitated before deciding to follow him in. She had never been inside a tavern, nor had she ever desired such an experience. Her only other choice, however, was to wander the streets until she found the church or somewhere better to sleep. Bracing herself, she took a deep breath of the clean air and followed him through the door.

It was even worse than she had imagined. A few dozen men and a couple of rough-looking women sat at wooden tables, which were placed as close to one another as physically possible. The floor was even stickier than the grubby chairs and tables she tried to avoid touching as she walked. The stink of sweat and soured ale nearly made her gag. Gil was already sitting down at a table in the center of the room by the time she caught up to him.

"But where am I supposed to go? What should I do?" Ugh. She'd used all of her air. Now she would have to breathe again.

The peddler turned to answer her, wearing an exasperated look. "See here, lass, my family lives in the forest. Now I feel bad for you, I do. But agreeing to take you away from Ward was a big enough risk as it was. It was done from the kindness of my heart. But I can't be putting my own family in danger now. I got you here. Live as you choose. Go where you will, I don't care. Just leave me and mine be."

"The kindness of your heart and a sack of gold." Liesel glared at him.

He reddened under the scrutiny of her gaze. "Look, you're pretty enough to find work somewhere. Save some coins and go to the capital, wherever you want. Just leave me alone."

"Aye," the tavern keep spoke, eyeing her from the table he was clearing. "I need another serving girl here."

A new kind of anxiety filled Liesel as she looked around, suddenly aware of a different type of predator. Sure enough, there were at least half a dozen men staring at her with an expression that made Liesel blush. And this time, Kurt wasn't there to save her. She felt suddenly as though she might throw up.

"Please," she turned tearfully to Gil, "just take me to the church." Taking asylum in the house of the Maker wouldn't solve all of her problems by any stretch, but it would be safer there than anywhere else.

"And what might you be needing the church for, young lady?" a new voice from behind her asked.

Liesel turned to see a tall, well-dressed man a bit older than her father would have been. His voice was smooth and confident, and he spoke more eloquently than anyone she'd heard since leaving Weit. She wanted to answer, but froze, unsure whether she should trust this genteel stranger or not.

He turned to the tavern keep and frowned a bit, his black and silver eyebrows pulling together as he handed the man a little parcel. "Your wife needs this tea for her headaches. Make sure she gets it. No trading it away for favors the way you did last time." At this, the tall man looked even sterner, and the tavern keep turned bright red.

"Are you in some sort of trouble?" He turned back to Liesel, his voice gentler this time.

Faintly, Liesel nodded. She wanted nothing more than someone to trust. But how could she know if this man was as kind as he looked?

He seemed to sense her fear, and stepped back a bit, giving a little bow. "My name is Ely Becke. I am the town healer here."

"I'm Liesel," she replied softly.

"I believe I overheard this man offer you a... position?" He spat the word out like a sour grape. "If you are in need of employment, please consider my offer instead. My wife needs someone to help her around the house, and I could use some assistance in my shop. Do you know anything of herbs?"

Liesel swallowed before nodding. "My mother taught me."

He raised his eyebrows in approval. "Well, it is growing late. If you wish, I can bring you to my house to meet my wife." He paused. "Or I can take you to the church if that is what you desire."

Liesel finally managed a smile before nodding and following him out the door, but she didn't feel as confident as her expression. Back outside in the moonlight, she grew more and more afraid. Staying in the tavern was never an option, but leaving it with a complete stranger was frightening, too.

She nearly cried with relief when a woman met them at the door of the house he led them to. It was rather spacious and more beautifully furnished than any place Liesel had seen since coming to the forest.

Once his wife confirmed that they did indeed need help, Liesel tried to convey her willingness to work starting that very night, but Ros would hear nothing of it.

Tall like her husband, Ros was a handsome woman. She kept her silver streaked brown hair pulled into a thick braid that was pinned back up into a loop on her head, and her clothes were stylish but practical. She reminded Liesel a great deal of her grandmother. Instead of letting her work, Ros insisted on feeding Liesel a late supper of stew before finding her some old bedclothes and tucking her into bed like a small child.

Liesel could tell that the couple was curious about her story, but they didn't ask, and she didn't share. Her head was too muddled from exhaustion, fear, and confusion to do much but fall into the bed of the small upstairs room they had given her.

As Ros blew out the candle, Liesel tried to recount how exactly in one day she had gone from her own cottage to running for her life to this lovely, but distant, safe haven. She couldn't, though. There was just too much to remember.

As she drifted off to sleep, there was only one thing that marred the relief she should have felt in the cozy little bed. She couldn't help but wonder what Kurt's family would do to punish him for sending her away. Would it have been better if she'd given herself up? Her fear had kept her from doing such a thing, and it shamed her to think she might have helped him, but hadn't. He had done so much for her with no true explanation as to why.

And what had she done for him? Telling him a few stories from a book was hardly comparable to the way he had sacrificed everything to keep her safe. The slumber that should have been sweet and peaceful was tainted by her guilt, and the last sound she heard before sleep took her was the single mournful cry of a wolf.

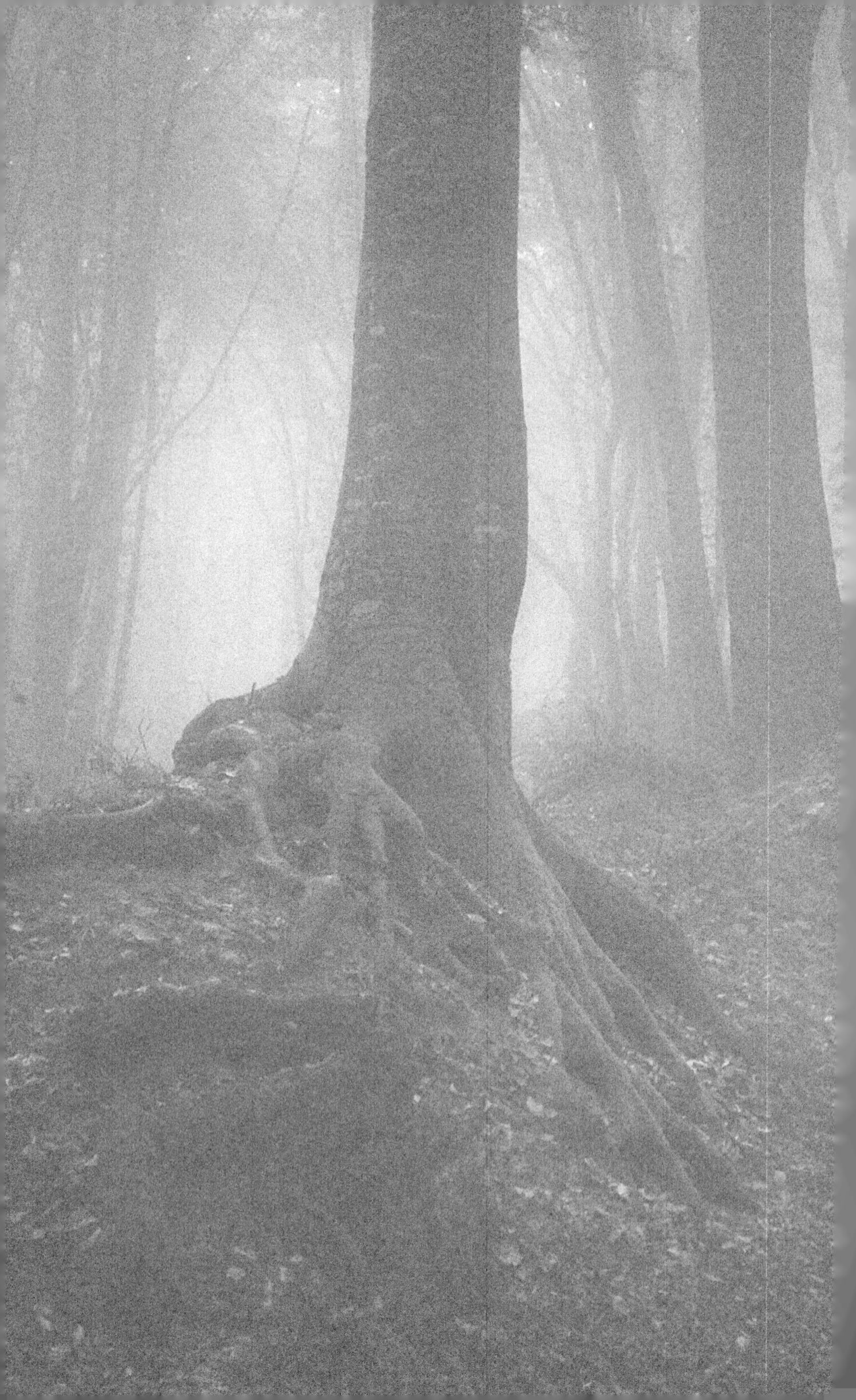

FOUR YEARS LATER...

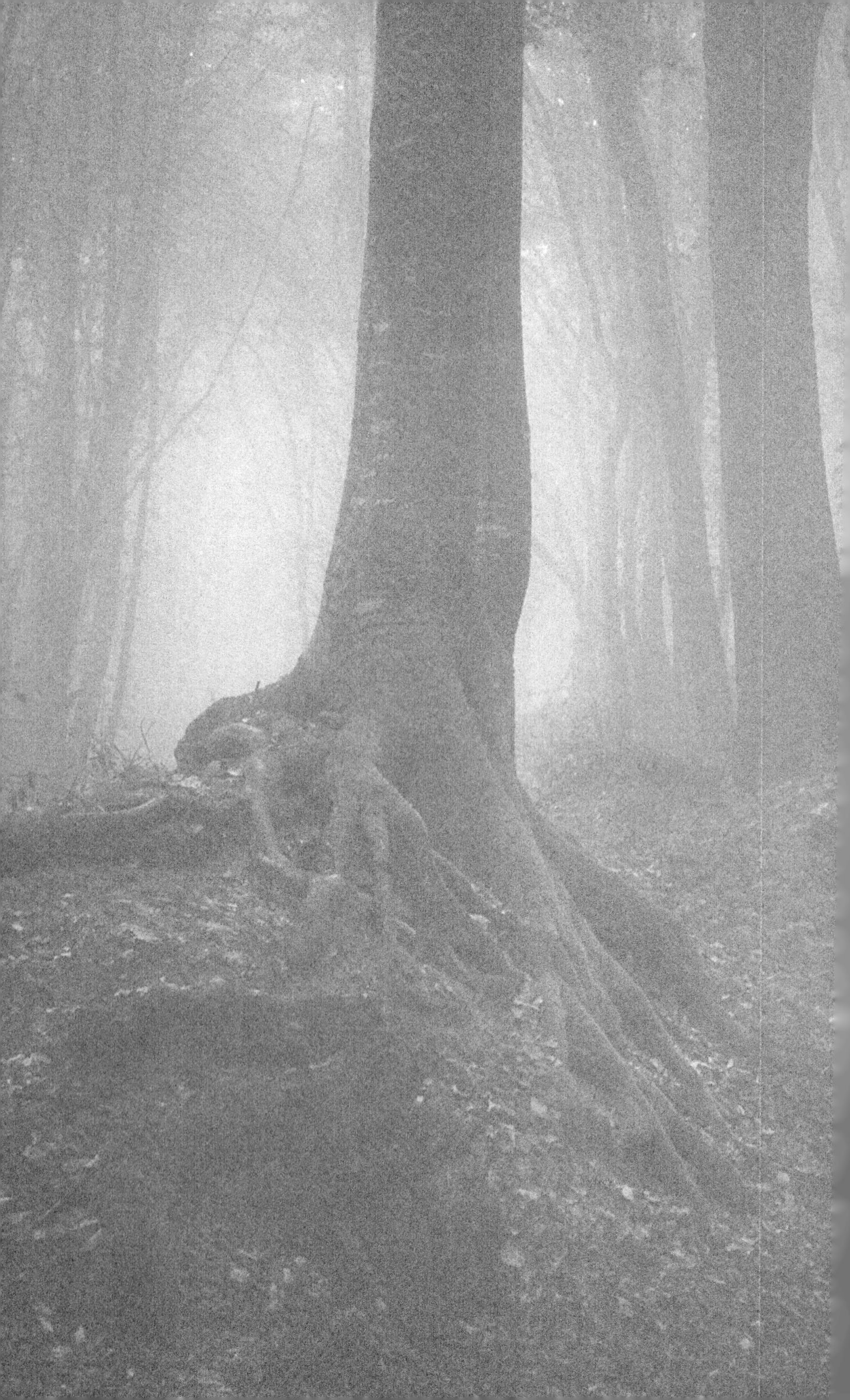

CHAPTER 13
WOLFSBANE

It didn't matter how long Liesel basked in the beams of sunlight. She would never tire of it.

Opening her eyes, Liesel looked down at the apple she held and squeezed it with satisfaction. It would be perfect for the pie Ros was going to bake that afternoon.

"I will take four," she told the man behind the stall. Ros only needed three, but Liesel was hungry. She smiled again as she thanked the Maker for the generosity of her patrons. It had been a long time since she'd gone hungry.

"Whether we like it or not," she heard a woman one stall over remark, "it's time to put out the Wolfsbane again."

"Aye, they were loud last night. I sent my Ada for some first thing this morning," Mrs. Thull answered dryly.

"Pardon me." Liesel moved closer. "But what is Wolfsbane?" She had already seen three children running about that morning with armfuls of the long purple stems, yelling out that they had Wolfsbane for sale.

"Didn't you hear the wolves last night?" Mrs. Thull asked.

Liesel shivered a little. She had done her best not to.

"The wolf mother must have died," the other woman said. Liesel didn't know who this lady was, but she was short and somewhat plump, dressed from head to toe in yellow. "The wolves must be looking for their new one."

"How long have you been in Tag, Liesel?" Mrs. Thull studied her.

Liesel shifted uncomfortably. "Four years."

"That would be it." Mrs. Thull nodded at her friend knowingly. "You weren't here the last time we had to put out Wolfsbane."

"It's been twenty-two years," the woman in yellow laughed, affectionately slapping Mrs. Thull on the arm. "She wasn't even alive then! Just us old birds." She turned to Liesel, still chuckling. "But where are you from, child? Even the babes know the story here."

"Weit," Liesel said softly. Telling people where she was born was easier than telling them she had come from Ward. It didn't matter how often she tried to relate her story to her friends in Tag, she just couldn't do it. Eventually, the Beckes had stopped asking her, and so had her other friends as time went by.

Liesel had once overheard Ros telling an acquaintance that the girl's past must have been difficult because she could never get more than a word or two out of Liesel about it. Liesel was thankful that they didn't press harder. Try as she might, she just couldn't bring herself to utter a word of her confusing past to anyone in Tag. Every time she tried, it was as though her mouth had stopped working.

Although she missed her grandparents sorely, coming to Tag had been the next best thing that could have happened to Liesel. The three years she had spent in Ward had been full of confusion, fear, and loneliness. The more time she spent in Tag, the stranger she realized her life in Ward had been.

Not long after her escape, Liesel had made the conscious decision to try and forget everything that had happened to her in Ward. And she'd succeeded for the most part. She no longer flinched when passersby turned to look at her. She came and left the Beckes' house without feeling afraid. She had friends, and the Beckes treated her like the daughter they'd always wanted. There were even two men who were determined to win her hand.

And yet, there were parts of her past that she couldn't shake. She found ways to block them during the day, to stay busy and productive, but at night, they came to visit her where she couldn't escape. Last night had been one of those nights, particularly in thanks to the distant cries of the wolves, something she hadn't heard since coming to Ward.

"Legend has it that there's a pack of wolves that live outside Ward," the woman in yellow began. "They live in the depths of the forest where the wood is the darkest. They're no ordinary wolves now, mind you. They can walk about as men, and you wouldn't know them from your neighbors. But they cannot remain in human form always. They need a wolf mother of human blood to keep the magic alive so they can continue to appear human. When the wolf mother dies, they must find a new one, or the magic will overwhelm them. That's what the Wolfsbane is for, to keep them away from the doors of good human families with daughters they might steal." The short woman's eyes shone with excitement as she spoke, but Mrs. Thull rolled her own eyes.

"Now look what you've done, gone and scared the poor girl with your stories." She waved her hand dismissively at her friend.

Liesel realized her mouth had fallen open, and tried quickly to pull herself back together. "No, I understand that it's just a story, but," she paused, "is the Wolfsbane effective?"

Mrs. Thull shrugged. "Who knows? Most parents put it on their porches now just to scare their children and keep them from straying too far into the woods. But it doesn't hurt, I've always supposed. I'll tell you one thing, though. I've lived here all my life, and every family that I have ever seen move to Ward has stayed there. Not one has ever left. Not one. Ada!" she suddenly called out to her small daughter. "Don't touch that!"

In a moment, both Mrs. Thull and her friend were gone. The story weighed heavy on Liesel's mind, however, as she walked home. There was too much to the legend that reminded her of her old life. They had laughed that it was just a children's story, a legend to keep little ones home and safe. And yet, it was somehow too familiar for comfort.

Liesel hurried home with her little basket of apples, too lost in thought to acknowledge the people she met on the street. As she reached to open the carved wooden door that adorned the Beckes' home, she realized she'd been rubbing the scar on her right hand.

It tingled. *Nonsense,* she thought. The scar hadn't hurt in years. It was just her imagination.

"Oh, there you are, Liesel." Her mistress greeted her with a mischievous grin. Despite the fact that her hair was graying, it was easy to forget Ros's age when she was up to some mischief. "Fridric was here again. He left you–"

"Flowers in the hall." Liesel rolled her eyes and smiled, briefly forgetting the troublesome Wolfsbane. Right on time. Fridric never missed a morning.

"You really should give him a chance." Ros shook her head indulgently. "He truly does like you, unlike Benat."

Liesel gave an unladylike snort. Fridric was, in fact, a sweet young man, if not a bit too obsessed with his horses. Very tall and so lanky he appeared almost skeletal, he had approached Liesel the first time she'd attended Holy Day with the Beckes, and there he had declared himself in love with her on the spot. Despite her assurances that she wasn't currently looking for a man to attach herself to, he had persisted, certain that being the wife of a horse breeder was what she desired in her heart of hearts.

Liesel had done her best to avoid him at first, but very quickly, she'd realized that meant staying cooped up in the house. Fridric's parents were good friends with the Beckes, and the families talked often. In time, she had learned how to handle the kind, somewhat overly sensitive man, especially when his imagination got the best of him. If she was honest, managing Fridic was rather akin to handling a very large child.

Benat Hass was another story. An older, less enthusiastic man, Ros reported that he had a bad habit of chasing every unattached woman that came through Tag. Sure enough, as soon as he'd noticed Fridric trailing about after her, Benat had simply followed suit. He was older than Fridric by at least ten years. Old enough, according to Ros, to know better. He was even taller than Fridric, and he was also broad. His thick, bushy mustache was only as wide as his mouth, and it reminded Liesel of the caterpillars that used to crawl into her mother's garden back in Weit. Rather than using his knowledge of horses to impress Liesel, as Fridric tried to do, however, Benat simply attempted to assert himself as Liesel's protector wherever she went.

"I am quite safe with the Beckes," she had assured him once, exasperated after he'd seated himself next to her at the church on Holy Day, and had spent the whole service resting his arm on the bench behind her. It had unnerved Liesel so much at one point that Ely had been forced to call on him and have a very stern discussion about the appropriate way to treat a young woman that was not his wife.

Fridric had somehow gotten wind of the conversation, though it was meant to be private, and there had very nearly been a fistfight in the town square, which Liesel knew would not have ended well for Fridric. The only way she could think to prevent the inevitable duel was by announcing to everyone that she was saving money for the journey back to her grandparents' home in Weit. It was a truth she had been hoping to keep to herself, as she knew it would pain the Beckes, but it did at least stop the fight.

Since then, the two young men had backed off a little, but only just. Fridric still picked wild flowers for her daily, and Benat still made sure he had the seat next to her at every public event she attended.

"I wish the poor man would spend his time and flowers on another girl." Liesel shook her head now, looking at Fridric's most recent bouquet. "I have told him a hundred times that I am not staying here."

Ros sighed. "I know. I just wish you would reconsider. We will miss you terribly when you're gone."

Liesel drew the older woman up in a hug. She still missed Amala every day, but Ely and Ros Becke had been the healing her soul had needed after the brutal and abrupt deaths of her parents. Though she was technically the hired help, the Beckes spared no expense when it came to taking care of her. It pained her to think about leaving them.

Her only comfort was that the journey back to Weit was quite expensive, so saving up for it was taking a long time. Going back through the forest would have been more economical by far, but Liesel knew better than to even consider that route. Instead, she would take the long way home that went around the woods completely. For such a journey, she would need to save for at least another year. But thanks to the Beckes, that was just fine.

In a desperate attempt to distract her mistress from the sad conversation they seemed to have every day after Fridric's flowers arrived, she held up her basket of apples.

Ros smiled as she pulled one out and felt it. "Perfect for my pie! Let us begin, shall we?"

It wasn't until that evening that Liesel remembered the Wolfsbane conversation. Supper had been served. The pie was baked and set out to cool. Ely was sitting in his favorite chair making notes about a new herb he'd purchased from a foreign peddler. Ros, looking neat and proper as ever in her blue day dress, was sewing, and Liesel was seated on the floor between them, using a mortar and pestle to crush dried herbs for Ely. She balked at asking about something as silly as a legend, but as much as she wanted to forget her past, the cries of the wolf she'd heard last night were too real for her to ignore.

"I have a question," she blurted out, not sure how else to begin such an assuredly awkward conversation. Ely looked over his spectacles and raised one eye. "Yes?"

"I was at the market today, and I heard... I heard two women discussing Wolfsbane." Liesel didn't miss the exchange of glances between Ros and Ely as she spoke. She tried to make her voice sound jovial. "I was told it's all just a legend, but they said it was time to put the Wolfsbane out when the wolves cried. If the people here believe it's just a legend, why do they still put it in front of their doors?" She forced a laugh. "I know simply a story, of course. I am only curious." Her trepidation grew, however, when Ros put her sewing down, and Ely removed his spectacles.

"Part of it is superstition," Ros began cautiously.

"But?"

"It's not entirely false, either."

Liesel shivered, and it wasn't from the cold.

"The Wolfsbane part is legend," Ros continued. "Wolves will enter any place they like, Wolfsbane or none. If a wolf wants something, the only way likely to stop him is through an arrow to the heart."

"How do you know that?" Liesel hoped her voice didn't sound as terrified as she felt, her heart beating faster than it had in a long time.

"From time to time, people move to a small town called Ward in the center of the forest," Ely said. "We've known several families who have made the move. But once they are in Ward, they never leave."

"But I have heard that visitors and peddlers like Gil travel through there often. Why are they allowed to leave while others can't?" Liesel knew the answer, but the Beckes didn't know that.

"There is a difference between stopping at an inn for the night and choosing a place like Ward to raise your family in." Ely shook his head, disgusted. "The fools ignore the warnings every time."

"None of them escape?" Liesel struggled to keep her voice even. "I mean, after moving there?"

"Not one has ever returned," he answered solemnly.

"I had a friend once who disappeared the last time they howled like this." Ros picked up her sewing again, but frowned at it now as she worked. "We were just young women then, a bit younger than you are now. Her mother had always loved the forest here, but her father wanted to leave Tag. He was a restless sort of man. When a gentleman came to Tag to see if any of the men were interested in working in the storage houses, they left with him.

"My friend and I managed to send letters back and forth for a while by paying the grain masters, but I never saw her again." Ros's brown eyes grew more and more troubled as she spoke. "She wrote repeatedly about how strange the village was. No one smiled at her, and only a few would even talk with her. Then her mother died without warning. Just slipped away in her sleep one night. Her father died a year later in an accident while chopping firewood."

Ros shook her head. "I remember the night of the last howling. It was much like last night. I had gotten my last letter from her a month before. She was planning on returning to Tag, she wrote. Her uncle lived here, and she wanted to join him."

"She never came?" Liesel whispered.

"The poor man nearly went mad with grief when his sister died. So when his niece never returned, he set off to Ward to find her. That was the last we ever saw of him." Liesel's mistress paused, pain etched into her handsome face. It was the closest to despair Liesel had ever seen her. "It would have been easier to lose her if I could have known that she had at least one soul to turn to there."

Liesel felt as though her blood had frozen through and through. It took all of her willpower not to tremble. Memories she had long ago buried were resurfacing faster than she could count them. She swallowed to steady her voice. "But why are the grain masters, peddlers, and travelers allowed in and out of Ward if no one else can leave?" she asked again. "And how long has this been going on?"

"I asked a grain master once," Ros said. "He only said, 'People in Ward need grain and cloth like everyone else.' But that's all he would say, no matter how I pleaded to know."

Liesel was about to ask another question, but Ely interrupted her, his lean face stoic. "Liesel, we've been careful not to ask too much about where you came from. It was easy to see that you'd had trouble, and we didn't want to hurt you. But I am going to ask you something now, and you had better tell us the truth. Did you come from Ward?"

Liesel stared at him. For four years, she had hardly been able to utter the name of that wretched village. But finally, someone knew. Still unable to answer his question with a yes or no, she whispered, "How did you know?"

"That night I found you pleading with Gil Gaspar in the tavern, Gil had just come from Ward. I heard him tell one of his friends over the ale before we left."

Liesel stared at Ely, unable to utter a word as he continued to unravel her secrets all by himself.

"And to this day, Gil refuses to even look at you."

Though she was still unable to speak it, Liesel felt relief well up within her as she stared at Ely. No one had ever guessed she'd come from Ward. Gil wouldn't talk about it, and she hadn't been able to bring herself to discuss it with anyone else. She had always wondered why none of the other townspeople had ever guessed she had come from Ward. Now that she knew its history, however, perhaps it was because no one ever had escaped Ward before. Maybe she was the first. Well, the second. There was that girl named Ilsa...

"Liesel, what exactly happened there?" Ely's face was severe, but after living with the healer and his wife for four years, Liesel knew he was only concerned.

She wet her lips and tried to tell them. Oh, she tried! But no matter how much she tried, no words would form in her mouth. She could only stare at them miserably.

"What about that scar?"

Liesel looked down to see that she was rubbing the back of her hand again. And again, it was tingling.

"I wish I could tell you," she whimpered.

It was a long moment as Ely and Ros studied her intensely. And as much as she wanted to tell them what they desired to know, her lips seemed to be sewn shut.

Ely stood up and stalked out of the room. A moment later, he returned with a small coin purse, one he kept hidden under a loose board in the staircase for times of need.

"How much do you have saved?" he asked.

That, she could answer. "Six hundred."

Without warning, the whole bag was shoved into her hands. Liesel gasped, but Ely shook his head. "That should be enough to pay the rest of your way."

Liesel began to protest, but Ros interrupted her. "You know we would love nothing more than to keep you. But Ely is right. You cannot stay here. I have no idea what happens in that awful place, but it reeks of evil." Her voice hitched at the end, and she suddenly remembered something she needed to do in the kitchen.

"You are leaving on the next caravan out," Ely said. "That should be in two days. Until then, you are not to leave the house at night. In fact, I want you to stay here as much as possible. You are only to leave if it is absolutely necessary."

Somehow, what had begun as a typical evening at home

became Liesel's way of escape. Part of her was thrilled. After seven long years in the woods, she had only two days more.

As she prepared for bed, she looked around her little room with a pang of sadness, however. It was simple, but she had felt at home from the moment she'd first stepped in. The walls were made of the same light wood as the sitting room, kitchen, and main bedroom downstairs. Her window faced the north, and through it, she could see the road that led out of the forest to the capital city. The trees that lined the road were tall, but they were spaced well enough to allow light in at all times of the day. Even now, as she looked up into the night, moonbeams fell through the trees and into her bedroom.

The first sunlight that had peeked through her window the morning after her wild ride with the peddler had been the first sign that Liesel would love Tag. The yellow bedcovers with its little purple embroidered flowers had calmed her many times when the tears had threatened to come. This room had been her place of solace. It would be hard to leave it. It would be even harder to leave the ones who had given it to her.

A piercing howl interrupted Liesel's thoughts and sent tremors through her body, reminding her of why she was leaving. Though the room was warm enough, Liesel went to the wardrobe and pulled out her cloak. Wrapping it around herself, she huddled in her bed, attempting to get as close to invisible as possible under the covers.

The howls brought back unwelcome memories of the time she'd last heard such cries, not counting the night before. They were longer and more forlorn this time. Tears slipped down the sides of Liesel's face as she scrunched her eyes shut. She had escaped the nightmare where wolves and men hunted her. She had spent four happy years in a comfortable house with adoring guardians.

But what had become of Kurt? It was the same question she asked herself every night.

Blocking out thoughts of him during the day was easier when there was always something to do, but the nights were hard. While she lay in bed there was nothing to occupy her mind but memories. How many times would she be tortured by the smile on his face as he teased her, or even worse, the sadness that would often creep into his eyes? She couldn't close her eyes without seeing him. She couldn't fall asleep without remembering how it had felt when he'd pressed his lips softly to her cheek.

Aside from Fridric's sweet but overzealous obsession with horses, and Benat's awkward obsession with himself, there was a reason Liesel had never attached herself to any of the more eligible bachelors of Tag. And it wasn't for a lack of offers. It wasn't even because she was planning to leave.

The reason Liesel stayed alone seemed so far-fetched that even she was inclined to admit its unlikelihood. And yet, deep down, Liesel hoped and prayed like a little girl that Kurt would remember his promise to explore the world with her. Because deep down, Liesel truly missed the boy.

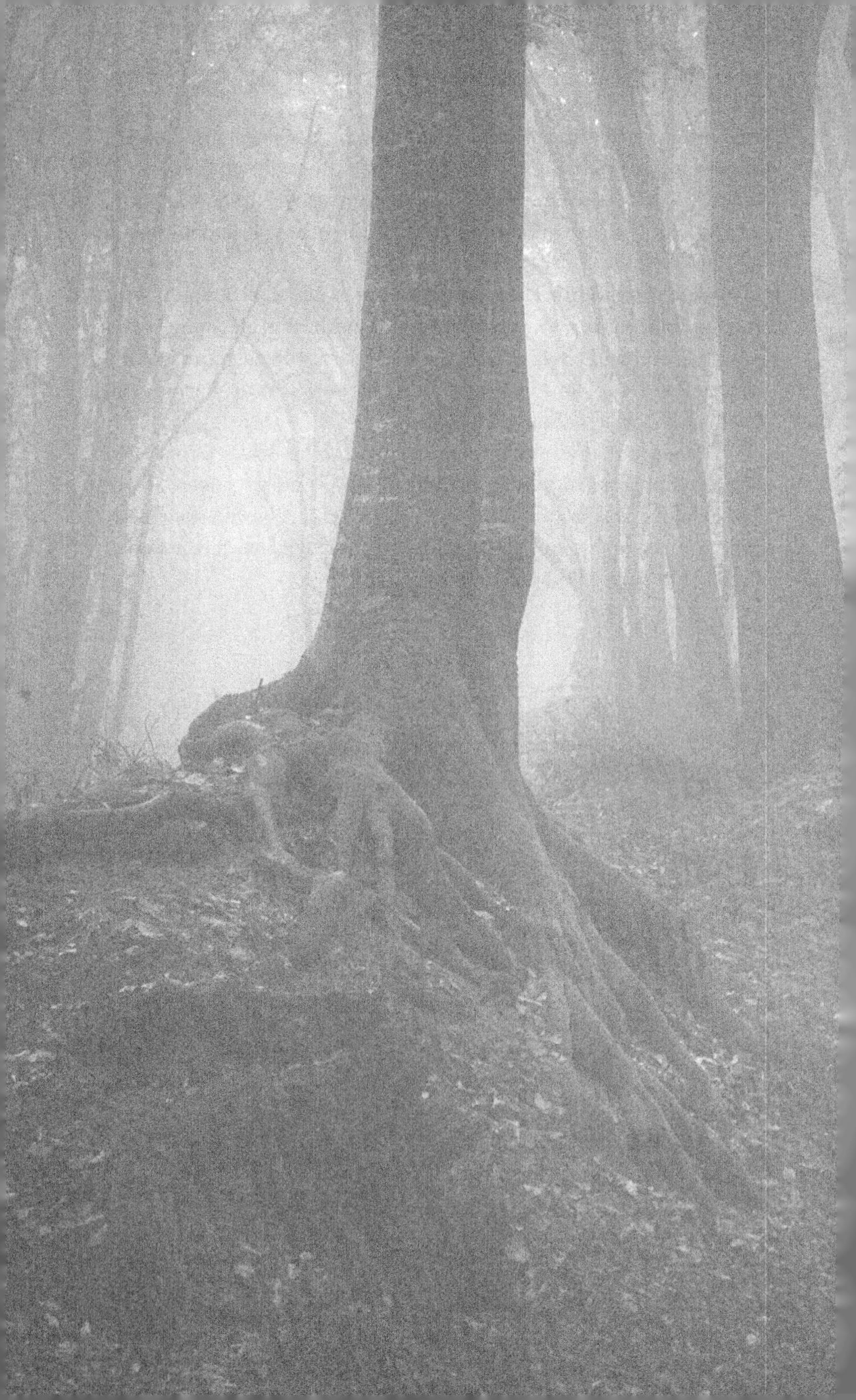

CHAPTER 14

PURE BLOOD

"And where are you going?" Ros eyed Liesel's cloak and basket suspiciously as she came down the stairs.

"I ordered a pair of shoes from the cobbler two days ago. I need to tell him not to make them after all."

For a moment, she feared Ros would order her back upstairs. After the howling that had taken place for the second night in a row, allowing no one to sleep, Ely had specifically ordered Liesel to stay in the house until her caravan departed the next day. Liesel had begged, however, for leave to say goodbye to some of her friends. She would stay in town, she had promised.

"Let her go," Ros had gently urged him. "She's not a child." It seemed now, though, that Ely's concerns had gotten to his wife in the time that had passed since that morning, because she now gave Liesel an uncharacteristically severe look. "You are not to set foot in the forest," she warned. "And here," Ros ran back to the kitchen and returned with the apple pie she had baked the day before, "bring this to Mrs. Dunst. She's on the way. But promise me that you won't go any closer to the woods than her house!"

Smiling, Liesel gave Ros a quick kiss then turned and fled before she could change her mind.

The cobbler's shop was all the way across town, but Liesel didn't mind the walk. It was late summer, and the air smelled of honeysuckle. Children shrieked with joy as they raced after one another, some of them stopping to wave at Liesel as she walked by. As Liesel waved back, she reflected on how the life where people had feared and avoided her seemed nothing more than a bad dream here.

Many women were taking advantage of the lovely day to clean the outsides of their homes. Tall, with pointed, sloping roofs, many homes lined the square stood proudly. Tag citizens liked to boast of their architecture to outsiders. Built to withstand the vast amounts of snow that fell every winter, the buildings were much sturdier than anything in Ward had been. But then, Ward, because of its thick forest ceiling, had never gotten nearly as much snow.

Bells jingled on the door as Liesel entered the cobbler's shop, and a short, barrel-chested man greeted her. "What did I tell you?" He shook his finger good-naturedly at the couple he was talking to. "I would know that red cloak anywhere! Your timing is perfect, Liesel! When you were in the other day I forgot to ask you which leather you wanted me to use."

Liesel smiled apologetically. "Actually, I came to tell you that I won't be needing the shoes after all. I am leaving tomorrow to return to my grandparents."

The cobbler's mouth dropped open. "Is that so? Well, it won't be the same around here without you, that's for certain." He gave her a long look over the rims of his spectacles. "This wouldn't have anything to do with the wolves now, would it? Put some Wolfsbane out on your porch, and when all is done, we won't hear any of this nonsense again for years. I promise you that."

Liesel did her best to sound unruffled by his insight. "In truth, I've wanted to return for years. The... opportunity simply arose sooner than I was expecting."

"Well then, we're happy for you, Liesel." The wife smiled sweetly. As the mother of four boisterous boys, she had told Liesel before how much she understood the importance of grandparents, particularly on days when the boys were livelier than usual.

"Say, who is the pie for?" The cobbler peeked into her basket.

Liesel slapped his hand away and laughed. "Ros wants me to drop it off at Mrs. Dunst's on the way home."

To her surprise, the cobbler frowned. "I stopped at her place just this morning, but she wasn't there. See if she's in now, will you? Don't just leave it on her doorstep."

Liesel nodded. Mrs. Dunst was rarely more than ten or twenty paces from her front door. It was indeed odd that the cobbler hadn't been able to find her. So after saying her goodbyes, Liesel headed to the old woman's home.

It was slow work getting to the widow's little house. News spread fast in Tag, and soon people Liesel didn't even know were wishing her farewell. By the time she arrived at Mrs. Dunst's cottage, it was almost time for supper, and Liesel knew Ros would worry if she wasn't home soon. She would have to make the visit quick. As she drew closer, however, she realized the front door was open. Cautiously, Liesel stepped inside.

"Mrs. Dunst?" she called out. "It's Liesel. I brought you a pie." There was no reply, though, and it made Liesel even more uneasy.

Maria Dunst was the oldest woman in Tag. Over ninety years of age, she could be found every day sitting in her little garden, offering lunch and advice to anyone who would take them. Liesel had understood immediately why the cobbler was suspicious when Mrs. Dunst hadn't come to the door that morning. In fact, if she had known about it earlier, she would have checked on the old woman first instead of on the way home.

Liesel went through every room of the house, but the woman was nowhere to be found. Tension brewed in her stomach as she went out and checked around the back. She called out again and again, but there was no reply.

She had nearly given up and gone to fetch Ely when she heard an odd scratching sound. The sound came from behind the house, but it wasn't until Liesel had followed it for a few minutes that she realized she had left the town behind her and was at the edge of the woods.

As if she needed another reason to worry, a single howl broke the silence of the evening. Liesel froze, suddenly wishing more than anything that she was back in the Beckes' home like she was supposed to be. Just then, however, a low moaning came from the bushes and a movement caught her eye, nearly invisible in the light of dusk.

"Mrs. Dunst?" Liesel called out once more.

Sure enough, the little old woman was hobbling along some invisible path with her cane, whimpering in low, woeful tones. Liesel hurried to her side. How long had she been out like this?

"They've taken her!" the woman sobbed. "They've taken Greta!"

"Who's Greta?" Liesel took the old woman gently by the shoulders and tried to turn her back toward Tag. "And who are *they*?"

But the old woman acted as though Liesel wasn't even there as she continued to try and wander deeper into the trees. "My daughter has been stolen by the wolves!" she continued to cry.

Fear tried to strangle Liesel's heart, but she took a deep breath, and forced herself to lead her charge back toward the town. It was not easy, for the old woman was convinced her daughter was nearby. Finally, after many long minutes of struggling, Mrs. Dunst quit fighting Liesel and allowed herself to be led back toward her house.

Another wolf howled, and Liesel prayed for speed for the old woman. She walked ever so slowly, leaning on her cane as she inched along the path. It didn't help that she continued to moan and sob until they were finally back on the cobblestone streets of the town. Only then, in the yellow flame of the street lamps, did Mrs. Dunst seem to notice or recognize the young woman. She turned to Liesel and gasped.

"Liesel! What are you doing here? You must go home! Don't you hear the wolves?"

Liesel took a big breath of relief, happy the old woman was finally coming to her senses. Curiosity got the better of her, however, and as they continued to walk toward Mrs. Dunst's cottage, she had to ask.

"Mrs. Dunst, did the wolves truly take your daughter?" She hoped deep down that the cries had simply been the mumblings of an old woman.

The haunted look in Maria Dunst's eyes told Liesel otherwise, though, even before she answered. And when she did speak, her thoughts suddenly seemed as clear as water. She motioned for Liesel to follow her into her little house when they arrived.

"My husband and I had just moved the family to Tag. We knew nothing of the rumors about Ward. We thought the other forest villages would be like this one." She gestured at the window. "My eldest girl wanted to be a dressmaker, but we had no money with which to apprentice her here." That made sense. Liesel had wanted to apprentice with the new healer after Doffy had died in Ward, but it was too expensive. She would slow him down and he would lose money, he had told her.

"A man came to Tag and said that the dressmaker in Ward was looking for an apprentice, that he would charge much less than the one here. Greta was fourteen at the time. She wanted to go." A strange gasp escaped the old woman before she composed herself again. Liesel's own heart hurt, as she knew what turn this story would be taking.

The old woman stiffly sank into her chair before continuing. Liesel had been in the house enough times to know where the tea supplies were kept, so she began to gather them up as Mrs. Dunst sat. The old woman had an unhealthy pallor to her cheeks. As Liesel bustled around, Mrs. Dunst closed her eyes and resumed her story.

"She was there for a year before the letters stopped coming. My husband went to see her a few times, but each time they spoke, he knew something was amiss. But she wouldn't tell him what! And then, she just disappeared. And when my husband searched for her, it was as if she had never been there. No one would even speak of her!"

"But how do you know the wolves took her?" Liesel asked.

The old woman leaned in, as though she were sharing a secret. "She always sent letters at the end of the month. The howling started three days before she would have sent her letter, after which we never received another."

Liesel studied the old woman. She felt a bit skeptical. There was no proof the girl had been taken by the wolves. But then, everything she had suffered in Ward made anything seem possible.

Once the old woman had finished her story, Liesel finally convinced Mrs. Dunst to drink some tea. After a few sips, the old woman apologized. "Sometimes I forget where I am, or even how old I am." She sighed. "But the wolves were so loud last night. I just knew if I looked hard enough, I could find..." Her eyes welled up with tears visible even in the weak light of the hearth, and Liesel decided she had pushed the widow hard enough. By the sound of it, they all had another long night ahead of them.

It was very late by the time Liesel started home. Ely might have even gone looking for her by now. He never would have known where to look, though, Liesel thought guiltily. She had been strictly instructed to stay out of the forest, and that was exactly where she had gone. She was twenty, after all, and far beyond the age of such foolishness.

It was a few minutes into her walk that Liesel realized she was going the wrong way. For some reason, she had begun to head east. Liesel shook her head to try and clear her tired mind. Tomorrow she would sleep on the caravan. The Maker knew she needed it. She had hardly slept in two days with all of the howling. Still, it was odd that she should have taken the wrong turn. She knew Tag too well for such errors. She was not lost, though, and even with the misstep it wouldn't take long to reach the Beckes' home.

To her surprise, however, when she turned the corner, she once again realized she was still going in the wrong direction. Determined not to get lost in her thoughts once more, she pictured the next street she must turn down to get back to the Beckes' house. But to her dismay, each street took her farther from her destination, and closer to the forest road.

No matter how she tried, her feet acted with a mind of their own. Tears threatened to spill down as she tried again and again in frustration to alter her course. What was wrong with her? She must stop, she decided, and wait until someone found her. She would not be bullied by whatever force was manipulating her.

But when she tried to halt, even that was denied her. It was not long before Liesel was leaving Tag and walking directly toward Ward. And to her dismay, the scar on her right hand began to ache. Panic built in her chest, and she wanted to scream. When she tried, however, nothing came. She couldn't even speak, she found, only sob softly as her feet carried her away from freedom and back to the torment she thought she had escaped.

After more than an hour of walking, Liesel was spent. Wearily, she let the darkness draw her onward, too tired to fight anymore. It was as if she were watching her body from afar. She knew what she was doing, but there was nothing she could do about it.

At some unseen marker, she abruptly left the road and headed into the woods. Kurt had taught her to walk in the deep underbrush quietly, but she was still out of control, and tripped twice. Soon, as the limbs overhead began to thicken, choking out the moonlight above, she made out two shapes standing just ahead of her. As she neared them, she could see that the taller shape was a man astride a horse. The other was a horse with an empty saddle. Stopping before them, she was startled to recognize her old horse, the gentle mare that pulled her family's cart all the way from Weit.

Without a word, the man climbed down from his horse and bent to help Liesel mount hers. At first, she wanted to icily reply that she could climb on by herself. But when she tried to mount, even with his help, she found that the walk had tired her more than she'd thought.

Still silent, the man stiffly hoisted himself back up on his ride, then turned and began heading east again ever deeper into the woods. Of course, Liesel's horse followed, and still bound to obey, Liesel did, too. Soon, however, she realized she was no longer mute. After trying repeatedly, she found that while she couldn't scream, she could talk.

"Why are you doing this?" she asked through indignant tears. "What evil are you using to bind me?"

The man slowly turned his head and looked at her curiously. In the light of the dimming moonlight, he appeared older than she had first thought, at least as old as her grandfather. His hair was silver, and though he sat tall in his saddle, there was much sorrow carved into the lines of his face. He didn't answer her incessant questions, though.

Liesel searched her mind desperately for something, anything that might make him at least slow his horse's steady pace toward Ward. "If you don't let me go, my friend Kurt will find us! He lives deep in these woods! Then you will regret treating me like this!" The threat was nonsense, of course. Liesel had no idea where Kurt was, nor did she know what he could do to help her against such an evil, but it was all she could think to say. Besides, there was a small but very irrational part of her that wished it was true.

A low growl interrupted her wishful thinking, and Liesel almost shrieked when she made out the nearly invisible silhouette of a wolf not three feet to her right. Another throaty grumble notified her to the presence of a second wolf a few yards behind them. The farther they went, the more wolves accompanied them. In her terror, Liesel recalled with stark vividness the day Kurt had saved her from his uncle and his wolves, and a minuscule bit of hope rose within her. Could Kurt possibly be nearer than she thought? Could he save her again?

After hours and hours of riding, Liesel was so tired she nearly dozed and slipped from her horse three times. The aching of her scar was the only thing that kept her awake. It tingled so much that it hurt. But she eventually did begin to make out a small beam of light ahead of them through the trees.

At first, Liesel was sure her eyes were playing tricks on her, but as they drew closer, she could truly see the glow of a fire. The outlines of four men came into view, two older and two younger. And one of them Liesel would have known anywhere. He stood hunched over the fire, his hands behind his back and his head bent as though deep in thought.

"Kurt!"

Stiffness and exhaustion forgotten, Liesel's body finally obeyed her as she threw herself from the horse and stumbled into his arms. All of her self-control came crashing down as she sobbed into his chest, shaking so hard it felt as though she might burst. "Help me!" she clutched at his shirt. "They used some sort of magic to bring me here! I don't know what! Just help me, please!" Fear suddenly made her dizzy, and she had to hold on even harder so she wouldn't fall.

As she cried, she felt his arms slowly close around her. His embrace was bliss. When she finally stepped back to look up, however, his face was an odd mix of sadness and severity.

"I know." His voice was even deeper than she remembered it, no longer on the cusp between boy and man.

She fell back a step. "You know?"

"I'm the one that sent them."

Liesel gasped. The air was suddenly too thick to breathe. She searched his face for any hint, any sign he might be sending her that all would be well, that he was just putting on an act for those who surrounded them. But his face remained stern, and his jaw was set tightly.

She finally broke her gaze with him to look at the other men watching them. She recognized Kurt's younger brother, Keegan, and with a shiver, his Uncle Lothur. The fourth man could only have been his father. And they all stood silently behind Kurt, waiting for her response. Liesel tasted bile in her mouth as she pulled out of his arms and started to back up.

Kurt sighed. "Liesel, how far do you think you'll get running from the wolves?"

For a long moment, she peered back behind her into the blackness of the forest. As she did, her hand began to burn once again, and all hope of a quick escape died. Finally, she faced him miserably, looking into the golden-brown eyes of her once savior.

"Come here, child." The man she guessed to be his father finally spoke, his order ringing with authority.

She stared at him, fear quickly giving way to anger. Her hand burned even more, a white hot pain, ordering her to go to him, but she didn't budge. She could see displeasure in the man's face, and he drew himself up to his full height, which was quite impressive.

A small wave of fear rippled through her body. What would he do to her if she didn't obey? As they continued to face off, however, she decided she didn't care. She was beyond caring. This awful family had caused her too much pain. So instead, she glared at him.

"Father," Kurt said softly, "give me a moment alone with her."

"She needs to be–"

"That won't work with her," Kurt said, giving him an earnest look. "Please. She's had a long night. Ordering her about is the last thing she will listen to."

His father gave him a skeptical look. After a long moment, however, he finally nodded and began to walk away, gesturing for the other two to follow him.

Kurt's younger brother, now lanky and even taller than Kurt, with stubble growing unevenly all over his young face, didn't leave as quickly as his elders. "Be careful," he whispered to Kurt as he walked by.

Kurt said nothing, though, waiting until he and Liesel were all alone to speak. Then he took a big breath and looked at her with an expression Liesel finally recognized. He'd worn it often when they had sat staring at her mountain. "I know you're angry with me," he started.

"Angry cannot even begin to describe what I am feeling," Liesel squeaked out through gritted teeth. Betrayal. Lies. Secrets. Everything Liesel had ever trusted in Kurt seemed to go up in smoke. And it hurt so much. "All those years," she hissed, "I thought you were trying to protect me! But here I am, and I don't even know why I'm here, or what evil you used to bring me!"

As she spoke, she tried desperately to recall the stories the women in Tag had told her, but she couldn't focus. Suddenly wearier than she remembered ever being in her life, she sat on the ground and pulled her legs up to her chest, hiding her face in her arms.

"The bite."

She did her best to pretend to ignore him, but Kurt continued to talk. "My father's youngest brother bit you when you first arrived."

Liesel risked raising her head enough to send him a resentful glare. He had known all this time. Then his words sank in.

"Your *uncle* bit me?" She covered her mouth.

"We're not complete animals." Kurt turned toward the fire, disgust dripping from his words.

It was a moment before Liesel could speak again, but when she did, her voice was ice cold. "Then what are you?" Any being that could in good conscience kill her father and then abduct her was, to Liesel, the very definition of an animal.

Kurt frowned. His words were barely whispers. "Two hundred

years ago, there was a wizard that lived in these woods. Often hunted by the townspeople for his practices, he wanted a sure way to protect himself. So he crafted a spell that would allow him the mind of a man and the strength and body of an animal. He even invited others to join him, petty thieves, misfits, those who wanted to stay hidden from the king. Not many joined him, but twelve were better than one. They would be the superior creatures, he promised. Wolves with the minds of humans surely couldn't be challenged.

"When he had gathered the people, he cast the spell. It was a failure, though." Kurt kicked a pebble. "So their descendants have been here for the last two centuries, stuck in two worlds. Everyone over sixteen years is constantly hovering on the cusp between man and wolf."

Liesel could only cradle her tingling hand and listen as he spoke, too horrified to interrupt.

"The only thing that has kept us from losing our humanity completely is the union of a pure-blooded human to the pack leader. Ever since, each generation has had to send the townspeople of Ward out to find us new Pure Bloods."

Liesel felt as though she might pass out.

"I know you always wondered why Ward was so desperate to bring your family here, and why it seemed impossible to leave." He took a deep breath before continuing. "When the steward found your grandparents' vineyard, he was looking for girls around your age. He'd met a number of them along the way, but you were perfect. Living outside of a large town meant your disappearance would go largely unnoticed. Of course, your grandparents might tell others, but you were far from the center of activity. Your absence would soon be forgotten."

Liesel wanted to argue, to scream and shout that he was wrong. But in truth, everything had taken place just as he'd said. No one had come for her. No search parties had been sent. Not even her grandfather had tried to come after her.

"When Izaak found out about your mother's illness, it was too perfect," he continued. "Your father was dying to leave. All Izaak had to do was convince your father that you would all be better off here. Once you arrived, you were marked, and all we had to do was keep you within the forest until it was time." Kurt swallowed hard before finishing. "And now that my mother has died, it is your turn to be our Pure Blood."

It was a moment before Liesel could speak. So the cowardice of a man who had lived two hundred years before was to blame. All of the pieces were falling into place. And yet, her newfound knowledge didn't make her any less miserable. But there was one question she had to ask, tears running down her face.

"Why did my mother have to die?"

"That was the overzealous doing of Odo." Kurt sighed. "He wanted to make sure you didn't get away. If your mother awakened, he was afraid she would convince your father to return to your grandparents."

"And why does the town care so much?"

"That's the agreement. As long as they bring us an acceptable Pure Blood, we leave their daughters alone."

That was why the baker had feared so for Karla and Mitsi. And now that Liesel knew why, she couldn't blame him. But what was it exactly that she had saved Karla and Mitsi from?

"And what does a Pure Blood do?"

"Marry the pack leader and continue the line," a deep voice boomed from behind them. Kurt's father joined them once again, but without Lothur or Keegan.

Liesel's heart nearly failed. Did he mean himself or his son?

Kurt must have read her stricken expression because he softly said, "My father is stepping down. I will be pack leader after we wed." His eyes were cautious as he studied her reaction.

Liesel had no idea as to what he saw, though, because not even she knew what she felt. There was too much to take in. Swallowing hard, she tried to clear the sudden lump in her throat. "And where will I live?" Her words were barely audible even to her own ears.

Kurt's face twisted. "Oh, Liesel." He groaned and ran his hand through his hair. "Are you really going to make me answer that?"

"You will be here, where you're needed, protecting the pack," Kurt's father answered for him, his eyes flat. He had a square face, sharper and deeper than Kurt's. There was a resemblance, but only just. Kurt looked much more like his mother. But then, Kurt had never looked that cruel either.

"No!" Liesel stood clumsily and grabbed Kurt's sleeve, which brought on another round of dizziness. "I cannot live like this forever! I can't live without the sun!" She searched his face for a sliver of pity, some sign of hope. But when he looked back at her, Kurt wore a mask of resolve, suddenly looking far older than twenty-one.

"Stop your blubbering." Kurt's father shook his head. "The magic called you back, and that is all there is to it. Best get on and accept it." As he began to stalk off, Liesel felt Kurt grasp both of her arms. He said something, but Liesel couldn't hear him. The woods began to tilt, and the ground rose up toward her with a surprising speed.

"That was cruel." Kurt's tone was quiet but disapproving.

"She needed to hear it." Heavy steps crunched in the dirt, but then paused again. Kurt's father's voice was suddenly old but maintained its ring of authority. "I know you think you know her, but this one will cause you only heartache if you don't kill all hope of escape now." He sighed heavily. "She has captured your heart, and that's how it should be. But you must break her before you can heal her. They're all the same."

A hand gently stroked Liesel's hair. It suddenly occurred to her that she wasn't upright. She didn't even have her eyes open. Instead, she was being cradled like a child.

"Perhaps I don't want my wife to die of a broken heart before she's gray." Kurt's voice was sharper than Liesel had ever heard it, quiet but cutting and smooth like a knife.

"Hold your tongue, Boy, and have some respect for the dead!"

"How many died before Mother? Two? Three? It took a fourth wife to survive long enough for children. Believe me, I have more respect for Mother than you ever did."

"Do you really think your girl is the first to get upset?" his father snarled. "Mark my words! When she sees what kind of life you are chaining her to, it doesn't matter how much you think she loves you. She will try to run, and you will have to bring her back. Sometimes again and again before she knows her place. And even when she stops, she will hate you for what you've done to her. And it will get worse when you give her children, and she must watch them change."

Liesel was still too disoriented to even try standing, but his words cut off all thoughts of trying to leave Kurt's arms anytime soon. Her head swam as she laid there like a limp doll.

The father and son were both silent for an immeasurable amount of time before the father spoke again. All the anger was gone from his voice this time, however, and he just sounded tired.

"The sooner she can find any shred of contentment, the sooner she will be able to accept it. They all do eventually." With that, Liesel heard him walk away.

Kurt sat holding Liesel for a long time. The way he cradled her made Liesel want to weep. How many times in her daydreams had she imagined him holding her this close? Even after she'd left Ward she had dreamed of Kurt. Why did her dreams have to come true like this?

Exhausted beyond anything she had ever known, Liesel was nearly unconscious when Kurt pressed his lips to her hair and whispered, "I've missed you."

When Liesel woke up, she had a ravaging headache. Slowly, she pushed herself into a sitting position before daring to open her eyes, afraid the world might spin again if she tried it too fast.

When she finally succeeded in prying her eyes open, she found herself in a spacious room made of sturdy logs, with a large bed, washstand, bedside table, and wide window. It was still black outside the window, which had dried pink flowers hanging beside it, but an impressive stone fireplace and a number of scattered candles lit the room, making it fairly easy to see. A tall, thin bookshelf stood across from the bed where she lay, and a little white desk sat in the corner near the door. The curtains were made of pink lace but were so old they looked ready to fall apart. The bed covering matched the window, but it seemed a little less dusty at least. And the whole room smelled of cedar. If she hadn't been forced here, the room wouldn't have seemed so bad.

But, Liesel sighed, this seemed to be the room where the dreams of women had died for two hundred years. Each piece of cloth and furniture had a slightly different look, as if each one had been chosen by a different woman. There was a sadness to the air. It was palpable.

Liesel briefly looked through the crevice under the door. Boots stood outside her room. She had expected no less. When she looked back down at where she had been lying, however, her throat caught. Not only was there a plate of potatoes, onions, and carrots waiting for her, still steaming, but also something far more precious.

Reaching out, she gingerly touched the familiar spine. When she opened it, the pages crinkled just as she remembered. The leather cover was a little worse for wear. But it was hers.

If nothing else, she would have her grandmother's stories after all.

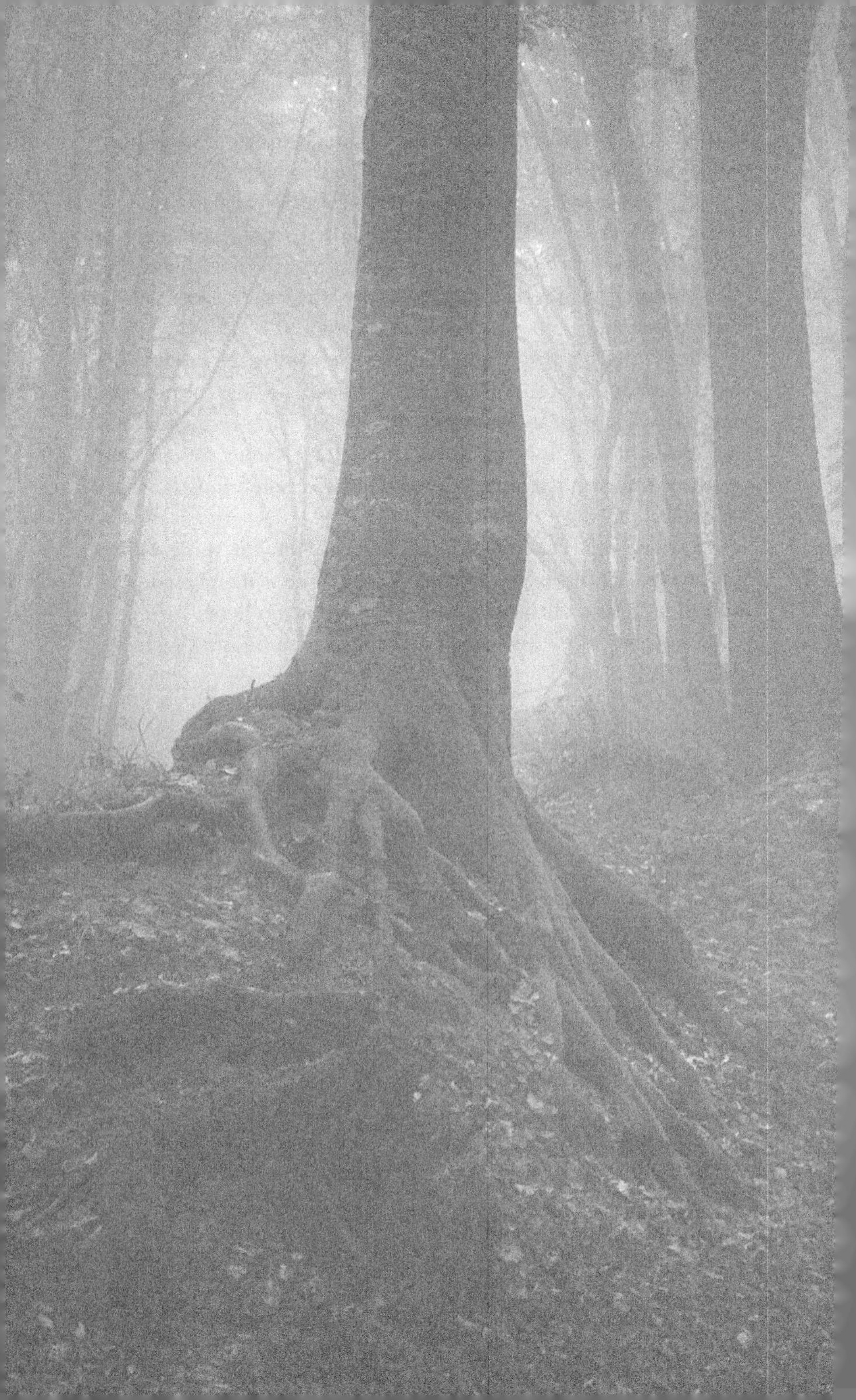

CHAPTER 15
A Boy's Hope

Voices awakened Liesel. Strangely, they were coming from the wrong side of the room, and it took her a moment to realize she was no longer in her little attic in Tag. She made out two men's voices from the other side of the door.

"Would you at least consider what he is saying? She believes in magic! She could end it once and for all if she was willing! With her help we could find a way!" The young man who spoke sounded like Keegan.

"I consider everything our uncle says, but with more caution and less zeal," Kurt responded dryly. "Now don't let Father hear you talking like that, or you and Uncle will get an earful."

As she blinked in the gray of morning, the events of the night before trickled back. Wolves, Kurt, magic, everything returned to her in the smallest of detail. She could even still taste the earthy carrots. The empty plate now lay on the short bedside table beside her.

When she had discovered the food the night before, Liesel had considered leaving it untouched, simply so they would know she wasn't at all in cooperation. But it had been a long while since she had eaten anything, so Liesel had decided to prove her displeasure in some other way. She would need her strength if the chance to escape arose.

As she lay there remembering, a rap on her door sent her into an annoyed tizzy as she searched for her robe, only to remember that she was still in her dress from the day before.

"Liesel, it's Kurt."

"Just a moment," she huffed. As angry as she was, Liesel had no desire to look as discomfited as she felt. If she was going to be held against her will, she was determined to appear at least somewhat dignified. She ran over to the wash basin and mirror and did her best to tame her rebellious golden locks, and chase the dark circles from beneath her eyes.

When she was as close to satisfied as her face and hair would allow, she finally opened the door to see Kurt standing there with a plate of eggs and biscuits and a cup of tea. Liesel hated to give her captors the upper hand, but the food smelled delectable, and much to her horror, it made her stomach growl loudly.

Kurt tried to hide a smile as he held them out to her. "As it's nearly noon, I thought you might be hungry."

With a sigh, Liesel took the food and went back to sit on her bed. Kurt pulled the chair out from under the desk and sat in the doorway. Liesel tried very hard to focus on her food and not at the striking young man intently watching her, but even without looking at him, Liesel was very aware of the fact that Kurt now looked every part a man.

What she really wanted to do was study every inch of his face to see if any trace of the boy she had loved still lingered. Not only would that be highly inappropriate, however, it would also encourage him to think she might actually submit to the pack's plans for her. And as confused as she felt about Kurt, no one emotion would allow her to simply accept this fate.

"When you're finished, I have something I need you to see," Kurt finally said after an awkward silence.

Liesel gave him a cold look, then nodded before returning to her food. It suddenly tasted sour, though. If it had been any other circumstance, she would have given him every snide remark she could think of. He'd lied to her, knowing all along what the townspeople and wolves had wanted. And even after he had sent her away, he'd brought her back to this place of loneliness and horror.

The only thing that kept her from pouring every drop of vehemence upon him was knowing that his mother had just died.

After dawdling for as long as she could, Liesel finally sighed and put her tea down and stood. Whatever he wanted to show her must be important. He had that sound to his voice, the same sound she'd heard the day he had brought her to see the waterfall for the first time. Grudgingly, she followed him out of the house.

Once they were outside, Liesel could see that it was the same log house she'd stumbled upon years before, a long log cabin situated at the top of a gently sloping hill. This time, she was in front of the house, though, and she was surprised to see that it stood watch over an entire town.

Sheltered by trees of monumental proportions, little cottages were huddled in clumps as far as the eye could see. They were much like the homes in Ward, made of logs with thatched roofs, and people came in and out of the houses as they might in Tag, or even Ward. But something was off.

"I know you're hoping to run." Kurt's voice was as collected and calm as though he were discussing the weather. She met his eyes with defiance, and he gave her a small, knowing smile.

"Don't they all?" she muttered.

"Despite the obvious futility and danger involved in trying to escape a town of nearly two hundred and thirty wolves, yes, some do." He frowned as he watched the bustle of the people below them. "But many stay."

"*Why?*" Liesel nearly regretted the rudeness of her question, not missing the fleeting pain in Kurt's face. She hadn't meant to add more pain to his loss by insulting him. But the idea of choosing to stay in such a wretched place after being dragged away from everything one knew and loved seemed ludicrous. That, and she was still terribly angry with him.

"I'll show you." Kurt's voice was a little more subdued as he led her down the first street.

It was somewhat unnerving when the townspeople returned her gaze. There were no smiles, and the only laughter came from the children. No one even spoke so much as a word, except to rebuke the children here and there. They just worked as silent as stones, pausing only to watch Kurt and Liesel walk.

"Wait here." Kurt motioned for Liesel to stay put as he turned into a small yard. She couldn't see why at first, and considered making a run for it as he strode up to the front door. Her own curiosity got the better of her, though.

"Steffen," he called, looking up above the door.

Liesel watched, confused.

"I know you're up there," he continued. "If I have to go up there and get you myself, your grandfather won't be very pleased."

A moment later, a little head of blond hair peeked out from behind the chimney. Wide-eyed, the little boy stared down at Kurt.

Kurt called out again, his voice stern but kind. "I told you, it's not safe to play on the roof. Now, can you get down, or do you need help?"

The boy didn't respond, but a moment later, he disappeared and then reappeared on the ground before them, still staring up with wide eyes. Kurt ruffled his hair and told him to go play with his sister before rejoining Liesel.

"His parents died last winter," Kurt explained as they walked. "He and his sister live with his grandfather now." As Kurt spoke, he nodded greetings to the people they passed.

The deeper they went into the heart of the town, the more Liesel felt pity for these strangers despite her resolve to stay unattached. She knew that the more she saw them as pitiable victims, the more defensible Kurt's actions would be. Keeping her eyes averted was hard, though.

For a village of two hundred years, the people were sadly lacking. To begin with, Liesel saw no shops. When pressed, Kurt said that some people sold their services from their homes, like the tanner, the tailor, and the butcher. Others simply did odd jobs, scrimping up a living in whatever way they could.

"We've tried to build shops," Kurt said, frustration creasing his brow. "Tradesmen have been brought in from Ward repeatedly to teach. We've assigned jobs and organized community building projects, such as bridges and a storehouse. And they've listened, doing what they were told, but..." his words trailed off as he came to a stop at the saddest town square Liesel had ever seen.

"They don't want to?" Liesel asked in spite of herself.

"You must *want* to thrive in order to do so."

"They've given up," Liesel whispered, more to herself than Kurt. Most of the villagers' clothes were torn and dirty. Hair, if cut at all, was chopped off roughly as though with a dull blade, even worse than Kurt's had ever been. In the gray light of the forest, everyone appeared tired and listless, although it was still barely noon. No work songs were shouted out, as Liesel had grown used to hearing in Tag. Although she had been determined to stay as disinterested as possible in order to fight the pack's plans for her, Liesel could finally stand it no longer.

"What happens without a Pure Blood?" She remembered something about failing magic in Mrs. Thull's story, but how much could she have really known? Rumors were often just rumors.

"Without a Pure Blood, everyone here above the age of sixteen would lose every drop of humanity left, and every child would be left alone and without a guardian."

Liesel faltered a moment, and finally looked Kurt straight in the eye. "Even you?"

"Especially me," he answered seriously. "Every pack needs a leader. My wolf blood runs even thicker than anyone else's."

"Why?"

"The wizard was my ancestor." The look in his golden-brown eyes was so fierce that Liesel chose to stay silent after that, simply following Kurt's lead as he walked them through the remainder of the town. There were a few people that greeted them, but most simply stared with woeful eyes.

He eventually moved them to the outskirts of the town, then back out into the forest, leaving the people and houses. It wasn't long before they were simply walking as they had when they were younger. Liesel was dying to ask him all the questions that were swirling around in her head, but she remained silent.

"Liesel, stay still!" Kurt's voice was strained and low.

Liesel suddenly realized she'd wandered off a bit, still following him, but meandering the way she used to. Startled by the urgency in his voice, she looked up to see Kurt staring at the ground near her feet. A nest of baby pigs lay just a few feet from where she stood.

"Walk slowly to me." Kurt kept a low, tense tone. "Stay quiet."

Liesel held her breath as she took a step backwards. When she did, however, a deafening crack echoed through the trees. Too late, she saw the stick she'd stepped on, and with its crack came ear-piercing squeals as one of the little pigs awakened. Liesel froze in horror as she heard something much larger begin to run toward them with startling speed.

For a split second, Liesel locked eyes with the sow. Its fur bristled out as it charged out of the bushes. Before she could react, a vicious snarl came from behind, and a blur of silver fur streaked past her, diving at the boar. The force of the wolf's blow knocked the sow over on her side. Without hesitation, the boar leapt back up and bit the wolf's neck.

Liesel watched in terror as the two creatures rolled around in the brush, snarls and squeals exchanged in quick succession. Just when it seemed as if neither would surrender, they stopped as quickly as they'd begun, the sow in front of its nest and the wolf crouched before her.

"Kurt," Liesel tried to call to him, her voice nearly inaudible. "She was just protecting her nest. Let's go." She hoped he would hear her, but she had no idea of how much of the man was left inside the creature. The memory of how he had protected the deer as a boy tugged at her heart, though, making her hopeful.

This time, however, there was no response. The wolf and the boar only continued to stare one another down. Nearly as tall as her waist, the wolf Kurt was lean and covered in muscle. The gray fur almost glinted like silver in the dim light of the woods. Tentatively, she stretched a hand out and gently laid it on his back.

Huge jaws snapped less than an inch from her hand. Though the golden-brown eyes were still human, they were flat and dangerous, their familiar warmth gone. It took Liesel a second to realize that Kurt had very nearly just bit her. Her voice dried up as the wolf continued to snarl, this time at her.

Without knowing what she was doing, Liesel began again to

slowly move backwards. He watched her the whole time. Not a hair moved. Once she was a stone's throw away, she turned and ran as hard as she could. She'd imagined a hundred ways to escape during the night before, but none of them had involved being pursued by Kurt himself. Surely he wouldn't be able to hurt *her*, she'd reasoned. But now as she ran aimlessly through the trees, driven on solely by fear, Liesel could see that she had been dead wrong.

After crashing and tumbling through the woods for several hundred yards, Liesel was spent. Despair took her as she heard her pursuer closing in from behind. Able to run no farther, Liesel dove behind a large tree. Sure enough, the footsteps continued to come closer. It wasn't until she heard only two feet round the corner and stop before her that Liesel realized the wolf was no longer in charge.

"Liesel, I... I'm so sorry!" His voice cracked when he spoke. When she didn't respond, he knelt beside her. She could see the hand he stretched out to touch her face, but without thinking, she flinched. The heartbreak was evident in his expression as he slowly withdrew his hand, but it couldn't erase what she had just witnessed. Nor was she ready for his touch.

"We can find somewhere more comfortable..." he stammered, but she shook her head and tucked it back in her arms. She heard him give a resigned sigh, and he moved to sit a few yards away.

With a little space to herself, Liesel took a deep breath and tried to gather her thoughts. His transformation shouldn't have been such a surprise. But after he'd told her all about it the night before, she hadn't been able to reconcile man with beast in her mind. Kurt had plainly told her he was a wolf, and yet, it hadn't felt real until the creature had stood right before her. Liesel had never forgotten the way the people of Ward had looked at him on the night of the dance, and now she understood why they had looked so stricken. And she hated it, because that was how she saw him now, too.

Opening her eyes, Liesel warily studied him. He was sitting on a boulder, his eyes distant and his body hunched over. His stare was like that of a blind man, unseeing and lifeless. For the first time, she noticed the dark circles beneath his eyes. He looked as though he'd slept even less than she had lately.

His face had become more angular in the years she'd been gone. Still the color of bark, his unruly hair was as badly cut as ever, but it looked as if he'd actually attempted to tame it that day, despite their surprise run. The clothes he wore were patched in several places. Still, they were slightly nicer than the ones he'd always run around in as a boy. And though he was still wiry, she could distinctly see the powerful frame beneath the ragged, ill-fitted attire. It made her heart beat in ways she wanted to ignore. To distract herself, she asked, "Is that why so many die?"

But Kurt didn't respond, just continued to stare dully out into the woods.

"Kurt!"

"What?" Kurt startled.

"You said your mother was your father's fourth wife." Liesel tried to keep her voice calm and deliberate. "Do they die because of... incidents like that?"

Shame and understanding filled Kurt's face before he lowered his gaze to the ground. "There have been some. Unfortunately, no Pure Blood is completely safe until she's married. Once she is wed to the pack leader, the magic protects her from any harm we might cause her in wolf form. That's why the wedding happens so quickly. We have one month before the magic dies, but for the sake of the woman, we try not to wait."

"Only some die of accidents?" Liesel raised her eyebrows, and Kurt shifted uncomfortably.

"My father's first three wives were only here for a short time before they died." He stood and gazed out at the gray wilderness before them. "My father calls it a weak constitution, but I always thought it was something else."

"So when you turn, you can't control it?"

"Fear is what changes us in the first place. It doesn't matter how much we wish to remain human." Kurt sounded annoyed. "If we truly want to rule over the animal mind, we must give up part of our humanity to marry the two. A few, such as my uncles, are willing to give up much of themselves. But most of us," Kurt shivered, "would rather lose control some of the time and keep what little humanity resides for the rest of it. When you turn, instinct takes over, and there is very little left of the man to inhibit that raw nature until you settle down again. To control it well, you must accept it. You must welcome the wolf as a part of you, something few are willing to do. There are times that are harder, like back there, that catch me off guard. The only thing that saves us from ourselves overall, however, is that we must listen to my father. As pack leader, he can direct us even when we're in animal form."

"How was it that you never turned when we were together?" Liesel thought particularly of the evening of the dance. He'd looked terrified.

"You sacrifice what you must." Kurt's words were nearly inaudible.

Liesel frowned. "Kurt, tell me the truth." She looked him straight in the eye. "What exactly did you sacrifice to stay human around me?"

But he shook his head. "For your sake, it was worth it."

Seeing that he wasn't about to go any further, Liesel decided to ask another kind of question. "So why bring me here now?" She didn't have to ask the other obvious questions. Why not just take her when she had arrived in Ward? Why toy with her? Why let her think she had a fighting chance and send her to Tag?

"I told you that my mother died."

"I heard that... and I'm sorry." As livid as she was, Liesel meant it. The seven years since her own mother's death had done little to heal the gaping hole in her heart.

Nodding a bit, he simply said, "I saw what being chained to this place did to my mother. While I couldn't stop the magic, I wanted to spare you at least a few more years if I could."

Liesel considered this. As much as she hated to admit it, it made sense. Kurt was kind but dutiful. After spending as much time with him as she had, she knew he was telling the truth. And yet, it still hurt to know he had chosen to keep her in the forest when she'd had the chance to run. Twice.

"So what happens if the Pure Blood escapes?" Liesel was thinking about the girl named Ilsa, but Kurt gave her a hard look.

"Within one month, the people here would lose themselves to their animal selves." He closed his eyes and rubbed his temples. "No one likes it, Liesel. No one wants it. But we're stuck, and there's no way out." He nodded back in the direction of the village. "Perhaps you can see now why my mother chose to stay. It's not just my humanity at stake, or even my family's. It's all of them, including the little ones who would be left behind, such as Steffan and his sister. It would be the people of Ward and all of the surrounding towns that would have to deal with hordes of wolves. It would be all those who wish to keep their own selves, and not lose their minds to the animal." He shook his head. "When the one named Ilsa escaped, we had to choose another from Ward, and quickly. If we hadn't, many people would have died."

"It makes no sense," Liesel muttered.

"And why is that?"

"All curses can be broken."

"Says who?"

"Look," Liesel turned to face him, "the curse allows you to keep your humanity as long as there is a Pure Blood within the family. That's already a positive step. In the worst of possibilities, you would all have been wolves from the start. The line would have begun and continued with ordinary wolves. But I think this might be the Maker's way of saving a remnant, preventing you all from being lost. The curse is simply waiting to be broken."

When she finished, Kurt stared at her with an unreadable expression. "There is one more thing I think you should see." Getting up, he headed back toward the town. This walk was less eventful than their earlier adventure. Once they were back in the cabin, Kurt instructed Liesel to wait in the front room of the house. He disappeared down the hall, leaving Liesel to examine the room she stood in.

The walls were a darker wood than the Beckes had in their house, and the beams had been left round, rather than being cut flat and smooth the way they were in the houses in Tag. Though the room was sparse, it was oddly warm and friendly. Liesel remembered walking through it that morning to the front door, but it had been dark and the fire had been unlit, so she had seen very little.

A cozy fireplace centered one wall, and a soft, green rug, nicer than anything Liesel had in Ward, lay before it. At the other end of the room was a simple wooden table with six stools beneath it. Along that wall, another door was open to what looked like a kitchen, unusual for the people even of Tag. In Tag, only well-to-do citizens, such as the Beckes, had separate kitchens. Everyone else simply cooked over their fireplaces. The only other furniture was a worn wooden writing desk and its stool a few feet from the door. There were two books that lay on top of the desk. Liesel stepped closer to see what they were. One was the Holy Writ, and the other a small, green leather book.

"Everyone else is gone," Kurt said as he walked back in, "so we're safe to talk here." Joining her at the desk, he picked up the little green book and brought it over to the table where the light was better.

"Don't tell my father about this." He gave her a smile that was faintly ornery. "Only the pack leaders and their sons are supposed to know this exists."

He didn't have to tell her to take care when he handed it to her. Liesel could tell immediately that the book was ancient. The pages were yellow and stained with time, and brittle to the touch. Gently, she opened the book to discover that it was a journal.

The pages were filled with all sorts of drawings and scribblings. There were countless sketches of wolves, detailed enough to make Liesel shiver after her run-in that morning. There were various herbs and flowers, too, most of which she knew from her many hours spent with Ely in his shop.

One flower in particular that was unfamiliar to her, however, appeared again and again. It had long, pointy petals that nearly looked like needles, hundreds of them, and its center was filled with what looked like fuzzy spores. The drawing was so intricate that she could make out the waxy shine of the petals. Liesel was sure she had never seen this flower in her life. She squinted to make out the words beneath it, then looked at Kurt in confusion.

"What language is this?"

"This is the journal of the wizard," he answered. "It is all we have left of him, aside from our stories and our unusual second natures."

"Does it prescribe how to break the spell?"

He shook his head ruefully. "No one knows how to read the wizard's tongue. We keep it though, if nothing else, as a reminder of what can happen when courage flees us as it fled from him. I poured over it repeatedly as a boy. I thought I could interpret a few words, but never got anything specific. You can sense the magic, though, when you hold it close."

Liesel held the book up and sniffed. Immediately, a strange dizziness washed over her, the same feeling that she got when Kurt stood too close.

"After years of searching," he took the book back and turned it over in his hands, "I simply decided it was better not to know. Not that any of us would be foolish enough to dabble in the dark arts after our ancestor's blunder."

A small feather fell out of the book as he closed it, and Kurt frowned as he picked it up. "Except for maybe my uncle," he growled. As he spoke, Liesel had a sudden vision, a memory long stowed away.

"What did your uncle mean all those years ago when he said I was the one who believed in magic? And your brother this morning?"

"You are not to give heed to a single word my uncle says. Do you understand me?" Kurt's voice was suddenly rigid. Liesel was a bit taken aback. He had never ordered her to do anything before. She nodded silently. His eyes softened a bit, however, when he saw her expression.

"I'm sorry. I don't mean to be harsh. It's just that I've been trying to protect you from my uncle since we met, believe it or not. My brother has good intentions, but he's spent too much time with my uncle. And Lothur would not hesitate to sacrifice you or anyone else if it meant breaking the curse. He wants you to believe in magic because he thinks you will be more likely to follow along with his plans. In truth, he does little more than study this book. It irks my father to no end. It's one thing to be interested in the writings, but the investment he has in it is something else entirely."

Kurt put the book back on the desk and headed toward the door. Liesel followed suit, although she didn't know where she thought she was going. It just felt natural to shadow him the way she had once shadowed the boy.

"We need to go now," he mumbled, pausing with his hand on the door.

"Where are we going?"

He paused before answering, seeming suddenly embarrassed. "I'm supposed to take you to the dressmaker's home to get you fitted for the wedding gown."

Liesel's breath caught in her throat. For just a little while, it had felt like the old days. But his mention of her wedding gown made her new nightmare real once again.

Quietly, they left the cabin. Somewhere down the road, Liesel's shoe caught on a rock in the path and she stumbled. Instead of getting up, however, tears filled her eyes and made it impossible to see. She stayed where she was and silently wept.

She wasn't ready.

This would be her life. This dark town without smiles or sunlight would be her home forever. She would never see her grandparents again. She would never again climb her mountain, and she would only ever dream of touching the salty froth of the sea. And not even her children could take up the dreams that she would leave behind. And though she was loathe to stay, how could she doom an entire village to ensure her own happiness? This was where she would die, just like all the others.

Kurt knelt beside her. He placed his forehead against her own and softly cupped her face in one of his rough hands, but she pulled away.

"I'm sorry," he whispered after a moment, his own voice strained.

A sob broke forth from her chest as his touch had sent her head spinning in more ways than one. "How long have you known?" she demanded tearfully, staring only at the ground. "I just need to know the truth."

"My father called me one night when I was fourteen, the night you arrived." Kurt's voice was husky as he stood. "My mother pleaded with him to let me be, but he said if I was ever to be the pack leader, I would need to know what to do one day when the need arose."

Liesel couldn't help but wonder if Kurt's next need would be for himself or his son after him. His father had gone through four wives. How long would she last?

"He sent his youngest brother, my Uncle Egon, to do it, but we were to watch from a distance. I was excited to be going with the men. I wasn't old enough yet to turn, so it was a privilege to be out so late at night." Kurt sat on the ground a ways from where Liesel knelt. "I was enjoying myself until I saw the look in your eyes. You were terrified." His voice grew quiet. "The next day was even worse, when I realized that the same deed had been done to my mother. I felt sick to my stomach for days after that. I think that's when I truly began to grow up. I had once longed to turn sixteen, but no more.

"My father made it clear, however, that without a Pure Blood, I and all the others would lose what precious little humanity we did have. And without that humanity, there was a very good chance that I could choose to spare you one day, only to accidentally kill you the next."

Liesel finally looked up at him, tears still sticking to her eyelashes and making his figure blurry. "If you knew all of this, why did you promise me we could leave together one day?" She felt rather silly for asking. It seemed foolish that she had held on to a promise made at so young an age. But if Liesel was honest with herself, the hope she had put into that promise had been the fire that had driven her on for so long. It had become her anchor every time her life became a storm.

"It was a boy's hope," he said quietly.

"Would you go if you could?"

"I'm afraid I cannot afford to dwell on such thoughts anymore. I have others to care for."

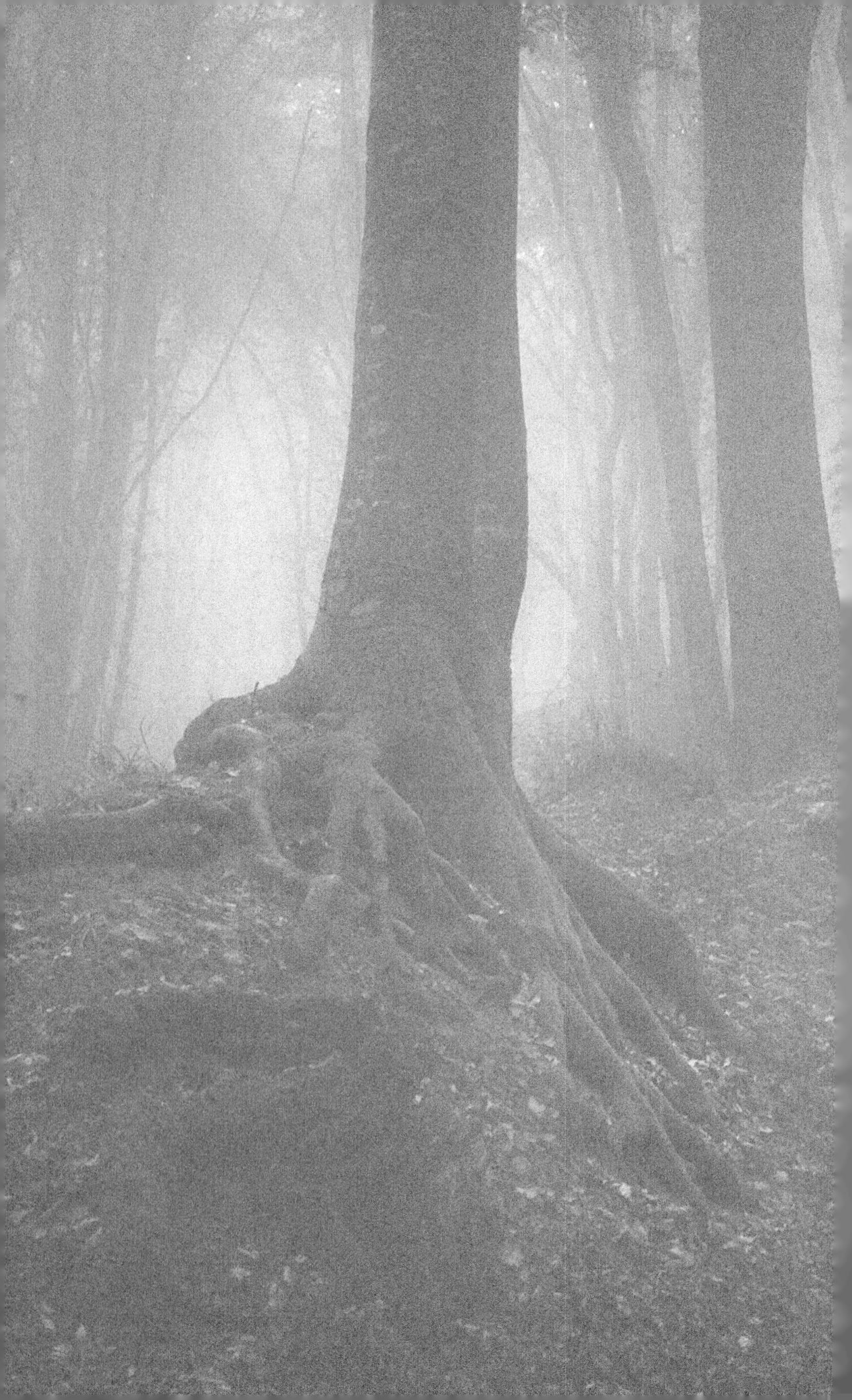

CHAPTER 16
ON ONE CONDITION

The dress was old, possibly as old as the curtains in her new bedroom. That it had been altered repeatedly was obvious, as the white lace was worn far more at the hems than anywhere else on the raiment. Still, the basic shape was becoming, or at least as becoming as a dress could be that had been worn by countless other women on other such unhappy days.

Liesel was silent as the woman finished her fitting. The two women had hardly spoken a word since Kurt had dropped her off. The seamstress had a kind smile, but Liesel couldn't bring herself to make small talk.

"When she's finished with the fitting, you may walk around the town a bit," Kurt had told her when he'd delivered her to the woman's home. "My family knows you like to explore. I've told them to leave you be." Of course, what he was really telling her was not to run away. Liesel set her jaw stubbornly. Would this really be her whole life? Perhaps it wasn't heartbreak the Pure Bloods died of, but rather boredom.

"You couldn't wed a better man," the seamstress said from the floor as she pinned Liesel's hem.

But Liesel pouted. "A good man wouldn't have lied to me."

"That wasn't by his choosing," the woman mumbled, her mouth filled with pins. She took them out and paused in her work to look right at Liesel. "His father forbade him from telling you.

The boy was so taken with you from the start that Old Garrit knew he'd fare better giving Kurt guidelines to follow instead of trying to separate you two completely." The seamstress nodded to herself and went back to pinning. "Things really couldn't have turned out better."

Liesel looked at her incredulously. "Couldn't have turned out better?" she echoed in disbelief. "My father was tricked into taking us far from our home. I watched both my parents die unnecessary deaths. Now I will never leave this wretched forest again! In what way could that be for the better?"

"Old Garrit could have laid claim to you."

Liesel felt the color drain from her face, but the seamstress continued talking on as she worked.

"Most pack leaders marry again and again until they die. So don't you go thinking this pack leader has no feelings. Garrit's a tough old thing, but he loves his son. When he realized Kurt was sneaking off every day to see you, he told Kurt's mother that you would be Kurt's and no one else's." The seamstress looked a bit smug, nodding again to herself. "I know because she told me. Good friends we were, despite her being Pure Blood and all. And there." She turned Liesel before the mirror. "This will be all done tomorrow. You'll be a lovely bride."

Liesel wanted to cry as she looked in the mirror. Dressed in an ancient, shabby lace gown without any family or friends was hardly her idea of a lovely wedding.

Instead of crying, however, she decided to force another question in an attempt to steady herself as the woman helped her step carefully out of the dress and back into her own.

"Why is everyone so quiet here?" Even in Ward, the people had laughed and talked when she wasn't near. But here, she noticed that there was very little conversation going on... anywhere. Only the children seemed to remember how to speak. And the seamstress, of course.

"That would be the magic," said the woman as she gently laid the gown back on her work table. Liesel frowned, confused, and the woman sighed. "When we're born, we are very much human. As Kurt, I'm sure, has told you, though, we begin turning at sixteen. Fear is what turns us. You learn quickly, however, that the human heart fears much, and then you eventually realize you can't live your life that way, constantly letting the wolf rise up. People get hurt, and you start to lose your mind. So we simply work to stop turning." She lifted the gown into her lap and began to sew.

"With every choice to stay human, however, we give a bit of humanity to the wolf. We might keep our human form, but a piece of us dies. As we feed more and more of ourselves to the wolf, we lose the words that were once within our minds. Some of us have more words than others, of course. Take me, for example." She gave a sad chuckle, then sighed. "But even I've begun to find moments, spells of time when the words don't come because the wolf doesn't have any to give. I fear if I live long enough, there will be a day when even I speak my last."

The seamstress's words painted a haunting picture. Liesel quietly thanked her, more for the conversation than the dress, then left.

It wasn't until Liesel had stepped out into the street that she realized she had nowhere to go. Though she'd craved freedom since arriving, the looks the townspeople threw her were almost more depressing than she could bear. Despairing eyes were everywhere, with not a smile to be seen.

Suddenly, Liesel wanted very much just to hide in the bedroom with the lace curtains and to read her grandmother's book. Out here, she felt exposed, especially as barks and snarls could be heard scattered throughout the town. She did not have to stand there for long, however, before a girl with light brown hair suddenly appeared beside her and grabbed her by the arm.

"Let us go," she whispered excitedly before yanking Liesel down the street behind her.

"Where are we going?" Liesel had to work to keep from tripping and being dragged along the ground. The girl didn't answer, though. Instead, she came to a halt and whirled around.

"You can leave us alone now, Keegan! I can handle her for a few minutes." She scowled, and Liesel couldn't help but feel a little unnerved. Had Kurt's brother been following her? Keegan seemed to appear out of nowhere, but Liesel could see now that he had been hunching to blend in with the street crowd.

"You might let her go." He frowned back.

The girl huffed. "Really, Kee, do you think me so daft? You have no business watching women relieve themselves in the woods." At these words, Liesel was suddenly grateful. She really had needed to go since arriving at the seamstress's cottage. "Besides," the girl added, "I'm fifteen, and more than old enough to know what happens if I lose her."

Keegan stood uncertainly for a moment before nodding once. "Fine. But I will be checking in on you."

The girl stuck her tongue out at him before flipping back around and breaking into a run. And as she still had a good grip on Liesel's wrist, it was all Liesel could do to stay upright as they ran.

The girl was strong and quick. It wasn't long before they were out of the town and in a part of the forest that Liesel had never seen before. Though there was still no sun, it was a little brighter here. When the girl finally released her, Liesel realized that they could see the cabin and most of the town from the little knoll they had just climbed. Gigantic, cone-laden trees still towered above them, but there was less brush, making it easier to see the town as a whole.

The little hill would have been lovely, had it been discovered under different circumstances. Purple dew-laced flowers carpeted the ground and even the bases of the tree trunks. Various boulders and stumps provided places to sit, but not enough for the space to appear crowded.

"If you truly do need to relieve yourself," the girl said nonchalantly, "I would do it now. I'm not sure how long Keegan will be able to contain himself."

As confused as Liesel still was, she hastened to do as the girl advised. When she returned, the girl was examining a tear in her skirt, muttering under her breath, something about how the seamstress would have her hide this time.

"Finally." She glanced up when Liesel approached, then returned to looking at her torn dress. "I was starting to think you'd run, and I would have to hunt you down." Liesel's expression must have been one of horror because the girl laughed and rolled her eyes. "It was a joke. Now, on to more important matters. Do you love my brother?"

Liesel stared back. "I'm sorry, but who is–"

"Oh, yes. I forgot. I'm Lora, Kurt's younger sister." As soon as she said it, Liesel could see Kurt's golden-brown eyes in the girl's face. The siblings didn't look greatly alike, but the girl was very pretty, despite favoring her father. "So, do you love him?" she asked again.

"I... don't know," Liesel faltered. And in truth, she didn't.

Lora studied her for a moment before finally nodding. "I think you do."

Liesel wasn't sure how qualified the girl was to make such judgments, but she held her tongue. It wouldn't do to offend her new friend... her new sister.

"This is for you." Lora shoved a parchment at her that was sealed in blue wax. Liesel's own name was written in a lovely script on the front. Liesel looked at Lora quizzically, but Lora just shook her head. "I didn't write it. But I *can* tell you that it is going to help you break the spell."

Liesel frowned. "This spell has been at work for two hundred years. Why should I suddenly have the answer?" She looked at Lora. "Wouldn't you be more... suited?"

"It has to be you. You're a Pure Blood. And on top of that, you want it more. No other Pure Blood has ever loved the pack leader the way you do." Lora climbed up on a round boulder and stared down at the town, her voice resentful. "Kurt used to believe. But Father drove that from him as fast as he could." The way the girl sounded made it seem as if she knew everything about Kurt and Liesel's unusual relationship, as if theirs was a lovely tale for children before bed.

"But what can I do?" Liesel looked up at her with doubt. The girl returned her gaze, the determination suddenly returning to her face.

"*We* are stuck here. But *you* can leave."

"I can?"

"It's in the letter." She hopped down and began to walk back the way they'd come. "Supper is in two hours back at the cabin. If you don't show, Keegan is going to eat me alive."

Liesel stared at the letter for a long time without opening it. So many times, she had come close to escaping. She didn't know if her heart could take another fall.

And if he found her trying to escape, what would Kurt say, even if it *was* for the pack's good? Would he believe her or resent her forever? She was tempted to simply refuse. At least for now, her intended had some sort of affection for her.

And yet, a memory flitted through her mind. A boy and a girl, bent over a book, plotting the twists and turns of their one-day adventure. How sweet the air had seemed during those days. The world had been theirs. They only needed to wait a few years before gaining the freedom to chase their dreams.

A part of her, an irrational part, still dreamed as that girl had. She still imagined the boy holding her close as they set off on their travels. She could almost sense his warmth beside her as she closed her eyes each night, whether under stars or a roof. She could almost feel his lips caressing her own, smiling beneath them as they watched the sun set over the ocean.

With shaking hands, she broke the seal.

Dear Liesel,

I knew who you were the moment I saw you, and in that moment, my heart both broke and rejoiced. I mourned because I knew what they were taking from you. I rejoiced because I knew you would bring much happiness to my son. The Maker knows he needs it.

Kurt has told me you are losing your grandparents. I was seventeen when I was marked for Garrit. I would have been marked long before I was called, except that the Pure Blood before me had died suddenly. I wish you could have had longer before you were marked, but the pack does it that way, marking girls before they need them. It's easier then if the current Pure Blood dies suddenly. The next one is nearby. It sounds cruel, but I suppose it makes sense.

I have instructed Lora to deliver this note to you before you wed my son because what I have discovered is of the utmost importance. Unfor-

tunately, I learned too late, but the moment I saw you, I knew you could be the one to break the spell. You have life in you still. It hasn't been beaten out of you like it has so many of the girls by the time they're brought here. (At least, that's what I've been told.)

I am writing this now because I can sense the life within me draining. My husband would deny it, but the pack unwittingly draws life from the Pure Blood. There's nothing in the legends that says it is so, but I can feel it. The world has lost its color, and I can no longer taste the sweetness of honey. I pray to the Maker that this slow death is never yours, nor does it fall on any other woman. If you can break the spell, it won't.

From the time I die, the pack has thirty days to carry on without a wedded Pure Blood. Tradition gives them four days before a new one is joined. Three for mourning and one for a wedding. You must leave before you are married, for if you leave the pack's boundaries after you are wed, the people will be lost. Your only hope of this is to convince Kurt to let you go.

Because of his place in line, he has the authority to suspend the magic and let you go, just as he had the authority to call you. But this must all be done before my husband realizes you are out of the forest. Even with Kurt's blessing, you cannot escape Garrit's direct summoning while still within the boundary of the woods. If you can escape those, however, you are free.

Once you are out, you will have no more than the month to find the way to break the curse and return. Sadly, I cannot tell you where to find that. A fairy, perhaps, or a wizard could help. I can only hope someone shall know.

I have told you this in the absolute faith that you care for Kurt. I could see it in your eyes the day he found you near our home. If you decide to run or are too late to return, everyone here will lose what humanity they have left forever. So consider your choices wisely.

Tell my Kurt that I love him. Although I was taken against my will, I have no regrets, except that I couldn't save them myself. The Maker has given me three beautiful children, and I would not trade them for the world. And don't resent Garrit too much. He is gruff and obstinate, but he means well. My husband wasn't always the way he is now. Actually, he was much like Kurt as a young man. Over the years, he's given much of himself to the wolf to keep order in the town. With each piece he sacri-

fices for others, he loses a bit of himself. He's a good man, and like Kurt, never had a choice in what happened two hundred years ago. They're as much prisoners in this forest as we are. They cannot leave, and they cannot let their people die. Please be the one who breaks this cycle of evil for all our sakes.

Your friend in hope,
Wanda

LIESEL'S HEART hammered as she folded the letter back up, afraid to read its contents again. And yet, hope had already sprung up within her. Breaking it out once more, she memorized the lines. That the spell could be broken she had no doubt. As to how that could be done in less than a month was another matter entirely. The suggestion that she use the plan as a ruse to escape danced across her mind, but she knew she couldn't do that, even before the thought was complete. As Kurt's mother had stated, it would be impossible to leave Steffan and his sister and grandfather and all the others to the spell's sentence. And Kurt. She couldn't do that to Kurt.

Was Lora right? Was she in love with Kurt?

Liesel had to wonder at her girlish assumptions about the future. Though they had never discussed it, Liesel had always assumed she and Kurt would marry. It would be the two of them and the rest of the world. She would give him children, and they would be happy, just like her grandparents had been. How little she had known when she'd dreamed up such ambitious plans. But somehow, she still wanted them. Despite all that had happened, she still wanted him.

But if they failed, if Kurt said no, or if she was just too tired to try, the outcome was simple. She would return and live out her short existence here as Wanda had done. It would be the easy thing to do. She would only have to follow the rules. She could still be his wife and the mother of his children, and they would stay together until death did them part. In fact, the ease of simply doing as she was told was tempting. Liesel was tired of fighting. Would it be so bad to simply let the spell have her?

"Lora said I would find you here." Kurt sat down on the stump next to hers. Liesel turned to tell him that she would do as he wanted. She would marry him. The pack would live. She was done fighting. As she looked into his eyes, however, his eyes glazed over, and his jaw went slack.

"Kurt?" Liesel frowned and leaned a hair closer. When she got no response, she gingerly reached out and touched his shoulder. "Kurt, what's wrong?"

Slowly, Kurt turned his head toward her, but his eyes were still vacant. It was the same look she'd seen on him that morning when she'd asked about the early deaths of the pack wives. The emptiness in his eyes made him look... dangerous, and it frightened her. What had happened to her friend while she was gone?

A deadly determination burned within Liesel. Whatever was happening to Kurt had to be part of the magic, and a strange urge to protect him from it suddenly invigorated her. It seemed odd that she should feel any need, much less harbor any ability to guard the one who had been her guardian. But none of that would matter if Kurt's mother had been right.

So Wanda's plan it would be after all, Liesel resolved as Kurt blinked back to life, completely unaware of the change that had just taken place within her. She wanted to ask about whatever had just happened, but decided it could wait for later. They had more important matters to discuss.

"I've been thinking," she began slowly, hoping he was ready for such a conversation. "You want me to marry you for the sake of the pack."

A myriad of emotions crossed his face, but he finally gave her a simple nod.

Liesel took a deep breath. "I will do so on one condition." Kurt raised an eyebrow, but said nothing. "We must use our month's time to try and break the spell."

Her words rushed out faster as he looked more and more skeptical. "I can go back to my grandparents and ask if they know how it can be done. They've been all over the world, Kurt! They knew where my father could have found a real cure for my mother—"

"You know we only have twenty-seven days. You miss that, and everyone here becomes a wolf forever. We would have to find another Pure Blood in your absence." The look on Kurt's face was accusatory, as if she had already abandoned him. "We would have no way to communicate, no way to know if you were alive or dead, whether you had found the answer or not. You might return on the last day to find some other woman in your place simply because we didn't know." He shook his head. "It's just too risky."

Liesel could see that she was getting nowhere. She thrust the letter at him. "Read this!"

He gave her an odd look, but obliged. Just a few lines in, he made a choking sound. "Where did you get this?"

"Lora gave it to me."

As he read further, he began to pale. When he looked up finally, tears were in his eyes. "We killed her," he whispered.

Liesel sighed. "Kurt, you know it wasn't your fault. The magic took her, just as the magic turns you against your will."

Kurt stayed still, though, staring out into the trees. When he finally spoke again, his words were soft. "The legends say the first Pure Blood lived nearly as long as her husband. As the years have gone by, they've begun to live shorter lives." He groaned. "How did we miss this?"

"Perhaps the larger the pack grows, the more humanity it needs to continue. Perhaps it isn't a broken heart that kills them after all. Maybe their own life is how they sustain the pack. Some people were just meant to live longer than others, and those are the women that make hardier Pure Bloods," Liesel suggested.

Kurt stood and began to pace, his face taut. After a few long moments, he strode back to her. He took her shoulders in his hands.

"My mother only lived twenty-two years after marrying my father. Our pack had thirty less back then!" It took a moment for Liesel to realize he was thinking about her. Kurt straightened his shoulders resolutely.

"So I can go?" Liesel's heart leapt.

"Not by yourself!" He looked at her as though she'd lost her mind.

Liesel put her hands on her hips. "You don't trust me to go alone?"

"Do you have any idea how dangerous the road is for a young woman traveling by herself?"

Liesel nearly smiled. "Who knows? I might be taken by a pack of weasels or bears who need my magic."

Kurt scowled at her. "Not funny."

"Well, if I'm not allowed to leave, then what do you want me to do?"

"We're going together."

"But you're not allowed to leave the forest!"

"I can leave if I go with you." He took her by the elbow as he'd done when they were children and began to lead her back toward the town.

"When are we leaving?" She suddenly felt breathless with exhilaration, lightheaded with joy.

Kurt paused. "Well, as the wedding is first thing tomorrow, we had better go tonight."

They'd begun to walk again when a man with gray hair, the one who had escorted Liesel through the woods, stepped out of the trees and onto the path ahead of them. His arms were folded, and he did not look pleased.

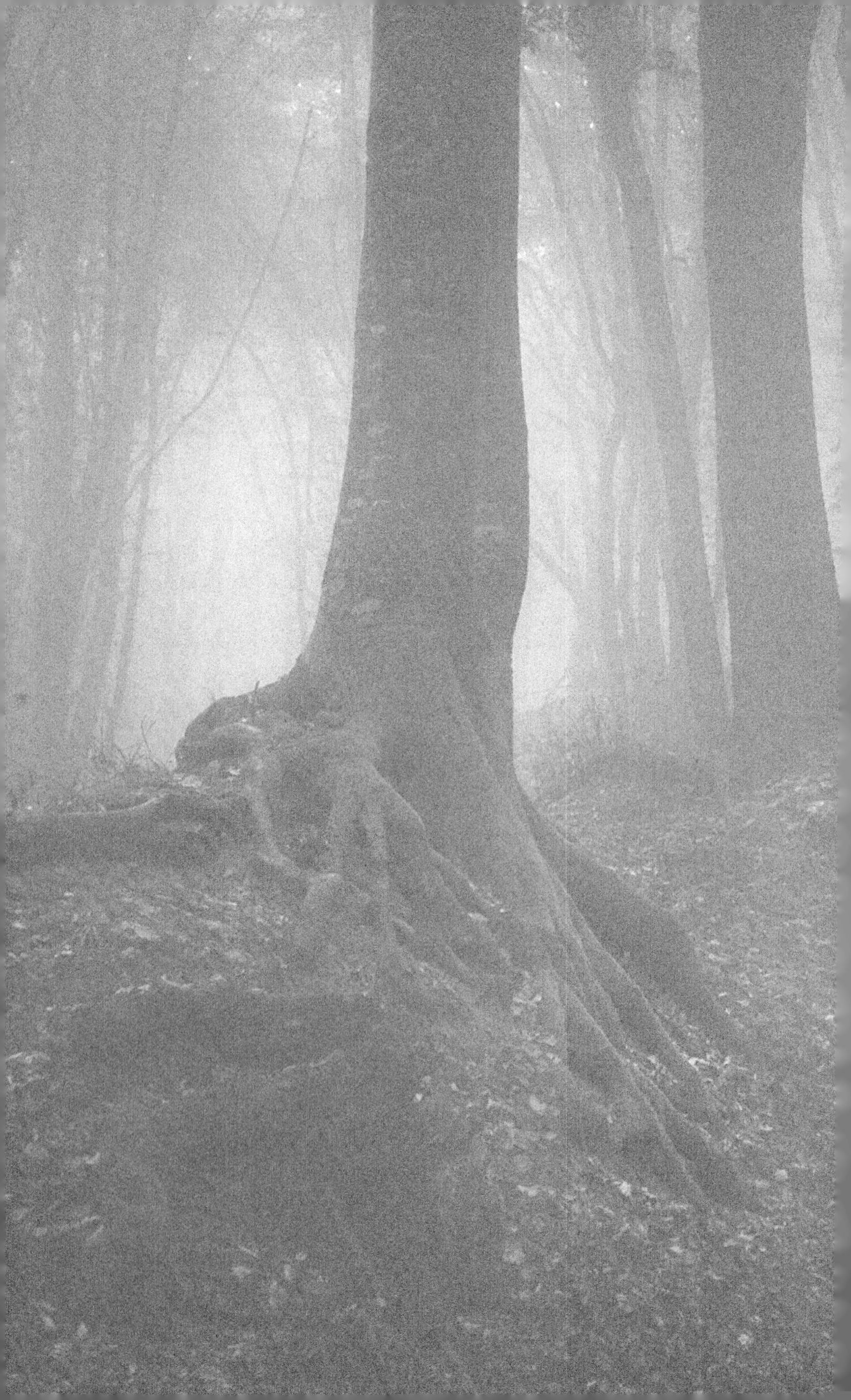

CHAPTER 17
ESCAPE

Under the scrutiny of the old man's fierce glare, Liesel could not think of a single word to say, but after a long, awkward silence and withering looks from the old man, Kurt finally pulled himself together and managed to lose his look of shock. Liesel didn't fare quite as well quite as quickly. But to her surprise, it was the old man who spoke first.

"The two of you are going nowhere alone. 'Tisn't proper for a young lady and a man not her husband to be traveling the road together." He raised an eyebrow at each of them in turn.

Liesel felt her face redden, and Kurt looked irritated. "We wouldn't–" he began testily, but the man held up a hand to stop him.

"That's why I'm going, too."

"You're not going to tell them?" Liesel was the one to find her voice this time.

The old man shook his head and grimaced as he rubbed his bristly chin. "Nah, I know what you're planning. Lora told me." Who else had the girl told, Liesel wondered. "Besides," he said to Kurt, "your mum made me promise to take care of you. And that is what I'm doing."

"You know my father won't take this lightly, Johan," Kurt said quietly. "If they catch you, it will be far worse than last time."

Liesel startled a little when Kurt spoke the old man's name.

"Johan? You were the one who ran with us when Kurt sent me away?"

The old man simply nodded before turning back to Kurt. As he did, Liesel shuddered a little to think of what his punishment must have been after he had helped Kurt with such an act of defiance. "So where are we going?"

"But I thought you lost all control when you turned," Liesel interrupted.

"Remember, some don't mind giving more to the wolf," Kurt murmured to her before turning back to Johan. "We're going to ask Liesel's grandparents for help. They live at the foot of the mountain."

"We don't have much time."

"I know. That is why we are leaving tonight."

And so they planned their escape. Johan would run through the forest in either wolf form or human form, depending on the need, but Kurt would carry Liesel.

"My tracks are all over this forest," he explained when she protested. "It won't take them long to find our scent, but if they can't smell you, it might delay them just enough for us to make it out of the woods."

"But what about your father? Your mother said I can't leave if he orders me not to."

Kurt thought for a moment before giving Johan a sideways glance. "Schnartchen?"

Johan rubbed his chin thoughtfully. "Your mother always kept some in your kitchen, to put the poor animals to sleep that your father brought home from hunting. See if your sister can slip some in his tea. Wouldn't do, though, for them to suspect her after we're gone."

"He hasn't had a strong drink for a while," Kurt said. "I could offer him some at supper."

The suggestion made sense, but Liesel understood the sudden look of guilt on Kurt's face. She had learned of the Schnartchen flower while living with the Beckes.

The purple plant would surely put Kurt's father to sleep. No matter how hard they tried, no one would be able to wake him for hours after he'd drunk it. Unfortunately, putting it in a strong drink would also make him appear weak and foolhardy for drinking more than his share. Sometimes, as a prank, the men in Tag would slip it into one another's drinks at the tavern, and the next morning, their wives would come running to Ely's shop, sure their husbands were close to death. Still, Kurt's plan made sense. For the sake of the pack they would have to try.

"Better put some in Lothur's, too," Johan added.

Kurt rolled his eyes and simply nodded. He didn't seem nearly as sorry to put his uncle to sleep.

Johan agreed to meet them outside of the village just before midnight. As they watched him walk away, though, Liesel caught Kurt's sleeve. Something was bothering her about the old man.

"Before we go," she hesitated, "I have a question... about Johan."

"What about him?"

"He's helped us so much that I hate to ask, but... what is his stake in all of this? Why does he want to help us so much?"

Understanding lit Kurt's eyes as he began to lead them back toward the cabin.

"Johan's wife died in childbirth. His daughter was about my mother's age," he said softly. "Or would have been, anyways. After his wife died, the girl was Johan's world. One day, when she was only four or five, his wolf form had taken over, and while he was gone, she disappeared. Just wandered off into the forest. I guess." Kurt shrugged. "I'm told that's why he's given so much of himself to the wolf. Actually, tonight was the most I've heard him speak in years. He doesn't spend much time in town, and is usually off in the woods by himself. My father never really liked him to begin with, and after he helped me send you away, he was nearly exiled."

"Oh," was all Liesel could say.

"When my mother was called to the pack as the next Pure Blood, Johan somehow realized she was about the same age as his daughter would have been. I suppose he just needed someone to take care of. Wild or not, he missed his daughter. So when my mother showed up, alone and afraid, he took it upon himself to care for her. He was her closest friend. My father never said as much, but I could tell that it always irked him when Mother would ask for Johan's opinion on decisions she had to make instead of asking his."

Liesel just nodded thoughtfully. Though she couldn't imagine the wild wolf man being close friends with anyone, she could understand the desperation of the young Pure Blood to seek his guidance. Johan's gray eyes were a little too bright, and the way he carried himself was even more feral than Kurt. But if Kurt hadn't been there for her when she had been called to the pack, Liesel would have clung to the first sympathetic soul she could find. And now that she knew his story, she felt much better about Johan's involvement.

Supper was held at the cabin, where, apparently, everyone in the family lived. Lora sent them a slightly relieved smile when Liesel followed Kurt inside, which Liesel took to mean she was glad Liesel hadn't decided to run. Kurt seated Liesel at the table, then excused himself, claiming that the pot was too heavy for Lora to carry in from the kitchen. Lora began to protest until he gave a very pointed look at Liesel.

Just a few minutes later, Kurt returned with the pot, and Lora followed, carrying the drinks. There was tea for the women and ale for the men. When Kurt's father raised his eyebrows at the drink, Kurt mumbled something about needing to take the edge off before the wedding. At that, Garrit's eyes softened and he simply nodded, and Liesel had to remind herself not to stare anxiously as he finished the mug.

To distract herself, she wondered if every night was like this, or if this was a special supper because of her added company. Kurt's father sat at the head of the table with Kurt on one side and Kurt's Uncle Lothur on the other. When Lora announced the supper was rabbit and vegetable stew, Liesel didn't ask about how they'd acquired the rabbit. She decided she would rather not imagine it.

Instead, she sat between Kurt and Lora and listened quietly to Garrit's explanation of how the wedding ceremony would proceed the next day.

Apparently, the seamstress would bring the dress to Liesel's room in the cabin, and they would prepare her there. The wedding would take place in the town square where the entire pack would be in attendance. As was the custom, the priest from Ward would be brought in to officiate the ceremony.

Liesel wanted to shut it all out, to imagine herself instead on the road back to the mountain with Kurt and Johan, where they hoped to be the next morning. But, she sighed to herself, if they failed, if there was no way to break the curse, this would be her lot anyway. She should listen and prepare herself for that time in case it did come. And despite her assurances to Kurt that her grandparents would have somehow heard about the spell's remedy through their travels, failure seemed inevitable.

Supper took forever to finish. Kurt and Lora attempted to draw Liesel into conversation now and then, but Liesel didn't feel much like talking. She just wanted to stare at Garrit and make sure he drank every drop of ale.

It seemed like a lifetime later that Lora began to collect the bowls, and Kurt walked Liesel to her bedroom. They said little, afraid to give away any hint of what they were planning. As soon as she shut the door, Liesel laid down on the floor to peer underneath the door. Sure enough, someone was standing just outside of her room. A quick peak outside at the moving torch showed that another body paced outside her window. Afraid she would draw attention by walking about the room as she wanted to do, Liesel laid on her bed so as not to rouse suspicion.

Still, she worried about the guards. Kurt hadn't factored them into the plan he had drawn out for her. Regardless, after the fire in the main room had been allowed to die, and the candles in the hallway had been extinguished, she heard a low voice from the now dark hall. It sounded like Kurt, but she couldn't make out what he was saying. A moment later, there was a soft thud on the floor.

"Liesel, open the door!" Kurt whispered. When she did, Kurt dragged in a body. Liesel stifled a gasp as he pushed the body into a corner.

"He's not dead," Kurt grunted. "He's just going to give us a head start on our run." Then he motioned for Liesel to step up on the bed, and in a moment, she was perched on his back and they were on their way.

Liesel was very glad no one else was awake to see them as they silently made their way out of town. She felt most undignified, more than she had felt since she was a child, the day her father had had to carry her home after she stepped on a bee. Her grandmother would have given her a lecture on inviting scandal if she could have seen Liesel clinging to a man's back like a baby swan sitting upon her mother. Still, it wasn't unpleasant to feel Kurt's warmth beneath her in the cool of the evening.

"You just had to keep the red cloak, didn't you," he muttered as soon as they were out of town.

She scowled down at him in the darkness. "I wasn't exactly planning to–" Her rebuttal was cut short by the low growl from the bushes. Liesel froze, but Kurt whispered,

"It's just Johan telling us to keep quiet."

And so they ran.

Kurt was fast, even in his human form. But how much farther could he go at this pace, Liesel wondered. Beads of sweat trickled down his neck and back as she clung to him. That he was tired was doubtless. He had been carrying her on his back since they had fled the town's edge. As tired as he must be, however, she doubted that the tremors in his shoulders had anything to do with his exhaustion.

"I can run," she whispered in his ear again. But he shook his head vehemently.

"Too unpredictable!" he hissed back through clenched teeth. Liesel nearly gave him a sour retort until she realized he wasn't talking about her, but about himself. Johan's human voice came from ahead of them, his whisper thick with impatience.

"If you two don't stop arguing, you'll have nothing left to argue about!"

A howl echoed his warning, long and shrill, raising the goosebumps on Liesel's arms as she clung to Kurt. Kurt put his head down and pushed harder. The branches and underbrush were becoming visible as the gray light of morning started to penetrate the trees. It was already much lighter here than it was anywhere near Ward, and Liesel was shocked at how far the men had run in just one night. She didn't have long to ponder, though, as the leaves rustled behind her, giving their pursuers away. They were less than a stone's throw back.

"Kurt!" She cringed, hiding her face in his neck as well as she could, awaiting the sure attack.

"Almost there."

Then she saw it. Up ahead was the forest's edge. Despite her ragged breathing, Liesel's heart fluttered with relief. She could see the golden rays of sun lining the wood's edge with the glorious fire of morning. Every branch, trunk, flower, and leaf was alight with it.

But before she could touch that fire, Liesel found herself breathless and on the ground, looking up at a very large gray wolf. Before she had time to scream, another wolf launched itself at her attacker, and strong human hands grasped her by the arms and dragged her out of the forest. Within seconds, Johan followed them through, beginning his leap as an animal and landing it as a man.

It was the first time Liesel actually witnessed the change. It was as if Johan was dissolving into thin air. But before he disappeared completely, the air began to shimmer, and where a wolf had been, a man took its place. He hit the ground running.

Liesel thought that since they were out they would surely rest, but instead, Kurt picked Liesel up again and continued to run. They finally stopped to catch their breath when the forest was far behind them, visible, but not clear. They were far enough that it took a moment of squinting for Liesel to see the lone figure standing at the edge of the trees.

"What are you doing?" It was Keegan's voice that called out to them, and his words were filled with confusion and abandonment.

"I will be back, Kee," Kurt called back. "I promise."

"But she was the one—"

"And that's why I have to do this," Kurt called to his little brother, his voice kind. "This has to end."

"It can! I told you that Uncle found a way!"

"That's not a way I can live with." Kurt shook his head. "I promise we will be back in time. I left a letter for Father on his desk. Make sure he finds it."

Keegan continued to stare after them, but Kurt turned and began to walk toward the road without another word. His expression was determined, but Liesel didn't miss the hint of a tear in his eye as he turned his back on his brother. Johan followed. After one more glance behind, Liesel hurried to catch up with the men.

She tried to rid herself of the sadness in Keegan's voice by focusing only on the mountain ahead. It loomed in the distance, a bright purple in the early rays of morning. She was leaving death and sorrow, loneliness and the failure behind her. Liesel was going home.

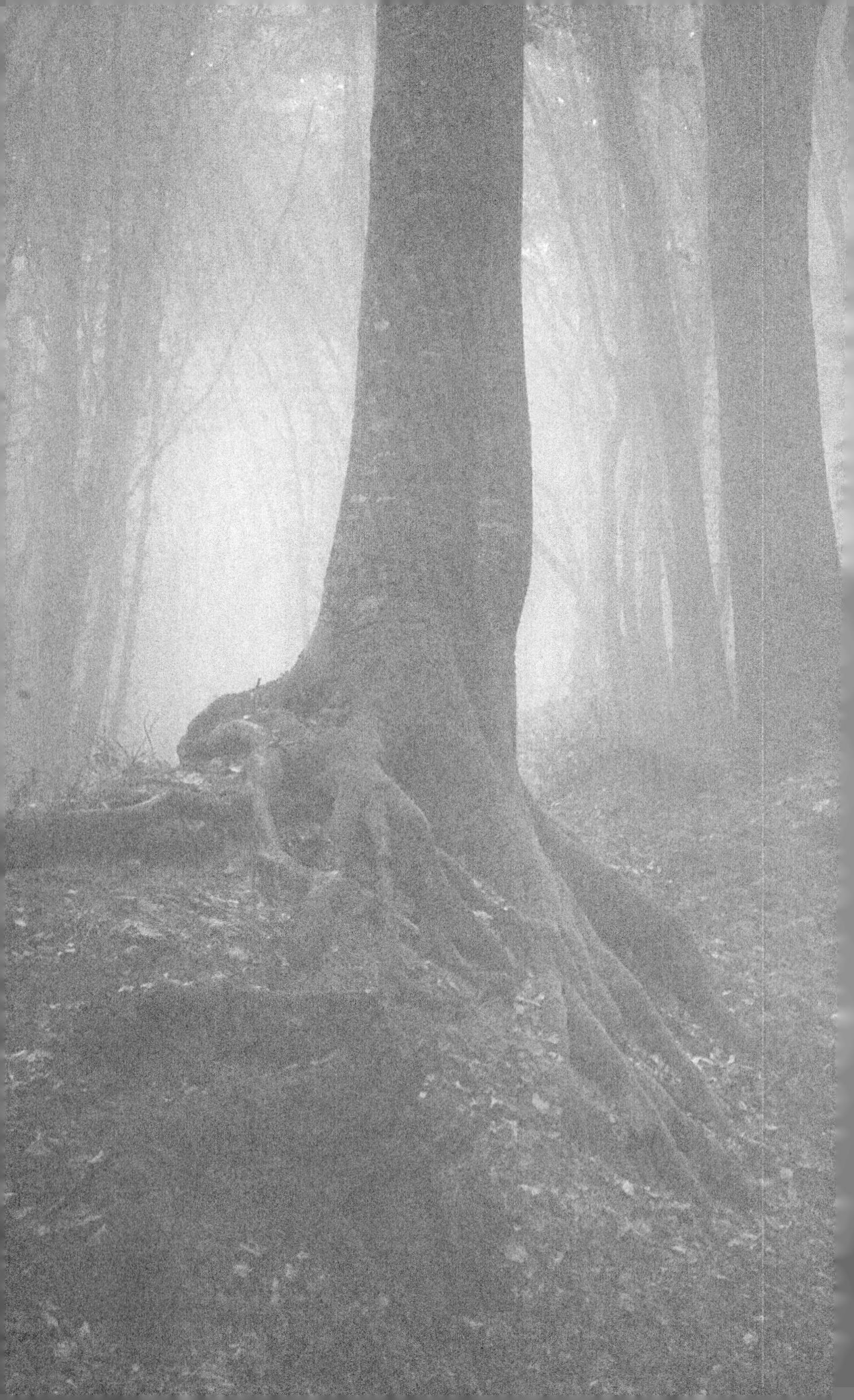

CHAPTER 18
TO GRANDMOTHER'S HOUSE WE GO

As they walked along the road, Liesel realized she had forgotten how soothing unadulterated sun felt, how it wooed one to a lazy sort of peace. It made the fields, the trees, the road, and the sky itself too bright, too glorious to look upon for long. With a grin, Liesel closed her eyes, spread her arms, and ran ahead. She felt as though she could fly.

"Liesel, where are you going?" Kurt called out nervously from behind her.

"Isn't it magnificent?" She ignored his question, her eyes still closed. With a smile on her face, she stopped and began to twirl. She hadn't felt this giddy, this free since she was a child. "There's so much space! So much room to move!" She stopped twirling and looked back at Kurt and Johan. Instead of smiling, though, they were staring at her as if she had gone mad. Johan simply shook his head and began walking again, but Kurt drew closer to her and said in a low voice, "You shouldn't get too far away."

"I was hardly running away," Liesel pouted, but Kurt glanced around furtively.

"It's not that. I just don't know how close we have to stay to you to keep your protection."

"My protection?"

"We can only travel outside of the forest with you. That's why

Keegan couldn't follow us. You were too far away. He was afraid he would have turned while he tried to reach us."

"And how do you know this?"

Kurt let go of her arm and began to walk toward where Johan was waiting for them. "There have been several Pure Bloods that needed healing, those who were accidentally injured before the wedding. No healers in the forest would touch them." He snorted. "The fools thought the magic might stain them. Anyhow, the pack leaders learned that they could accompany the women out of the forest if they stayed close."

"Have they ever tried to leave after the wedding?" Liesel couldn't stop the bit of hope that surged within her.

"The Pure Bloods died," Kurt said, looking straight ahead, "even with the people in tow."

Liesel felt her heart drop. So Wanda had been right. This was their only chance.

They walked until they came to a town, where Kurt produced a bag of coins that looked suspiciously like the one Liesel had saved up while working at the bakery. It didn't take long for her to figure out his plan, though, as he headed toward the closest building to the road, which happened to be a church.

"We don't have the time to walk the whole way," Kurt answered her unspoken question.

"So we're buying a horse?"

"Two, actually."

At that, Liesel giggled.

"What's so funny?"

"I don't know what you think you are going to find at the church, but it surely won't be horses." She continued to giggle until she was doubled over laughing.

Kurt frowned. "Well, where do we find them?"

Liesel did her best to smother her laughter, reminding herself that if she'd grown up in the forest, she would be confused, as well. "Usually the tavern has some that have been left by customers who couldn't pay," she suggested.

It wasn't difficult to locate the tavern. Kurt went in to talk with the owner while Liesel waited outside with Johan. She would be happy to never set foot in a tavern again after her experience with the peddler in Ward. She didn't have to, though, as it wasn't long until Kurt returned and waved them over to the back of the ramshackle building. Liesel wasn't sure he knew the wiles that most tavern keeps were prone to, but she followed anyway, curious to see how he would bargain.

The stable around the back of the tavern was acrid, and glancing in at the horses' feet, Liesel could see why. The hay hadn't been changed for days, and the flies were so thick that it was nearly impossible to breath without inhaling one. Liesel coughed as a man in a stained apron met them there.

"These 'uns been left by their masters."

"Left?" Kurt raised an eyebrow.

The man shrugged. "Well, some's left. Others' owners been killed. Some stays as... payment. Anyhow, I keeps 'em till some 'un else wants 'em." He led a skinny gray mare forward for them to see. "Ye said ye needs to travel?"

Kurt was already reaching for the reigns when Liesel shook her head. "This is ridiculous," she said, stopping Kurt mid-reach. "That poor creature will be lame in a day. Look at how unsteady her left back leg is."

The men all stared at her for a long moment before she sighed and entered the stinking filth herself. Holding her breath, she stepped over the piles of muck, searching each and every stall. By the time she'd nearly reached the end of the row, Liesel had almost given up on finding any decent beasts fit for the distance they needed to travel. To her relief, though, in the last stall, she discovered a pair of black horses that were quite handsome. Despite the mess, they were relatively clean, which made Liesel think they couldn't have been at the tavern for very long. Their thick necks arched proudly, and their legs were strong and sturdy. As she led them out, the tavern keep cried out,

"Them's ma' best two! Can't ye do with the little gray over there?"

Liesel gave him a hard look. "Do you want us to buy horses here or not? We can just as easily go to the next town."

Kurt started to say something about time, but Liesel threw him a nasty glare. He caught it and was quiet. A long silence stretched between Liesel and the tavern keep, but Liesel was determined not to give in.

It wasn't long after that that Kurt and Liesel rode proudly out of town, Johan keeping pace with the horses on all fours. Liesel thought it strange how the horses didn't spook in such proximity to the wolf, but then, she thought, there were many things about the pack's magic that didn't make sense. The wizard had botched up his spell worse than any of the wizards in her grandparents' stories.

"Where did you learn to buy horses like that?" Kurt chuckled. "I certainly wouldn't want to cross you in a trade."

"I have always wanted to travel," Liesel stared hard at her mountain as she spoke. "My grandfather took me aside when I was eight, and he said if I was going to roam the world, I had better know how to buy a horse without getting conned." A small smile escaped her. "The way you almost did back there."

Kurt scoffed. "It's not like I've ever had to buy a horse." He thought for a moment before adding, "If nothing else, at least this journey means you got to try your hand at it."

"Yes," Liesel said quietly. "I suppose it does." She knew Kurt meant well, but his words were more easily translated, *If we fail, at least you had the chance to pretend this was a journey.*

They were silent for a long time, breaking the long stretches between towns with short bursts of galloping, which seemed to greatly appeal to Johan. They met few strangers on the road, but Liesel knew that any day harvest would soon begin, and the road would then be filled with people transporting their goods to markets all over the valley. She grew excited at the prospect of seeing so much food and so many people until she realized that they would be returning before harvest season was at its peak. It was a pity. Harvest had always been her favorite time of the year.

They rode on until deep into the night. Johan turned back into his human self for supper, which they had purchased at a market in some little town along the way. As he handed out the strips of dried meat, bread, and cheese, Kurt's eyes continued to dart about into the night beyond the fire they'd built.

Finally, Liesel could stand it no longer. "Kurt, is something wrong?"

"I don't like this." He shook his head. "We're too exposed."

"We're right next to the road."

But Kurt just shook his head again. "At least in the forest you can shelter to avoid trouble. Out here, it is as if we're just waiting for some sort of trouble to find us." He nodded at her cloak. "That thing certainly doesn't help."

"Well, I like it better out here," Liesel said. "You can see if something is coming at you, rather than being ambushed from above or behind or whatever direction the forest goes. Where are you going?"

Kurt stood up and stalked away, ignoring Liesel's calls. She nearly got up and followed him, but a second look at his face revealed the blank look once again.

"Don't take it personal," the old man said, his first words since that morning. He took a worn pipe from his coat and lit it. "It's nothing you've done."

"You wouldn't know it," Liesel grumbled. Then she sighed. "He's different now. I mean, I suppose I knew he would be. But still..."

The old man shook his head. "The lad changed after you left. To start with, he got in royal trouble with Garrit and Lothur for sending you out of the pack's territory. They almost gave the pack leader seat to Keegan."

Liesel nearly choked on the bite she'd just taken. While she didn't dislike the young man, the thought of being married to Keegan instead of Kurt was sickening.

"He convinced them to let you be for a few years. Told them you could still be called back anytime, despite the boundary."

"Lora said he lost hope after sending me away?"

"He existed to be with you."

"What happened when I left?" Liesel asked softly. It was the question she had been asking herself for four years.

"Garrit told the boy that if you married before they called you back, Kurt would have to find and mark a new wife for himself."

Liesel was silent for a moment as it all sank in, all of the what-ifs running through her mind like a pack of wild horses. What if she had married Fridric or Benat? The magic could have been broken that easily, she realized. It would have taken so little work, far less than what they were attempting now.

And yet, some other girl would have belonged to Kurt. Being the good man he was, he would have treated her kindly and with affection. They would have had a family, and though Liesel knew it would have taken time, his new wife would have come to love him, and he, her. Despite her current horror at the life ahead of her, the near other future suddenly made Liesel feel ill.

"What happened after that?" she whispered.

"The boy shut out the world. He's talked more since you've been back than he has since you left." This surprised Liesel. Kurt had seemed somewhat reserved. The old man looked as if he was ready to go to sleep, so Liesel tried to squeeze in one last question.

"Why does he keep doing that?"

"Doing what?"

"When he got up, and he wouldn't speak to me?"

Understanding lit the old man's gray eyes. "It happens to all of us. The more you give to the wolf, the more the wolf rules. Kurt's given a lot not to turn around you."

It was just as the seamstress had told her. Liesel just hadn't expected the strange silence to affect Kurt like it had everyone else. He was too real to fall prey to such power. And yet, she couldn't deny what she had seen. "So... it might get worse?"

"Without a doubt it will," the old man said, tucking his pipe away. "Happens to all of us eventually." And before Liesel could ask any more questions, the man had shimmered into a wolf, tucked cozily into his tail for the night.

***

LIESEL DIDN'T REMEMBER when Johan and Kurt changed places, but when she woke up, Kurt was the one laying on the other side of the fire, although, unlike Johan, he slept in human form, it seemed. He was awake, lying on his back, staring into the early morning sky. Liesel wondered if he was still in whatever state of mind Johan had told her about the night before. She didn't have to wonder for long, however, because just then, he stood up and began to gather their packs.

"Think we'll reach them today?" he asked. Liesel took a deep breath, feeling both relief and excitement. This was the day she had been waiting for.

"I know we will."

Just as she predicted, they were approaching the foot of the mountain by early afternoon. The house looked just as Liesel remembered it. The long, wooden building stretched out to show its many windows that ran along the front, something uncommon to most people, even the wealthy merchants that lived in Weit.

"My grandfather's wine is sold as far as the capital," Liesel told them proudly. Even without her words, the other two looked clearly impressed. Kurt, who had continued glancing around nervously all morning, had finally stopped searching for trouble, and was staring with huge eyes at the rows of neatly laid vines that seemed to go on for miles. Johan, a wolf again for the travel, had even stopped to stare. Liesel felt her heart vacillate between swelling with joy and shaking with trepidation as they neared.

For so long, she had pictured everything returning to the way it had been. She and Kurt would marry and go on adventures of their own. Then they would return here and spend their lives happily in the shadow of the mountain with her grandparents.

Shaking her head, she tried to brace herself for the reality she knew lay ahead... or rather, didn't lie ahead. Seven years was a long time. Would they even recognize her? And how would they react when told that she was simply there to search and not to stay? Would she have to break them a second time? Her stomach was suddenly jittery, and she felt her moment of imagined joy fast approaching sorrow and heartache.

"Liesel."

She turned to see Kurt looking at her with wide eyes. "Are you all right?"

She plastered a smile on her face and nodded. "Just a little nervous, I suppose. It's been a long time. Perhaps you should take your human form again, Johan." She looked down at the wolf. "It might be a bit of a fright for them if they see me traveling with a wolf."

"They'll be happy to see you," Kurt offered kindly. Liesel could tell he was nervous himself, though, and for the first time, she wondered what they would think of Kurt and Johan when they discovered what their errand truly was. She could only hope the amount of magic her grandparents had seen throughout their travels had prepared them for what her little group had in store.

As they neared, Liesel's grandmother came out of the house and began to hang laundry on the line stretched out in the yard. A strong gust of wind blew the garment out of her hand and when she turned to chase it, she caught sight of the three. Without a moment's pause, she shouted at the house for Liesel's grandfather before running toward them, her speed impressive for her age. Liesel hardly had time to get off her horse by the time Ilsa was there.

"Liesel!" She drew her in tightly, and Liesel nearly cried as she breathed in the familiar scent of sage. She had imagined being held in those arms countless times, and yet, their comfort far exceeded any of her dreams. "My baby is home! My baby is home!" Ilsa continued to cry as she stroked Liesel's hair.

Liesel looked over her grandmother's shoulder, expecting to see her grandfather join their embrace any minute. To her surprise, however, he was standing about twelve paces back, glaring furiously at her companions.

Liesel pulled out of the embrace slowly as she watched her grandfather glower, her grandmother following suit. Finally, he began to walk toward them.

"Ilsa, get Liesel back in the house." His voice was low and rough. Liesel had never heard him sound so menacing.

"Grandfather, they're with me," she said quickly. But her grandfather didn't even acknowledge her. Liesel looked desperately at Kurt and Johan, but to her dismay, Johan was glaring, too.

"I don't believe it," Johan muttered. "You survived."

Kurt looked sharply at his companion. "You know him?"

"I should," Johan growled. "He's the one that got away."

Kurt's eyes grew huge. He looked at Liesel. "Your grandmother's name is *Ilsa?*"

"Yes." She wanted to run between them to stop whatever clash was brewing, but Ilsa stepped closer and grasped her arms tightly. Kurt turned back to her grandfather, who was still standing before Johan as if ready to fight.

"Because it means your grandfather is one of us."

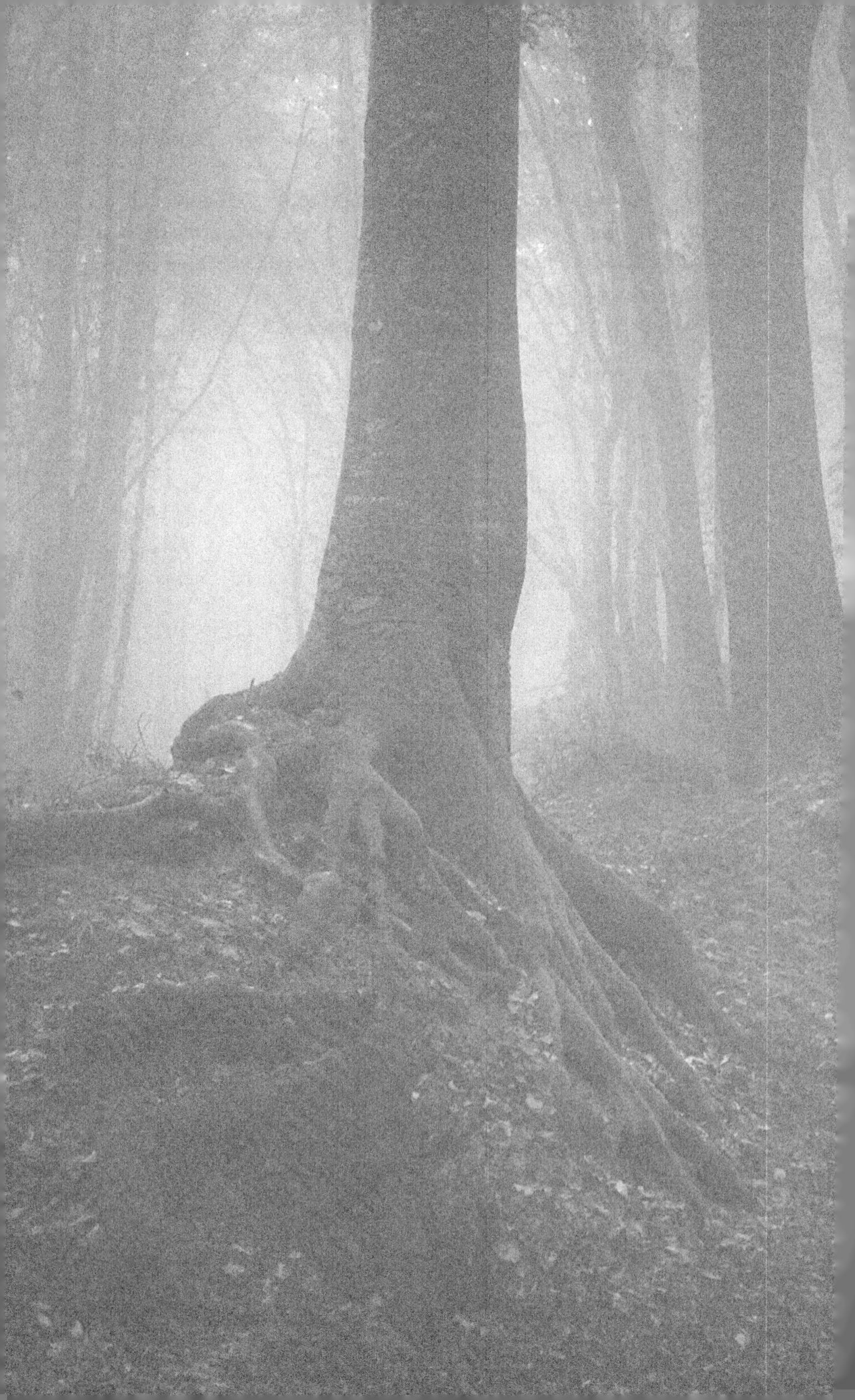

CHAPTER 19

BAD BLOOD

Before Liesel could respond, both Kurt and Johan had shimmered into wolves, and her grandfather had thrown his long walking staff up into a defensive position.

Liesel shrieked. It would be more than she could stand if one of them hurt another. She tried again to run to them, but her grandmother held her with a surprising strength.

"Your grandfather knows what he's doing," Ilsa whispered fiercely. "You will only get hurt!"

Liesel watched in horror as Kurt made the first lunge. Bernd expertly feinted to one side, then the other, which was impressive, considering his age and stiff knee. Kurt fell for his trick, and in the blink of an eye, her grandfather had the young wolf pinned to the ground with the staff. Johan began to move in with a growl, but her grandfather stopped him with a look.

"I won't hurt him, but he's staying here until he comes to his right mind."

To Liesel's surprise, Johan let out a slight snarl before laying down. Her grandfather firmly held Kurt beneath the staff for what felt like hours, until the wolf stopped thrashing and lay still. Liesel wondered how it was possible to keep the animal under the staff until she looked closely to see small, silver flecks sticking out the side of the wood. Were those miniature knives?

Finally Kurt shimmered back into his human form once again.

He lay still, glaring up at her grandfather from beneath the staff, but he didn't change a second time.

"Now, I am going to ask you this once," Bernd said. "What are *you* doing *here* with *my* granddaughter?"

"We came here for help!" Liesel yelled. Now that the danger seemed to be over, she found herself furious that everyone else knew something she did not.

"Everyone inside," her grandfather ordered without looking at her. "We will discuss this at the table."

The joyful reunion Liesel had envisioned was suddenly over. Ilsa let Liesel out of the tight arm hold she'd been keeping her in, but she kept a desperate grip on Liesel's hand as they walked, and Liesel could feel her anxious stare the whole way. Falling behind, Bernd called over one of the hired hands.

"Tell the others you're all free for the rest of the day," he said in a low voice. "I have visitors."

As everyone filed into the house, Liesel paused for a moment to watch her grandfather as he slowly made his way behind them. Despite his expert use of the staff that she had just witnessed, Bernd walked like a man who had been bested by the world. He no longer held his head up but stared at the ground as he went, moving as though it was not only his body that ached, but his soul as well. The hair that had been peppered gray and black when she'd left was all gray now. Lines that had covered his face and neck when Warin had taken them had seemed to branch and grow, leaving three times the lines in their wake. Liesel's grandfather, an unusual specimen of youth when she'd gone, had aged far more than seven years.

In spite of the awful start to the visit, Liesel found herself nearly smiling as they settled around her grandmother's large wooden table. Just as she recalled, the large stone fireplace was still topped with the thick cedar shelf covered in trinkets from her grandparents' travels. The wide window on the east wall looked out over the entire vineyard and beyond, filling the room with light and contrasting greatly with the dark wood of the walls. She marveled at how one could see so much without the forest to block her view. The world was just so *big*.

As Liesel drank in the wide open space, she felt arms envelop her from behind, and she let her head fall back on her grandmother's shoulder, inhaling deeply. If only she could stay right here, she would be content never to journey again. Sorrow washed over her, though, as she realized what grim news she bore. Though it had been seven years since Amala's death and four since Warin's, she'd not even been able to send a letter to tell her grandparents of the loss of their only child. Turning, she felt her voice break.

"After we arrived, Mother—"

"I know, love. I know." Ilsa stroked Liesel's hair gently, and Liesel wondered how she knew, but was immensely grateful that she didn't have to actually say it.

She was slightly aware that Kurt and Johan were deep in some whispered conversation, but she didn't care for the moment. For now, all she wanted to do was to stay in her grandmother's embrace.

The moment was short, however, because Bernd rejoined them soon after. Locking the door behind him, he went and sat at the head of the table. With a sigh, Liesel joined the men, and her grandmother prepared to make tea. This would not be an enjoyable conversation.

As Liesel watched her grandfather search for words, however, she decided to take the reins while she had the chance. "I want to know what is going on," she said. Looking at each of the men in turn, she tried to keep her voice steady. The frustration of being kept in the dark even now was too much. She was done being the last to know what forces were controlling her life. The others looked at one another warily. Kurt looked as though he might speak after an awkward pause, but her grandfather spoke first. "I want to know—"

"No." Liesel had never interrupted her grandfather before in her life, but she was too angry now to stop. Despite her resolve to stay strong, her voice quivered, and furious tears lingered at the brinks of her eyes. Still, she went on. "*I* want to know what Kurt meant when he said you were one of them. And what Johan meant when he said you were the ones that got away." As her grandparents exchanged pained glances, she softened her voice. "I deserve to know."

"Yes," her grandfather let out a gusty breath. "Yes, you do."

"My father was a baker," Ilsa began as she served the tea. As she spoke, the realization suddenly hit Liesel that her grandparents had never spoken of their youth before marrying and traveling the world.

"We lived in a small town called Aussehen. It lies just on the outskirts of the woods."

Liesel knew it. It had been the town where they'd purchased the horses.

"My father was working in my grandfather's shop when they came to us. They needed a new baker, they said. The idea of having his own bakery appealed to my father, so it wasn't long before we were in Ward." She shivered. "I was marked a few days later while I was out gathering firewood." She paused before asking Liesel wistfully, "Did they hurt you too badly?"

"Mother had died just hours before," Liesel said, feeling numb all over again. "I didn't really care."

Ilsa put her hand to her mouth, and Kurt looked uncomfortable. It was a moment before Ilsa went on.

"I met your grandfather not long after that. He found me stumbling around the woods less than a mile from our cottage. A fog had filled the forest, and I was as lost as they get."

A faint smile filled Bernd's lips. "I knew who she was by the mark, and I also knew I wasn't supposed to talk with her. Still, I was already breaking the rules by straying near the town. I thought I might as well save the pack some time and bring her home while I was at it. It would do them no good to lose her to fog, of all the worthless things."

"But you went back?" Liesel asked.

"I couldn't help myself. She was so full of life..." he broke off for a moment before leveling a stubborn look at Kurt. "You know what it's like there."

Kurt only frowned, but to Liesel's surprise, Johan spoke up, his voice a low growl. "There was just one problem."

"What?" Liesel asked.

"He wasn't pack leader," Ilsa answered. "A few years later, your grandfather came to me the day before the old Pure Blood died and said that if we ever wanted to escape, it would have to be then, before the pack leader called me." She lowered her eyes and said in a soft voice, "They had already managed to kill my parents. I didn't know what else to do."

"They always kill the parents," Bernd said gruffly, turning the teacup in his hands. "Whether it's the town or the pack that does the deed, if the family is there, it doesn't survive for long."

"So you ran and we were forced to take your best friend in your place," Johan interrupted, his eyes fiercer than Liesel had ever seen them. Ilsa's own eyes tightened before she closed them and mouthed a quick blessing.

"So do you still turn if Grandmother isn't around?" Liesel tried to picture a time when she was younger that her grandparents had ever been farther apart than a field or two.

"No."

"Why not?" Kurt spoke up.

"It doesn't matter how far apart we are if the spell is broken."

"So you did it," Liesel breathed out. Never in her wildest dreams had she considered her grandparents would know the answer because *they* had been the ones to break the spell.

"How?" Kurt asked.

Her grandfather gave him a hard look. "We got as far from the woods as we could go, but even that wasn't enough. I had to find peace with my new place in life."

"How long?" Kurt's voice was tight.

"A lot longer than thirty days." Bernd leaned in toward Kurt. "Because no matter what happens or where you go, deep down you know you'll always be an animal." With that, he stood up and stomped outside, slamming the door on the way out.

"Bernd." Her grandmother was quick to follow. No one else at the table spoke, but Liesel suddenly felt as though she might pass out. How she had gotten roped into the same tangled mess her grandparents had left behind was beyond her. Of all the girls in the world, the pack had found *her*... by accident. It was obvious from

Kurt and Johan's initial looks of shock that they were as surprised as Liesel.

Standing up, Liesel woodenly excused herself. She slowly walked down the hall to her old room. As she pushed the door open, a wave of sadness drenched her in memories. This had also been Amala's room when she had been a girl.

Her grandparents had an unusually large house, thanks to their thriving vineyard. Most families in and around Weit had homes with only one room, the kind Liesel and her father had shared back in Ward. To have enough rooms for the children to sleep alone was nearly unheard of outside of noble and royal circles. The room was small, but large enough for a raised bed, as opposed to a pallet, as well as a nightstand, wash basin, and mirror.

The smell nearly made her cry. It smelled just as her mother always had, of dried chamomile blossoms. And nearly everything was red. The doll on the shelf wore a red shawl the same color as Liesel's cloak. The blanket on the bed, the window coverings, even the braided rug was a bright crimson. Liesel didn't have time to linger on past remembrances, however, when she realized that her grandparents were talking just outside her window. Thankfully, the window coverings were still drawn, so Liesel was able to simply listen in. A part of her knew it was rude to eavesdrop, but the rest of her was too frustrated to care.

"–just finished mourning," her grandfather moaned.

"Liesel is alive," her grandmother said gently. "There's no need to mourn that."

"And we're just going to lose her again!" Bitterness filled his voice this time. "This is the Maker's way of punishing us. We could have gone back, Ilsa! He's angry with us!"

"What if this isn't punishment? What if this is a chance to make things right?"

"That boy will never learn in time. They can't have more than twenty-five or twenty-six days left! No, she'll have to stay here. We can't let her go back."

"Have you seen the way she looks at him?" her grandmother asked gently.

"She's young. She just thinks she loves him."

"We were younger than they are." Her grandmother sounded uncertain. "If Liesel is determined to stay with him, I doubt we'll be able to do much about it, short of tying her up in her sleep." Ilsa paused, her confident tone slipping. "Can't we at least try to enjoy this evening with our granddaughter? We can discuss this later."

Bernd began to respond, but Liesel realized they were walking back toward the front door. Bolting up from the bed, Liesel darted back out to the table, nearly tripping on a stool leg as she flew back into the main room. Her grandparents didn't seem to notice, though, as they walked back in. Bernd stopped at the door and folded his arms, his white bearded mouth setting in a stubborn line Liesel knew well. He had worn the look often when Warin was around.

"Since you're here with an escort, I can only guess you hold the wizard's blood in your veins?" He glared at Kurt.

Kurt simply nodded.

"So what's your interest in all of this?" Bernd asked. "Why do you care enough to bring her back here?"

Kurt's lip curved into a sneer as if he'd been insulted. "You should know as well as anyone. This existence is Torment on earth."

Bernd sent an unhappy glance to his wife, who nodded once. "I'm going to help you then," he said, "but you need to swear to me that you will live by my rules. That means, first of all, that you will be sleeping in the barn, where it's proper."

"Grandfather—" Liesel started, but Bernd just held up his hand. "Also, you will be learning how to fight." When disbelief flashed across Kurt's face, Bernd said, "You asked how I found peace. It was while studying the staff. I learned to quiet my mind in the movement. If you want me to teach you, this is the only way I know how. So, do we have a deal?"

Kurt looked at Johan, who gave a reluctant nod. "Don't suppose I have a choice," Kurt muttered.

"Good. We start now. Johan, I'll need you to help me if he turns again."

After the men finally left the room together, it was only Liesel and her grandmother. Ilsa took Liesel's hands in her own and kissed them. Tears filled her eyes and ran down her cheeks as she reached out and stroked Liesel's face.

"You're so beautiful, so like your mother," she whispered as sobs began to shake her body. "I never thought I'd see you again." Liesel felt her own breath catch as they clung to one another. Ilsa let out a shaky laugh. "I suppose I should have known you would find a way back. You were always such a determined little thing."

"Why didn't you tell me?" Liesel pulled back and searched her grandmother's face.

"Believe me, love, I tried so hard. But the magic wouldn't let me." She sniffed. "We've escaped every part but that. No matter how hard I tried, it just wouldn't let me speak. I knew, though! I knew the moment I saw your father speaking to that pale man before you left. He thought he had a secret, but I knew. I just didn't think he would leave so soon, though. I thought I would get at least another day or so."

Quiet settled over them. So many times, Liesel had imagined telling her grandmother about all that had happened while she was gone. For years, she had longed to tell Ilsa how she had saved up the money to ride on a grain wagon, and about how she had found a home in Tag. But the details, the pieces of her life that had once seemed so important, were suddenly mundane, useless. Because now she was here trapped in a web far stickier than anything she could have imagined even a few hours before.

The mood lightened a bit when it was time to prepare supper. Liesel enjoyed helping her grandmother in the kitchen, and Kurt and Johan were happy to see the food. Whatever they had been doing, it had plastered them with mud, sweat, and grass, and with a laugh, Ilsa ordered them all out to the well to wash up.

It wasn't long before Ilsa's gentle nature had her guests at ease as she told silly stories about Liesel's childhood antics. Even Johan smiled a few times. The only one who seemed aloof to the merriment was Liesel's grandfather. He wore a pained, contemplative look the whole evening, and it bothered Liesel.

As she lay in her little bed that night, Liesel breathed in the familiar scent of her surroundings and tried to soak it up. She prayed to the Maker that it would be better after this. She tried to think of ways to help Kurt find the peace her grandfather said he needed to break the spell, but she was too weary.

Her grandfather's threat to keep her from returning with Kurt, the difficulty of the task at hand, and the sheer weight of their responsibility, held Liesel's thoughts captive. The future was difficult to imagine without giving into worry or tears. For this one night, Liesel decided, she would just stay in the here and now. Because for now, all the people she loved were near. And that was more than she had thought she would ever get after all.

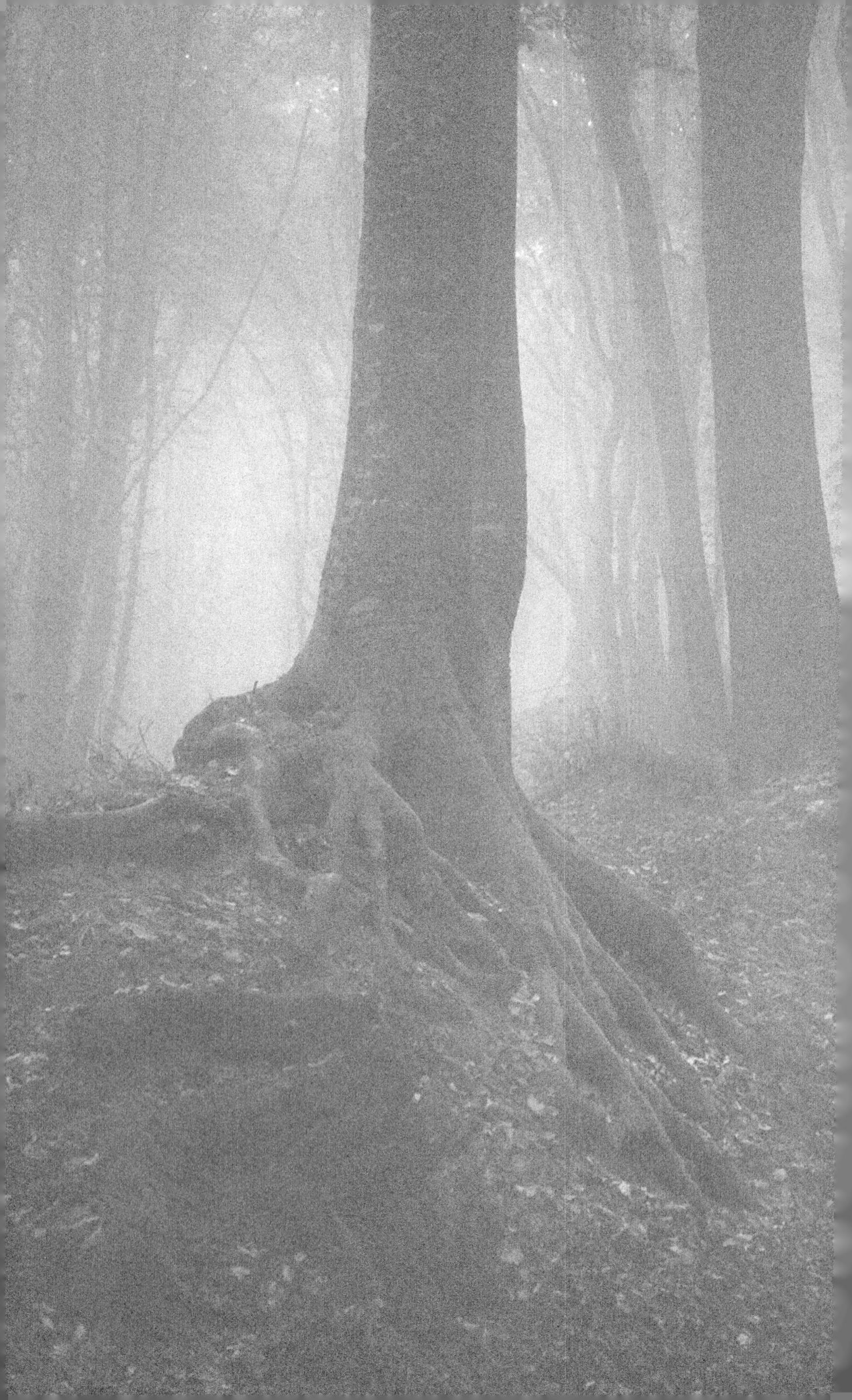

CHAPTER 20
FAIR

"Liesel, get back inside!" Bernd hollered as he tossed a staff to Kurt.

Liesel frowned but stood and did as she was told. Of all the changes returning home had entailed, being treated as though she were still thirteen was most irksome. Seven years had held unimaginable change for Liesel, but apparently, her grandfather was determined not to see it. At least, he had chosen to ignore it in the two weeks they had thus spent at the vineyard.

"He's terrified of losing you, you know," Ilsa said without looking up as Liesel walked inside. She was cutting potatoes at the table. "He's trying desperately to find a way to keep you here."

Still annoyed, Liesel picked up a knife and joined her grandmother in chopping vegetables. "What happened to his leg?" she asked, changing the subject. It was a topic she had been curious about since they'd arrived, but her grandfather had seemed determined not to discuss it. Every time Liesel asked him, his brows would furrow and some sort of undone chore would suddenly be remembered, and Bernd would shuffle off in a stony silence. Eventually, she had given up on asking him. Even now, her grandmother hesitated, her hands slowing just slightly as she chopped.

Compared to Bernd, Ilsa hadn't aged much since Liesel had gone. She was still a very handsome woman. There was more gray in her yellow hair, and she had run more slowly to Liesel through the yard than the last time she'd chased them in their cart. But she still held herself straight and proud as she stood at the table. Her long, thin face was just as Liesel remembered it, perhaps with just a few more wrinkles at the corners of the eyes and mouth. That mouth was now turned down as it spoke.

"He was trying to save you."

Liesel nearly dropped the knife, but her grandmother went on.

"As soon as he arrived home the next day from that hunting trip, and I told him where your father had taken you, he immediately found his horse and made the chase. Didn't take food or water, the old fool. He wore his horse out on the way and nearly lost him to exhaustion. By the time he arrived at the forest's edge, several people from Ward were waiting in case someone decided to follow you in.

"When they discovered his intent, they refused to let him pass. He fought hard, but he was tired, and they chased him back to the main road. He always swore he should have gone straight through the forest after that, but his ankle was broken in the fight, and it was all he could do to return home."

Liesel tried to swallow the lump in her throat. To think he had been that close when her mother had died. Her gaze shifted out of the window to where the men were training.

Despite his bad ankle, her grandfather used the staff now as though it were a part of him. He whirled it around his body so fast that it was nearly invisible. Johan hovered in his animal form, ready to intervene in case things got out of hand. Bernd was instructing Kurt on how to move his own staff, directing Johan to sometimes step in, acting as an opponent, feinting one way and then another. Again and again they practiced.

"Is this how Kurt is supposed to find peace?" Liesel asked doubtfully, changing the subject again. Every day, they practiced, and every day the whole lot of them came in dirty and out of sorts.

Her grandmother gave a dry laugh. "Your grandfather finds staff work relaxing. He trained with one of the masters during the years we lived in the east in Toku. That's actually how he broke the spell. He says there is something in the movements that helps him focus and put life in perspective. Nothing magic, of course. It just helps him think." She shook her head at the window. "I can't see how anything so demanding can relax him so, but it does. It may not seem like it, but he's doing the best he knows to try and help Kurt."

True as her grandfather's intent might be, Liesel wasn't so sure the staff practice was relaxing Kurt the way her grandfather had hoped. Sweat poured down the young man's face and neck, and made his thin work shirt stick to his chest and back. His figure was slim, but powerful as he moved.

Liesel didn't realize she was staring until her grandmother laughed at her. Her cheeks warmed with embarrassment as she became conscious that she had been caught gawking. It was just so hard to believe that Kurt was the same boy she'd left behind. As a boy, his arms hadn't been so defined, nor had his back held such a fine arch. She had seen the sharp angles of his face and the steady set of his jaw countless times in the last two weeks, but she still couldn't get used to them. As foolish as it seemed, Liesel actually felt a bit awed. She knew he was the same person, and yet, he sometimes felt like a stranger in a way that made her feel ridiculously young and shy.

"It might surprise you what two people in love can accomplish," her grandmother said, her voice gentle.

Liesel turned away from the window. In the weeks since they'd arrived, she had avoided this topic. It only made her cross.

"What is it?"

"What is what?"

"You're upset."

Liesel took a deep breath. "It's not fair."

"What's not fair?"

Liesel forced herself to look her grandmother in the eyes. "What if Grandfather is right, and we can't break the spell?"

Ilsa only stared back sadly, so Liesel turned again to the window. "I can't let those people die. So many lives... and they all depend on me, whether I want them to or not." She shook her head. "How can the Maker give me such a choice? I don't want it. I don't want this choice to be mine."

Ilsa put down her knife with a little more force than necessary.

"Sometimes the responsibility of doing what's right isn't idyllic like in the stories, Leese. It is given to us without pomp or glory. And we are the ones who have to make the choice of doing what is right or doing what is easy."

Nothing more was said until the potatoes had all been sliced and they were both seated with needlework in their laps.

"Your grandfather and I have had a wonderful life," Ilsa said quietly, "but never going back to tell them we'd found the way... that was the decision we made. And we've had to carry that burden all these years. We always will. That's one reason your grandfather is taking this so hard. If we had gone back and risked our happiness to show them the way out, you probably wouldn't be in this mess. And now you are paying for our wrong. So no, it isn't fair. But," she nodded at the window, "it seems the good Maker has deemed it fit that you should have a partner, that you won't be doing this alone."

Liesel usually hated sewing, but at least it provided her a bit of peace and quiet to mull over what her grandmother had just said. She didn't get much of a break, however, because at that moment, the men came crashing through the door like a herd of wild animals.

"Ilsa, get water and rags."

"Mercy! What happened?" Ilsa exclaimed. Blood dripped from a gash above Kurt's eye, and a knot on Bernd's forehead was beginning to redden and swell.

"Practice got a bit out of hand," her grandfather muttered.

Kurt didn't say anything, but he looked livid.

"Grandfather, I will take care of Kurt. In fact, there's something I need to show him. I think you should take the rest of the day away from practice."

"Liesel, if he can't find a way to do this before—"

"I am going to show him *my* attempt at finding peace." Liesel nearly laughed. "I don't think your way is working." Kurt looked relieved as she dragged him out to the well to clean his wound.

"Just stay within sight," her grandfather called after them.

"Don't worry, Johan will be nearby," she called back.

"It looks like you made this session without turning," Liesel said as she drew water from the well. Kurt sat beside her on its little stone wall. "At least that was a knot on his head and not a bite," she continued. Kurt reddened a bit. They'd had a number of turnings in the past few weeks that had resulted in bites to Johan as he had attempted to keep Kurt and Bernd from seriously harming one another.

"I wasn't afraid this time. I was angry," Kurt muttered. "He says he wants me to learn to relax and find peace, then he repeatedly hits me with a stick. If it were not for your stake in all of this, I wouldn't think he would really want me to succeed at all."

"Well, never mind him." Liesel dipped her rag in the bucket. "Tonight we are going to try something new." Gently, she began to dab at the gash. Once the blood was off, it really wasn't very large.

For some reason, however, she found herself enjoying the moment, and drew it out just a bit. There was something comfortable in being the one to care for Kurt, as though she had been made for that very purpose. In fact, it was nearly unnerving how very natural it felt to be so close, to turn his face gently from side to side as she finished cleaning his brow, even with the eddies of dizziness that moved through her every time she touched his skin. When she was done, she realized he was staring right up at her, not politely avoiding her gaze as she had been doing with him.

His eyes looked starved, as though he had never seen her before. In response, her fingers lingered on his chin, and she felt her breath catch.

"If you're going to get up and down the mountain before dark, you had better go!" Bernd shouted from the doorway. "I want you home before supper, Liesel. And remember, where I can see you!"

Liesel inhaled deeply and closed her eyes in an effort to control her temper and answer him evenly. "Yes, Grandfather." He knew her well enough to have read her thoughts, and that was slightly annoying.

As soon as they heard the door slam, Liesel threw the rag down on the stone wall and took Kurt's hand. "I'm going to show you how *I* find peace." Breaking into a run, she pulled Kurt behind her all the way to the foot of the mountain, and without hesitating they plunged up the path.

In her effort to respect Bernd's attempt to help Kurt, Liesel had stayed away from the mountain, biding her time so she wasn't too far from Kurt or Johan for the magic's sake. But now, as she hopped lithely from rock to rock, she immediately wondered why on earth she had waited.

It didn't matter that seven years had passed since she had last touched her beloved mountain. She could have taken the trail blindfolded. The crunch of the dirt and rocks beneath her feet was a welcome sound as she followed the trail, greeting every familiar tree and bush with delight. The grass wasn't as vibrant as it would have been in the spring, but the variations of yellow and green were lovely as they became caught in the little breezes that danced by. It was funny, Liesel thought, but the trail had once seemed much steeper than it did now. But then, she had grown a good deal taller since she had last followed it.

Neither Kurt nor Liesel spoke as they made their way up. She did eventually have to let go so that the dizzy spells wouldn't knock her off of her feet, but she did glance back often to see the wonder in his eyes as he took everything in. That made her smile even more. Since they'd met, she had wanted nothing more than for him to love her mountain as much as she did.

Nearly half an hour later, she stopped. A ledge nearly as wide as her bedroom jutted out over the valley. The drop over the edge was almost straight down, but it was deep enough for six or seven to sit comfortably on the natural little seats that the wind and rain had carved into the mountain. She heard Kurt gasp as he took in the sight below them.

Like a bowl, the valley gently sloped down from the mountain. The great forest lay on their right side, and another mountain range lay to their left. The neat lines of her grandparents' vineyard gave way to individual plots with houses and gardens, as well as pastures for cattle and sheep, dotted all over with blue ponds that reflected the crystal blue sky. They could see the road they had taken from the forest to her grandparents' house as it passed the forest's edge and went on toward the capital city. And far off, so distant it was nearly invisible, was the thin line of the ocean. Well, perhaps that was the ocean she saw and perhaps not. Either way, she knew it was there. Liesel closed her eyes, smiled, and drank in the sweet scent of pine.

"Don't look down," she said without opening her eyes. She could hear Kurt sit heavily beside her, as if he had half fallen back against the stone cliff.

"You're not joking," he muttered. "Are you sure this isn't going to crumble?"

"I came up here almost every day as a child." Liesel opened her eyes and took it all in again. "See, out here, there's room to *breathe*. You're not stifled by the trees or cut off from the sun."

"You can breathe in the forest," Kurt scoffed. "And you don't feel as if you are about to fall off the edge of the world." He caught Liesel's eye and smiled, "But you are right. It is special." He paused before adding, "I've always tried to imagine what the sky looked like outside of the woods. I could never have conceived this. Not even from the waterfall."

"What I don't understand is why people stay in Ward at all." Liesel shook her head, curiosity getting the best of her again. "If I were one of them, and I had the choice between this and the dark forest of Ward–"

"To begin with, most people aren't as well informed as you or your grandparents." Kurt tousled her hair playfully. "When you imagine the world, you see freedom because you remember the stories you grew up with, the tales of adventure. The people of Ward know nothing else. It has simply always been this way. For my people, we have a desire to escape because of the constant pain of the curse. Still, even with our stories, most have no idea of what life is like outside of our village. We desire a new life, but we have no idea of what that life would truly look like." With a bit of hesitation, he added, "After your grandparents escaped, my grandfather forbade anyone from leaving the village and its immediate vicinity unless ordered to do so." He glanced at her almost shyly. "I was the first since to break the rules."

Liesel couldn't help the smile that crept up, along with the blush she felt rising in her cheeks.

"To answer your question, though, the people of Ward have always lived that way, and we strive not to make it too difficult for them to continue. We try only to take what we need from the supply wagons, as we have no trade routes of our own, and we try to keep the dangerous animals away from their border. Not that we're much better." He gave a rueful smile. "Although my father did sometimes take a bauble or trinket for my mother now and then."

Liesel shifted uncomfortably.

"What were your parents like? As a couple, I mean."

He shrugged. "It wasn't ideal, but I didn't really start noticing something was off until the night you were marked." He sighed. "My father really did love my mother. He didn't always know how to show it, but he tried. He tried to find ways to make her smile, to make her feel at home. It frustrated him that he couldn't make her want to stay. It also frustrated him that she was so determined to raise us as if we were completely human. She was the reason he didn't go after the hunter, the one that killed his brother to save you."

"He wanted to kill Paul?" Liesel shuddered. She never forgot to mention him in her nighttime prayers.

"After bringing me home, Father was going to turn right around to find and kill him, but Mother begged and pleaded him not to spill more blood, that the hunter was only doing what he thought was right. My father finally agreed not to kill him, but he was never the same after that. He distanced himself from everyone but Lothur and me." Kurt looked at his hands. "It must have nearly killed him when I left."

Liesel hesitated. She knew her next question would seem callous, but she had to know. "Was he the one that killed my father?"

"No, that was my Uncle Lothur. He caught wind of your father's threat to leave and decided to take care of it himself. Once you are out of the forest, the magic of the call doesn't work anymore." He shook his head. "Very few of us have given enough of ourselves to the wolf to have that much control. But my uncle is strange that way. As much as he's given of his mind to the wolf, he values his humanity exceptionally. Up until now, he has been the one most obsessed with breaking the spell. My father didn't like what he did to your father, but after it was done, he agreed it had been a necessity."

Liesel closed her eyes and breathed the mountain air deeply again. The sight of her father, bloody and still, would always be there with her. They were quiet for a while as she fought back the dreadful memory.

"Do you think it was worth it?" she eventually asked as they stared out at the valley. "Coming out here, risking everything for a hunch?"

Kurt turned and stared at her with his deep golden-brown eyes. "I do," he answered seriously. "If for no other reason than to see why you're so strange."

She smacked his arm. "I am not strange."

"Oh, it's not your fault," he answered innocently. "It's this mountain air. It makes you do crazy things."

"Like what?"

"Like this." He leaned forward and planted a swift kiss on her cheek before standing and launching himself further up the trail. It was so fast Liesel didn't even have time to feel dizzy.

"Kurt!" She scrambled up to follow him, laughing. "Be careful! It's easier going up than down!"

By the time she caught up to him, he was on a slightly higher ledge, staring down at the valley again, a look of reverent awe on his face. The setting sun behind them was casting a rainbow of colors all over the valley. It had always been one of Liesel's favorite moments on the mountain, the seconds that just preceded the sun's descent, but as the sunset burst into all of its glory, Liesel couldn't tear her eyes away from him.

His face was serious again, his dark brown hair ruffling in the breeze. Taking her by the arms, his voice was nearly a whisper. "If this doesn't work, I will marry you knowing you only have a few years to live. I might live longer, but it won't be long before I have to give more of myself to the wolf than any pack leader ever has before. In the few moments of clarity that I may receive on my deathbed, I don't want to look back on this time and say we didn't try."

Liesel caught her breath as he slipped his arm around her and pulled her close. Gently, with his free hand, he tipped her face up toward his. Liesel could feel her heart beat recklessly in her chest as he held her. The world swam around her as the gold flecks in his eyes reflected the dying light of the sun, making him look momentarily *other*, as though he could disappear at any moment in a cloud of smoke. But the strong hand that held her jaw and the arm that encircled her waist were very warm and very real. Slowly, he had begun to lean down when her grandfather's voice, somehow floating up on the wind, broke the stillness of the moment.

"Liesel! It's getting dark! I want you back home soon!"

"Cliffs or no cliffs, we should have climbed higher," Kurt grumbled.

Liesel begrudgingly broke his gaze to look down and see her grandfather standing at the bottom of the path. He was staring right up at them. The moment was gone. Sighing, she pulled out of Kurt's arm and did her best to smile at him.

"Come on, mountain goat. I need to teach you how to climb *down*."

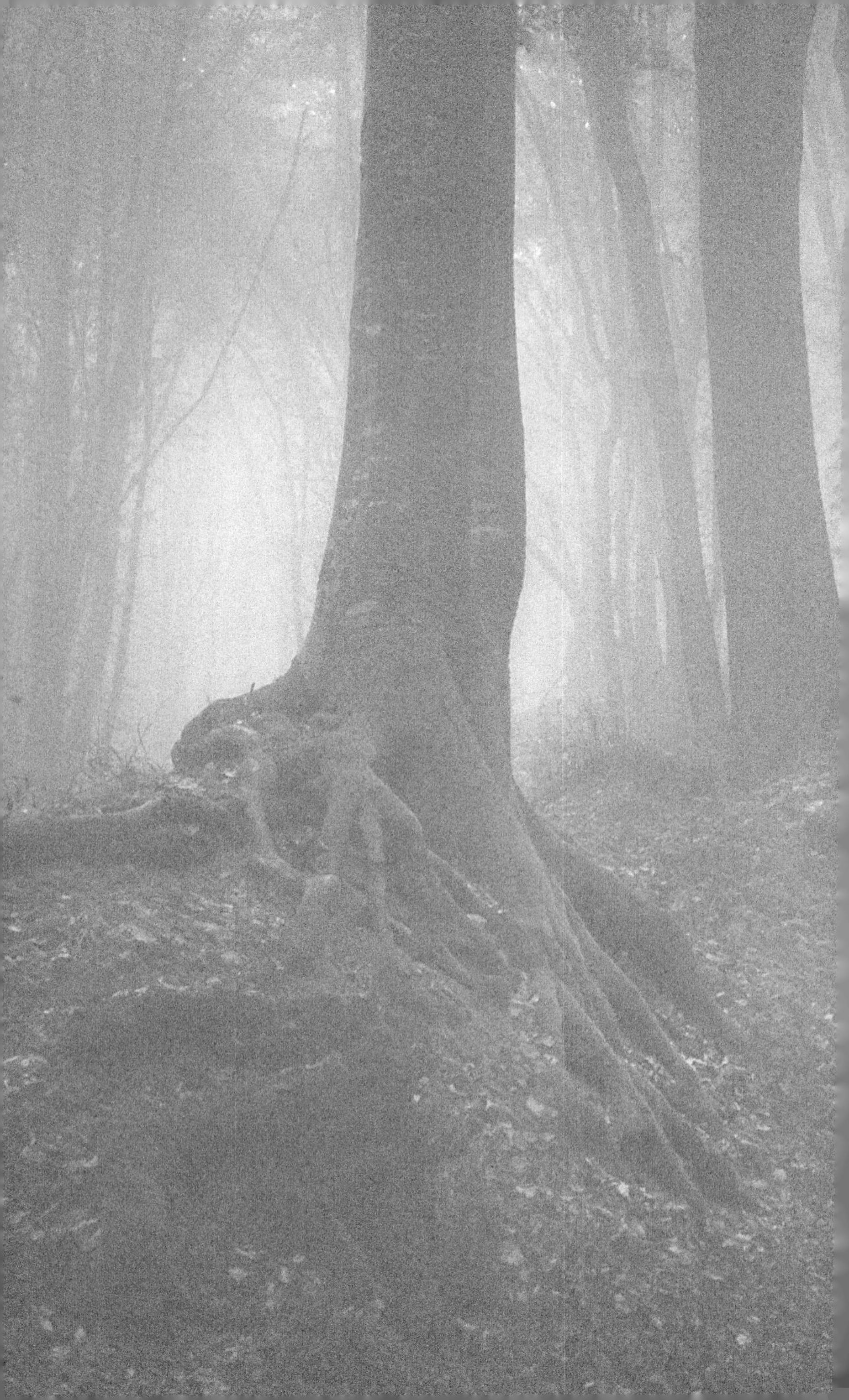

CHAPTER 21
GRANDFATHER

Liesel felt as though she was walking on clouds in the days following their trip up the mountain. It was odd, considering nothing had really changed. Kurt had not yet found his peace, and her grandfather still couldn't seem to find a single thing he liked about Kurt, but Liesel couldn't stop smiling.

The day after they had climbed the mountain, Kurt had chosen to work in the fields after telling her grandfather that staff practice just wasn't helping him. Her grandfather grumbled, but upon Ilsa's advice, consented, reasoning that a hard day's work did a man's soul good after all. Liesel would often pause and watch them in the fields, and she couldn't help but pretend this was how it would always be.

By the time they were halfway through their third week at the vineyard, Bernd was pushing the hired hands hard to prepare for harvest. Any day, he would shout across the rows of vines, the grapes would be ready. And so Kurt and the hired hands had worked long hours every day so they could be ready when that moment came.

The noonday sun made Kurt's pale skin shiny and red, and on his first day, the heat had made him lightheaded. The other workers had teased him about his strange sensitivity to the sun, but they hadn't laughed for very long. Kurt was surprisingly adept at the field work he was given, despite never having done it before, and he labored hard. Even Bernd, after the first few days of work, had been forced to admit Kurt's worth as a worker. Liesel gloated quietly about this now as she made her way to Kurt.

"Liesel, don't keep him too long. The days are growing shorter, and we need this fruit gathered!"

Liesel rolled her eyes and nodded to her grandfather before handing her bucket of water to Kurt. Kurt shook his head in disbelief as Bernd continued walking down the row, shouting orders at anyone he could find.

"He has a lot of strength for an old man. Too much, actually. Shouldn't he be inside resting at his age?"

At this, Liesel had to laugh. "You wondered why I believed in magic when I came to the forest. Stories weren't the only things my grandparents procured in their travels." When Kurt gave her a quizzical look, Liesel leaned in and whispered, "Have you noticed they drink tea every night before bed?"

"Yes. So?"

"Have they ever offered their tea to anyone else?" Kurt thought about this for a moment before Liesel winked and added, "I saw my grandmother steep a long, strange root in her tea once when she thought I wasn't looking. I believe it came from the Far East as well. They just don't tell people about it. The town would assume it to be witchcraft if they knew."

"Well, is it?" Kurt prodded.

Liesel shook her head scornfully. "Not at all. It's just–"

"Liesel, I mean it. The boy needs to get to work!"

Liesel huffed as Bernd shouted at them again from the other side of the field, and Kurt gave the old man a baleful glare as he lifted the bucket and drank deeply from it again.

"He wasn't always like this," Liesel told him as he drank. It was only midday, but the air was unusually hot.

"I find that hard to believe." Kurt wiped his mouth and gave Liesel a doubtful look. "The way he orders you about makes it seem he thinks you incapable of any thought at all."

But she smiled and shook her head indulgently. "When I was little, he was stern, but he took me on the grandest adventures–"

She was interrupted by the sound of an approaching horse.

They were in plain sight of the house, close enough that it would seem awkward if they left or ignored the visitor, so Liesel reluctantly took the lead to greet the rider. She recognized him as a rancher that lived a few farms down the road. A bit younger than her father would have been, he was dirty, with a mop of graying black hair, wide-set eyes, and a very broad nose. Liesel thought she remembered him being widowed right before she left. As she approached him, Kurt followed and her grandparents came out as well.

"I know you were wanting another calf, Bernd." The man jumped down and walked back to the animal he had been leading on a rope. "I thought this one might be to your liking." He paused for a moment before asking, "Is that Liesel?"

"Yes on both accounts," her grandfather grunted. As Bernd went over to inspect the calf, the man did the same to Liesel. Kurt cleared his throat when the man's eyes lingered just a bit too long. Looking up, he finally seemed to notice Kurt for the first time.

"And who is this?"

Everyone froze, unsure of what to say. They had agreed to stay out of the town for a while to avoid being asked questions the curse wouldn't allow them to answer. Aside from the hired hands that lived on the vineyard and slept in the barn, this man was the first person they had seen since arriving. Finally, to avoid looking any more suspicious than they already did, Liesel blurted out, "My betrothed."

The man nodded and mumbled a greeting, but Liesel didn't miss the sudden fury in her grandfather's face.

"Will you all be at the Adler wedding?" Their guest finally looked at Liesel's grandmother.

"We haven't decided yet," Ilsa said in a strained voice. "The harvest is later coming than usual this year."

"You know, folks are starting to talk about you all up here alone," he said nonchalantly. "They want to send someone up to see what all the hiding is for."

Ilsa and Bernd exchanged looks before Bernd said, "The harvest looks to be unusually good. We're trying to keep pace. In a couple of weeks, we'll be done."

"But I think we will be at the wedding," Ilsa chimed in.

Seeming momentarily mollified, the man turned back to Bernd to discuss the calf, but Liesel got the feeling that the dissonance between Kurt and her grandfather that had been building since they'd arrived would be coming to a head as soon as their guest left.

"Liesel," Bernd sternly said once the man headed back down the road, "that was quick thinking on your part. But after this, I don't want to hear that nonsense again."

"Nonsense?" Liesel asked.

"I would hardly call a betrothal nonsense." Kurt took a step closer to Liesel.

"That's it!" Bernd threw down the calf's reigns and turned to Ilsa. "I'm through! I just can't pretend any longer. I can't act as if I'm allowing my granddaughter to go back and marry into a pack of dogs!"

"Because you were such a better choice for your wife, old man." Kurt sneered.

"I actually *worked* to change for my wife. I didn't just dance around breaking the spell when I felt like it!"

Seconds later, Bernd's nose was bloody, and Kurt was on the ground. Her grandfather had swept out his feet with the staff, and without hesitation, brought the stick down hard on Kurt's chest, knocking him back down as he tried to stand up. The pain was evident on Kurt's face as he rolled over and tried to get up again. Again, the staff came crashing down.

Without thinking, Liesel grabbed the nearest rock she could find and threw it at them. It missed but succeeded in getting their attention. When they finally looked at her, Liesel heard herself utter words she had never spoken to anyone in her life.

"I hate you both!"

With that, she turned and took off for the mountain as fast as her feet would carry her. She initially heard footsteps behind her, but her grandmother must have stopped them from following because Liesel remained alone for the length of her run. Still, she plunged on ahead as though evil spirits were at her heels.

It wasn't until she'd gone about ten minutes up the mountain path that she stopped. She couldn't go too far from Kurt and Johan, no matter how angry she was. Still, unsatisfied with the proximity to the path and all familiar landmarks, Liesel deliberately left the path and headed into the sparsely scattered trees until she found a large, flat, sunny rock to flop down upon.

Images of what could have happened kept flashing through her mind. Kurt could have lost control. Bernd might have broken one of Kurt's bones or worse. Despite the time that had passed, Liesel could remember exactly what death had looked like on her own parents' faces. She might go mad if she lost another loved one so senselessly.

Since they had come, Liesel had been aware that her grandfather didn't approve of Kurt. He had made it a habit of sending him disapproving glances every chance he got, and nothing Kurt could do was quite good enough for perfection. But she hadn't thought he would go so far as to forbid her from returning to the pack. Of all people, Bernd should have understood her need to help them. To fix, she thought darkly, what he and her grandmother had not. Because of their mistake, Liesel had made a promise. Somehow, she was going to keep it.

Liesel let her mind slip into the sounds around her, closing her eyes and simply soaking up the sun. She had learned to do so when her mother was ill and she was afraid. Bernd had actually been the one to teach her.

"When life gets hard, Leese," he had crouched down and pointed at a swift clinging to the side of a tree trunk, "just come up here, close your eyes, and remember that the good Maker does care. He wouldn't have made all this if He didn't."

Liesel did her best to concentrate now the way he had taught her all those years ago. When she did, she heard a brook trickling behind her. Birds on their journey south sang goodbye songs as the summer showed signs of aging. Air whistled through the thin branches, and a toad croaked to her left.

So relaxing were the sounds of nature, that Liesel had nearly dozed off when a rustle in the leaves behind her made her glance back. After a moment of looking, however, she saw nothing, so she turned back and closed her eyes once more. Just a moment later, whatever it was moved again.

Her second glance found her staring into the bright eyes of a lynx. Its pointed ears twitched, but nothing else moved as it crouched, staring her down. Liesel's body went cold as fear paralyzed her where she sat.

She had climbed the mountain nearly every day of her early life and never once had she seen one of the big cats. The neighbors had spoken of them stealing chickens, and parents warned their children that the big cats could sneak in and eat naughty children who didn't go to bed on time. But, Liesel had always thought, those were stories for people who didn't understand the mountain and its animals.

And now one was going to kill her. Sure enough, it began to crouch even deeper, when an arrow whizzed right past Liesel and straight into its heart. A second arrow followed, ensuring the great cat stayed down.

Liesel was still staring at the dead animal and catching her breath when she heard heavy footsteps pounding up the path. She turned to see a young man racing toward her, nocking a third arrow as he went.

"Are you hurt, Miss?"

It took Liesel a moment, but she realized that she recognized the man who was now standing over her, his eyes wide. Grown up or not, the red-bearded face was impossible to mistake.

"Manny!" Liesel scrambled to stand, but her knees still shook.

Her old friend stretched a large arm down to help her to her feet. "Liesel?" His mouth fell open. "What... When did you get back?"

In spite of her still-injured feelings, Liesel couldn't help smiling a little. "A few weeks ago."

"I haven't seen you in town. You must have snuck in and out if your presence was kept a secret this long." He ran his hand through his fiery hair and laughed. "Old Mrs. Klatsch would have told all of Weit by now if she'd seen you."

"She's still alive?" Liesel laughed with him. The old woman had been the town gossip and as old as dirt for as long as Liesel could remember. She had a nasty habit of creating rumors that were more than just a little false.

"Of course! Who else would guess at all the neighbors' goings-on?" Shaking his head, he studied her with a look of awe. "I have to say, Liesel, you've really grown up."

Liesel blushed. Though a wisp of unease floated up from her stomach at the way he was still staring, she couldn't ignore the subtle thrill of being noticed, either.

"You've changed, too, you know." She waved at him, suddenly feeling ridiculously shy. The ornery little boy she had once run the streets with was far from little now. Everything about Manny was massive. His arms, his legs, even his chest and neck looked as if someone had stuffed them full of rock and packed it firm. He towered over Liesel, and would probably stand even a bit taller than Keegan.

"Are you hunting for your father's shop?" Liesel pointed at the weapon he held.

"What? Oh, this. I had some time away from the shop, so I thought I might look for some small game. Things are slow this morning. And no, my father died three years ago."

"I am sorry," Liesel said. And for his loss, she was sorry, but not excessively so. Manny's father had been a drunk, but unlike her father, he had made it a habit of beating his children when he came home in the wee hours of the night, and his inflictions were visible for weeks after, never disappearing completely before a new set was doled out.

"What about you?" The young man shifted uncomfortably. "Is your family back to stay?"

"No," she said quietly, remembering suddenly why she had fled to the mountain in the first place. "No, I'm just visiting my grandparents before my wedding." It felt so strange to say, and when she did say it, his face fell just slightly.

"Ah... I see. So is your betrothed here, too?"

Liesel nodded.

Finally, he cleared his throat. "What are you doing up here alone anyway?"

"I miss the mountain," she said slowly, careful not to give too much away.

He snorted. "You of all people should know better than to run off by yourself. You're invisible from the trail."

"Did that stop us when we were young?" Liesel teased, hoping to deflect further questions.

Manny grinned. "No, I guess not. Can... Could I at least escort you down? You didn't seem too keen on handling him earlier." He pointed with his bow at the large cat lying still on the ground.

Liesel smiled as he picked up his prize. "Thank you. That sounds good."

Thankfully, he queried no more about Liesel's personal situation as they walked down. Only after he had brought her to her grandparents' porch did he ask whether or not they would be at the Adler wedding.

"My grandmother says we will be there."

Manny smiled more broadly this time and nodded before turning and heading back down the hill toward town. Liesel watched him go, feeling satisfied with the reunion until she recalled her initial reasons for running.

"Who was that?"

Liesel jumped. Kurt's voice was low and dangerous as he stepped out of the evening shadows. At the same time, her grandparents emerged from the house. Liesel was about to reply, when Bernd sent Kurt a scathing look and Kurt returned it. The hatred in their expressions rekindled her anger for both men, and instead of replying to Kurt, Liesel looked over to her grandmother instead, and spoke only to her.

"Manny Rinder walked me home." As she said it, Liesel didn't miss the dark anger that flashed across Kurt's face.

"Well, I suppose that was kind of him," her grandmother said a bit hesitantly. "What did he need to do that for?"

"A lynx found me, and he happened to be out hunting."

"Mercy! Are you all right?" Ilsa began looking for blood, but Liesel shrugged.

"He killed it before it could touch me. Now, if you don't mind, I am tired, and I want to go to bed." She began to walk into the house, but stopped. "Grandmother?"

"Yes, dear?"

"If they don't already know, please tell my grandfather and Kurt that if they try anything like that ever again, I will not be speaking to either of them for as long as I live."

Her family was silent as Liesel made her way back to her room and shut the door. And as soon as she was alone, large tears began to fall as sobs shook her body.

As much as she tried to push them out, the images of what could have been bombarded her once again. Her grandfather, still and white, covered in blood just as her father had been. Kurt, lying on the ground from a swift blow to the head with her grandfather's hateful staff.

And it wasn't just the fight that hurt Liesel. It was the betrayal.

Warin's fondness for strong drinks meant he had often spent many of his days and nights in the tavern, even when Amala had been alive. It hadn't been lost on Liesel, even from a young age, that her father wasn't at home much of the time. Even on Holy Days, he could often be found sleeping off a night of fun instead of going to the church with his family. Though he wasn't gone to the extent that he was later on in Ward, Liesel had grown to hate his ways from a young age. Even worse than his drinking, however, were his aspirations for Liesel.

It had all culminated the day she had arrived home from visiting her grandparents to announce she was going to follow their suit and see the world.

"Your fancies are pretty, as are you my dear," her father had slurred. "But it's best if you keep those hopes to yourself, Leese." When Liesel had demanded to know why, he had simply shrugged and patted her head. "Women don't need to see the world. You're pretty enough to land a smut with enough money to keep you and your little pack of mongrels fed and warm." He'd let out a raucous laugh. "Just like your mum."

Liesel had been so upset she'd turned right around and run all the way back to the vineyard in tears. As much as she loved her mother, Liesel had no desire or intention of ending up like Amala.

She had been so angry and ashamed of her tears, however, that she'd hidden out in the middle of a field, crying alone and slamming her fists on the ground in protest for hours.

It had been Bernd who had found her, finally quieted and staring silently out at the other fields below as her grandfather's men readied to leave for the day. Without saying a word, he'd simply seated himself on the ground beside her and waited until she was ready to speak. Liesel had never forgotten how comforting it had been, just sitting beside her grandfather in the dirt and knowing that, unlike her father, he was listening.

"Father says I can't see the mermaids," Liesel had finally mumbled in a sulky voice.

"Oh?" Bernd had asked. "And what does he want you to do instead?"

Liesel's young eyes had burned with tears once more. "He says I have to stay here and marry someone like him."

Before she knew it, she had been drawn up into her grandfather's strong arms. While she had sobbed like a baby, he'd cradled her fiercely, his arms holding her protectively.

"No, you won't, Leese," he had whispered with fire in his voice. "You are going to see those mermaids... and the rest of the world as well."

"But what about Father–"

But he was already shaking his head, his beard tickling her forehead. "I won't let them hold you here. The choice will be yours when the time comes. I promise."

And Liesel had believed him. They had sat like that until Ilsa had come looking for them.

Liesel had wondered as time passed if the promise had been an attempt from her grandfather to have revenge upon Warin for marrying his own daughter. And if she was honest with herself, she couldn't blame him. From that day forward, Bernd, and not Warin, had become her protector and her confidante. Ilsa had liked to tease that while other girls were learning to enjoy sewing and cooking, Liesel could always be found trailing along behind Bernd in the fields.

And now, after promising for all those years to allow her to choose her life, her grandfather's hatred for the one she had chosen to love cut deeper than any knife ever could. And Kurt's own hatred just made it worse.

"Liesel?" Kurt whispered from the other side of the door. Before he could say anything else, though, Bernd spoke from down the hall. Liesel couldn't make out what he said, but Kurt's retort was acidic. "If by some miracle we pull this off and break the spell, old man, don't expect me to ever bring her back here again."

Just when she thought her heart couldn't hurt more, Liesel felt it break.

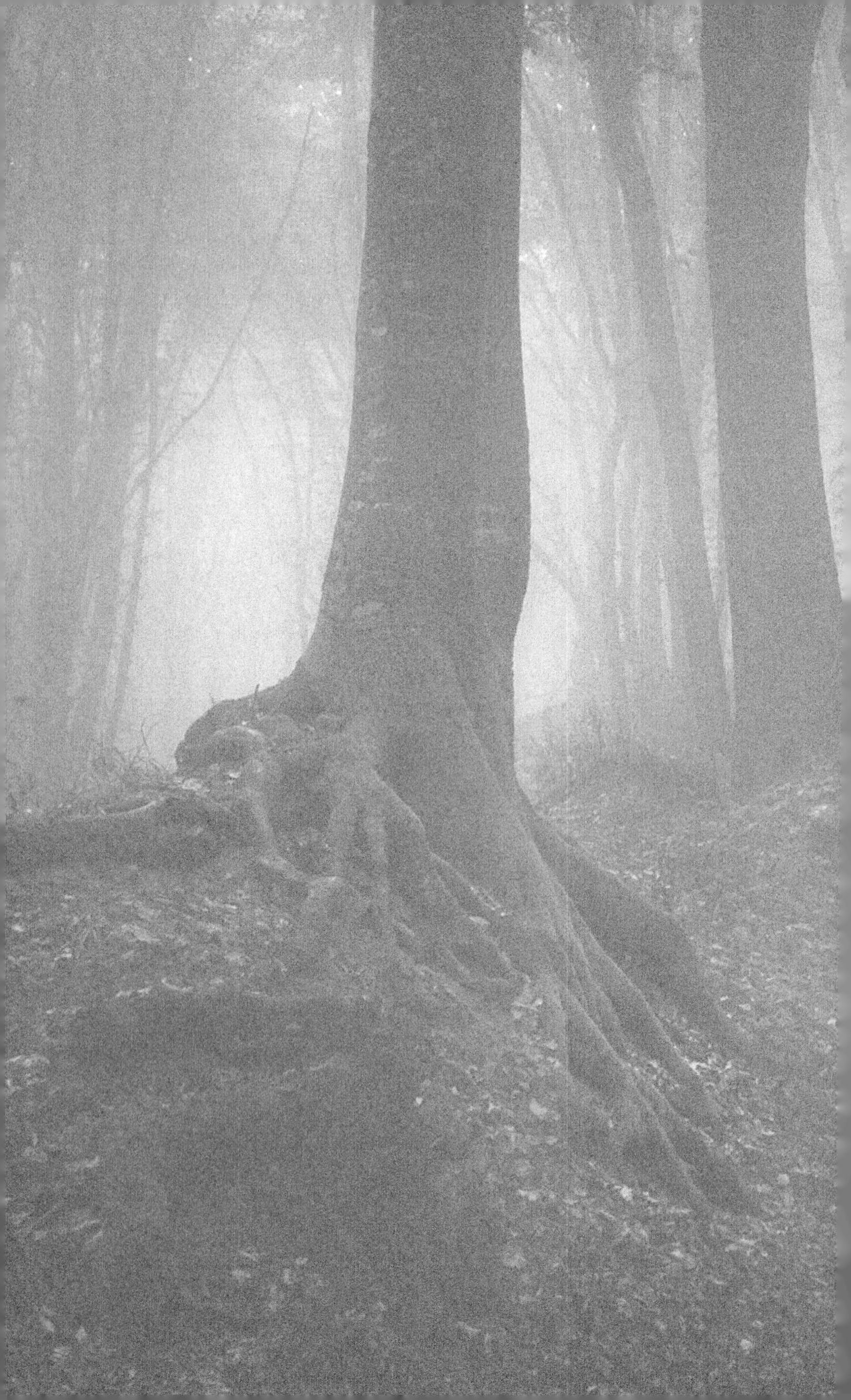

CHAPTER 22
DISSONANCE

True to her word, Liesel spoke to neither Kurt nor her grandfather after the fight. Days passed, and she ignored them so well she impressed even herself.

"Silence can feel empowering, Liesel," her grandmother warned, "but it accomplishes little."

"If I speak to either one of them, it will accomplish even less," Liesel retorted. "Because it won't be a word, but rather, a shout." And so, she continued to simply watch and wait.

There weren't any more fights, but there was no peace either. Kurt now disappeared with Johan instead of working in the fields, and only came back to the barn when it was time to sleep. Bernd worked as many hours as possible, and when he was inside did little besides shuffling around, mumbling that the young fool would never break the spell.

Though Liesel said nothing about it, she secretly feared her grandfather was right. Kurt had gone from training with Bernd every day to avoiding the family as much as possible, only joining them for supper when Ilsa insisted by shouting out the window that if he wanted fresh hay for his bed in the barn, he would be coming to eat at the table like a decent human being. Kurt would appear, but the meals were never enjoyable. Kurt glared at his food, speaking only to Ilsa when asked a direct question. Bernd stared his food down with a look nearly identical to Kurt's. He spoke to no one. The only one who seemed unaffected by the awkward silence of the room was Johan. Speaking as little as possible was in his nature.

It was during such a meal one night that Liesel decided she'd had all she could take of Kurt's new countenance. His sullen silence galled her, and she resolved to get him to speak that night, even if she had to do it out of spite. Guilt tried to nip at her even as she spoke the words, but she ignored her conscience and asked anyway.

"So who is the preferred bachelor of the dance this year?"

The question was directed to her grandmother, but Liesel could sense Kurt tense up as he bent over his food. Satisfied with some sort of reaction, she looked expectantly at Ilsa. Either Ilsa didn't care or didn't see what she was up to, because her answer was as even as ever. "Actually, I think it was Manny who won the draw this year."

"Are there any ladies he's rumored to favor?" Liesel continued casually.

"Not really." Ilsa raised one eye at Liesel, suddenly sounding suspicious. "Why?"

"It's always just fun to see a little competition." Liesel shrugged, sneaking another glance at Kurt.

His mouth had turned down in a way that assured Liesel he was angry. Good, she thought, trying to quiet the nagging rage of her conscience. Perhaps he would get angry enough to stop sulking.

Nothing more was said of the dance, but when Liesel excused herself to relieve herself after supper had ended, Kurt immediately excused himself as well, ignoring the warning glare her grandfather leveled at him. He quickly overtook her in the darkness, grabbing her hand and pulling her out of earshot of the cabin. Liesel could feel from his grasp that he wasn't fooling around. But then, she steeled herself, neither was she.

"What do you think you're doing?" Kurt's voice was low and tense.

"I haven't done anything." She glowered up at him.

"Oh, please. You've not spoken to me in days, and now you're thinking and teasing about *him*?"

Liesel jerked her hand out of his and glowered at him through the darkness, sure he could see her better than she could see him, but she remained silent.

"Liesel," he suddenly sounded exasperated, "I don't know what you want me to do!"

The question caught Liesel off guard. What did she want him to do? It took her a moment to find her voice, and when she did, much to her annoyance, it was very close to cracking.

"I wish you would at least *try* breaking the spell. I wish you would stop acting like a child around my grandfather. I want you to *fight* for me." Liesel stopped as her voice broke and a sob forced its way out.

Kurt didn't speak for a moment, but when he did, his voice was somber. "What do you think I've been doing since the day we met?" And with that, he walked away.

Liesel went to bed feeling ill that night. Heat rushed to her face, and her cheeks burned with embarrassment as she thought about his words over and over again. What had possessed her to be so blind, she wondered. While his avoidance of her family still exasperated her, she realized now that it was foolish to think that he would stop trying to break the spell just because of his squabble with Bernd. Perhaps she had assumed wrong when she'd believed he was only out hiding as a wolf. Even more guilt was heaped on her as she realized she had inadvertently called Kurt a coward to his face as well.

Liesel sobbed angrily into her bed as she wrestled with herself. No, Kurt's behavior certainly hadn't been perfect as of late. But that gave her no excuse to be cruel. And she had been vicious.

The next day was the Adler wedding, and it was quieter than ever around the big house. Only Ilsa seemed to speak, barking out orders at everyone she came across. "Fight or no fight," she had threatened Kurt and Bernd, "I won't have all of Weit thinking I let the men around here look like buzzards."

For the first time in his life, Kurt was given a sharp haircut and a set of clothes without holes in them. Liesel had nearly broken her silence when Ilsa was through with him.

The even cut of his short hair chiseled his face even more sharply, and made his golden-brown eyes stand out more. The dark shirt and pants he was assigned fit him becomingly as well, making his wiry figure look even taller. It took all of Liesel's strength not to gawk, so it was a good thing when Ilsa shooed Liesel to her own room to get ready.

"There, that's the first smile I've seen in days," Ilsa teased her as she sat back on her heels and looked up at her handiwork.

Liesel smiled a little more in spite of herself. The dress her grandmother had made for her was lovely. The deep green velvet skirt billowed out when she turned. The sleeves and collar were white, and the bodice was made of a darker green. It all made her red cloak look even more vibrant as she tied it over the top.

Despite the dress, her conversation with Kurt from the night before weighed heavily on her shoulders. Every time she tried to meet his eyes today, Kurt looked away. And as foolish as it seemed, she wanted so much to hear what he thought of her new dress.

She didn't miss the way his eyes widened when she walked out in the ensemble for the first time. That brought at least some satisfaction, but not enough to erase their sharp words from the night before. Kurt quickly looked away and mumbled something about getting the horses.

It was a long, silent ride to the wedding. Liesel tried to feel excited. She was going to see old friends, she reminded herself, and after the wedding, there would be dancing, food, and wine back at the bride's home. The family had already agreed that if someone asked where Liesel had been, they would answer that she had moved to Tag and apprenticed under a healer. The spell would at least allow for that much to be shared honestly.

The church was even busier that evening than it was on Holy Days. The service brought little joy to Liesel, though, despite her desire to be happy for the new couple. The bride was surrounded by her family and friends. Her mother cried and her father looked gruff and cleared his throat often. The groom looked as though he might pass out, but when he saw the bride, his fidgeting stopped and his eyes followed only her. And Liesel wanted it all so much that it nearly hurt.

She snuck glances at Kurt throughout the ceremony, but he gave nothing away, simply staring at the ground the whole time. Her grandfather studied the ceiling. Johan watched with vacant eyes, but Liesel expected nothing else from him. Ilsa was the only member of the family who managed to look reasonably happy and say all the right words of congratulations. In spite of Liesel's best efforts, it was impossible to even pretend she was enjoying herself.

After the ceremony was finally finished, Ilsa had sharp words for the lot of them. "Now remember, *all* of you," she turned and pointed her finger at them each in turn before entering the house where the festivities were being held, "unless you want questions that we can't answer, at least *try* to be civil to one another."

It wasn't long before the dancing began. Planks had been laid out on the ground to create a level dancing floor in the space behind the house. The dozens of people twirling arm in arm brought back with strange clarity the night of her one and only dance with Kurt. He had been so nervous. And yet, his eyes had shone with hope. That had been the first time she had been close enough to feel his magic.

Suddenly, Liesel longed for that once again, and in spite of all their recent fights, she suddenly felt a fierce hope rise up within her that Kurt would ask her to dance tonight. When she turned to him, however, all thoughts of dancing fled when she saw his blank look.

"Your betrothed hasn't asked you to dance yet?"

Liesel jumped at the man's voice. Turning, she saw Manny. He had trimmed his red beard, and his hair was combed back. He looked even bigger in his blue trousers and clean white shirt than he had a few days before. The expression on his face as he stared at Kurt was one of open disgust.

"Kurt isn't feeling well," Liesel stuttered, racking her mind for something to distract Manny from his obvious competitive curiosity. He had been that way as a boy as well, Liesel suddenly recalled, always needing to have the upper hand.

"Why don't you dance with Manny while Kurt recovers

himself," her grandmother said loudly. From the expression on Manny's face, he couldn't have been more pleased with the suggestion. Grateful to her grandmother for the distraction, Liesel stood and smiled.

"If you were my betrothed," Manny whispered as they headed toward the dance floor, "I wouldn't let you out of my sight even if I was on my deathbed."

Liesel gave a nervous laugh, wishing very suddenly to change the subject. She didn't have to worry, however, as the musicians picked up the pace, and everyone joined arms for a group jig.

As the jig began to move her into the arms of other partners, Liesel began to enjoy herself. The smiles and laughter of her old neighbors and friends were delightful as word spread that she was back. The music gave little time for chatting, but that was fine with her. The recognition in their eyes was enough. Manny soon muttered something about being tired of the movement, and excused himself to get a drink, and it wasn't long after that the partner dances began again.

After Manny left, Liesel realized with some guilt that she was having fun. The men continued to line up to partner with her dance after dance, and Liesel couldn't help but wonder if this was what her life would have been like had they never left. If she had been given the chance to be the Summer Maiden like her mother had, would she already have been married to one of the young men that now politely asked for a turn with her? How would he have proposed? Liesel imagined something romantic, perhaps out on her grandfather's vineyard, or on the porch under the stars. Anything would have been more romantic than the deal she had struck with Kurt.

Liesel didn't realize how long she'd been dancing until the church bell tolled the hour. Withdrawing her hands from those of another would-be suitor, Liesel tried to find Kurt. Guilt and disappointment warred within her when she saw that his chair was empty. Part of her felt sorry for allowing so many men to seek a dance, but a deeper part felt hurt that he hadn't even tried to cut in. There was no way his blank spell had lasted that long. Was he so angry with her that he was done with pursuing her completely?

"I need some air," Manny spoke into her ear above the din. "Keep me company?" Though the question was posed, he gave her no choice, grabbing her above the elbow and pulling her away from the crowd. Rather than make a scene, Liesel let him take her. After seeing Kurt's empty chair, she suddenly needed a bit of breathing room herself.

The night was clear, which meant they weren't the only two people in the gardens. Liesel made sure to stand far enough from her old friend, however, to ensure no one could suspect them of the same kind of engagements others in the garden were participating in. There was a bonfire a ways away that someone had lit, and a number of men stood around it smoking pipes. The sounds of the music wafted out of the yard toward them, but it was more muted out here. The branches of the apple trees were heavy with fruit, hanging down by their faces. Manny picked two and offered one to Liesel as they wandered. They walked without speaking for a few moments, but that suited Liesel just fine. When Manny finally did speak, however, his words were unexpectedly gentle.

"It wasn't the same after you left, Leese. Some said your father had gone seeking a fairy for your mother. Others said she'd died and he'd lost his mind. I never thought it was fair that they took you, though, no matter what your father sought."

Liesel stayed quiet.

"I always knew you'd be beautiful," he mumbled. "I just never imagined you'd be as beautiful as this."

Liesel felt herself blush. "That is... very sweet of you. But–" She made the mistake then of meeting his eyes. They were suddenly burning, reflecting the light of the distant fire.

"What do you see in him?" Manny's voice rose to match his eyes.

"He's a good man," she said, taking a step back, wondering suddenly how much of Manny's boldness was due to the drinks he'd been consuming. It was one thing to catch up with an old friend, but it was quite another to try and steal another man's betrothed when he wasn't there to defend himself. "He cares for his family and works hard to protect them."

"I could be a good family man if you gave me the chance," Manny grumbled.

"I think I am going back to find my family." Liesel turned.

"Wait, Liesel." He tried to take her hand, but she pulled free. Undeterred, he grabbed her arm just above the elbow and held fast. "Just listen to me!" His face was open, pleading, but his meaty hand gripped her arm so tightly it hurt. Pulling her close, his whisper grated on her ear. "I could love you if you gave me a chance!"

For the first time, Liesel smelled the ale on his breath. Memories of her father's drunken nights on the floor came to mind, and with the memories, her temper flared as well.

"Get off me!" She brought her free hand around and bloodied his nose upon contact. Without hesitating, she followed the first blow by bringing her knee up as hard as she could. The large man doubled over in pain. Liesel whirled around to run, but before she got three steps, he'd reached out and twisted her arm. She let out a cry of pain as he yanked her back to him.

A snarl ripped the air as a gray blur launched itself between them. Liesel was knocked to the ground but not nearly as hard as her attacker. Manny screamed as the wolf stood over him with hackles raised and teeth barred. Manny was drunk and cruel, but he wasn't a boar, and if Kurt killed him, Liesel knew it would haunt him for life.

She tried desperately to find her voice. "Kurt." Not loud enough. She wet her lips and tried again. "Kurt!"

The wolf continued to growl down at the man it held pinned, but the man flipped his head to stare in disbelief.

"*That* is *him*?" His voice cracked.

The wolf snapped his jaws just an inch from Manny's face, returning the drunk man's attention back to himself. Unfortunately, he drew the attention of others as well. Those milling in the garden who hadn't heard Liesel's cries of pain now heard the snarls of the wolf.

"Quick! Bring a light!" someone yelled. Liesel could hear others begin to echo him, and knew they only had moments before the entire wedding was after them.

"Kurt! Leave him be! We have to go!" She shouted now. The voices of men shouting grew closer as they searched the trees and bushes for the animal. Upon her shout, however, Kurt did not run, but instead, turned to her and snarled.

Still on the ground where she had been pushed, Liesel froze. Slowly, Kurt stepped off of the man and turned toward her. Liesel began to crawl backwards, pleading as she went, praying for him to remember. But his eyes remained glazed and his fur bristled as he crept closer. Inches from her face, Liesel could feel the heat from his muzzle. His growls vibrated in her chest, and his red gums seemed to grow larger as he curled his lips back.

"Please," she whimpered. "Remember who I am."

A howl interrupted her pleas. Liesel turned to see Johan hidden in the shadow of the house, still howling at his friend. To her great relief, Kurt began to retreat, slowly at first, and then he broke into a run, following Johan. As soon as she could get her legs to work, Liesel was up and running after them.

"So that's what it is!" Manny yelled from behind her. She could hear the people gather around him as he still sat on the ground. "She's cursed! That wolf has cursed her!"

Liesel rounded the corner of the building to find Johan and Kurt back in human form. Kurt was breathing hard, his hands on his knees, but Johan was already taking off in the direction of the stable where they had left their horses. Liesel nearly collapsed with relief when she saw that they were both in their right minds, but the look Kurt gave her when their eyes met was doleful. She couldn't think of anything to say as Johan returned with the horses.

"How much did they see, Johan?" Kurt asked, still not breaking his gaze with Liesel.

"Just enough to give spirit back to old bedtime tales. I set fire to one of the trees to buy us a few extra minutes just in case," Johan muttered as he handed them the reigns of their respective horses. "But we need to go now."

"Go?" Liesel looked first at Johan and then at Kurt. "No... No, I'm not ready to go! I can't!" Her breaths began to come in and out too fast, and the world no longer looked exactly level. "I'm not ready to live without the sun!" Liesel knew her words were hysterical, and her voice rang with an odd pitch, but all she could think about was accepting the life she had been pretending didn't exist for the last few weeks.

"We only have three days," Kurt said. "I was hoping tonight..." his voice trailed off as he watched her sink to the ground and fall to pieces.

How had she lost such track of time? Liesel sat in a daze, tears streaming down her face as Kurt and Johan gently lifted her onto her horse. Somehow, she managed to stay upright, though she wasn't sure how. More shouts rang out as the crowd drew near, but all she could think about was leaving. She would never see her grandparents again. She would never be able to tell her grandfather she was sorry. She would never rest in her grandmother's embrace. She would live a life without sun, watching Kurt lose himself to the animal, and dying before she was gray.

"Liesel!" Kurt's voice broke through her reverie. He was calling to her over the din of approaching shouts. Liesel came to her senses just in time to see the mob encircle them. Torches had been lit, and weapons of all sorts had been made out of farming tools, whatever could be found on such short notice. Liesel winced at the scythes in particular as it dawned on her just how many people now surrounded them. After frantically searching, she finally found the distressed face of her grandmother hidden deep in the rowdy crowd. But where was her grandfather?

"After all these years..." one man stepped forward with a torch. Liesel thought she recognized him as one of the city council members. She had been good friends with his daughter when they were little. "You've returned to bring a curse on us?"

Before Liesel could even think of an answer, a small popping sound was heard. Immediately, the circle began to fill with a thick, noxious smoke. People cried out as it filled their eyes and burned their noses. Liesel briefly had time to recall her grandfather telling her about such oddities he'd found in the east, when a rough hand grabbed her horse's reins.

"Liesel!" her grandfather's voice was urgent.

"Grandfather!" Liesel's eyes grew even wetter as she began to cry in earnest.

Gently, he took her face in his hand. "Help him find his peace!" His voice was low and compassionate. "You were right, and I'm sorry for being so hard on you. You're his only hope now... so go!" With that, he slapped her horse and she was off.

It was surprising how fast the two horses and the wolf made their way through the coughing, gagging mob. As they galloped off into the night, Liesel turned to look behind her once more, but she could see nothing above the smoke balls her grandfather had lit, and the torches enveloped in the thick cloud of smoke that continued to cling to the ground.

THEY DIDN'T STOP RUNNING for a long time and then only long enough for the horses to rest before taking off again. Thankfully, the moon had come out, and it made the world around them glow blue. Liesel was aware of the concerned glances Kurt kept throwing her way, but she didn't meet his eyes. She couldn't believe they had failed. As much as she'd felt the pessimism rise up within her during their time at the vineyard, she only now began to realize how much hope she'd clung to.

Instead of following the road, they moved into the wood's fringe as soon as they could see it, continuing the rest-run pattern even after the sun rose. Liesel knew she was hungry, but she really didn't care. She drank when Kurt told her to at brooks and streams, but not of her own choosing.

By the time they finally stopped the next night, she still hadn't been able to speak a word. Kurt built a fire, and Johan took the first watch while Liesel sat and simply stared at the tongues of flame licking the darkness. She was aware that Kurt sat across from her, but she didn't look at him. After a long stretch of silence, he finally spoke in a low voice.

"I am aware that I'm being a hypocrite, saving you from a fate with him only to force you into one with me." His voice broke a bit. "I just don't know what else to do. I don't want to hurt you. But I can't let my people die. We tried, Liesel. We did our best." With that, he stood. "I'm going to get some firewood. I'll be back," he mumbled.

"Don't let his sense of duty fool you." Johan, back in his human form, sat on the log Kurt had just left. "He hasn't been the same since the first time you left. Tortured himself for years over what to do about you." Staring down at his pipe as he lit it, he quietly added, "And don't mistake his sense of duty for indifference. He could never be indifferent about you."

Liesel didn't reply, simply continuing to stare into the flames as though they held the answers she was seeking. As the hour drew late, though, she began to grow fidgety. A look at Johan confirmed her suspicions.

"Should've been back by now." Johan stood. Liesel stood with him, although she wasn't sure why. It wasn't as if she could be of any help. Johan disappeared into the thick brush, but Liesel began to pace.

The longer they were gone, the worse she felt. Finally, she heard two sets of human footsteps approach. "Thank goodness you're back!" she said as she began to push through the leaves. Instead of seeing Kurt or Johan on the other side of the brush, however, Liesel was shocked to find herself staring right into the face of Lothur.

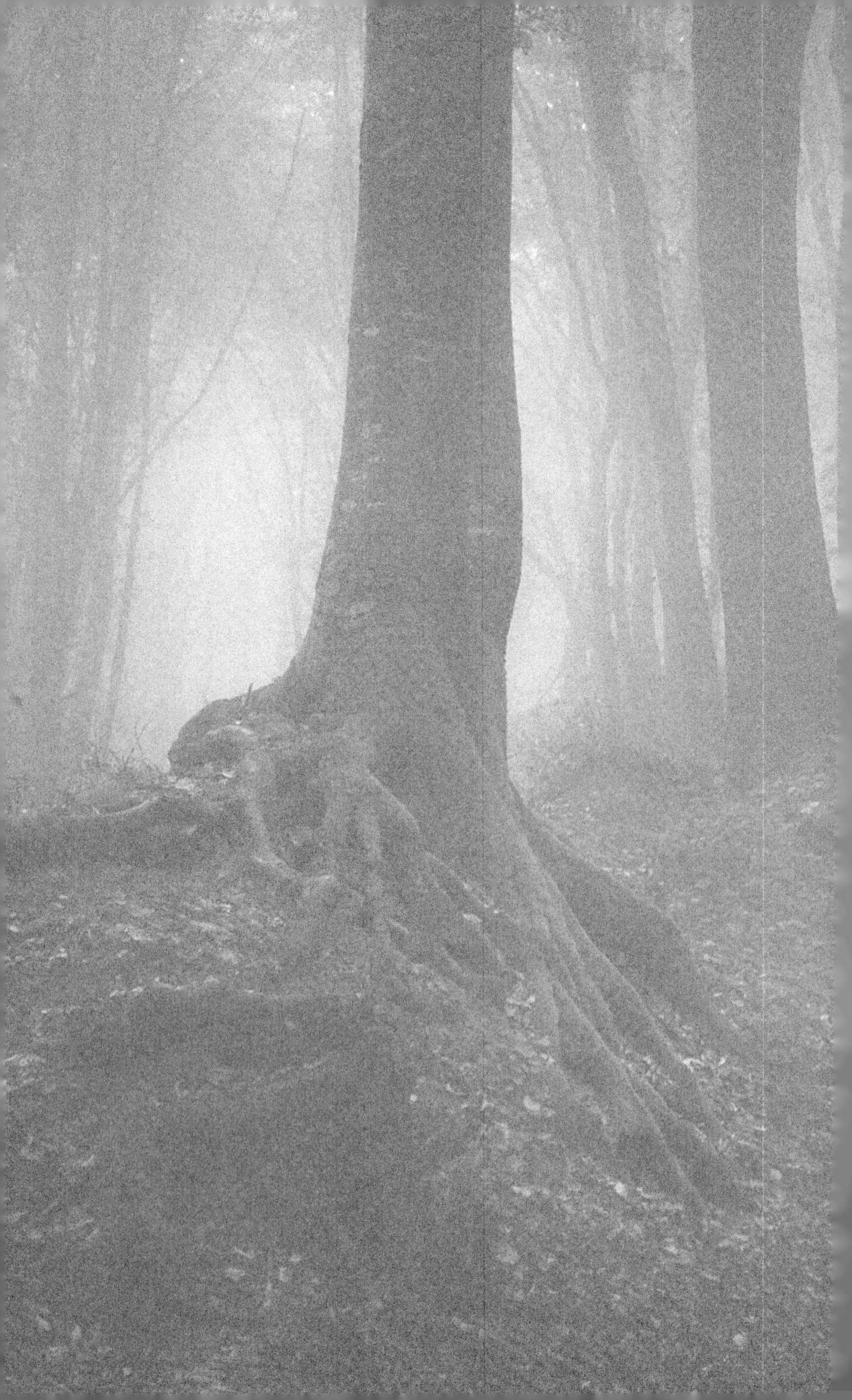

CHAPTER 23
MORNING GLORY

It was a long moment before either of them spoke. Liesel thought about running, but dispelled the thought before it was even complete. She knew too well how fast the wolves were.

"Liesel," Lothur said, then paused. He seemed almost nervous. "Thank goodness you said something. I might have turned had I thought you an animal."

Liesel was silent.

"If you'll just come with me," he continued, "I can escort you safely back to the town."

Still, she hesitated. But the more she considered it, the more she realized she had no choice. Kurt and Johan were gone, and she had no way to defend herself. Finally, she nodded and followed him back through the forest.

It felt like a death march, the way she imagined a criminal might feel while being walked to the gallows. Liesel had never seen a hanging. Amala had been adamant such events were no place for young ladies. Still, she'd heard enough from her friends who had attended to know what went on at one. And she could only feel that her own noose was waiting for her back in that long log cabin.

Lothur let her stew quietly until they ran into a few other men dragging a disgruntled Johan in tow. He was in wolf form, snarling and wrenching his body from side to side, but their ropes held, and they pulled him like a common, disobedient pet. But where was Kurt?

She didn't have to wonder for long. Keegan soon stepped into the clearing followed closely by Kurt. Neither of the brothers looked very happy. Keegan kept sending his older brother wary glances, but all Kurt did was glare at his uncle. Liesel quickly made her way over to Kurt, who hugged her tightly to his side away from Lothur. As they began to walk, she wondered why he didn't use his authority to tell his uncle to let them go. From the looks he kept sending to Keegan, however, all she could guess was that they weren't simply being escorted back to the town. Something else was amiss.

After about an hour of walking, the group reached the southern edge of the town. As they moved, Liesel decided that something was most definitely different. Instead of staring at her silently as they had the first time she'd visited, the townspeople now avoided her gaze completely. Not one person made eye contact as she walked through the streets. They looked away as though they were... guilty. It sent a cold shiver up her spine. They had known she was being forced to marry their pack leader the last time they'd seen her. What had changed?

"Where's Father?" Kurt asked as soon as the door was shut back in the cabin. Lothur excused the guards before fixing him with an unnerving stare and answering, "Your father fell sick soon after you left."

Kurt paled. "I need to see him."

Lothur looked as though he were about to say no, but Keegan stepped forward. "I'll take him."

Lothur leveled a suspicious stare at his youngest nephew. "I need to be sure you won't be—"

"We've already come this far." Keegan shook his head. "You needn't worry, Uncle."

After studying him carefully for a long moment, Lothur finally nodded, and Keegan motioned his brother down the hall. Their uncle turned to Liesel and Johan finally with an apologetic look.

"I'm sorry we had to meet again in this situation. It's just that something has changed."

"We were coming back—" Liesel tried to speak, but Lothur held up his hand.

"I know, and I'm not angry. I understand you were looking for your own answer to the spell, and that I admire. But now that you're back, I need to make sure you remain here for the time being. Now, Liesel, you look exhausted."

Liesel hadn't felt tired until he mentioned it. But as soon as the words left his mouth, she realized she was close to fainting. It had been two days since she'd gotten any decent sleep, and suddenly it was as if she could hardly bear to stand any longer.

Lothur caught her as she swayed, and much to her chagrin, he had to support her as he led her down the hall to her room. Inside, she was screaming and crying to be released so she could go find Kurt, but her body would have none of it. It wasn't long before she was dead asleep.

When Liesel awoke, she had no way of telling how long she'd been asleep. The inky blackness through her window told her that it was night. No fire had been lit, nor had any candles been. Groggily, she pulled herself out of bed and, holding her hands out before her, she made the slow trek to the door. It was locked.

Just as the lock caught, however, she heard soft footsteps outside. Liesel scrambled through the dark to step beside the door so that she could still hear, but wouldn't be immediately visible if someone opened it. Fears raced through her as she stood there, heart pounding and breaths coming too fast. Where was Kurt? And Johan? And why was everyone being so secretive?

All of Liesel's hope of breaking the spell had dissipated as they'd escaped Weit. Now, Liesel thought miserably, she would be grateful to simply be reunited with Kurt for the wedding. Locked in a dark room without an inkling as to why, however, made even that dream seem vain.

Whomever was in the hall walked up to her door and stood there silently, as if listening. Liesel held her breath and wondered if she should risk jumping back in the bed and pretending to sleep. It didn't matter, though, because the listener eventually walked away. Liesel let out a huge breath.

The door rattled and clicked open. The figure turned to Liesel and clamped a hand firmly over her mouth. Whoever it was had known exactly where she was hiding. As she struggled to suck in the air for a scream, a rough whisper was breathed into her ear.

"If you make a sound, my uncle will hear, and you will never make it out alive."

It took Liesel a long moment to recognize Keegan's voice and an even longer moment to process his warning. She wasn't sure she could trust the intentions of Kurt's younger brother, but dealing with his uncle would be decidedly worse. Reluctantly, she finally nodded, and he carefully let her go.

He surprised her then by taking her hand and leading her from the room. She expected him to light a candle, but instead they walked in the darkness, and it was all Liesel could do to keep herself upright and to avoid bumping into the walls. Keegan made no sounds as he moved through the darkness.

After what felt like a century to Liesel, she heard the unmistakable click of another door. Since no moonlight moved through the thick trees, it was nearly as dark outside as it had been in the house. Liesel was amazed and frightened at how quickly she had forgotten the true darkness of the forest. She gripped Keegan's hand tightly as they moved, for she could see nothing distinguishable, not even her own hand. After walking a brief distance from the house, they stopped and she felt herself lifted onto a horse. Once she heard Keegan alight his, her horse's reins were tugged forward and she allowed him to lead her without question.

As they rode in silence, the dark slowly began to lift. Liesel hardly noticed, though, for she felt sick trying to imagine where Kurt could be. If they were sending her away in secret, which she knew Kurt must have had a hand in, something must have gone wrong. The future Kurt had discussed only an hour before his disappearance had still involved both of them. If she wasn't going to their wedding, which she couldn't imagine would be taking place so far from the town they were leaving behind, where was she going? Where did that leave him? Liesel opened her mouth to ask, when her eyes rested on the still form of the most terrible creature she'd ever seen.

Her eyes, though not clear, had adjusted well enough to the shadows to see that the creature was at least twelve feet long where it lay stretched upon the forest floor. It lay just a short distance from their horses and looked like a wolf upon first glance.

But the longer Liesel stared at it in the dim light of the woods, the less recognizable it appeared. It had gray fur like a wolf, and the fangs sticking out of its mouth were nearly as long as her hand. Still, the creature appeared almost... human. And not just human, but woman-like. Its torso extended out abnormally in the front, and the animal's hips were wider than those of any wolf Liesel had ever seen. Likewise, its front limbs were outstretched like arms reaching, rather than legs running. The snout was much too short, which made its fangs look even more grotesquely out of place. Leaning forward to further examine it, she then noticed an arrow protruding from the back of its neck.

"So that's where she went." Keegan's words were nearly too quiet to hear.

Cold bumps raised up on Liesel's arms. "Keegan," she began in a low voice, but he'd already turned and had begun to lead their horses away. "What hap—"

"Don't!"

The force behind his words surprised Liesel, and he turned to glare at her with a look she had never seen on his young face before. Something instinctive warned her not to press any further, despite her morbid curiosity. For a long moment, the young man looked dangerous as his nostrils flared and his neck tightened, and as she decided she had no desire to deal with a wolf at that moment, Liesel swallowed her questions and nodded faintly before he began to lead their horses again.

They stayed quiet for a long time before he finally muttered something about that part of the woods being full of strange creatures. Liesel rolled her eyes at the obvious lie but chose not to push the subject. Instead, she chose to ask the question that had been burning in her mind since she'd awakened.

"Keegan," she whispered hesitantly. When he didn't respond,

she tried again. "Keegan! Where is Kurt?" Her only answer was a soft shushing sound, which for some reason annoyed her greatly. Feeling for the reins, she found them and jerked them out of his hands. She could hear his horse stop a few feet ahead of hers. "I am not going any farther until you tell me what is going on!"

Keegan finally gave a small sigh. "If I explain while we move, will you give me back the reins?"

Liesel sent him a skeptical look, which she hoped he could see through the darkness, but finally acquiesced.

He took the reins again, and when they began to move once more, his whisper was nearly inaudible. "My uncle has found a way to break the curse."

"Isn't that a good thing?"

Keegan paused before answering. "I thought he was doing something great, sacrificing the good of one for that of the pack."

An involuntary shiver moved down Liesel's spine as Keegan's words to Kurt came back to her from that first morning in the cabin. *She believes in magic! She could end it once and for all if she was willing!* What did her belief in magic have to do with sacrifice?

"But," he continued, "after witnessing what he truly meant to do to you, I couldn't do it. Harming you would kill Kurt, human or not."

Liesel swallowed hard as she tried to imagine what Lothur might have been planning. But then, she shuddered, perhaps it was better that she didn't know. But that still didn't answer her question.

The early gray of morning finally began to peep in earnest through the great trees that surrounded them, which meant they were close to the edge of the forest. Liesel didn't recognize this part of the wood, however. They were going in a different direction than she'd ever ventured in, north. As the light grew, so did her ability to read the terror written all over the young man's face. He still wasn't telling her something.

"Where is Kurt?"

Keegan just looked at the ground and shook his head like a whipped dog.

"Keegan." Liesel worked to make her voice more authoritative while still whispering. "Where is he?" As she spoke, they broke through the trees, and the golden rays of the sun momentarily blinded her.

"This is as far as I can take you." Keegan held out her horse's reins. Liesel took them as if in a daze.

"I'm free?" she whispered. Keegan nodded as he turned his horse back toward the forest. "But what about the spell?" she called after him.

"Kurt says it's no longer your responsibility. Because he's first in line, he has the authority to grant you that much." He paused at the edge of the woods. "He wanted you to see the world." For the first time, Keegan brought his eyes up to meet hers. They were far too sad for a man his age. "My brother is sacrificing a lot for you," he said with a solemn voice and pleading eyes. "Don't waste the life he's given up for you."

In a daze, Liesel gazed out at the serene scene before her as Keegan slipped back into the forest. She was free. After fighting for seven years, she was no longer bound to the destiny she'd feared so much. As she blinked in the sunlight, she tried to comprehend that she was going to drink it in every morning after this.

She would never have to wake up again dreading the gloomy gray of the deep woods. She would see the ocean. Her grandparents could see her grow and marry, and she could show her children the world without dreading the day they became the wolf.

Her children. But not Kurt's children. It seemed highly unlikely to Liesel that Lothur would truly break the curse, no matter how convinced he was that he'd discovered the cure. Instead of gaining their freedom, Kurt's children would never see the ocean from afar. They would never know what it meant to step out onto a road and follow it just to see where it went. Kurt's children would be sentenced to a life of shadowy magic in a dark forest without hope. His sons would have to abduct their wives, girls with families and futures. And Kurt would be left to drift away.

He would marry some unsuspecting girl like the baker's daughter, Karla, who would be haphazardly kidnapped for him after Liesel's absence was discovered. And knowing Kurt, he would never tell his new wife about how the wolf would take his mind.

He would simply let it eat away at him, wasting away slowly until he was as rigid and cold as his father. Her beloved friend and protector would be no more.

Liesel looked to the west at the contour of her beloved mountain. Freedom was hers. All she had to do was stretch her hand out and take it.

And, she thought, live life as her grandparents had, knowing her happiness had cost an entire village its chance of escape. Forever the wolves would howl for her, and with guilt she would think of the boy who had loved her more than life.

Without another glance at the morning glory, Liesel turned her horse and pressed back into the heart of the woods. She prayed only that she could make it in time to stop the wedding.

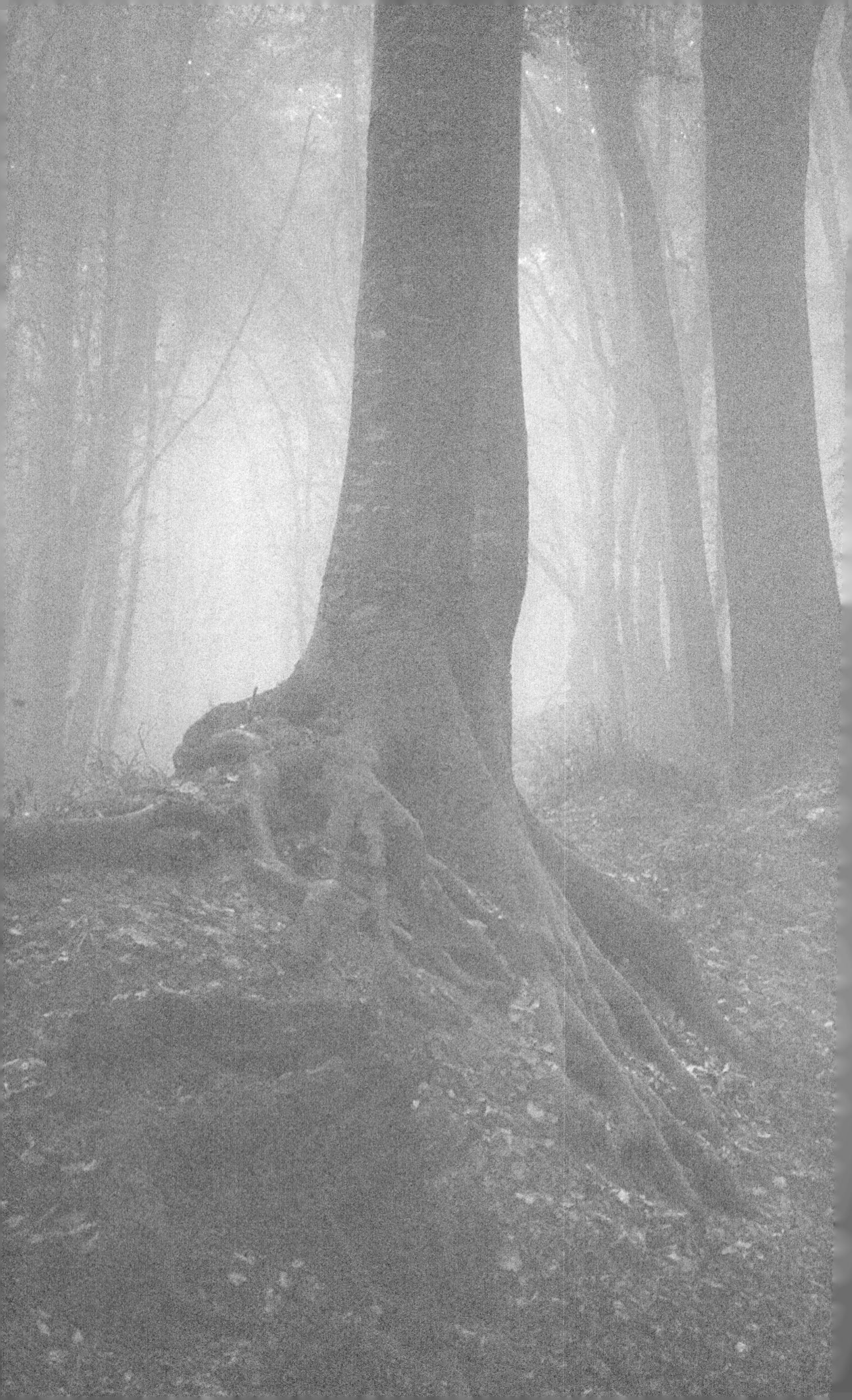

CHAPTER 24
CHOICES

Pressing her horse hard, it took Liesel less than an hour to cover the distance Keegan had taken her. Thankfully, the horse seemed to know its way home. She had to slow, though, as she neared the village town, praying no wolves would accidentally stumble upon her while she was alone. Her prayers were answered when she spotted Lora in her human form, perched on top of a stump on her beloved hill. Liesel thought about calling out, but decided against it, climbing off her horse instead and scampering up the knoll.

Despite her anxiety, Liesel's heart went out to the girl as she got closer. Instead of the bright hope that had been on her face the last time they'd spoken, Lora now looked shaken and terrified and even paler than usual, if that were possible.

"Lora," Liesel called softly as she approached. The last thing she needed was for Lora to change forms because she was frightened. "Lora, it's Liesel!"

The girl turned toward her, tear-streaked cheeks ashen and eyes puffy. They grew large, however, when she recognized her. "What are you—"

But Liesel gave her no time for queries. "Where is Kurt?"

"You shouldn't be here!" Lora shook her head a little too emphatically, which irritated Liesel. She didn't have time for an argument.

"I am not leaving! Now where is he?"

Lora studied her with troubled eyes before getting up and climbing noiselessly down the hill. Liesel tried to follow her just as quietly, but despite her best efforts, Liesel's steps seemed ridiculously loud as twigs snapped and leaves crunched beneath her feet. They wound their way around the town and snaked through the trees behind the cabin before coming upon another knoll a few hundred paces away. Liesel's courage nearly failed her as she began to make out muffled snarls and yelps that grew louder as they walked. Lora led them into a large thicket that bordered the hill. Inside the thicket, carved into the side of the hill, was a door.

"He's not himself," Lora whispered, tears gathering at the corners of her eyes again. "Keegan was going to keep it a secret the way Uncle had told him to, but when he saw Kurt, he just couldn't do it." She paused before unlocking the door. "When he comes to, he's not going to be pleased to see you." She shuddered. "He's going to be so angry with me!"

"Let me worry about that." Liesel tried to make her smile confident as she laid a hand on the girl's shoulder. "Thank you."

With a quick nod, Lora was gone. Liesel briefly mourned the fact that Lora would have been a wonderful sister, had things ever gone as they were supposed to. But the time for wishful thinking was over. Without even the slightest idea as to what she was doing, Liesel gathered her skirts and opened the door.

It was so heavy that she'd barely squeezed through before it slammed shut behind her. The drop-off into the underground space was deeper than she'd expected, and the misstep sent Liesel sprawling onto the dirt floor of the small cavernous room.

The ferocity with which the wolf lunged at her was shocking. Liesel shrieked and fell back into the wall. When she finally realized she was still alive, Liesel dared to look up. The wolf continued to rush at her, but as her eyes adjusted to the dim light, provided by a single torch hung high on the wall, Liesel saw that Kurt was chained around the neck. The chain had been somehow mounted into the wall so that there was no way for it to work loose. That it had been done with magic, Liesel could only guess.

As her eyes continued to adjust, Liesel's heart broke in two.

Kurt's fur was bloodied all over from where the chain dug into his body from his savage lunges. His eyes were glazed over, and his teeth snapped with surprisingly loud clicks.

"Kurt?"

The wolf paused for a moment before launching an even more vicious attack, snapping and snarling faster and harder than before. Liesel tried to get her shaking legs to stand, but when she finally did, it seemed to agitate him even more. She knelt back down so that she was curled up with her knees to her chest, her face at the same level as his. Her mind felt as fuzzy as the light around her, making it hard to focus. The dizzying magic she felt every time she was especially close to him seemed to double in the enclosed space.

"I'm sorry," she began, saying the first thing that came to mind. "I'm sorry for treating you the way I have lately, for being angry. I know it's not your fault." She swallowed hard, knowing that if she stopped talking she might not have the courage to start again. "None of this is your fault. And it was never you that I blamed. I just... I just wanted to be the one to choose. I've been forced into this forest... this life time and time again, and every time I tried to choose a new path for myself, I lost everything."

The wolf continued growling, but his attacks had turned to pacing, and the fur on his back no longer bristled. For the first time, Liesel dared to peer into the wolf's eyes. It was so strange to see their golden-brown depths resting in the face of bloodied silver fur.

"I suppose you never had a choice either. You were assigned me in a way, assigned to lead these people." She paused, as the truth of her ramblings sank in, filling her with an even deeper understanding and gratefulness for what he had done. "And for some reason, you loved me. You were good to me without reason, even when I wasn't good to you."

Liesel felt her face burn as she thought back to the many days of stony silence she'd inflicted upon him in her anger. The hurt had been there in his eyes when she'd returned with Manny, and then when she'd ignored his pleas for her attention. "But just so you know," her voice shook, "I choose you now." She paused and then added in a whisper, "And I'm not leaving until you're safe."

The wolf no longer paced, but had frozen in the center of the damp cave. The expression he wore was very human, a look of excruciating pain. Before she could utter another word, the animal dissolved into a cloud of silver dust, and in its place knelt a man. He groaned as he tried to get up, but Liesel hurried to his side just in time to push him back down.

"Rest." She tried to soothe him as he moaned again. The pain in his moan was raw and vulnerable like a child's. As she laid one hand on his head and another on his back, Liesel realized that most of the sticky residue on her hands wasn't sweat, but blood. Warily, her eyes traced the bloodstains down his limbs.

"You..." he gulped, his voice coming out like sand. "You have to go."

"I'm not leaving you again."

He stopped struggling and stared into her eyes. Slowly, he lifted a hand from the ground where he still knelt and traced the contour of her face with trembling fingers. She turned her face into his shaking hand and he pulled it near. His breaths were labored and came out in rasps, and the sweaty, raw sheen of his pale skin showed through the shreds of what used to be his shirt. He said nothing, but the look in his eyes was immeasurable. Their moment was short-lived, however, as the door behind her opened with a loud creak.

"Right on time," said a still, serene voice, as if finding the young woman in a secret cave was the most natural thing in the world.

"You don't have to do this!" Kurt shook his head, gasping for air between his hoarse words.

"She's a good girl," Lothur said, continuing to stare at Liesel in the same quiet, unnerving way he'd looked at her the first time they'd met. "She'll come."

Kurt shook his head vehemently. "I told you! We found another way to break the curse!"

"I heard you the first time. Unfortunately, however, it seems that your way isn't as... expedient as mine."

"Keegan didn't seem to approve of your way, whatever it was." Liesel frowned at him.

"If you don't mind, Liesel, I think Kurt needs to rest. In the meantime, I would like to discuss this at length with you. I think you'll want to hear what I have to say." Lothur gestured at the door. "If I may have a word in private?"

"No!" Kurt tried to yell, but his voice was nearly gone.

Liesel turned back to him and gently took his face in her hands, pulling him so their foreheads touched. "You've done everything you can to free me," she whispered. "Now it's my turn." With that, she stood and did her best to ignore his screams of protest as she followed his uncle out the door.

They didn't talk on their way back to the cabin, but she studied the lean man as they walked. He wore the long coat she'd always seen him in, but the blood on one of his sleeves told her he'd indeed gotten his hands dirty. She had no intention of trusting him, but if he did have a way to break the curse, she would simply have to tread carefully. There wasn't time for anything else.

"Tea?" He held up an empty cup as she seated herself on a stool at the table. Liesel shook her head. With a shrug, he poured himself a cup and took a seat. As he did, Liesel felt another wave of unease. Kurt still didn't have complete control over the pack, which meant Garrit must still be alive. But his malady must have been great if he hadn't interfered with any of Lothur's plans.

"How is Garrit?"

"Unfortunately, your little adventure took more of a toll on Kurt's father than I think Kurt expected. He hasn't spoken since reading Kurt's letter." The brief shadow that passed over Lothur's face was the only hint that he might know about the Schnartchen flower. He said nothing of it, however. "And before you ask, Johan is well. Skulking around somewhere, I'm sure, licking his wounds." Liesel must have looked fierce, because Lothur snorted and waved a hand at the window. "Only his pride has been wounded, I assure you. My brother gave him an unusual amount of freedom after his daughter disappeared. He's not used to being told what to do."

Liesel considered that. She was a bit distracted, however, by the intensity with which Lothur studied her as he stirred his tea.

"Why is Kurt bound so tightly?" she finally asked, shifting uncomfortably under his scrutinizing gaze.

"Just a precaution. It's an unfortunate part of this life, but for his own safety and the safety of others, we couldn't let him run about the town in such a state. That cave was a gift of our ancestor. He knew by nature that we would need it."

"But he will be let out soon?" Liesel pressed, ready to use her cooperation as a bargaining tool if need be.

But his uncle just shrugged again. "Of course. As soon as he's calmed down, he will be freed." He stopped stirring his tea and raised a brow. "Does that not suit you?"

"I want to know why he was upset." Liesel mustered her courage and sat as tall as she could, narrowing her eyes at him. "And why you locked me up."

"For that, I must apologize. Kurt rather took us by surprise. You don't know the territory the way we do, but your little party had wandered back onto our land. As you know, the month is almost up, and we feared you might run if your companions caught wind of our scent. As for Kurt's agitation, I have a bit of a longer story to share. Garrit was more than disappointed when you left, but *I* understood your desire completely."

Liesel frowned at him in surprise, and Lothur held up his hands.

"Honest, I do. I don't know if Kurt mentioned it, but I've been searching to break the spell my entire life. So when you left and Garrit became indisposed, I was free to do some of my own searching, something my brother had never allowed." Lothur reached into his coat and produced the little green journal.

"The people of Ward want this spell lifted as much as my people do, so it wasn't hard to persuade them to find an enchantress, one who reads the ancient tongue written here." He pushed the little book toward Liesel, who took it hesitantly.

She flipped it open again the way she'd done with Kurt. This time, however, there were new notes scribbled into the margins. To conceal her reaction, she kept her face down as she skimmed the pages. "Did you find it?" she asked.

"We did."

Unable to help herself, Liesel looked up. She'd never seen Lothur smile, and she found that the slight grin he wore was disconcerting.

"So why was Kurt angry?"

"Kurt loves you." Lothur fixed his dark eyes on her and leaned forward, a new intensity in his low voice. "He would do anything to keep you safe. Actually, he already had when he sent you away this morning, despite the needs of his pack. But I knew you would return," he continued, "because you love him as well. And you have a good heart. You couldn't have the deaths of these people on your conscience."

"What do you want?" Liesel quit fiddling with the journal and leaned back. She was tired of games.

Another small smile formed on Lothur's thin, pale lips. "As I said, there is a way to break the curse. Unfortunately, there is risk involved."

"To the Pure Blood."

"Precisely." He nodded.

Liesel sighed and closed her eyes. This was what Kurt had feared. He had known she wouldn't be able to resist. "And that is?"

Lothur stood and began to pace. "When you left, the pack panicked. It took us quite a while to calm everyone, which you can imagine, was no easy task. To appease the people, I decided to make Keegan the heir in Kurt's absence. The magic wouldn't transfer, of course, until the marriage ceremony was complete, but with Garrit ill, I thought it the next best thing. We didn't know if your party would return, and there was only a week left after the enchantress had come and revealed the first wizard's error. We quickly marked a new Pure Blood for Keegan, and our attempt to break the curse began."

"And failed," Liesel finished. Obviously, if it had been broken, she wouldn't have just witnessed Kurt bloody himself nearly to death.

Lothur nodded once. "She wasn't strong enough. Fear can be crippling, Liesel. If this is something you're willing to do, you must face the possibility that you, too, will die trying."

Liesel swallowed. Of course Kurt would want to stop her from this. "What must I do?" The small smile returned as Lothur stood and walked toward her in his quiet way. He lifted the green journal and opened it to the drawing of the purple spiked flower.

"I know Kurt told you of this journal." Liesel didn't respond to the bait, so after a moment, Lothur continued. "I'm sure also that he's told you of my interest in it. For years, I've tried fruitlessly to understand its secrets. Ever since I was a boy, I longed to end this fear, this unpredictability. I despise chaos, and that's exactly what this spell is. It makes one go mad. My ability to read the writings, however, was non-existent. But if you are strong enough to follow through with what the enchantress said, we shall both get what we want."

"And this flower has something to do with that?" He still hadn't told her what she was supposed to do, and that made Liesel even more uneasy.

"The flower is usually poisonous, but when mixed with the right herbs, as the enchantress explained, its effects are incredible. It can not only draw poison, but magic as well." He pulled a leather waterskin from his coat and took her empty teacup. After opening the skin, he poured a bright red liquid into the cup, then handed it to Liesel.

She sniffed it. It was sweet, pleasant at first, but there was the subtlest hint of sourness that lingered behind the sweet. "If I drink this, it pulls the magic out of the pack? But how?"

"It doesn't work immediately. When you marry the pack leader, what happens to him happens to all. If you are able to contain the magic it pulls from him, they'll all be free."

"How?"

"The drink will pull it from them, and in its place, your humanity will be poured back into them. But it's a risk. As I said, the last girl sickened and died." He left Liesel staring into the depths of the cup as he strode over to the window. "I told them she was too frail," he muttered under his breath.

Liesel continued to stare into the cup. She had wanted so much for her grandparents' answer to work, but she had to face the harsh reality that it hadn't. Kurt had not found his peace, and now seemed further than ever from discovering it. With the month soon ending, there wasn't any more time for guesses. It was this or nothing.

A small part of Liesel had to wonder if Kurt's uncle was telling the truth. There was nothing about him that lent itself to trust. In fact, she had been truly surprised when he'd admitted that his plan could possibly kill her.

"What is your interest in this?" Liesel placed the cup back on the table. She suddenly felt as though she were bargaining for a horse, and the merchant had something to hide about the goods, a bad leg or rotting teeth.

"You mean aside from killing the animal inside of me?" He scoffed. "I told you, I hate chaos. Everything about this life reeks of it."

"No," Liesel shook her head. "There's something else you're not telling me. If this drink is possibly going to be the death of me, I want to know everything." She folded her arms and did her best to stare him down and make him squirm the way Bernd had taught her to do with tradesmen.

Lothur didn't squirm, but after holding her stare for a few long moments, he nodded once. "Kurt tells me you grew up with stories of magic. I, too, grew up with stories, but they lacked the shine of those in your book."

He must have read her grandparents' book in her absence. For some reason, this annoyed her greatly.

"Worry not," he sighed, "it's still in your little room, just the way I found it. Anyhow, the only story that ever mattered to us was the wizard's story. It explained who we were. And the others, my brothers and the rest of the family, accepted that. But it was never enough for me." He clasped his hands together and rested his chin on them, looking intently at her.

"You and I aren't so different, you know. You see, when I heard those stories, I wasn't listening to tales about our past. I wanted to know about the world we'd left behind. Trolling merchants' carts every so often in Ward to see what the world had created without us was never my idea of living. But even that would have been tolerable if it weren't for this monstrous nature we keep."

He paused for a moment. The cool smirk had slipped from his

thin face, and Liesel finally saw a man consumed by grief. When he spoke again, it was as though another person suddenly occupied his body. "Kurt doesn't know this, but I was born a twin. Mary and I weren't expected to survive the birth, but somehow, we did. My sister and I were dissimilar in every way. As I had a tendency toward sickliness when we were young, she would often stay in to make sure I–"

Shaking his head, Lothur broke off the thought. "I won't bore you with details, but suffice it to say, she was much braver than I ever was, and as a result, I turned before she did. We had just celebrated our sixteenth year," his voice grew quiet, "when we were out together one day. I can't even recall what it was, but something spooked me, and I turned."

Despite her great dislike for the man, Liesel couldn't help but pity him for whatever was coming next.

"I'd never turned before." His voice was a whisper. "When I did, I lost all control. She didn't even see me coming." He closed his eyes as he spoke. "The life you think has been so trying is nothing but charmed compared to my youth. You haven't suffered until you've awakened to find your sister's blood caked on your hands, dirtying your fingernails and powdered in your hair, dry enough that it's already turned to a red dust." He shook his head and walked over to the window again.

"My family doesn't speak of it. It's just one of the heinous parts of being what we are, and I wasn't the first to do such a thing, either. So you're right, I do have a deeper motive for searching. It was a game as a child, a puzzle for a boy bored with his sickbed. For a man, it's the hope for redemption. And the hope that no one else will have so much reason to hate himself as I do."

Liesel gazed at him for a long time before once again lifting the cup. But this time, she drank.

If the red nectar had smelled sweet, its taste was sweeter by tenfold. Thick and surprisingly cool, it glided down her throat as smooth as glass. Only after she'd emptied the cup did the sour aftertaste bite her. Liesel nearly gagged. It took all her focus to stay upright and not to heave it all back up. As she gripped the table, she heard Lothur quietly thank her as he stood and turned to go.

"The wedding will be in two hours," he said softly without looking at her. "The seamstress will be over soon to help you prepare. I'd appreciate it if you remained here. It will make it easier to find you when it's time." And with that, he was gone. It took another ten minutes before Liesel could drag herself from the stool to begin her trek down the hallway toward her room.

Just as she reached her door, however, a thump from another room across the hall startled her. Cautiously, she walked to the door and placed her ear against it. This time, she heard not only thumps but muffled cries as well. As silently as she could, Liesel ran to the end of the hall to make sure Lothur had indeed left the house, and was happy to see him through the window, still walking toward the village.

Running back, Liesel opened the door to find Keegan bound and gagged, stretched out upon his bed. The young man's lanky body was so long, his feet dangled off the edge of the pallet. Liesel felt guilty as she realized he'd probably been locked in for escorting her out of the forest. She tried to loosen the gag first, but it was no easy task. She wanted to ask how he'd been taken, but as soon as the rag was off, he blurted out,

"Did you drink it?"

"Keegan, what happened to you?"

But he sat straight up, hands still bound, and shouted again, "Did you drink it?"

And as she saw the terror in the young man's eyes, a new dread filled her stomach. "Yes."

The silence that filled the room was pregnant with unasked questions, but Liesel could only watch him as he bowed his head and his shoulders drooped. "I promised Kurt I would keep you safe," he finally moaned in a low voice.

"It was my choice." She tried to comfort him but he shook his head violently.

"You don't understand. I was here when the enchantress was found, and I heard what she said. My uncle lied to you."

"He told me it was a risk," Liesel said in an uneven voice.

"It's not a risk," Keegan spat. "It's as sure as the dark of night."

"How do you know?"

"The girl who died was my wife."

Liesel froze.

Keegan continued, his voice bitter. "My uncle told the girl from Ward that her humanity would fill them, and the wolves would no longer be cursed. What he didn't tell her, and what I'm sure he didn't tell you, is that the black magic needs somewhere to go. So when you marry my brother, we will regain our humanity. What happens to the pack leader or his heir happens to all."

"And me?" Liesel's fingers refused to loosen the knots, so she stopped trying.

Keegan kept his eyes on the ground as he spoke. "You'll gain the form that they're discarding."

"You mean I will become a wolf?"

"Not just any wolf..." Keegan's voice trailed off.

Panic hit her as the form from that morning's escape lit her memory. "That beast?"

Keegan just nodded. Liesel tried to speak, but her voice suddenly felt just as brittle as her body, ready to break with the slightest movement.

"The nectar of the flower you drank isn't magical by itself, but it acts as a bridge, allowing whatever magic resides in one spouse to flow into the other, and because Kurt is the pack leader, the magic of the entire pack will flow into you with his."

"Why..." Liesel had to lick her lips and try again. "Why didn't it work the first time? If she took the wolf form—"

But Keegan was already shaking his head. "She wasn't strong enough to take it all, just enough to become that... thing." He shuddered. "Liesel, I married her, turned her, and then hunted her down!" He suddenly glared at her. "And now you have sentenced Kurt to do the same thing to you."

Liesel didn't hear when Lothur returned and gently threatened Keegan with further punishment if he attempted to escape again. She didn't even notice when the seamstress kindly helped her rise from the floor and return to her room. She didn't see her reflection when the seamstress placed her before a mirror to see how the new lacy blue gown draped elegantly from her shoulders and hips. The woman spoke sweet words, but there was nothing Liesel could say that would fully express the horror she felt from within.

Numbness was better than trying to create words. It was with a hollow heart that she was escorted from the cabin to the center of town where everyone was gathered. For it was only with an empty heart, she reasoned, that she could marry the man she'd always loved before becoming the very monster he loathed.

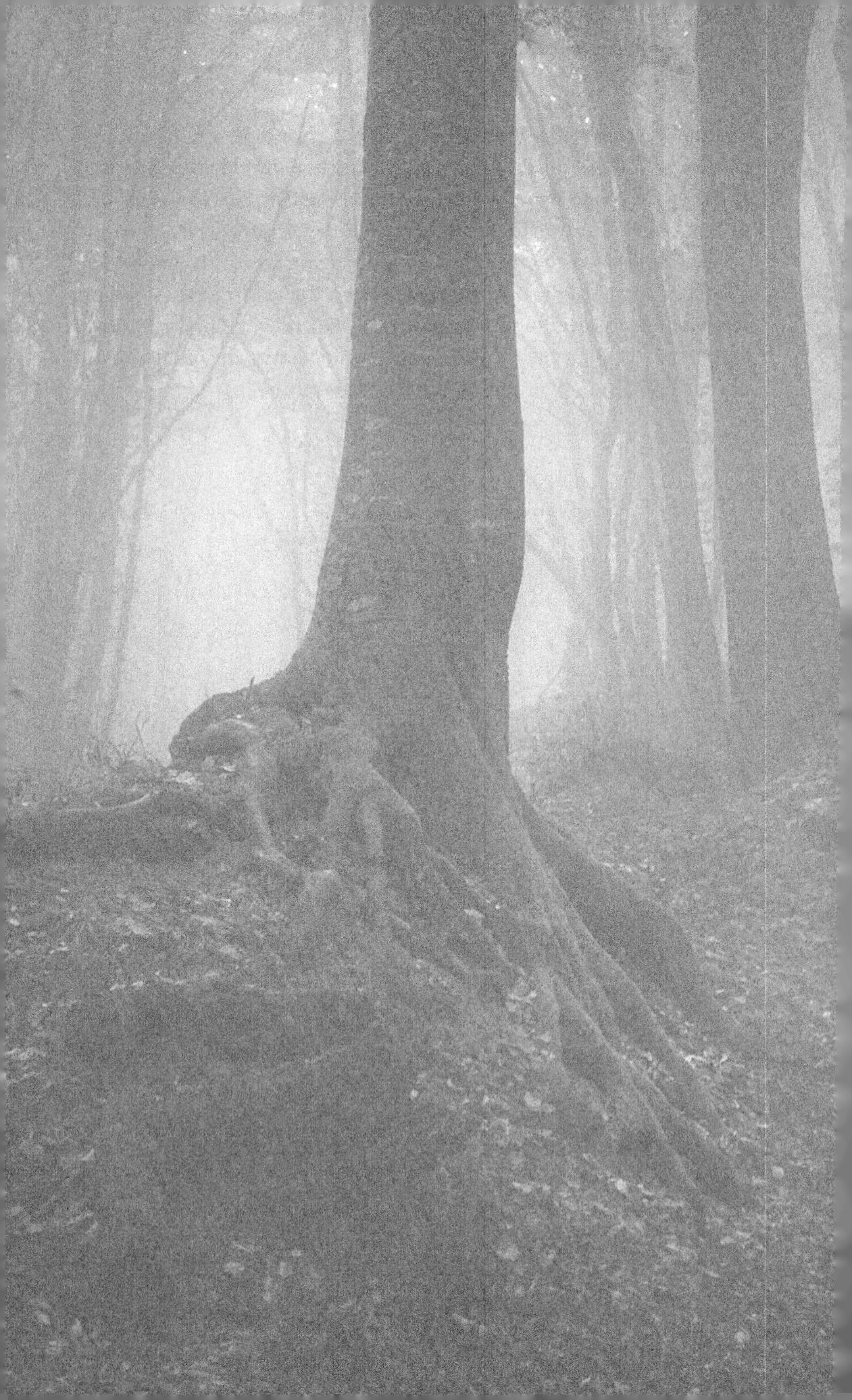

CHAPTER 25
THE WEDDING

It wasn't until she saw Kurt that her hollow heart shattered and released a flood of tears. The people who surrounded her looked uncomfortable, refusing still to meet her gaze. Even the seamstress could no longer look her in the eyes. They knew exactly what Lothur had done, and though it made them uncomfortable, the prize of freedom was worth the cost of her life. They simply didn't want to witness it for themselves, Liesel thought sourly.

As she stared down the dirt aisle between two rows of benches, Lora solemnly handed Liesel a bouquet of wildflowers, the kind Kurt had shown her the day he'd led her on their first forest adventure. And for a moment, Liesel wasn't sure what to do. There was no father to give her away. Not even a grandfather.

As she took her first step alone, however, she felt a calloused hand gently take her by the arm. To her surprise, Johan suddenly stood beside her wearing a determined frown. She almost managed a smile for him, thankful that at least she didn't have to complete this one act alone.

After sharing a long look, they began their walk down the aisle. As tradition dictated, the groom waited for her down at the end with the priest. Liesel purposefully kept her eyes averted until she could stand it no longer. She knew that once she met his gaze, she wouldn't be able to pull her eyes away. It didn't seem fair to have to look into the eyes of the future she could never have.

The cuts and bruises all over his face looked less severe in the gray light of the forest day, and most of his other wounds were hidden beneath the new clothes he wore. He was so handsome, Liesel mourned. He stood tall, his lips pressed into a tight line. She tried not to meet his eyes, but in her peripheral vision, she could feel his eyes burning curiously as he watched her.

Why? Liesel asked the Maker. Here was everything she'd ever wanted staring at her through golden-brown eyes. *Why does this beautiful moment, this perfect happiness, have to be so flawed?* They'd tried so many times to beat the sin of his ancestor, and now both were caught up in a bottomless pit of sorrow instead. They would both lose. Man and wife were destined for loneliness, it seemed.

Finally, they reached the end of the aisle. Before placing her hand in Kurt's, Johan faced her and gave her hands a gentle squeeze. It was then that Liesel realized there was no pipe sticking out of his coat. "Do what you need to do, and I'll be ready to go with you when you're done," he whispered. Despite the haze that seemed to cloud her mind, Liesel managed the tiniest of smiles.

"I'm afraid there won't be anywhere for us to go," she whispered. It overwhelmed her that the lonely old man would be willing to accompany them wherever he thought they were going.

He leaned in a bit, though, and returned her sad smile. "I know. But however far you're going, I'll be going with you just the same."

It was a moment before Liesel realized he knew. "But I won't be myself," she choked out. "I might kill you without knowing!"

To her surprise, the gruff old man just nodded. "I've been a wolf too long to do well as a man. After I lost my girl, I swore I wouldn't let the forest take another the way it took mine. I'm not going to let this damnable wood have you, too, all alone like she was."

A lone tear escaped down Liesel's face. With another small smile, the old man finally placed her hand in Kurt's before turning to take his seat. Liesel felt as though she might break, but Kurt still held that same curious expression of ferocity.

"Dearly beloved..." The holy man's voice warbled like an

adolescent boy's as he began the ceremony. Liesel recognized the holy man from Ward. They must have dragged him up from the town just for the special occasion. He was clearly ill-at-ease in the company of the human wolves. But as Liesel strained to read Kurt's strange expression, she forgot to listen to the words of her own ceremony until the holy man asked if anyone had a reason that the two should abstain from matrimony.

A sob broke forth from deep in Liesel's chest. The priest paused as the sobs came faster and harder, and Kurt gently cupped her face in his hand.

"I'm so sorry," she whispered. "I did what you told me not to, and I drank the potion." Her weeping echoed strangely through the town square as everyone watched her fall to pieces. Not that she cared anymore. The only person that mattered was standing before her wearing a mixture of gentle pain and concern on his face.

As more tears fell, he tucked a stray lock of hair behind her ear. "I know," he whispered back.

Liesel caught her breath. "You know? But how?" Again, not that it mattered.

"I knew you would do it," Kurt said, rubbing her cheek with his thumb. "You have a kind heart, and you do stupid things for the ones you love, like wearing a red cape in a forest full of danger."

"He lied to me." Liesel shook her head.

"I know, I know." Kurt soothed her as he glared at his uncle, who sat just a few feet away. That only released another barrage of tears from Liesel.

"I'm sorry," the holy man interrupted. "But I can't do this." When Lothur raised an eyebrow, the priest raised his hands helplessly. "I cannot marry this girl against her will. It is not what the Maker ordained me to do."

"If you refuse to marry them," Lothur stood, "you will be responsible for all of these people around you turning to wolves permanently with your town close by. Is that what the Maker ordained you to allow?" As the holy man stared at him, speechless, Liesel turned back to Kurt.

"I have to," she whispered.

Kurt clenched his jaw and swallowed hard as his eyes burned once again. Gently, he pulled her face close, and he rested his forehead against hers.

"You're going to be fine, Liesel!"

"How do you know?" she whimpered. "The last woman they—"

"Do you trust me?"

"Yes." If Liesel had learned nothing else over the last seven years, she had learned to trust Kurt.

"Enough to marry me?"

"I do."

Slowly, a smile spread across his face as he released her and took her hands once more. He closed his eyes for a long moment, drew a deep breath, and when his eyes opened once again, they were calm. Oddly, Liesel felt more peaceful herself. She couldn't explain why, but the serenity that Kurt exuded was palpable. It felt peculiar to smile, but Liesel knew one rested on her own lips as she stared into the eyes of her dearest companion.

"Go on," she said softly to the holy man. "I am ready." When the older man hesitated a moment longer, she fixed her steady gaze on him and nodded. Finally, he began reading from his large leather book once more. As the words were spoken, Kurt's grip on her hands tightened, and the fierce determination on his face was nearly frightening and grew more so as the ceremony neared its end.

Soon vows were exchanged, and just before the holy man announced them man and wife, Kurt suddenly drew her in and wrapped his arms around her tightly, holding her close to his body.

"Now I need you to hold onto me," he breathed into her hair. "Things are going to look a little strange in a moment."

"How do you know that?" she asked, fear suddenly chasing away all the calm from moments before.

"I can feel it. I've lived with magic all my life."

Liesel did as she was told. He'd never held her so close, and the proximity made her head swim. It wasn't in any way unpleasant, however. If this was the way she was to spend her last moments, in the arms of her beloved husband, Liesel decided she would choose no other way.

"Now close your eyes," he instructed, "and listen to my voice."

"What are you doing?"

"I'm not going to let you go." With those words, he nodded to the holy man.

"I now pronounce you man and wife." The holy man hadn't even finished uttering the words when a great wind began to whirl around them. Liesel scrunched her eyes shut and pressed her face into Kurt's chest. And although her eyes were closed, Liesel sensed bright flashes of light exploding all around them.

"Kurt?" As the wind blew harder, Liesel began to feel a part of her trying to slip away, as though the gales were going to snatch the soul from her body.

"I'm here, Liesel." His voice was strong and warm, and when she heard it, she felt strengthened. Not enough, though, to stop the raging tides that warred within her. A foreign darkness began to burn inside her chest, and her heart's cadence rose and fell in unusual rhythms.

"*Kurt?*" Liesel's call was frantic as panic set in.

"Listen to my voice!" he shouted above the din. Liesel nodded into his chest, so he continued. "Your grandfather was right!"

"How?" she breathed.

"I had to find peace with what I have in life. And I found it."

Liesel wanted to answer, but she was feeling faint. Kurt tipped her head up, and she briefly opened her eyes. Bright whirls of color swirled around them faster and faster, and it was hard to focus as Kurt held her head up.

"You came back for me. Before that moment, I was sure I would never find my peace, but when you came back I knew for sure that you loved me more than your freedom, more than your family, more than life."

The air began to push in on them, and Liesel began to see spots.

"Liesel?" he called out, a little louder this time, but Liesel couldn't respond. She gasped for air, but nothing came out.

"Liesel!" His voice rose. Still, she couldn't answer. "Stay with me!" he yelled above the storm. "I am not letting go, and neither can you!"

But Liesel felt as though she were being torn into another world, and her legs began to give way. She could only just feel his vise grip on her and the warmth of his chest as he crushed her against him. The colors began to run, giving way to the color of blood.

"It's taking me," she whispered.

"No it's not! I won't let it have you!" His words were steel, an anchor in the storm. "Because of you, my soul has escaped the spell." He bent and spoke in her ear, "So now we have nothing to give one another but light." With those words, he tilted her head and pressed his lips against hers.

Kurt's kiss was the most powerful touch Liesel had ever felt. Soft, and yet an act of war, it threw up battlements around her soul. The purity that flowed from his heart flooded her confusion, and though her eyes were closed, it chased away the blood-red darkness with a searing white light.

The winds screamed louder than ever, but instead of explosions, Liesel felt as though she were being wrapped in a rainbow of a brilliant star. Then, in one fantastic burst of light, the storm began to recede. Slowly, ever so slowly, the winds began to die, and the vivid brightness that had surrounded them started to fade.

Liesel had no desire to ever open her eyes again. Kurt still held her as though he battled, and his kiss was very much still warm and soft, and yet, triumphant. It wasn't until Liesel heard cheering that she realized she still stood before the rest of the pack. And she was every bit as human, or rather, even more so, than she had been before.

Likewise, the people before her no longer acted the part of a pack, skulking fearfully and silently. Instead, they clapped and cheered, smiles on the faces of all. In confusion, she looked back up at Kurt, who wore his own victorious smile proudly.

"How?" Liesel shook her head in confusion. It seemed too good to be true. "I shouldn't be here." She glanced down at her body. "At least, not like this."

"Weren't you listening?" Kurt chuckled.

"I was a bit preoccupied." Liesel gave him the slightest frown.

Kurt turned her to face the crowd. "Your grandfather was right when he said I had to find peace with who I was. I couldn't find that peace the way he did, however. I came close that evening on the mountain, but it just wasn't enough. But today, when I saw what you were willing to sacrifice for me, that you were willing to risk death for me, I finally understood that I was enough, that you loved me just as I am and not for what I should be."

He leaned down to place another kiss on her lips when his eyes flicked up and his body turned to ice. Moving her aside, Kurt stalked into the trees. Liesel was confused until she saw a second figure walking quickly just ahead of Kurt. Realizing what he was about to do, Liesel took off after them. When she found them, Kurt had his uncle by the neck, squeezing harder every time Lothur tried to speak.

"I should kill you, and rid the world of one more liar!"

Lothur tried desperately to loosen his nephew's hold, but Johan and Keegan were suddenly there at his side, holding his uncle in place.

"Kurt," Liesel cautioned, "think about this before you do something you'll regret."

"If you had died, your blood would have been on his hands!" Kurt thundered. "It would have been on all their hands!" He waved angrily at the joyful crowd through the trees.

"I'm not excusing him," Liesel said. "I want what's best for you. And killing your uncle in cold blood is not it. And as for them," she looked back at the people, "you're right about them, too. But can you really blame them? They wanted more for their children."

Kurt glared at the distant throng for a long moment more, but Liesel saw his eyes soften just a little. Keegan and Johan exchanged nervous glances. Finally, Kurt slowly loosened his grip on his uncle's neck.

"It would have been worth it," Lothur rasped as he clutched his neck. "All the deaths we've suffered in the last two hundred years would have been worth one more if she were to end it! And she did!"

Kurt made to move for him again, but Liesel grabbed ahold of his arm. "Just go." She glared Lothur.

Lothur scrambled up to straighten himself. No one spoke as he turned and started walking toward Ward.

The four of them stood there for a while even after he was gone. Without his pipe, Johan fumbled idly with his hands. Keegan looked miserable, and Kurt continued to glare at the merry people through the trees. And as much as Liesel wanted to go back to the cabin and just take a long, hard nap, it suddenly dawned on her that this was her wedding day, and strange or not, she was never going to have another one again.

It also occurred to her that the young man standing beside her was now her husband. And, she decided, she was going to celebrate that whether he felt like it or not. Liesel took both of his hands in hers. She had to repeat his name a few times before he pulled his gaze down to her level, his eyes still brooding.

"I don't care what awful things your uncle has done, nor do I care what *they* have done."

Kurt still frowned, but at least he was listening to her.

"What I care about right now is that this is my wedding, and my groom still has yet to ask me to dance."

Kurt stared at her blankly for a long minute before the shadow of a grin crossed his face. Liesel stared into his golden-brown depths until the smile was real. "My apologies," he murmured, lifting one of her hands to his lips and bowing his head. Holding her gaze, he slowly led her back toward the music that had just begun to play.

The people cheered as they walked to the center of the crowd. And as Kurt began to turn her in a circle in time to the music, Liesel's head began to spin again. But this time, it had nothing to do with magic and everything to do with the man who was holding her in his arms.

Everything she had ever asked of the Maker had been given to her. She had married her best friend. They were free. Just looking at Kurt, it was clear the darkness was gone from his mind, the pieces of him that the wolf had stolen were back to stay. He would never again stare blankly as he lost himself to the animal, and everything the beast had once taken was hers until the day they died.

THE REST of the day flew by in a blur of dancing, singing, and laughter. Liesel didn't even realize she'd fallen asleep until she felt Kurt nudge her awake in the middle of the night.

"Liesel?"

When she didn't respond immediately, he softly kissed her temple and whispered her name again. Liesel briefly considered not answering just so he would kiss her more. He would have none of that, though, letting out a low chuckle when she faked a snore. "You are a terrible liar. I know you're awake."

"Fine." She yawned and stretched before snuggling deeper into the covers. "You've found me out."

Kurt gave another throaty laugh, tapping her on the nose playfully. "About what you said in the cave earlier, that you couldn't understand why I love you..."

Liesel had been lightly tracing the contours of his face in the dark, but as he uttered these words, she stopped, suddenly fully awake.

"Do you really believe that?" he asked.

"I suppose..." she stuttered, "you just spent so much time—"

"Would you stop?" Kurt gently covered her mouth with his hand until she playfully shoved it off. "What I want to say is that you don't understand what it meant when you came into my life. I never saw you as a burden, Liesel. You were freedom to me!"

"Why?" Liesel asked breathlessly.

"From the first time I saw you, you had a spark in your eyes. You can't understand what growing up here was like... how disorienting it could be. But the light I saw in your soul was an anchor. It pulled me out of the pack's constant darkness, drew me toward the light of life hoped for. And you know what?"

"Mm?" Liesel was wide awake, but she lay quietly, drinking in the warmth of the moment. Being in his arms, listening to the soothing rumble of his voice without the threat of disaster looming above their heads was intoxicating. She could stay there forever and be satisfied.

"Do you know what a spark does?"

Smiling into the dark, Liesel mumbled a no.

He leaned closer, whispering right into her ear. "It creates a flame. And today, that flame saved a village."

"So," Liesel sat up on her elbows, giving up on sleep for the moment, "what do we do now?"

"Well, I think your grandparents might be interested in hearing about how things turned out."

At that, Liesel bolted straight up. "Really? Oh, Kurt! That would be... I can't even describe how happy that makes me!"

Kurt laughed. "First we'll need to see everyone off who wants to go, help them find a true trade." His voice fell a little. "And we'll need to take care of my father." Garrit had regained his consciousness that afternoon when the wedding bells rang, according to the caretaker who had been placed at his side, but he was by no means ready to take command of the village again.

"I have the feeling some might remain," Liesel said, thinking back to how Keegan and a few of the others had stayed silent as they'd discussed leaving the forest earlier that evening. And she didn't even want to think about what Johan would do without even his wolf self to turn to when he was lonely.

"But I promise you this," he said. "The moment the people can do without us, we are leaving." Kurt lay down again and drew her close. Liesel snuggled in as close as she could.

"And then?"

"We are never looking back."

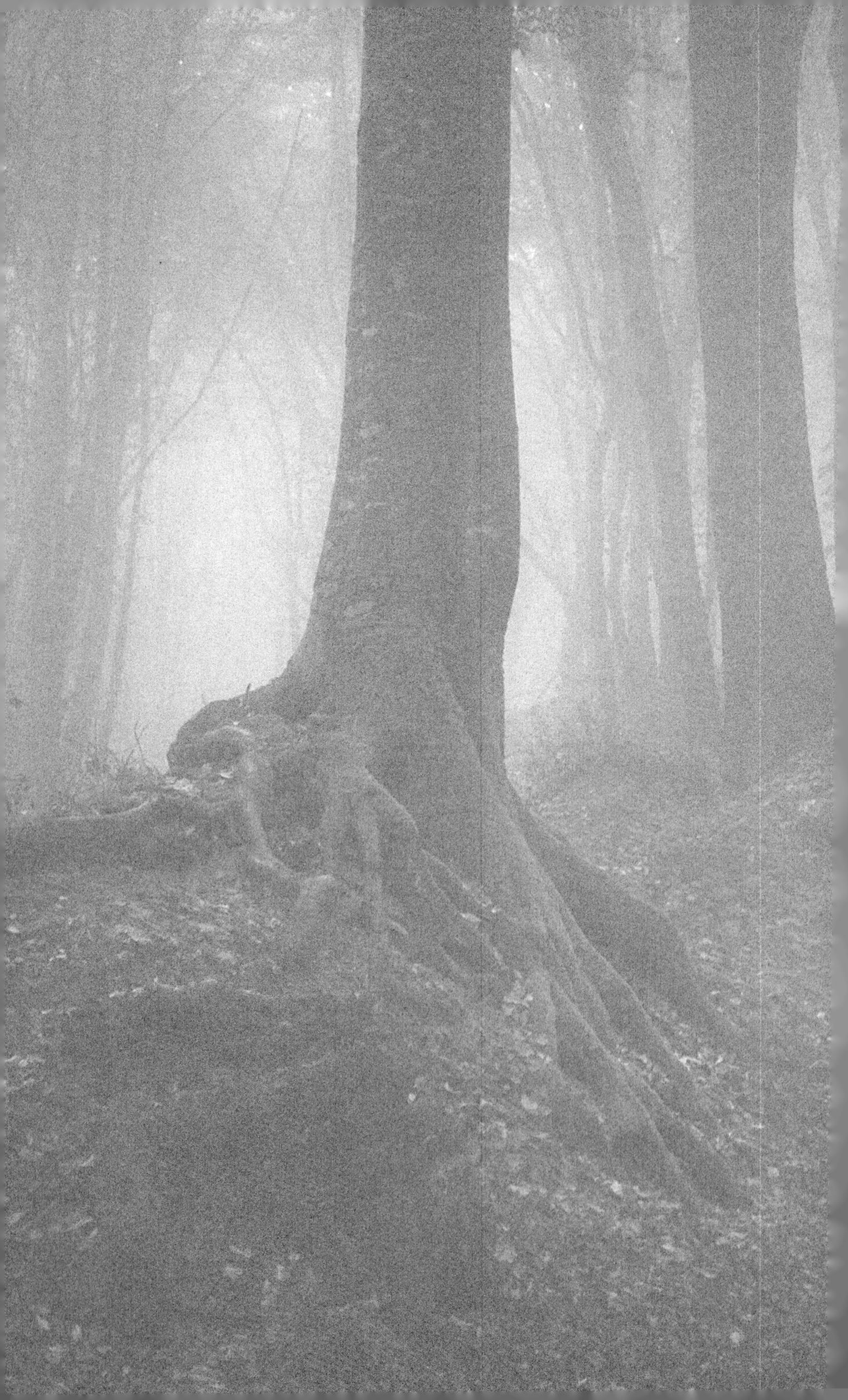

CHAPTER 26
EPILOGUE
THE GIRL IN THE RED HOOD

Leaving the forest took longer than Liesel would have liked, but anything was livable after what she had endured for the past seven years. The people of the pack were energetic, joyful in the wake of Kurt and Liesel's miracle.

But as their capacity for joy had grown, so had their capacity to fret and worry Kurt to death. Every man and woman, it seemed, was suddenly at a loss for what to do with him or herself. The menial jobs and gardens and cottages that had once sustained them were suddenly too dirty and insignificant to keep them a moment longer. And as Garrit was still recovering, the responsibility of setting the people at rights after being suppressed for two hundred years fell upon Kurt.

"Foolish woman!" Kurt stomped in one day, shaking his head and muttering to himself incoherently. In the midst of the constant crisis that seemed to be perpetually developing in the suddenly too small village, the members of Kurt's family had chosen to stay together in the large cabin while things were set to rights. It was a good thing, too, as everyone else was so intent on either leaving or rebuilding their own decrepit houses that there wasn't a spare work animal to be found. Even Ward was short on horses.

Kurt had done his best to negotiate for the individuals and families who wished to leave. They'd never had much need for gold, as while under the spell no one had cared enough to create many tradable goods. So Kurt had arranged deals in promise that his charges would pay back their loans in labor. It had taken him weeks to find enough carts and horses to borrow to get everyone moved, and now it seemed that not even what he'd wrangled would be enough.

"Who is it this time?" Lora rolled her eyes and tossed her big brother a biscuit. Kurt caught it and slumped down onto one of the stools, his head making a thumping sound when it hit the table. He left it there as he answered in a muffled voice.

"Mrs. Fisch is convinced she can't move to Ward without a wooden cart." Sitting back up, he threw his free hand in the air in frustration. "It's less than an hour's walk! But she wants me to take the cart from the Abel family the day they move so she can use it."

"The Abels have four children under the age of five." Keegan frowned as he looked up from the wood block he was carving. The tall young man had been even quieter than usual since the wedding. Liesel felt they might be good friends if he ever decided to speak more than a sentence at a time to her. A thoughtful look crossed his face. "I'm helping Mrs. Fisch's neighbor move, too. Do you think Mrs. Fisch would be willing to go sooner?"

Kurt studied his brother for a moment. "Come with me tomorrow. I could use your help."

"No." Keegan shook his head, staring at his carving block again. "I need to take–"

"I can care for Father." Lora raised an eyebrow and smiled knowingly.

Keegan gave her a long look before mumbling something about Kurt having it all in hand.

It took an entire evening of cajoling before he would even consider leaving the house to help Kurt. Later, when Liesel asked Kurt why, he said,

"My brother has always looked up to my uncle. Playing a part in his plan, the failed wedding, my capture... they all made him even less confident in himself than he already was." He sighed. "Whether he knew her or not, Keegan exchanged vows with the girl from Ward. She was his wife. And he was the reason she died such a horrible death. It will take time before he's ready to move on."

If Keegan was a mess, Johan was worse. Liesel had always assumed everyone would benefit from the removal of the spell, but after weeks of watching Johan help others move, only to see him disappear by himself at the end of every day, Liesel could stand it no longer. She watched and waited one day, about a month after the spell had been lifted, until she saw him begin his daily walk out of town. Grabbing the basket of apples she'd bartered for at Ward's market, she set out to follow him.

He walked farther than she first thought he might until he was deep in the woods where there was neither sign nor sound of anything human. Just when Liesel thought her feet might fall off from walking so far, Johan sat on a fallen log, lit his pipe, and just stared into the trees.

Wordlessly, Liesel went and sat beside him. When she held out one of her apples, he took it and turned it slowly in his hands, examining the fruit without really seeing it.

"Seems ungrateful to the Maker," he finally said, letting out a gusty sigh, "but I miss it."

Liesel just watched the old man carefully.

"At least the wolf was able to swallow up some of the shame," he said again. "In that form, I could at least forget about losing her for a little while."

Liesel's heart hurt as she looked into the weathered face that stared down blindly, a single tear gathering in its corner. They sat like that for a long time. There were no words Liesel could find that would help. She knew nothing of losing a child. Until that moment, she hadn't realized the extent to which he had relied on the form that everyone else hated. Silently, she called out to the Maker, asking Him to give Johan something, some sort of closure to the pain, some sort of hope.

Johan was still weighing heavily on Liesel's mind the next day as she set out on an errand of a different sort. Though she had stayed busy trying to help Kurt in whatever ways she could, there was someone else she needed to thank before they left the woods.

Now that the spell was broken, the people of Ward would at

least speak with her. And though they weren't exactly friendly, they were at least willing to help her try to find her person of mystery.

"Paul?" The mayor rubbed his chin thoughtfully. He was one of the only individuals who seemed to go on as if nothing had happened after the curse had been broken, as if he hadn't helped deliver Liesel to a pack of wolves. "A hunter, you say? I think I do remember someone by that name. He lives a ways off, half a day's ride on horseback. What do you want him for?"

"It's a long story." Liesel shook her head. "How do I find him?"

The next morning, Liesel slipped out of the cabin before anyone else was awake. She was sure Kurt wouldn't be keen on her riding so far by herself, but she tried to comfort him in her note by assuring him that she would be home before dark.

The mayor's directions were correct, much to Liesel's relief. After about three hours of riding straight west, Liesel came upon a large cabin in the middle of the great forest. It was surprisingly well-kept for something so deep in the woods. Praying she was right, and that this truly was the hunter's house, she dismounted from her horse and gave a timid knock on the door.

"Yes?" A woman with graying brown hair answered. She looked confused, but Liesel thought she had kind eyes.

"I... I'm looking for a man named Paul." Liesel tried to sound confident. "I was told this is where he lives?"

"Aye." A man answered as the door opened wider. Sure enough, it was him. He looked a little older, perhaps, but Liesel knew his voice immediately.

"I don't know if you remember me," she tried to smile, "but while you were out hunting seven years ago, I had been bitten by a wolf and—"

"Ah, yes!" Recognition lit his eyes. "You were the girl I brought back to Ward! Come in, please! My wife will get you something to drink. Joseph!" he barked. A boy who looked to be about ten or so ran up to them. "Get our guest's horse to the stable. See it's taken care of."

Liesel's trepidation quickly melted as she walked into the cozy, glowing cabin. It was simple but neat. The fire roared, and stew was cooking above it. A few other children, older and younger, showed themselves as Liesel seated herself in one of the comfortable wooden chairs offered her.

The hunter's family was just as kind as he had been that first night, but nothing struck Liesel as out of the ordinary until she asked where they were from. As she listened, however, her heart began to pound, and she had the sudden, desperate need to return home. The Maker had answered her prayer.

The next morning, Liesel was banging on Johan's door before the morning light.

She had been right. Kurt hadn't been very happy with her at all when she'd returned the night before. When she had insisted that she was taking Johan back with her the next day, however, he relented a bit. And when she told him why she needed to take Johan back with her, he had grown nearly as giddy as she was.

"Be careful, though," he cautioned her after sharing her initial excitement. "If you're right, this will be the answer to our prayers. If it's not her, though, it just might kill him."

Liesel thought about that as she waited impatiently for Johan to answer her knock. She had nearly chickened out of telling him, but the conviction that she was right was too strong for her to give up. Convincing Johan to accompany her out into the forest wasn't difficult at all. Until they reached the cabin.

"Ho, now. What are we doing here?" Johan balked at the cabin uneasily.

"There's someone here I think you should meet," Liesel answered, already knocking on the door. She wasn't going to give him the chance to get nervous and escape back into the woods.

The hunter's wife answered the door again. She smiled when she saw Liesel, but her smile wavered and then disappeared when she saw Johan.

The old man stood as though chained to the ground, as though vines had grown up around him. The woman and the old man stared at one another for a long time before she finally whispered, "Do I know you?"

Johan tried to speak, but it took him a moment to gather the breath. "Probably... Probably not." His breaths came fast and heavy. "But I could never forget..." He stopped and looked at Liesel, the confusion and hope warring in his eyes. Liesel just smiled and nodded. "Hanne?" he finally asked.

As if in a trance, the woman nodded. Then her eyes widened. "Papa!"

THOUGH THE LARGE cabin made Johan a bit wary, he was immediately enchanted with his daughter's family. He did still insist on taking Liesel home, and she accepted out of consideration for Kurt's already frayed nerves, but she could tell it was killing him to leave his daughter even for such a short trip. As she waved goodbye to him for the last time, she thanked the Maker. Johan had finally found his peace.

Unfortunately, the pain wasn't so easily resolved for all the others Kurt and Liesel helped. Keegan still doubted everything he said or touched. Much to his surprise and everyone else's, however, once the young man showed his hand at managing the anxious villagers, he proved to be quite capable. It was only a few weeks before Kurt made the announcement at supper that he wanted to hand down the leadership to Keegan.

Keegan's brown eyes grew large. "But Father–" he started, but Kurt just shook his head.

"Father is recovering, yes. But you know he won't be able to lead anymore, Kee. Those who stay here will need someone strong. You can ask him for advice, but the people will need *you*."

Keegan had continued to argue, but Kurt wouldn't hear of it. After supper that night, he took his little brother on a long walk.

"Well, did he accept?" Liesel asked anxiously when they got back. Keegan's acceptance was the key to their escape from the forest. The people couldn't be left alone in the state they were in.

Kurt's grin was so broad that words were unnecessary. Liesel nearly shrieked with joy. It had only been a few months since the wedding, but she was more ready than ever to leave the dark confines of the woods.

Leaving the depths of the woods, when they finally did go, was surreal. Liesel half-expected sentries from Ward to appear on the dirt road and order them back. But they made it out unaccosted, and their first stop was Tag to thank the Beckes. And then they headed to Weit.

Given the circumstances of their departure, they agreed that it would be best not to appear in the town itself, but Liesel wanted to make amends with her grandparents before they set off on their own journey.

As they rode up to the grand house once again, she nearly trembled for fear of what her grandparents would say. Not that they could separate the happily married couple, but that didn't make her angst any less. Even if her grandparents had come to terms with her choice, she wondered what the town had to say about them remaining at the vineyard. Had her actions caused them trouble?

Still, she wanted their blessing. She prayed desperately to see the happiness in their eyes at her marriage, something they had never worn for her mother.

Ilsa wept even harder at Liesel's return than she had the first time. Bernd was the most surprising, however. He walked stoically out of the cabin and down the hill behind his wife, as always, leaning on his staff. As Liesel and her grandmother embraced and cried in one another's arms, he looked at Kurt.

"It is over?" he asked. "For all of them?"

Kurt simply nodded.

Bernd swallowed hard, and to everyone's surprise, fell to his knees and began to weep. Everyone stopped to stare as the big man cried, and in that moment, Liesel knew that all was forgiven. The nightmare was over. Her grandparents could shed the guilt they'd born for so many years.

"But what about Weit?" Liesel asked them over supper. "They couldn't have wanted you to stay after what happened."

"No." Ilsa turned her teacup in her hands. "No, they weren't happy at all."

"In fact," Bernd snorted, "they wanted to run us out of town."

"What stopped them?"

"The holy man, of all people." Her grandfather chuckled. "He told them all that if we left, they'd have no wine for the holy sacraments in church."

"They leave us alone now more than ever." Ilsa smiled wryly. "Not that being alone ever bothered your grandfather."

It was with joyful hearts that Liesel and Kurt soon departed. Though she knew they would miss her and she them, Liesel had peace in knowing her grandparents were happy for her.

Before she mounted her horse, Liesel handed her grandmother her beloved book. Ilsa took it reverently and traced the leather spine with her hand. To Liesel's surprise, however, she handed it back to Liesel with a twinkle in her eye.

"There are empty pages in the back. I want you to write your own stories here so your children can see. And if you ever decide to come home, your dear old grandmother, as well."

"We don't know when we will return," Liesel said apologetically as Kurt loaded their little cart.

Ilsa just smiled and took a lock of Liesel's yellow hair, stroking it with affection. "Go where the Maker leads you. You will return when He appoints. Who knows where else He has work for you to do? You're so young, Leese. You're just getting started."

And so they journeyed, and after weeks of slow, blissful travel, their journey led them right to the edge of the sea.

"Kurt, I can see them!" Liesel pointed to the ocean, having climbed as close to the edge of the bluff as she dared while Kurt unloaded the cart. "Come see! Quickly, before they go!"

"I won't be able see you or the merfolk if I don't get a fire going soon." Kurt shook his head in false annoyance as he went to join her.

Despite his protests, it wasn't long before the fire was built and strips of meat were smoking over it. Liesel sat quietly, mesmerized by the smell of the sea and the wetness in the air that floated all around them. Kurt added some logs to the fire before coming over and sitting next to her on the back of the cart.

Without breaking her gaze at the glittering ocean that moved without ceasing, Liesel reached back and grabbed his hands, rubbing them contentedly while she closed her eyes and simply existed.

Kurt fingered the garnet ring he'd purchased for her from a trader they'd met back in Tag on their way out of the forest. "This bluff would be a lovely place for a house," he said.

Liesel laughed and poked him. Kurt had said such things about every place they had stayed at since leaving her grandparents' home. Each night he said it, and each night she reminded him that they hadn't yet seen the ocean.

"No, it wouldn't." Liesel shook her head. It took every bit of her self-control not to burst as she waited for his reply.

"And why not?"

"Cliffs aren't good places for children."

When Kurt didn't reply, Liesel finally turned and looked at him.

"Wait... you mean it?" Kurt immediately looked down at her dress, but Liesel just laughed again. It would be a few months before he would be able to tell just by looking.

"If we have a boy," she snuggled deeper into his arms and looked up at the stars that filled the heavens above them, "I hope he's just like his father."

"A boy would be nice, but so would a girl. She could be just like her mother."

Liesel gave an unladylike snort. "And what would that be?"

"Too willing to talk to strangers." Kurt smiled. "Particularly odd boys in the forest."

"We will have to warn her about those." Liesel nodded soberly.

Kurt just chuckled, then continued in a warm voice. "She'll have a hunger for adventure. She might just change the lives of an entire village. And everywhere she goes, people will say, 'Look, there goes the daughter of the girl in the red hood.'"

Silent Mermaid

A Clean Fantasy Fairy Tale Retelling of The Little Mermaid

"If you absolutely must go, then at least wear your black camicett." Renata eyed Arianna from her perch by the tower window. Though Arianna's aunt rarely used her monocle, as she claimed it made her look old, she peeked through it now, her leaf and pressing knife still in hand.

Arianna would have protested on any other occasion, but her guilt was too great this night to argue. That Renata wasn't reporting her disobedience to her father was a gift enough in itself, so she flipped back into her little chamber and changed into the black camicett as requested.

Arianna inwardly groaned at the tight, slick material as she pulled it over her head. Wearing the night apparel felt much like she was wrapping her top half snugly in waxy leaf paper. Her aunt was right, though. Swimming about at night was a trifle to most merpeople. For them, the black camicett was simply a precaution, a preventive measure against being seen by pirates. A mermaid without a voice, however, couldn't be too careful, and the sleek black shirt would make her less visible in the inky waters of the eve.

As she launched herself through her tower window, Arianna felt a shiver of dual fear and excitement run all the way from her shoulders to her tail. Her father would pop a scale if he could see what she was doing now. Darkness had begun to fall, and the sea already felt different. The waters were eerily silent, no longer filled with the working songs the merpeople spun throughout the day. Only the Protector songs of the distant guards were audible as they continued their constant murmurs at the edges of the Deeps.

The water was still warm from the day, but all the pleasure its heat should have brought her was chased away by the guilt that gnawed at her stomach. True enough, Arianna broke the rules daily with her excursions to the surface. Amadeo rarely reprimanded her, though, and even the guards turned their backs whenever she swam by. The absolute warning in her father's voice earlier that evening, however, had been steel and stone. He did not want her going to the ball.

Though she had wavered in her determination as he spoke of the ways she might be tortured, should she be captured by pirates, his threat itself was what had made up Arianna's mind entirely. If her father wasn't going to treat her as a member of the family, then she didn't need to act like one.

Or at least, that was what she had been telling herself all evening. Even now, she nearly turned back as the moon rippled into view above the surface she was fast approaching. By the time she broke the surface, doubt had nearly killed her determination completely, and she had resolved to simply glance at the party and then scurry home to her aunt in their lonely tower. But then she glimpsed the ball.

Taking care as she always did to keep the end of her tail in the water, Arianna pulled herself up onto the lower ledge that jutted out just below the Sun Palace's terrace.

Despite the dark of twilight, the terrace was nearly as light as day. Dozens of torches stood several feet above the heads of even the tallest people, their flames not only yellow, but also blue, green, pink, and even purple. Tables lined the terrace's edges, and from the way the guests hovered around them, Arianna could only guess that those tables held all varieties of food. Lalia swore that human food was nothing special. Most of it was so dry it was inedible, she'd complained once to Arianna after a similar event a few years before. But now Arianna was sure her sister was only feeding her own prejudice. There were too many smiling people standing around the tables for the food to be bland or dry.

The people themselves were stunning. Arianna gawked as men strode around with confident swagger in their steps while the ladies flitted, their fluffy, lacy skirts swishing gracefully from side to side. Arianna stared at the colorful gowns longingly. Merpeople never wore so many clothes. Not only was it unnecessary, cloth hindered swimming significantly. Still, despite the impracticality of the humans' clothes, as Arianna was sure that they could have been covered adequately with less than half as many clothes, their attire was so very pretty.

It didn't take Arianna long to spot her family. Her sister and mother were standing close to her father's elbows, watching the human merriment with cool, collected eyes. Her father's scowl was so deep that Arianna first feared he'd seen her watching them.

Before she dove back into the water, however, she realized that he was scowling at everyone and everything. The food, the dancing, the children running about underfoot, and especially the Sun Crown himself. At least, Arianna guessed he was the Sun Crown, judging by the oversized golden diadem on his head and the horde of admirers encircling him.

It took her a moment longer, however, to locate her brother. Rinaldo was chatting animatedly with another young man. When the young man turned, Arianna sucked in a quick breath.

Prince Michael wore black trousers and a brown doublet that made his olive skin look tan even in the dark of the evening. His curly black hair had been cut more neatly than Arianna had seen in a long time. Arianna smiled to herself as he tugged nervously at the bottom of his jacket. The fitted coat did indeed look restricting. But, oh! The effect of the clothing on his shoulders made her chest tight and her breath catch in her throat.

His charms clearly weren't lost on the human girls, either. Arianna's delight in his appearance quickly disappeared as she noticed a number of them eyeing the prince as well. All too soon, the young men finished their conversation, and Prince Michael turned away and bowed to a young woman nearby. They promptly began to dance.

Arianna's annoyance about the forced proximity that human dances required was interrupted by a small splash behind her. She nearly dived back into the water when Rinaldo's head popped up from the waves. Arianna felt the color drain from her face.

"And why am I not surprised?" he asked.

Arianna couldn't meet his eyes. Instead, she stared at his drenched shirt.

"Not to worry," he said, following her gaze. "The charm will dry them as soon as I get out of the water." He paused for a minute, and Arianna finally dared to sneak a peek up at his face.

His brow was furrowed, but his mouth was set in a crooked grin. Arianna dared to swallow. Did that mean he wasn't going to tell their father?

"I shouldn't be doing this, but since you're already here . . ." He bowed his head and removed the fiber string from around his neck.

Arianna's heart beat fast as he handed the little shell to her. "Just a few minutes, then I need to get back."

Arianna stared at the charm, still afraid to put it on. It was too good to be true. But her brother only shook his head as he took it back and put it around her neck himself.

"I really do need to get back. So get on with it."

Arianna's mouth fell open as her tail began to quiver. The trembling grew so strong that it itched, but her discomfort was forgotten as a black skirt began to extend down from the bottom of her camicett. And at the bottom of the skirt appeared two little slippered feet.

Rinaldo let out a deep laugh as Arianna turned and bolted up to the edge of the terrace. She wondered at how easily her new legs moved. Bending and turning, they moved in directions Arianna had never even considered human legs moving. And every movement felt as natural as swimming. Kneeling behind a bush, Arianna watched the ball from a position she had only ever dreamed of reaching.

A new dance had begun, and Arianna wished more than ever to give her new legs use. Prince Michael had switched partners. Now he twirled with a girl with hair the color of ebony and skin the color of sand. Keeping perfect time to the music, the prince never once missed a step. Not until he turned and looked out at the ocean, that is. Arianna froze as his eyes swept the horizon. She was sure, if he ever saw her, that those eyes would be able to look inside her soul. At that precise moment, those eyes stopped their sweeping and settled on the bush she hid behind. Was it possible? Did he see her behind the leaves through which she now peered?

They stayed that way, Arianna holding her breath and the prince staring with a crinkled brow, until his partner said something and he returned those dark eyes to the girl instead. Arianna dared to breathe again when her brother's voice came from the water behind her.

"So I see you've found Prince Michelangelo."

Arianna turned to find Rinaldo's face twisted into an amused smile.

"He's highly sought after, for sure, but not unworthily, as many of his station are. The lad's a good one. I think the Sun Crown will be far better when he sits on the throne."

Arianna turned back to look at the dance floor, and a hollow ache filled her chest. If her father had only listened to her mother then she might be the one dancing with the prince now. She would wear the frilly dress the charm had formed on her—though she would have chosen her blue camicett instead of black—and her skirts would swish and sway gracefully in time to the strange but entrancing music.

But then, she sighed to herself, what would she have said to him? Nothing, of course. Even the charm couldn't give her a voice. Her parents had tried that long ago. No, she would have been the silent maiden, laughed at by the human girls and thought dull by all the court boys. The prince himself might even have thought her dimwitted. But no. She shook her head. Prince Michael was too kind for that. And even if he had thought it of her, he would still have asked her to dance. He was good like that, too.

"I'm loathe to do it," Rinaldo's voice had lost its laugh, "but I'm afraid I shall need that back. Father will be missing me soon if I don't return."

Arianna shot one last longing look at the terrace. Her normal view seemed suddenly far away when she returned to her perch at the bottom of the rocks, but at least it was better than being in her tower. As she removed the charm and handed it back to her brother, however, a flash of light off the darkened horizon caught her eye. It glimmered for no more than a second, like a flame extinguished upon the water.

Rinaldo had slipped the charm back over his neck when Arianna patted his shoulder and pointed to the west where the light was flashing again. He turned, and his eyes immediately hardened into an expression so fierce it was nearly frightening on his gentle face. "No human ship should be that close to the Deeps. Unless . . ." he let his words trail off. "Stay here," he muttered, tossing the necklace back at her. Then he plunged beneath the surface.

It occurred to Arianna that she might put the necklace back on and return to the party, but the look of dread on Rinaldo's face haunted her, and Arianna could only clutch the charm to her chest as she prayed for him to resurface and tell her it was only a falling star.

The wait felt like hours, but it could only have been twenty minutes before he was back. She sighed with relief when he rejoined her, but the set of his jaw told Arianna that the flame had certainly not been a star.

"I want you to go as deep as you can," he said as he put the charm back on. "Even lower than the tower. Stay there until you can't possibly stay down any longer." He began to climb the rocks as soon as his legs were returned to him. Before he could leave her, however, Arianna reached out and grasped his foot. When he turned his expression was grim, but upon meeting her eyes, his face grew soft.

"I promise, I'll be careful." He reached back and squeezed her hand. "Leaving you to your own devices would be a terrible thing."

Arianna held on for a moment longer before nodding once and throwing herself down into the waves. He had promised to be careful, she told herself over and over again. That was all she could ask.

Arianna tried to obey her brother's wishes. But only minutes after reaching the seafloor, she began to feel as though someone were poking her with urchin needles all over, and her head felt as if a manatee were trying to sit on it. Gasping, she pushed herself back up toward the surface, to the sky that now glowed orange. She began swimming back to her tower. It was built into the side of a sea cliff below the Sun Palace. Surely it would be safe enough if she and her aunt covered all of their algae lanterns.

But she swam only a few fathoms before Arianna realized the battle was raging in between her and the tower. The merpeople had been quick, particularly the Protectors. All of them, even her father, had taken off their charms and moved out toward the ship before she had even reached the seafloor. By the time she was on her way back up, their haunting, minor choruses had filled the sea like beams of the sun's light. Arianna could not imagine what kind of ship had risked sailing so close to the Deeps and then straight over her father's city. As she drew nearer to the surface, she could hear the voices of her people straining in their warfare.

The ship above her was neither large nor small, but something had to be wrong. So many merpeople's songs should have splintered it already. Arianna had seen her father's guards practice, and the song of a single Protector could burst a fishing boat in one or two minutes. This ship, despite the strongest songs of her people, however, continued to sail right toward her parents' home and the city that lay below it.

That was when she realized that there was not just one ship. There were ten.

An explosion so loud that it drowned out all of the voices from above brought Arianna to a halt. A strange red light filled the choppy seas above her. Arianna's stomach nearly heaved as the bodies of mermen and mermaids—their Protectors—began to go limp, drifting with the waves. Arianna wanted to scream.

Rinaldo's orders forgotten, she streaked up to the nearest body she could see, a female Protector who floated on the water's surface, a black contour against the orange-red sky above. Arianna hooked her arm through the woman's and pulled her down until they were deep enough to be free of the continuous barrage of explosions, songs, and human shouts from above. But a moment of listening to her heart confirmed what Arianna had most feared. The woman was dead.

Nothing short of another explosion was able to pull Arianna's attention back to the surface. Letting the tides take the body, Arianna raced back to the top for the next body she could see, praying the whole time it wasn't one of her own family. Lalia and Giana were Healers, so they wouldn't even be at the surface, much to Arianna's relief. They couldn't be dead.

She was so distracted that she forgot to watch her back.

The roll of cloth that was drawn about her mouth tasted sour, and Arianna choked as it was tightened behind her head. She thrashed about, trying to dive back below the waves, but whatever force had gagged her now grabbed her arms as well, and she was lifted out of the water and tossed backward, landing with a sharp crack at the bottom of a rowboat.

"Quiet now," a man standing at the back of the boat ordered, his dark eyes glinting orange in the light of the burning ship. "We wouldn't want you overusing that voice so soon."

Arianna tried to push herself back against the side of the boat, but she found that she was already as far back as she could go. A dozen men leered down at her from their benches until the man that had spoken to her barked at them to keep rowing. Arianna tried to move her arms up to untie the rag, but whoever had so expertly tied her gag had also bound her wrists tightly. She tried then to flip her body backward over the side, but her tail wasn't long enough or strong enough. Instead, her green-blue scales only glowed orange in the fire's light as she quivered.

"She's tryin' t'scape!" a rower beside her called back as he glared at Arianna. She glared back, particularly at his sand-encrusted beard.

The man who had addressed Arianna before now walked toward her, leaning heavily to stay upright as the boat tossed and turned in the waves. When he was nearly on top of her, he placed a thin hand beneath her chin. "She's young."

"Let her go!"

Arianna turned to see her brother climb into the boat, his charm dripping as he stood tall once again. The movement of the waves didn't seem to affect him or his balance as it did everyone else in the boat. Arianna reached out to him, but before he'd taken a step toward her, the man with the dark eyes pushed himself between them, his red coat slapping Arianna's face as he did. The other men looked back and forth between their leader and the young man who now stood on their boat. Arianna wondered if they could feel his power even when he wasn't singing. Whatever their reason, they looked nervous as their rowing ceased and their hands moved to their weapons.

"She's too young for you," Rinaldo said in a low voice.

"Actually, she's going to make me a good deal of money. I think the pearl farms will be our first stop, wherever those are. Then she'll take us—"

"She can't sing."

The man stared at him.

"She can't even speak," Rinaldo continued. "You would get nothing out of her because she has no voice."

"A mermaid without a voice."

Rinaldo only nodded, but the man laughed.

"I'm hardly a wise man, but you can't expect me to be fool enough to believe that." As he spoke, a particularly rough wave hit the boat, and they all tumbled forward. Before Arianna could right herself, however, she was lifted into the air by strong arms. Blessed, warm water enveloped her as those arms dumped her over the boat's side. For the first time in her life, Arianna swam straight down as fast as her fins could push her.

Continue Arianna and Michael's tale in Silent Mermaid: A Retelling of The Little Mermaid.

Dear Reader,
I want to thank you for journeying with me through Girl in the Red Hood. *Writing Kurt and Liesel's love story was so much fun, and I'm so glad you were along for the ride.*

If you like free stories (including more about Kurt and Liesel) visit BrittanyFichterFiction.com. *By joining my email list, you'll get free access to secret bonus stories, sneaks peeks, book updates, exclusive coupons, and more!*

And if you loved this book, please consider giving it a rating or review so other readers can find it to on your favorite retailer or Goodreads.com.

Sign me up!

About the Author

Brittany lives with her Prince Charming, their little fairy, and their little prince in a ~~sparkling~~ (decently clean) castle in whatever kingdom the Air Force has most recently placed them. When she's not writing, Brittany can be found chasing her kids around with a DSLR and belting it in the church choir.

Contact Brittany:

Subscribe: BrittanyFichterFiction.com
Email: BrittanyFichterFiction@gmail.com
Facebook: Facebook.com/BFichterFiction
Instagram: @BrittanyFichterFiction

GIRL IN THE RED HOOD Copyright © 2015 Brittany Fichter.

All rights reserved. No part of this publication may be reproduced, distributed or transmitted in any form or by any means, including photocopying, recording, or other electronic or mechanical methods, without the prior written permission of the publisher, except in the case of brief quotations embodied in critical reviews and certain other noncommercial uses permitted by copyright law. For permission requests, write to the publisher, addressed "Attention: Permissions Coordinator," at BrittanyFichterFiction.com

Girl in the Red Hood / Brittany Fichter. -- 2nd ed.

Edited by Mark Swift & Katherine Stephen